SONGBIRD

SONGBIRD

COLLEEN HELME

A Mundania Press Production
Mundania Press LLC
6470A Glenway Avenue, #109
Cincinnati, Ohio 45211-5222

To order additional copies of this book, contact:
books@mundania.com
www.mundania.com

Cover Art © 2010 by Ana Winson
Arien Graphics (http://www.arien-graphics.com)
Edited by Erena Kelley

Trade Paperback ISBN: 978-1-60659-241-0
eBook ISBN: 978-1-60659-240-3

First Edition • August 2010

Production by Mundania Press LLC
Printed in the United States of America

10   9   8   7   6   5   4   3   2   1

DEDICATION

To Tom
Thanks for singing with me!

ACKNOWLEDGMENTS

I would like to thank all those who read this book as a work in progress, especially Tom, Erin, and Melissa. Thanks for your support and also that from Clayton and Jason and the rest of my family and friends, Julee and Holly. Also a big thanks to Mundania Press, Ana Winson, for the amazing cover art, and my editor, Erena Kelley, whose suggestions helped make this a better book. You Rock!

Prologue

A huge meaty hand closed over her mouth, stifling the scream in her throat. Struggling against the tight grip made her captor increase his crushing hold, and he squeezed the remaining air from her lungs. Darkness closed around her and she fell limp against him. His hold loosened, allowing sweet air into her starving lungs, and sudden tears filled her eyes.

Terror clutched her chest when his blackened face swam into view. His eyes bulged white, and his nostrils flared red. The vicious smile froze her blood and he spoke with a threatening growl. "I don't like kids. So you'll either do what I say or I'll snap your head off." His burly arm slid around her neck and she choked, her small body trembling with fear.

"Don't!" she whimpered.

He laughed then, an evil laugh full of sadistic amusement. "I don't want to hear another peep out of you. Understand?"

She nodded vigorously, trying to hold back the tears. He shifted his hold, and tied her hands in front of her so tight that she gasped with pain. "What did I say?" He raised his hand to strike. She flinched away and lost her balance, toppling backward over his leg. With a grunt of irritation, he caught her by the arms and threw her over his shoulder. Before she could cry out, he started to run.

With each jolt slamming her stomach into his shoulder, Teya swallowed to hold back her breakfast. If she lost control now, she knew he'd kill her. The ground passed by in a blur and she tried to watch where they were going, but it was too hard to raise her head and keep the food down at the same time. She was moaning in rhythm to his steps by the time he finally stopped and lowered her to the ground.

Relief flooded her so sharply that her stomach cramped with pain, and tears flooded her eyes. She couldn't stop the tears, and cried as silently as possible, but the man turned on her with a curse. He raised his hand to strike, but before he could complete the motion, another man grabbed him by the wrist and forced him back.

"You fool! What are you doing?"

"I'm just going to shut her up."

"Hitting her won't accomplish anything. You don't know what she's capable of."

"I'm the one who got her here. If you think you can do a better job, then you take charge of her."

"Fine. I will." Her protector knelt beside her and pursed his lips, noting her pale tear-streaked face and the tightness of her bonds. He cursed under his breath. "I'm going to loosen your bonds to make you more comfortable, then you can have a drink of water. Would you like that?"

Something in his eyes calmed her enough to stop her tears. Once he loosened the rope, he rubbed her hands together to get the circulation moving, then retied the rope so it wouldn't hurt so much. She took the waterskin he offered and drank it greedily.

"How old are you?" he asked.

Somehow she found her voice. "Ten."

"Ah." He nodded. "I thought so." He paused, considering her. "I'm going to make you a deal. I don't want to see you get hurt, but there's only so much I can do." He looked meaningfully over at the monster. "We're going to wait here for a while. If you're good and don't cause any problems, I'll make sure you get home safely, but it all depends on you. Can you do that?"

"You'll…you'll take me home?" she stammered.

"Yes. But only if you do everything you're told."

"All right." She swallowed, still trembling all over. Why was she here? What did they want with her? Would he really take her home? Her eyes misted up again, and she choked on a sob.

The man frowned. "For your own good, you've got to stop crying." He jerked his head in the other man's direction. "Do you want him to hurt you?" Teya quickly shook her head, and tried to stop her tears, but they kept running down her cheeks.

"Listen," her protector whispered. "If you ever want to see your family again, you've got to be brave. That means that you've got to stop crying. That's part of our bargain. Find that courage, and I'll make sure you get home."

Teya took a deep breath and tried to find the strength he spoke of. She wanted to be with her family again, and vowed she would do whatever it took to return to them. With courage beyond her years, she buried her tears deep within herself, realizing they were a weakness that would only hurt her chances of survival.

The man nodded with approval. "Now, be a good girl and rest here. If you need anything, just ask me." He took the slack from the rope at her wrists and tied it to a tree branch, effectively leashing her to the spot. After a meaningful glance, he turned away from her and spoke in hushed tones to the other man.

Teya swallowed her fear and repeated the litany that she would be going home over and over in her mind. Her grandmother would be worried when she didn't return from her errand. Would her grandmother come looking for her? Maybe she would find the bags Teya had dropped on the path and know that someone had taken her. Then she'd send her father and brother, and all the others after her. That hope was like a balm to her soul and she settled back against the tree to wait.

The next few hours passed by slowly and soon the day faded into dusk. She wanted to ask what they were waiting for, but didn't dare. Each moment might bring her father closer. She held as still as she could, glad her captors seemed to have forgotten her. The monster glared at her often. It stopped her breath every time. He was evil, she was sure of it.

She tried working her wrists free. If she could slip away, she knew she could find her way home. The harder she pulled, the tighter they seemed to get, until she finally gave up. The other end tied to the tree was too high for her to reach, and with nothing sharp, cutting the rope was out of the question. Tired and disheartened, she curled up in a ball and closed her eyes, grateful for the warm clothes she was wearing.

It was full dark when soft cursing brought her awake. Many large shapes were crowded around the monster. They were arguing with barely controlled anger, but she couldn't understand what they were saying. The sound of approaching riders jerked them to attention and all talk ceased. Could it be her father? Had he come for her? Teya jumped to her feet and tried to scramble up the tree she was tethered to. Not able to reach the rope, she yanked at it, willing it to come off.

"It's him!" Someone shouted. "They got him out!"

A dozen or more riders entered their hiding place. One of them jumped off his horse and pushed through the crowd. "Where's the girl?"

Teya tried to hide behind the tree when a flare of light nearly blinded her. "Come out so I can see you," the newcomer commanded.

She peeked around the tree and glared up at the dark faces lost in shadow. She couldn't see the man that spoke, but the others seemed to leer at her with inhuman cruelty, and she faltered back a step. Stifling tears, she forced herself to speak. "I want to go home."

One of the men laughed, but the leader quickly cuffed him before addressing her from the shadows. "I'd like to take you back, but it seems they don't want you, so you'll just have to come with me."

What was he saying? Of course they wanted her! The other man told her she could go home if she was good, and she'd done everything they'd told her. With a burst of anger and defiance, she did something she was taught never to do. She screamed.

The sudden explosion of sound cut through the air like a sharp blade. Men instantly grabbed their ears and doubled over in pain. Horses shied, birds flew from their nests. Forrest animals joined her with wild screams of their own, splitting the air in cacophonic tones. The sky shimmered with electric heat and the earth trembled.

Only one man could stand, and he staggered toward her. With brutal finality, he slapped her hard across the face, and she reeled to the ground in a daze. The sudden silence wheezed over them, and Teya stumbled to her feet before turning to run.

The man grabbed her and quickly clapped his hand across her mouth. "You will never do that again," he hissed. He had something in his hands and snapped it around her neck. "You're lucky I have this, otherwise I'd have to kill you." He hauled her toward his men, and thrust her into the monster's outstretched arms. "There's no time to lose. You four take her to the king. The rest of you come with me."

CHAPTER ONE

The Escape

The ambassador had only been there five minutes when he was struck speechless. The crowd parted unexpectedly, and she stood only ten feet away. Raven-black hair flowed around her shoulders in feathered waves, in sharp contrast to her creamy white skin. When she looked up at him with startling aqua-blue eyes, his mind went blank.

After a short silence, the king's top advisor cleared his throat, and Bran came back to his senses. An embarrassing rush of color stained his dark complexion, and Bran cursed the fates that the king's advisor had witnessed his reaction.

"Don't worry," Chancellor Turner said. "The Songbird affects everyone that way the first time they see her. Beauty like that commands attention. No one is immune to her exotic looks. But don't be deceived; she is not to be taken lightly or trusted. None of the Kaloriahns are. That race of people has a penchant for evil. That is why we enslave them. The *kundar* keeps them under control. Without it, we would be nothing but dirt under their feet. She could devour both your mind and soul with one look into those eyes."

Bran was familiar with the *kundar,* although he didn't agree with the reason it was used. It was said that the Kaloriahns were evil because of their magic, but he wasn't so sure. If the Kaloriahns really did have magic, it still didn't make them evil. He wasn't one to believe tales told by power hungry men, and it sickened him that the king would force the subjugation of another race.

The Songbird was a symbol of that enslavement. Although they softened the truth and made it look like the taming of a wild bird, it was nothing short of bondage. She had no choices, no freedom, nothing. It was wrong, and it grated on him. Couldn't something positive come from a reciprocal relationship with people like her? People who had magic at their command? Bran pasted a questioning look on his face, and acted as though he hadn't been studying their culture for the last several months. "Is that it? The golden circlet around her neck?"

The chancellor turned his full attention on Bran. "The *kundar* is much more than a simple necklace. It causes excruciating pain if the Songbird uses too much magic. It is like the safety-catch on your weapon and, fortunately for us, she can't remove it." His eyes narrowed. "Neither can anyone else." His pointed look left no question of his warning.

Bran allowed a smile. "I was merely curious. My sole purpose here is to form a liaison between our countries that I hope will be mutually beneficial." The Chancellor nodded absently, returning his attention to the Songbird. Bran glanced at her again and found it hard to pull his eyes away. She was draped in a black gown, which clung to the willowy curves of her body before falling away in silky folds. Shimmering layers of diaphanous cloth fell from her sleeves, giving the impression of wings when she moved her arms. The square neckline emphasized the contrast to the creamy white skin of her long neck, and was edged with deep blue feathers. "She's very beautiful," he voiced his thoughts aloud.

When Bran pulled his gaze away, he was surprised at the raw hunger that quickly passed over Chancellor Turner's face. "There are many who would give up all they own for such a possession. But she belongs to the king and he guards her well. Believe me, there have been several attempts to take her, all of which have ended in death."

"Only a fool would even consider it," Bran said tightly.

"I'm glad we understand each other, but I'll be watching you just the same."

"That's the last thing on my mind." Bran reassured him. "An alliance between our countries would benefit us both. We have much to offer each other."

"Oh, I plan on exploiting that idea. Your weapons are intriguing. I've never seen anything like them. I'm sure we can come to an agreement, but that doesn't mean I will trust you."

Bran smiled in spite of himself. "I can see why the king values your opinion. I'll do my best to stay on your good side."

"You're a very wise man. Now if you'll excuse me, it's time to begin." Turner left the reception area at the back of the hall, and spoke to the servants who came forward to usher the large number of guests to their assigned places.

Bran was relieved to find his seat near the front of the hall just below the king's high table. Here, he could observe everything that happened without being obvious. When the Songbird took her place at the king's table opposite him, he could hardly believe his good fortune. From here, he could easily study her and see for himself if she was as dangerous as they said.

He didn't realize he'd been staring at her until she turned to him with an unblinking glance. Her gaze traveled over him with a studied blankness that was unsettling and he held back a shiver. When her attention shifted to a spot behind him, he let out his breath. She masked her feelings well. It was impossible to know what she was thinking.

Chancellor Turner stepped to the dais and announced the entrance of the king and queen. The applause turned into loud cheering as they made their way from the back of the hall to the high table. King Thesald carried a sybaritic energy about him that was both repulsive and fascinating at the same time. The force of his personality swept through the hall and demanded attention. Beside him, Queen Agnus was small and timid, deferring to him in everything she did. She had no real power and seemed resigned to whatever role the king wanted her to play.

Bran focused on the Songbird to gauge her reaction to the king, but her countenance held the same blankness she had worn all night. Her face was totally void of expression and he wondered if anything touched her. Maybe there was some truth to the rumors. From what he had seen, he had to agree that she didn't seem quite human.

"Tonight we celebrate our golden anniversary!" King Thesald said. For an old man, he seemed unusually spry and healthy. He had a full, thick head of reddish-brown hair that was only slightly gray at the temples. "Since I became king fifty years ago, our enemies have been destroyed and we have prospered in the land. There are none who would dare to oppose the strength of our mighty army. Our kingdom has spread from the sea, far to the North and we are now establishing trade and commerce with the people of Braemar. We welcome our honored visitors and guests who have traveled many miles to reach us. To everyone here, let the festivities begin!"

Amid loud cheering, more servants entered the room and placed platters of food on each table, filling up empty glasses with wine. An air of merriment flooded the hall and conversation grew to a high pitch. Seated with the other guests, Bran joined in the small talk at his table. As the ambassador from Braemar, he was shown civil respect from his table companions, but it was tinged with an air of distrust. He did his best to put them at ease and was soon rewarded with an open discussion of the happenings in the city. During the conversation, he kept his attention focused on the king's table and the Songbird. She never spoke, nor was she spoken to. It was clear she was only there to be seen like a prize.

Before he knew it, the tables were cleared in preparation for the rest of the celebration. It was almost time for the Songbird to sing, and his stomach fluttered with excitement. Ever since first learning of her, he had waited and planned for this moment. It would prove to him one way or another if magic was real.

The king stood proudly and the hall quieted before he spoke. "This is the moment we have all been waiting for. Our celebration would not be complete without hearing from my beautiful Songbird. She will now sing something specially prepared for this evening." He took her unresisting hand, and led her to a raised platform as though she were an honored guest. From where he sat, Bran heard the king's soft-spoken threat. "Do not fail me."

An expectant hush filled the hall and for the first time, Bran detected a flicker of emotion behind her cool exterior. Was it anger or defiance? As quick as it came, it was gone, and her face returned to the schooled blankness that made her seem remote and cold. The silence lengthened uncomfortably before she tilted her chin at a determined slant. It was when she took a deep breath that Bran caught the gleam of wildness in her eyes. His gut clenched with sudden apprehension.

The first few notes took him by surprise. It was not what he expected. The notes were light and clear as sparkling water under the sun, carrying an underlying tone of reverence. The tones conjured golden images of light, and bound to the intensity of her voice, created a feeling of wonder and awe. As the beautiful tones rose in volume, the air became drenched with sparkling light. Swirling around her, the light shifted in color and size, growing and changing with the music.

It was like watching fireworks with bursts of energy that trailed away into sparkling diamonds. The beauty of it was breathtaking, and seemed to enclose the entire hall in bursts of golden light. The steady light grew, and he watched with amazement as it encircled his body, even becoming the air he breathed. Incredibly, his skin seemed to glow. As he tried to understand what was happening, the tones grew in intensity and seemed to carry his soul to another sphere. To a place beyond beauty.

Time slowed, and almost stopped. Then the moment passed and he could breathe again. His senses reeled like he had just been taken for a wild ride. As he gathered his wits, a low echo filled the hall, soothing his nerves. The melody and harmonies changed, whispering of tranquility and peace.

Within this cocoon of warmth, his defenses fell away one by one. An air of complacency relaxed his breathing and peace surrounded him. He vaguely sensed his vulnerability, but couldn't do anything about it, nor did he want to. The very air he breathed seemed laden with hues of green and blue.

With his mind like an open book, the tones suddenly changed into a twisting dissonance. Bran instinctively covered his ears along with everyone else in the room. Startled cries of the crowd joined the dissonance, cutting into him like nails. The Songbird's beautiful face twisted with pain as she forced out the notes and struggled to stand upright. Fighting obvious agony, she continued to sing, and the notes rose in a crescendo that swirled in the air around the king. Bands of dark light descended over him and tightened like a vise.

All of a sudden, King Thesald jumped to his feet with a strangled gasp and clutched at his chest. Her song went on, but the effort sent her to her knees. With a pop, the *kundar* around her neck flared a bright orange-red, cutting off her voice and leaving the room abruptly silent. Moaning, the Songbird fell to the ground, clutching her stomach and writhing in pain. Her fall jolted everyone into action, and the guards nearest the king caught him when he slumped.

With the king overcome, Chancellor Turner took charge. He motioned the guards forward and stood over the Songbird's still form. "You will be severely punished for this," he said through gritted teeth. "Take her away."

Bran held his breath as they hauled her to her feet and half dragged her down the hall. Her pale face haunted him with abject defeat, as if she didn't care whether she lived or died. The change from the blankness she carried before unsettled him. If he ever doubted her humanity, it was erased by the passion of her song and the desperate act he had just witnessed. Her song had touched him deeply, and now her pain was like his own. True, she had hurt the king, but he understood her desire for freedom.

The attendants surrounding the king dispersed, leaving him sitting upright in his chair. The king mopped his brow and took a long drink of wine before motioning to Chancellor Turner, who held up his hands to quiet the whispering crowd. "I apologize for this small inconvenience. As you can see, King Thesald is unharmed and would like the festivities to continue. Please understand that every once in awhile, the Songbird gets out of control and tries to hurt the king. Do not be alarmed. It is her nature, the true nature of all Kaloriahns, but because of the *kundar*, she only ends up hurting herself."

He signaled, and a group of musicians and dancers came forward. With this diversion, the tension dissipated from the hall and Bran relaxed into his chair. He was stunned by what the Songbird had done, and had a feeling it was more than defiance that spurred her. From the defeat on her face, he almost believed it was a death wish. Could he blame her? In her place, he would do all in his power to gain his freedom, or die trying. Her song haunted him, and he couldn't seem to forget the flowing beauty that had surrounded him, nor the dissonant pain.

He also believed that the king had suffered. She'd hurt him; even now his face was pale and pinched. What would her punishment be? She must have felt it was worth it.

Coming from Braemar, Bran had only heard stories about the things that happened in the Old Country. Power and magic existed on this side of the wall, but not on his. The West had technological advances that made this society seem primitive, but there was no magic where he came from. That was one of the reasons he had decided to become a diplomat. Magic fascinated him. But now, everything had changed. Two months ago, strange things began happening on his side of the wall.

Things only explained by magic.

His country may be industrialized, but they were no match against magic, and the way things were going, his superiors could only believe that King Thesald was making plans to invade Braemar. What didn't add up was the stand Thesald took against magic. King Thesald identified the Kaloriahns as the only people who could wield magic, and because of this, the king had wiped out most of them, or collared them like the Songbird. No one trusted the Kaloriahns, especially the king. It didn't make sense.

Another piece of the puzzle surfaced three weeks ago. An informant led them to a drunken man who bragged about an elixir he claimed gave people magic—the ability to disappear, or disarm a man with the flick of a wrist, and many other uses. He called the potion 'sym' and explained that it wore off after a few hours.

An elixir that could give magical power. The demand for something like that was frightening. In the wrong hands, it could be used for all kinds of evil. If the king had enough for his army, they would be hard to defeat. The man claimed it came from the Old Country, but before they could find out more, he disappeared. Now it was up to Bran to find its origins, and the only key to this riddle was the Songbird. She was the only Kaloriahn with magic he knew of, and his only hope of finding others like her. There had to be a connection between them and the elixir.

The people at his table were conversing in low tones. Most of them were affiliated with the king and his minions, but Bran didn't know all of the connections. The others seemed to have recovered from the experience, although they were subdued. "I have never heard the Songbird before," Bran said. "It was incredible. Does she have a name or do you just call her Songbird?"

The man next to him shrugged before answering. "Her name is Teya."

"Hmm…that's an unusual name, but then, she's an unusual creature." Bran furrowed his brows. "Chancellor Turner said she would be punished. What do they usually do to her?"

The woman across from him narrowed her eyes. "That's a good question," she said. "He doesn't beat her, I know that much."

One of the other men began to shake his head. "This is all wrong. If the king would treat her as a beloved pet with special privileges, he would gain her loyalty and never have to worry about the scene that was displayed tonight. I've told him so myself, many times. If she were mine, I'd treat her differently, and she would never turn on me."

"So you say." The woman broke in. "But her kind are different. They don't think like we do. Didn't you notice that strange light in her eyes? She doesn't seem quite right to me, almost inhuman, and definitely not to be trusted."

"Of course she's human," the man scoffed. "That's just an old tale to keep people afraid of her, so the king doesn't have to worry about someone trying to steal her away."

This made sense to Bran, but since Chancellor Turner had made the same remark, it could be more than a rumor. How far was the king willing to go to keep his Songbird safe? Spreading a few lies certainly wouldn't hurt, and she seemed human enough to him.

"It's certain you've had your eye on her for some time now," the woman said with disdain. "I'd be careful if I were you."

The man shot her a venomous look. "Keep your warnings to yourself. I'm not a fool. Besides, I'm more interested in other matters." He turned his attention to Bran. "So, Ambassador Havil, what do you think of all this?"

Bran kept his thoughts from showing with an easy smile. "Quite remarkable. I never believed in magic before she sang. Now I'm still wondering if it was real."

"Makes you wonder what she could do without that thing around her neck, doesn't it?"

"Stop baiting him, Max," the woman beside him said. "It's not fair to our guest." To Bran she added, "This is a running debate between Chancellor Turner and Max that has gone on for years. We all know what would happen without the *kundar*. She'd kill every last one of us."

Max rolled his eyes but was saved from replying by a servant who requested that they all move to the other end of the hall where the king was leading his queen in the first steps of a dance.

Bran made his way casually to the far end of the hall, closer to the doors for his escape. He glanced at the people surrounding him. Those not dancing were enjoying the entertainment while drinks and trays of sweet confections were served. He chose a fruit bar dusted in powdered sugar and decided it had the right amount of nuts to be convincing. He glanced at his watch. It was time.

"Fine evening isn't it?" He asked the plump, pretty woman standing beside him. "Allow me to introduce myself; I'm Ambassador Havil from Braemar."

The woman seemed more than happy to make his acquaintance, especially with the attention he lavished on her. It was now or never, and with relish, he ate the cookie. Immediately, his throat began to swell. It wasn't too bad, but he acted the part, grabbing at his throat like he was choking. His breath began to wheeze in and out, and the woman quickly patted his back with wide-eyed concern.

"Ambassador! Is something wrong?"

"Can't...breathe." He took hold of her arm. "I need...my...assistant." He allowed her to lead him out of the hall and into the corridor where he collapsed against the wall.

He had picked the woman well, for she quickly took charge of the situation, shouting for help, and sending for Bran's assistant. Jax arrived right on queue and exclaimed that Bran was having an allergic reaction to something he ate. Jax fished through his pockets and produced a syringe, explaining that it would help Bran breathe. After administering the medicine, Bran's wheezing quieted and he was able to sit up.

"Thank you for your help," he told the woman, still a little breathless. "It probably saved my life."

She dabbed at the beads of perspiration on his forehead with her handkerchief. "Oh, it was nothing. I'm just glad you're all right."

Chancellor Turner appeared at her elbow. "What happened?"

"Oh, it was terrible!" the woman exclaimed. "Ambassador Havil had an allergic reaction to something he ate and nearly died! He couldn't breathe. It was quite frightful."

"Can I get you anything?" Chancellor Turner asked.

"I think I'd better go," Bran rasped. "My assistant can see to my needs and I don't want to interrupt the festivities. Please give my regrets to the king and queen."

"Very well," Turner said. "I'll have your carriage brought round."

Jax helped Bran to his feet and he swayed slightly. He caught his balance and bowed over the woman's hand. "Thanks again, my lady."

She smiled sweetly and gave him her handkerchief. "Take it. You look like you need it. I've got plenty of others."

He inclined his head in thanks. "Goodnight, then." He bowed to Turner as he passed. "Chancellor."

Jax followed closely as Bran led the way out of the palace and into the waiting carriage. He let out a sigh when he fell back against the cushioned seats and mopped his brow. Jax climbed in beside him and closed the door before turning a baleful eye on Bran. "What the hell do you think you're doing? That was real! You trying to kill yourself?"

Bran shook his head and swallowed. His throat was still swollen and his mouth was dry. "Is there any water in here?"

Jax mumbled in exasperation as he rummaged beneath the seat and pulled out a flask of water. Bran drained the flask to the last drop and his throat opened up, allowing him to breath easier. "Thanks. I guess I miss-judged the amount of nuts. That, or the nuts around here are stronger. At least Turner was a witness." When Jax didn't answer Bran continued. "Hey, I'm fine now, so you can stop scowling."

Bran took a deep breath that felt wonderful, and gave silent thanks that the medicine worked so well. He had probably pushed it a little too far, but having it real only made it that much better. No one would suspect the truth.

The carriage slowed to a crawl. "That's our signal." Jax cracked open the door and waited until the carriage rounded the corner before stepping out. Bran followed and was soon crouching beneath an overgrown bush. He and Jax scrambled to the other side and cut through the yard to a side street.

"I'm going to watch the carriage to make sure it gets past the guards at the wall," Jax said. "I'll meet you at the house in a minute."

Bran watched him go, then turned down an alley and pushed through the opening in a fence to a small, enclosed yard. The covered walk and secluded doorway were the main reasons he had picked this house. It was easy to go in and out without being seen. At least tonight had gone off without a hitch. By this time tomorrow, he'd know if the weeks of careful planning had worked. If they didn't, he'd probably be dead.

❧ ❧

The guards allowed Teya to change her clothes before they marched her down to the cellar and forced her into the 'box'. She took a calming breath, but it had little effect. Her stomach still cramped with pain, and the confined space in the tiny cell made it worse. With no windows and no light, the walls seemed to close in around her and she knew she had to gain control before she started screaming.

Her claustrophobia was King Thesald's greatest weapon against her, which was why it was the perfect punishment. It galled her that he was the cause of it in the first place, and now he used it against her whenever he could. She clamped her eyes shut, and tried to think of something besides the closeness of the walls and the sound of her tight breathing.

She envisioned the meadow of her youth, with the canopy of trees swaying gently in the breeze. Here, the green grass smelled like sweet hay. A small waterfall echoed on the rocks behind her and then flowed into a pool of crystal clear water.

She was ten years old the last time she'd been there, but the peace of the meadow had never been forgotten. It soothed her and softened the hard edge of her prison. She tried to picture her parent's faces, along with her older brother Hewson, but their images had blurred with time. Profound sorrow lanced through her heart. Ten years had passed since then. Ten long years since the king's men had captured her and carried her in a box, like an animal.

In her mind, she opened the box and stepped out, then poured all her anger, sorrow and hate inside. The box shrank until it was small enough to fit in her pocket. She would keep it there until the right time. In her pocket, these feelings couldn't destroy her. Humming softly to herself, she relaxed and fell into a fitful sleep.

When the guard opened the door early the next morning, he was unnerved when Teya calmly opened her eyes and stared at him. His face twisted with guilt and shame for what had been done to her, but also held a small amount of fear, which made him gruff. He turned away, not seeing the tears that silently slid down her cheeks.

"You can get out now. I'll escort you to your room," he said.

Teya swallowed the lump in her throat. She had vowed never to show weakness, but it was getting more difficult to mask her feelings. Her legs and back were stiff and cramped, and movement was painful and slow. She knew this guard, and although his manners were harsh, he had a good heart. He knew she wasn't an animal.

"Please," she said. "I can't seem to get up. Can you give me a hand?"

Her request startled him and he finally looked her in the face. His features softened, and with a quick nod, he clasped her outstretched hand and pulled her to her feet. She swayed for a moment, and he steadied her until the dizziness passed. His kindness opened a crack in her heart and the tears fell in earnest.

"Lady," the guard said. "Please don't cry."

Teya understood the unspoken plea. He put himself in danger to help her. By the king's command, no one was allowed to assist her in any way unless he ordered it. This guard could be stripped of his rank if someone reported him. The king had spread the lie that she was evil to keep her isolated. So far, it had worked well.

"I'm sorry." She pulled away from him and wiped at the tears on her cheeks, realizing they carried just as much anger as pain.

He hesitated, uncomfortable with her apology. "Come on then, let's go," he said briskly.

She was grateful that he walked slowly enough for her to get the kinks out. From the cellar of the palace, it was a long walk up several flights of stairs to her room in the north wing. They took the servants' staircase and no one saw them. Once at her door, the guard seemed relieved to be rid of her and quickly ushered her into Clare's capable hands.

Clare rose from her chair in a huff and sneered at Teya's hesitation to enter her own room. "Come in, you stupid girl. A fine mess you made of things. You're lucky they don't whip you for your disobedience. They should. It might teach you some respect."

Teya sighed inwardly and closed her mind to the woman's unending tirade on her lack of wits. Clare had only been with her a few days, replacing another woman who had loathed her even more. She wondered what Clare had done to displease the king. He had some hold over all of them, but Teya never found out any of the details. Her keepers never stayed long enough.

Teya learned to cope, mostly by not speaking. She found that her blank stare could unnerve the best of them and they backed off. After all, she wasn't totally defenseless. The small amount of magic at her disposal was enough to play a few tricks. Along with the rumors, it was enough to keep them from harming her.

Of course, it hadn't always been that way. Her first keeper, Bea had been kind and loving. She doted on Teya and told her how special she was. Bea took on the role of mother, teacher and mentor, bringing books and conversation to fill the empty hours. But most of all, she served as a buffer between Teya and the king.

Bea had been with Teya nearly four years before the king had her executed. A shudder of pain and anger knifed through Teya with the memory. It was her fault. She never should have tried to escape. Since then, her jailors had come and gone, serving their sentences with brutal vigilance no different from Clare.

After setting a tray of food on the small table, Clare left the room, bolting the door behind her. The sound of that bolt was like a stab to Teya's heart. She fell on her bed and let the tears flow. She was tired of her life, tired of being a prisoner. Nothing ever changed. Last night would have been the perfect time to humiliate the king. She had planned to lash out with her magic, no matter how much it hurt, even if it killed her, but the pain was too great. She had failed.

She tugged at the golden circlet around her neck. If it wasn't for this, she could have left long ago. Her magic was strong, but this was stronger. It was useless to fight it anymore. Revenge and hope that she could escape had been enough once. It didn't seem like enough now.

The day turned cloudy, and then started to rain, a reflection of her despair. She spent the time lost in misery and feeling sorry for herself. She knew the king would keep her locked in her room for at least three days and maybe longer, depending on his mood.

By the time evening came, she had bathed and changed her clothes. It quit raining, and she opened the windows between the bars to let in the fresh air. Outside it was spring, with the promise of new life, but inside, her heart was heavy with despair.

Clare came with her dinner, setting it on the table with a flourish. "I don't know what you did to the king, but he's been in a foul mood all day. You're lucky to be out of his way. The way he's been carrying on, he may keep you locked up for a week."

So, Teya had caused him some humiliation after all. Good. Clare continued, "I hope you think it was worth it."

Teya glanced at her with surprise. "It was."

"You never heard this from me," she whispered. "But I'm glad you did it." With that she swept out of the room, locking the door behind her. Teya hadn't planned on eating, but suddenly her appetite returned and she ate the light fare with enjoyment.

As the evening passed, however, her euphoria wore off. Tonight would be no different than hundreds of nights before. There was nothing to do, and her confinement wore on her nerves. The hours slipped by, but she refused to go to bed because it was one of the few choices she could make.

With a huff of despair, she left a candle burning on the mantle, and perched on the windowsill. The cool night air wafted over her, and she stared up at the stars, thinking of all the ways she could kill herself. But even as much as she hated her life, she couldn't bring herself to end it.

Half asleep and lost in her thoughts, she didn't notice when the door opened. The soft click when it shut startled her, and she gasped at the cloaked figure dominating her room. The figure turned in the dim light, and with surprise, she recognized the Ambassador from Braemar.

"Shh." He held a gloved finger to his lips and waited like a coiled spring for several seconds.

Teya's heart beat furiously. "What are you doing here? What do you want?"

"It's all right. I don't mean you any harm. I've come to get you out of here."

She clamped down the sudden flare of hope. "Are you crazy? It's impossible. You'll only get yourself killed. Believe me, it's happened before." He didn't know what he was doing. "Why would you risk your life for me?"

"I have my reasons, and I'll tell you what they are once we're away." He pushed the cloak back from his shoulders with a sweeping wave. Concealed beneath it were all kinds of tools, knives, and a rope.

As he moved to the window, she stopped him. "It won't work. The king has guards everywhere, and I'm watched all the time. We'll never get out of the palace let alone the city. They'll kill you."

He considered her for a moment. "I have everything under control. I can get you out. Don't you want to leave?"

His audacity shocked her, but he waited patiently while she gathered her wits. There was kindness in his eyes, and it was hard not to believe him. "Do you mean to keep me enslaved? Can you take this off?" She couldn't believe she was challenging him. Here was someone willing to get her out of this hell, and she was bargaining over the *kundar*. If she went with him, she would be out of her prison with a better chance of getting it off than she had now. She almost wished she hadn't asked.

He hesitated, staring at her with such intensity that she inwardly cringed. After a pause, he came to a decision. "I can't guarantee anything. But even with it on, I can promise you more freedom than you have now."

"So you can own me?"

"No. That's not my intention." Pity and anger creased his brow. "I think the way you've been treated here is deplorable, but I have to be able to trust you before I can take that thing off."

She didn't mind the anger behind his words, but his pity bothered her. "What do you want from me?" There had to be more to it. The risks were too great.

"I just need your help. After that you'll be free to do whatever you wish."

Right. How could she believe that? He didn't trust her, but he certainly expected her to trust him.

"There's no time," he said. "Do you want to leave, or not?"

What choice did she have? She had to take the chance. "Yes. But I'll not be used, ever again. By anyone." Her voice shook with conviction and she held her breath for his answer.

"I'll not use you. I just need your help."

He seemed genuine enough, and with a surge of hope she gave in. "All right."

He smiled, and her breath caught at the change in his face. His brow relaxed and the playful crinkles at the corners of his eyes held a promise of friendship. With a shadow of beard covering his strong jaw, and dark penetrating eyes, he also seemed dangerous. She suddenly hoped trusting him wasn't based on something as foolish as a handsome face.

"Good. We'd better get moving." Looking at his wrist he announced, "We have sixteen minutes to get out the window and down to the ground before the watchman comes back." He stepped to the window and tested the bars, then took out a tool, which he wedged into the space between them. When he rotated the handle on the tool, the bars began to bend out. He spared her a glance. "Put something in your bed to make it look like you're asleep, and then find some dark clothes to wear."

Teya watched him for a moment. Was this really happening? It was like a fantasy dream she had given up on years ago, and this man was even more handsome than the one in her dreams. He glanced at her with an arched brow and she sprang into action. After stuffing a blanket under the bedclothes, she rummaged through her wardrobe. She found her black pants and the black silky blouse that went with them. Her boots and belt were in the corner and she grabbed them, then pulled her closet door partway shut for some privacy while she quickly changed. She completed the ensemble with a black jacket that would help keep her warm in the cool night air.

He was waiting at the window. The bars were barely wide enough to squeeze through, and her stomach tightened when she realized that was the way out. "Hurry. Step into this." It was a belt with loops to go around her legs that cinched at the waist. He bent down and held it for her to step into. Her pulse leapt while he drew it up her legs to her waist and pulled the belt tight. After he attached a long rope, she hastily stepped away.

"I'll lower you down. There's someone waiting at the bottom. If you can, try to stay facing the wall. Don't hold onto the rope. Use your hands and feet for leverage. Understand?"

She swallowed, more afraid than she cared to admit. "How are you getting out?"

"I'll follow after you." When she hesitated, he continued. "I won't drop you. But we need to hurry."

Teya took a deep breath and moved to the window. A few minutes ago she would have willingly jumped out the window, so what was there to be afraid of now?

"Feet first."

She nodded, then with a deep breath, stepped over the windowsill into nothing. He held tightly to the rope, but it took all her courage to let go of the bars, and when she did, she automatically grabbed the rope. She started to twist when he lowered her down but could not seem to let go. Realizing that she could hit her head or shoulders against the wall, she finally released the rope and used her arms the way he'd told her to.

With her heart pounding, she glanced down to see how much further she had to go and gasped. It was so far! What if there wasn't enough rope? What if he lost his grip? She clenched her eyes shut. She had to trust that her rescuer knew what he was doing. After enduring a long moment of dread, there were hands reaching up for her and her feet touched the ground.

"I've got you," a rough voice said. "Now, let's get that rope undone...there." The man smiled to reassure her, but all she could see were white teeth in the dark. "Take cover in those bushes until Bran gets here." He pulled the rope toward him taking the extra slack, and then steadied it. Teya moved back toward the bushes and crouched down to watch the ambassador come out of the window.

He seemed to have a little trouble squeezing his shoulders and head through the bars, but he finally made it out, and was soon rappelling down the side of the building. Teya held her breath when a light came on in a nearby window. The man beside her cursed, but Bran didn't slow his descent. Once he hit the ground, he quickly untied the rope while his companion pulled it free of the bars. Bran reached for Teya and led them through the outer gardens to a small building at the back of the grounds. Teya knew this was the gardener's shed, and at Bran's tap, the door opened and a slight figure in black stepped out.

"Any trouble?" Bran asked.

"No. Everything went as planned. Hello Teya."

How could it be? "Clare?"

"Yes. Sorry about the way I spoke to you, but I had to be convincing."

"Oh." Teya was stunned. Clare must have been in on this from the beginning.

"You know Clare," Bran said. "And this is Jax."

"Nice to meet you," Jax said cordially. It all seemed unreal to Teya.

"Come on." Bran took the lead. "Try and stay low." Bran kept to the edge of a path and soon they were at the far end of the palace grounds. Now, only a rock wall separated them from the city, and Teya steeled herself at the alarming prospect of having to climb over it. Her trepidation quickly turned to relief when Jax and Clare moved some bushes away to reveal a crawl space under the wall.

Jax went first, followed by Clare. They gave the all-clear sign and Teya went next. The ground was wet and soggy from the rain, and dirt smeared all over her clothes and hands. She came out on the other side in full view of anyone who happened to be looking. Clare ushered her across the street and into a dark alley.

Bran soon joined them and nodded to Jax. "Get Clare out of here."

"But…" Clare began.

"No. You can't go back," Bran said. Clare let out a sigh, then reluctantly agreed. To Jax he continued, "I don't know how long we'll be, but watch for us at the inn, and make sure Clare stays out of sight."

"Be careful," Clare said, then she and Jax quietly slipped into the darkness.

"Where are we going?" Teya asked.

"We have to split up. It's easier this way. Come on, we need to get out of the city before they discover you're gone."

He led her through a maze of back alleys until she was totally turned around. She hadn't been out of the palace grounds since her capture, so nothing made sense to her anyway. Still, she was out, and this continually amazed her. Why had Bran done this? He said he needed her help, but what did he want her to do? What if it was something terrible? Would he really let her go after she'd helped him, or had he just said that? There were many who would pay handsomely for her. Was this a possibility? The thought curdled her stomach. He didn't seem like the type, but how could she know?

They neared the city wall and Teya sucked in her breath. It was huge. That was one thing King Thesald excelled at—building walls. How were they ever going to get over that?

Bran led her to the back of a church and through a gate that opened into a massive graveyard. As they carefully negotiated around the headstones, the shifting wind rattled through the tree branches with a soft moan. Teya shivered when an owl hooted ominously. Creeping through a graveyard in the wild hours of night, made it easy to imagine the bodies of the dead underfoot, and Teya moved closer to Bran.

At the far end of the cemetery, a mausoleum stood against the outside wall. They circled around it and found a staircase leading down to a bolted door. Bran deftly unlocked the bolt and motioned Teya inside. It was pitch black, and the sound of the closing door sent a shock of panic through her. Bran lit a candle, but the sudden light did nothing to stop the terror that froze her blood.

"What's wrong?" Bran asked.

A large coffin with an outline of a body lying on top took up most of the space. Teya tried to get her breathing under control, but couldn't seem to get enough air. "I have a hard time with closed spaces."

"Damn," Bran swore. "This is the only way out. Do you think you can make it? I promise it's not far."

"I don't know." Shut up inside this tiny space next to a dead body, Teya could feel the scream starting to rise. She clenched her fists in an effort to fight the panic.

"Look, there's a path right here." He held the candle toward a small opening in the wall. "It leads outside the city. Just think; with only a few steps, we'll be out of here and you'll be free. Come on, I'll be right here with you. We'll do it together."

Teya nodded, but couldn't seem to move. She wanted nothing more than to leave the coffin and small room behind, but that space was even smaller. There was no way she could walk in there.

Bran put his arm around her and pulled her close. His sudden warmth gave her strength and she leaned against him, clenching her eyes shut. "That's right," he said. "Keep your eyes closed, and pretend we're somewhere else. Hold on to me. You'll be fine. I won't let anything happen to you. I'll be right here all the way. Come on, just one step at a time. You can do it."

Teya took a deep breath, then moved with Bran, knowing that each step was taking her into a smaller, more confined space. But how could she stop now? After everything else, this was her only chance at freedom. Bran pulled her along, and even though she cringed, she stayed beside him.

She tried to imagine an open forest glade and took another step, but the dank, musty air wouldn't let her hold that image. Bran bent his head lower and pulled her closer to him, and even with her eyes closed, she could tell the space was getting smaller. A few clods of dirt fell on her arm and she gasped. Was the tunnel caving in? Would they be trapped in here forever? She trembled, and her stomach clenched with fear.

Bran coaxed and cajoled her, and she poured all her concentration on him. His voice was smooth and tranquil, with a slight accent that was pleasant to the ear. His arm was firm and strong, and she took comfort in his protective touch. She wasn't alone this time. He had promised he would get her through this. The smell of earth was strong, but with it came a gentle breeze and her heart quickened with anticipation. It couldn't be far now.

"All right," Bran breathed. "Look up. See the stars? We just need to climb this ladder and we'll be out."

Teya opened her eyes and took a deep breath. He was right; the stars were just above her. She climbed up the ladder with trembling legs. Bran was right behind her and they soon emerged in a copse of trees outside the city wall.

"Here. Sit down," Bran said. "I need to cover the opening."

Teya sank to the ground while the realization struck her that she was finally free! Her elation was tempered, however, by the uncertainty of what lay ahead. Bran started toward her, his face unreadable in the darkness, and her heart quickened. What did he want of her, and more important, would he free her from the *kundar*?

CHAPTER TWO

The Kundar

"I have horses hidden over the rise," Bran said. "Can you ride?"

"Yes, but I'd like to know where we're going." Now that they were out of the city, it was time he told her what he wanted.

"I'll explain after I get you to a safe place."

"No. I want to know now."

Bran huffed with impatience. "All right, but explanations will have to wait, understand?" When she nodded he continued. "I want you to take me to the Kaloriahns."

Shock sent a shiver down her spine. "Why?"

"There's no time to explain right now. We're still too close to the city. We have to keep moving."

He started up the hill and Teya hurried to catch up, her mind whirling with plausible reasons for his request. What could he possibly gain by finding the Kaloriahns? Did he intend to exploit her people? A knot of dread formed in her stomach, it was the one place she wanted to go, and now she didn't know if she should. Did he intend to exact a price for returning her?

The horses were just where he said they'd be, and Teya realized how organized his escape plans were. He could have taken her in the opposite direction to Braemar, instead they headed north, toward her people. She understood the need to get away from the city, but this direction was closer to his goal. He wasn't leaving anything to chance, and she hoped she wasn't just a pawn in his plans. She'd had enough of others being in control of her life.

From this vantage point, she was surprised at how far the city spread beyond the wall. This 'outer' city was almost as big as the one inside the gates. Inns and houses dotted the land in front of the city wall, which soon gave way to larger estates before filtering out to farmhouses and country roads.

Bran led her through the outside fringes of town, then into the countryside, skirting around homesteads and farms. Every once in a while, he turned in the saddle to look back. At first she thought he was making sure she was following, but then realized he was watching for pursuit from the city. It rattled her nerves that he thought there was a chance they could get caught, and when Bran wasn't watching, she cast surreptitious glances over her shoulder as well.

As dawn approached, they left the last of the settlements behind. Bran turned off the road and took another path through the trees, which led to a rocky ravine. He coaxed his horse into the ravine, and led her down a trail through dense underbrush. Leveling out near the bottom, the flat ground led to a small stream, which they followed into a space that opened up into a little valley. Trees and brush helped camouflage the small cabin that stood in the dense shadows.

Much to Teya's relief, it was here that Bran stopped to rest. She wasn't used to riding so long, and was exhausted after being up all night. Still, she couldn't rest until she knew why Bran wanted to find her people.

"It's not much, but I have food and extra supplies here," Bran said, dismounting.

Once she hit the ground, Teya held on to the saddle for a few seconds, making sure her legs didn't give way. When she was sure she could walk, she straightened and followed Bran to the cabin. The unlocked door swung open on creaky hinges and she was nervous about entering the enclosed space.

Noticing her hesitation, Bran stepped in ahead of her. "It's safe, and not as small as you think. Why don't you find something to eat while I take care of the horses?" He set a food pouch from his saddlebags on the table and turned to leave.

A deep fireplace lined the wall beyond the table and chairs, and a narrow bed took up the rest of the space on the other side. "How long are we going to stay here?"

"Not more than a few hours."

Teya stepped inside and took a seat at the table, but was too tired to eat. She rummaged through the pouch anyway, and found bread, cheese, and dried fruit, along with a waterbag. Her stomach chose that moment to growl, and she decided a little food wouldn't hurt. After she'd eaten as much as she wanted, Bran came in and sat beside her. He took an apple and bit into it, then settled back in his chair. His nonchalance took some of the wariness out of her and she relaxed. He had risked a great deal to get her out of the palace and gratitude swept over her.

"What do you think the king will do when he finds you missing?" Bran asked.

Teya considered it. "First, he'll send guards to search the grounds, and servants to search the palace. He won't let them rest until I'm found. I'm not sure what he'll do then, but it won't be pretty. He'll do whatever he can to get me back. He'll probably have the guard killed who escorted me to my room last night. If Clare was still there he would have her tortured before executing her." A spasm of pain shook her body. "He's shown such cruelty before. Anyone who ever cared for me is dead."

"It wasn't your fault."

"I know." Her voice was hard with anger. "Now, tell me why you want to find the Kaloriahns."

Bran frowned, pausing to choose his words carefully. "I'm here because of *sym*. Have you ever heard of it?"

His question caught her off-guard and her anger cooled. "No. What is it?"

"We don't have magic in Braemar. But recently we've uncovered an elixir that gives magical abilities. It's called *sym*, and it comes from the Old Country. The magic only lasts a few hours, but in the wrong hands, it's deadly. In fact, we have reason to believe that whoever is behind it is a threat to Braemar. I need to find out where it's coming from and the Kaloriahns are the only people who possess magic. That's why I want to find them."

"You think my people are making *sym*?" A flare of hot indignation surged through her.

"No, not your people," he said quickly. "But maybe some of them."

"The Kaloriahns would never use magic to hurt anyone," she said defiantly, then realized her blunder. "Unless it was the only way to defend themselves."

"Like you?" His eyes narrowed with accusation. "I know you hurt the king the other night, not that he didn't deserve it, but people were saying that was exactly why Kaloriahns needed to be collared. They're not to be trusted because they wouldn't hesitate to kill anyone who didn't agree with them."

"That's not true!" Teya said, outraged that he would believe this. "Those are lies. Kaloriahns love peace and treasure life."

"All Kaloriahns?" Bran asked. "There must be a few who don't feel that way. Not everyone loves peace, and ruthless ambition is everywhere."

Teya couldn't deny his reasoning, but she couldn't believe one of her own would use magic to destroy others. "I was only ten when I was kidnapped. My memories of home are filled with love and contentment. I was happy there. It was only after I was taken that I learned anger and hate." She held his gaze, challenging him to disagree. "That didn't come from my people, and none of them wore a *kundar*." Sudden comprehension dawned. "You never planned to take this off, did you?" She fingered the collar. "Are you afraid of me? Of what I might do without the *kundar* on?"

"Why shouldn't I be concerned? After everything I've heard, I would be a fool not to consider your power. You're right. You have learned anger and hate. You've been a slave for ten years. Without the *kundar*, how do I know you won't seek revenge?"

"Why should you care what I do to the king? He deserves to die." As the words left her mouth, she realized how vindictive she sounded. That was not the right thing to say to gain his trust. She softened her voice, hoping he would understand. "But I wouldn't go back now. Not before I returned to my people. You got me out of there, and because of that, I would honor our bargain."

He didn't reply, and it seemed as though a wall had gone up between them. How could she blame him for his caution? In his place she would probably feel the same way. Exhaustion overcame her and her shoulders slumped. "Why do you think my people would help you?"

"Once I explained about *sym*, they could give me an idea of who might be involved in making it, especially if it bothers them as much as it bothers you. I know the king has made it his business to capture or kill the Kaloriahns, but no one really knows where they come from. I've heard rumors that they've disappeared, but no one knows for sure. I just want to talk with them and I thought that if I brought you back they would be more willing to help me."

She glanced at him sharply. "Oh, I get it; you're using me to bargain with."

"I guess you could say that if you like." Now he was angry. "Do you want to go back to your people or not?"

"Of course I do."

"Then we're helping each other."

Silence stretched between them. Now that she knew he didn't trust her magic it was hard to tell him what she wanted. But if he didn't take it off now, she wasn't sure he ever would. "I can take you to them, but the *kundar* limits my sense of direction. I know we're headed the right way, but I can't sense them like I could without it. If you want me to find them, you'll need to take it off."

He glanced at her with surprise. "How do I know you're telling the truth?"

"I promise I won't hurt you. Not after you helped me escape." When he didn't respond she continued with the truth. "I'm afraid if you don't take it off now, you never will. I can't risk it. If there's a chance of getting caught again, I have to know

I can use my magic to defend myself. I won't go back. I would rather die first."

Her declaration seemed to hit a nerve with Bran and he hesitated before responding. "I need to think about this. Why don't you rest for a little while? I'll keep watch."

Without waiting for a response, he fled the cabin, probably eager to get away from her. She wanted to call him back to allay his fears, but what more could she say? Only time would convince him that she meant what she said. Time they didn't have.

Teya couldn't seem to open her eyes when Bran nudged her shoulder. It seemed like she had only been asleep for a minute. A very short minute. Bran was sitting on the edge of the bed, and for some reason, it soothed her to have him close.

"When you asked me if I could get the *kundar* off, I told you I wasn't sure I could. Remember?"

That woke her up. "You said there was a way."

"Yes, but I wasn't sure it would work."

"So what are you saying?"

"I'll try and get it off, but I can't guarantee anything."

Relief coursed through her. "What made you change your mind?"

"I tried to imagine what it would be like to be in your place. How I'd feel. I realized that I couldn't stand to have another man's collar around my neck. It's wrong. You deserve the opportunity to decide your own fate. Even if it's not what I want."

Something inside Teya cracked open. His kindness astonished her. It had been so long since someone cared about her feelings that she didn't know how to respond. Did he really mean it?

"I need to put this," he said, holding up an animal hide, "between the *kundar* and your skin to protect you, then I'll wrap this string around the gold. It's coated with an explosive powder, and once I ignite it, the metal should melt down. It is gold, isn't it?"

Teya swallowed. "I think so, but it has some kind of magic in it."

Bran hesitated. "Do you think it will hurt you?"

Teya suppressed a laugh. "This collar's been hurting me ever since I can remember, but I'll try anything to get it off." Bran nodded before he put the animal hide under the *kundar* and spread it as far as he could over her neck and face. The soft fur tickled her nose and she turned her head to the side.

"I didn't think you would do this," she said. "I'm not used to kindness."

"I just hope it works. This is ready. Hold still."

Teya held her breath when she heard the sizzle of fire. An acrid smell filled her nostrils before a small pop reverberated through her body. It was soon followed by a thin, high-pitched wail that made her eyes water. Then it was over.

"It worked." Bran grasped the broken ends and easily pried it open while Teya sat up. As he examined the *kundar*, the gold glittered brightly in the filtered sunlight coming through the window. As Teya reached out to touch it, she was surprised that her hand shook. Taking a deep breath, her fingers found the *kundar* cold and lifeless.

"Something died to forge this." She swallowed. "That wail was the sound of it dying."

"I'll bury it," Bran said soberly.

"No." Teya took it from him. "I want to keep it. It can't hurt me anymore."

Bran frowned in distaste, and she wondered why she didn't want to fling it as far from her as possible.

"We'd better leave, we've been here too long already. There's some water and a washcloth on the table if you'd like to wash up. I'll get the horses ready."

Teya nodded, grateful for some time alone. Slipping the *kundar* into her jacket pocket she dipped a soft cloth into the water and held it to her face, relieving the tiredness in her eyes. She still had smudges of dirt on her hands and wondered how bad she looked. She rubbed her face vigorously, until satisfied that no dirt remained. The cool cloth on the back of her neck felt wonderful, and as she pressed it against the front of her neck, she realized that this was the first time in years the *kundar* wasn't in the way.

It was really gone. Her pulse leapt in her throat, and something akin to joy floated up from her heart. For many long years, she had suppressed her feelings of anger and hate. The only way she'd survived was trying to live in a state of serenity where nothing could touch her.

This new feeling of joy surprised her. She'd lived without happiness for so long, it was almost overwhelming. She had Bran to thank for it. He had given her the most impressive gift of all. His trust. He deserved no less from her.

She gathered her things and gazed out the window, focusing on the blue sky and the sounds of the forest. The birds chirped as they called to one another, and all kinds of insects droned in a cadence of life. The removal of the *kundar* had not only freed her magic, but also freed her soul. As if she had been dead before, she could now take a place among the living. This moment was the beginning of a new life, and her heart swelled with gratitude.

"Teya? Are you ready?"

She fought for a measure of control, but when she faced Bran, his brows drew together in concern. "What's wrong?"

"Nothing," she managed to smile. "Nothing is wrong." When he didn't look convinced, she continued. "I'm free of that cursed collar. I'm free to live!" His smile sent a wave of pleasure through her. "I'll never be able to thank you enough."

Bran shook his head modestly. "I'm just glad it worked."

"After everything you heard, I'm surprised you even considered it, let alone did it." She wished there was a better way to express the joy she felt. "Thank you." On impulse, she hugged him close, then drew back, concerned she had overstepped.

Bran's eyes smoldered. With a smile, he gently touched her hair. "I've been wanting to do that ever since I first saw you. It's so soft. Soft and beautiful."

They were standing so close, that Teya's mouth went dry and her legs trembled. He leaned toward her, and for a moment she thought he might kiss her.

"We'd better go," she said, her heart beating fast.

Bran dropped his gaze and moved away. "I'll grab our things."

Teya stepped out of the cabin and took a calming breath to get her emotions under control. Bran confused and excited her at the same time. Getting involved with him would be like touching fire. One way or another, it would burn. He came out and packed the saddlebags, then helped her mount.

"Can you tell where your people are now?"

Teya knew without thinking. The direction came into her mind like a bird following a migratory path. "That way." She pointed north.

Bran smiled, then stilled at the sound of falling rocks. In the distance, a flock of birds burst from the trees. "Someone's coming," Bran said. "Hurry. There's a different way out than the way we came. It's this way." She followed him, urging her horse to keep up. On the other side of the cabin a small trail opened up, but the thick underbrush slowed the horses down. Behind them, the scuttle of hooves on rocks was fast approaching. Bran quickened the pace and the bushes gave way, but instead of open country, they faced a wall of rocks.

Teya's heart sank. How were they supposed to get out now? Bran pressed forward and she realized there was a small fissure just big enough for their horses to pass between the rocks. It was hard to see with rocks camouflaging the break. Beyond the opening, they picked their way up a sharp incline to the left and soon emerged at the top of a hill.

Bran set a grueling pace, riding deep into the forest. They followed a well-ridden track and kept to it for speed. After several miles, they came to a fork in the road and after taking one path, Bran cut through the brush toward the other.

The detour slowed them down, but she couldn't hear any signs of pursuit. They emerged onto the other road and sped up, hoping to lose their pursuers once and for all. When they came to a small river, Bran stopped to let the horses drink and rest for a moment.

"Did you see who it was?" Teya asked.

"No, I didn't have a chance, but I can only assume they were King Thesald's men. I don't know how they found us so fast." Bran frowned, his brows furrowed. "There aren't that many people who know about the cove."

Teya's shoulders tensed. Had Jax or Clare been caught? "If we weren't followed, then maybe taking off the *kundar* released magic of some kind that led them to us."

"There's nothing we can do about it now. We'd better keep going. They might not be far behind." He glanced at her hesitantly before asking, "Is there anything you can do to slow them down?"

His question caught her off-guard. Things were desperate if he wanted her to use magic, especially when she had no idea what she could do without the *kundar* around her neck. When she hesitated, he added, "Think about it. We've got a good lead for now and hopefully we can lose them in the mountains. Let's go." He urged his horse into the stream and Teya followed, still unsure of what to do. They went a few miles upstream until the river got too deep for the horses.

Once on dry ground, they headed up a rocky incline and dismounted at the top of a rise. Searching the forest below, Bran pointed to the riverbed. Two men on horseback had just entered the stream. "I wonder if they're using *sym* to track us."

Teya hadn't thought of that and it made her pause. If others could use magic against them, then what was she waiting for? "Let me try something." She concentrated on the stream. Its source was high above them, but if she could stir it up, it could easily become a raging torrent. She listened to the sound of the rushing water and formed the notes in her mind. Taking a deep breath, she drew out the notes, low and hard. Bending the current to her will, the water churned into a frothing whirlpool. She held the water back as long as she could before releasing the turbid mass.

The water crashed into the river with a powerful roar. Below, the riders paused before understanding dawned. In a sudden blur, the water surged over them with breaking waves. Thrown from their horses, Teya lost sight of the riders. Dread formed a knot in her stomach. She hadn't meant to kill them. An instant later, she caught sight of their dark heads bobbing in the water before they disappeared from sight.

"Do you think they'll survive?" she asked Bran.

He nodded absently. "No doubt they'll wash up somewhere downstream. I don't think we need to worry about them for the time being." His wary glance held new respect, and something close to fear.

She didn't know what to say. She'd never done anything like this before. It was both exhilarating and frightening at the same time. Still, she didn't want him to be afraid of her.

"Are we headed in the right direction?" he asked.

"Yes," Teya closed her eyes and felt the pull. "It's straight through there."

Bran nodded. "Let's keep moving."

Following Bran, she marveled at how easy it had been to summon her magic. She was so conditioned to having it cause her pain that she was almost afraid of it. Under the direction of King Thesald, she had used magic to influence people's minds, to calm them, or dazzle them with imagery, but mostly, to make them more amenable to the king's wishes. But with the *kundar* around her neck, she could only use a small amount of her magic before pain stabbed her like a thousand knives.

Without the *kundar*, she had no idea of what she could do. No one had ever used magic for anything like this at home, at least not that she could remember. Of course, not everyone could sing the way she could. Just before she'd been kidnapped, her grandmother had taught her to do simple things like light fire and heat water. Her grandmother had told her she was special, and that when she was older, she would take her place as Songmistress of the grove.

After all these years was she really going home? How would it be? Would her parents know her? Excitement warred with nervousness. Ten years was a long time, and so many things could have changed. Would they still want her? Were they still there?

She tucked her hair behind her ear and remembered how Bran had touched it. When he leaned toward her, she almost believed he was going to kiss her. Her pulse leapt at the thought, and she wondered what it would be like to kiss him. He was incredibly handsome in a dangerous sort of way.

But he had a mission to accomplish, and she was just a means to an end. Once he found out what he needed to know, he would leave and she would never see him again. Better to keep a distance and make sure he didn't get too close.

Dusk approached on a cool mountain breeze. Teya had no idea where they were, only which direction to go. The Kaloriahns lived in a valley deep in the mountains, but that was all she remembered. Her back ached, and she was grateful when Bran stopped in a small clearing.

"I think we'll be safe here for the night." He dismounted and began to set up camp. Teya followed suit and swallowed against the pain in her legs. She took a few small steps, stretching her legs out.

They worked in companionable silence and soon had a small fire going. "Do you know how far your home is from here?" Bran asked.

Teya closed her eyes, the pull was stronger now, the Kaloriahns had to be close. "Not far, maybe we'll be there tomorrow, but I could be wrong. When I was taken, it seemed further away."

"Things are different when you're young." He took some food and water from the pack and handed it to her. "I've heard a lot of things about the Kaloriahns. Most of the rumors are probably wrong. What can you tell me about them? Are all of them like you?"

Teya knew he meant her magic. "Yes, but only a few can use magic to do more than sing to the trees. My grandmother was one. She was the Songmistress of the Grove. I was supposed to take her place."

"Did she teach you anything?"

"She had just begun my training, so I was spending a lot of time with her."

"What about the day you were taken?"

Thinking of that day brought a swirl of anger and fear she would rather forget. "It was a day like any other, except that my grandmother was busy. Someone came to see her and she spent most of the day with him. Later when I went to her, she sent me away. I never saw her again."

"Where did she send you?"

"I don't remember, but I was always doing things for her, running errands or taking messages. It must have been something like that."

"And that was when you were kidnapped?" Bran asked.

"Yes. I've always wondered how my grandmother felt, if she ever blamed herself for sending me away." Teya wrapped the blanket tight around her to quiet her sudden trembling.

Bran wasn't finished. "The men who took you, are you sure they were the king's men?"

Teya opened her mouth to respond, then stopped. She had always assumed that they were King Thesald's men, but what if they weren't? "I think so, but now I'm not sure. They weren't wearing the king's insignia, but you could hardly expect them to. Their clothes were coarse and they were rough looking men with long hair and beards. After they caught me, they kept me tied up in a wooden box. It was like a coffin. It had three small air holes in the top, but that was all." Her stomach clenched just talking about it.

"That explains your fear of closed spaces." Bran shook his head. "I'm sorry to put you through this, but I have one more question that I have to ask."

Teya braced herself, knowing intuitively that it was something she would rather not hear.

"In all of the time that you've been gone," Bran said, "why has no one come for you?"

It was a question Teya had asked herself many times. At first she had believed that her father would be right behind her and she would be home that night. Then, as time passed and no one came, she made up excuses. She had to believe that someday they would come to get her. It never happened. Ten long years of captivity and not once had anyone tried to get her out. Unexpected tears welled up in her eyes, but she held them back with a burst of anger. "I don't know." She held back the unspoken fear that the real reason was because they were gone or worse, dead. From rumors she'd heard they had fled to another country, but if that were true, how could she know where to find them?

She was trembling when Bran sat beside her, but in her distress she didn't want his sympathy. He seemed to sense this and was careful not to touch her. Teya immediately regretted it, wishing she could turn to him for comfort, but afraid that if she did, she would start to like it. Sitting this close, he smelled of leather and horse with a deeper musky scent that was all his own.

"You know, the first time I saw you," he said. "I was struck speechless. That's never happened to me before. You seemed untouchable, like you were above all of us lowly humans. Then you sang and everything changed."

Teya was grateful to think of something else. "I noticed you as soon as you walked in. You were different. I remember you staring at me, but that's what most people do. I lost track of you after that. I guess I had other things on my mind."

"Like your song for the king?"

"Yes. I decided that I didn't care how much it hurt me, as long as I could hurt him too. Of course it didn't work, and I ended up spending most of the night in the box."

Bran went still. "What do you mean?"

"My punishment for defying him. It's a small, enclosed cell, with no windows for light, and barely enough room to sit comfortably. It was the perfect punishment for me because he knew how much I hated closed spaces. There were times when I thought I would go crazy in there. I always tried to imagine that I was someplace else. Sometimes it worked, but there were other times when I fell apart, especially at first. I never mastered that box. I don't think I ever will."

Bran bristled. "I wondered what your punishment was." His jaw clenched and she realized he was angry. "At least he can't do that anymore."

"You're right. He'll never be able to put me in a box again."

Bran seemed about to say something else, but held back. She suddenly wanted to thank him again for rescuing her, but knew he wouldn't like it. "I hope my people have the answers you're searching for." It was small consolation for everything he had risked.

"I hope they can answer your questions as well." Bran stood. "Get some sleep, I'm going to take care of the horses."

After he left, she sat listening to his movements, taking comfort that he was close by. He had risked so much to rescue her, and she considered that finding the Kaloriahns and *sym* might be important, but it seemed there was more to it. He actually believed that her captivity was wrong. Not only that, but he seemed truly outraged at how the king had treated her. The other thing she could hardly comprehend was that he trusted her enough to take off the *kundar*. She didn't know anyone who would do that. He seemed too good to be true, and that made her suspicious. Maybe there was something he wasn't telling her.

Finally giving in to her fatigue, she tried to find a spot that wasn't too rocky and snuggled into her blanket. As she drifted into sleep, Bran kept watch. Even with her suspicions, it warmed her heart. Somewhere deep inside she wanted to trust him. It was nice having someone on her side for a change and her spirits lifted. The dark cloud of oppression that was her companion for the last several years dissipated into a mellow contentment, and for the first time in a long time, she slept peacefully.

☙❧

The gray light of dawn filtered through the trees, waking Teya from a sound sleep. The horses were chomping on grass nearby, but there was no sign of Bran. Untangling from the blankets, she stood and used her fingers to comb through her hair. She straightened her clothes and brushed at the dirt on her pants. She wasn't used to being dirty and sleeping in her clothes, but found she didn't mind too much. Freedom was worth any price.

Light footsteps alerted her to Bran's approach, and set her heart pounding at the sight of him. He wore the same clothing, but his hair was wet and curled around his ears. He was quite tall, and walked with an easy grace that she admired. With a few days' growth of beard on his face, he exuded masculine strength that was more than a little exciting. His dark eyes danced when he smiled, and it left her speechless.

"There's a stream if you'd like to wash up."

Teya couldn't seem to think straight and merely inclined her head in acknowledgment before she fled his presence. Her heart was still pounding when she found the stream, but the cold water shocked her back to her senses. What was she thinking? Bran was her rescuer, nothing more. There could never be anything between them. He was taking her home and after that, he was leaving.

She realized that confiding in Bran last night had opened a crack in her heart. Even though she liked having someone to talk to, it left her vulnerable at the same time. It was a feeling she didn't like. Everyone she'd been close to was gone, and once he took her home, he would leave as well. It was better to keep a distance between them.

With a deep breath, she pushed her attraction to him aside. It didn't matter anyway. All that ever mattered was getting home, and hopefully, today she would be there. Excitement warred with trepidation. Home. It had been so long and her memories had faded, but not her feelings. Home meant love and warmth. She was willing to risk anything to have it again. But what if they weren't there? What if the king had killed them all? What if they had left to some distant place? She shook off these senseless worries and pushed them to the back of her mind. Now was not the time to get panicky. They were there, and she would see them soon.

When she returned to camp, everything was packed and Bran was tightening the straps on her saddle. "I was wondering," she asked tentatively. "What if the Kaloriahns aren't there? What will you do?"

He glanced her way, then continued with his task. "I'd keep looking until we found them." He turned his full attention on her. "Are you worried that I won't keep my end of the bargain?"

"No. I just want to make it clear that I'm not stopping until I find them, whether you're with me or not."

"I'm not your jailor. I released you from that, remember?"

She flushed, realizing she had just insulted him. After everything he'd done for her, she still had trouble trusting him. "I don't mean to sound ungrateful. I just needed you to know."

"I know that you've been living in hell for the last ten years, so I'll try not to be offended. I just hope you won't let that experience cloud your judgment. Not everyone is bad."

"I didn't mean to insinuate that you were. You've more than proven yourself. It's just that I'm new at this, and I don't know the rules."

"Rule number one, you can trust me. Rule number two, I'm not going anywhere until we find the Kaloriahns. Now, let's get going."

This coaxed a smile out of her, and she mounted her horse with a lighter heart. The morning was clear, without a cloud in sight. It seemed warmer than it should at this elevation, but Teya didn't complain. She was curious about Bran and his country. "What's it like in Braemar?"

A smile lit his eyes. "It's very different from here. We have a lot of things that you don't have."

"Like what?" Her curiosity peaked.

"Motorbikes. If we had one of those, we would have found your people yesterday." At her puzzled frown he continued. "They're machines that can take you anywhere you want to go. They have two wheels, and the front wheel has a handlebar on it that you can turn to guide it. You sit in the middle like on a horse."

"How do you keep from tipping over?"

He shrugged. "You learn. It has a motor on it that makes it go, and it runs on petrol, so it can go for miles." His brow tilted at a rakish angle. "And they're very fast."

Teya couldn't comprehend such a thing. "What do you do when you run out of petrol?"

"You put more in." At her puzzlement, he continued. "In Braemar, petrol stations are all over the place."

"I'm not sure I understand these 'motorbikes' but I can tell you love them."

He smiled. "Yes." Then with heartfelt excitement said, "Someday I'll have to take you for a ride."

She couldn't help the lurch of her heart, nor his contagious enthusiasm. "I'd like that. When was the first time you ever rode one?"

Bran regaled her with several stories, some of them downright hilarious. It was so easy to talk to him. He was different; he didn't look at her like she was a freak. She almost envied the freedom he'd had growing up, knowing it was nothing like the last ten years of her life. It was nice to carry on a normal conversation, and she was surprised when she actually laughed. She hadn't done that for years.

It wasn't until noon that she noticed the beginning of a change in the countryside. Small things were apparent at first. The grass had turned brown from lack of water, and the earth beneath was dry and dusty. There wasn't any new growth, and what did grow was spread out in patches.

"It looks like this area has had a dry spell," Bran said.

"It feels oppressive." But she knew this was the right way. Every time she thought about changing direction, she was pulled back to this course. Foreboding entered her heart and she shivered. They continued on, and the further they went, the worse it got. Soon the trees showed signs of stress. Instead of growing straight and tall, the trunks were misshapen and craggy. Some of the leaves had curled black with decay.

Further on, the trees leaned toward the earth, broken and bent as if struck by a whirlwind. The forest stood in silence. There were no birdcalls or the rustling of small animals. No wind stirred the grass. Clouds blocked the sun, and cast a gray shadow over them. It was as if all life had died.

Panic gripped Teya. Maybe her people were dead after all. She closed her eyes again and felt the pull. This was the right way, but what had happened?

Bran met her gaze with a troubled frown. "There's a rise up ahead, we should be able to see better from there."

Teya followed Bran up the rise and her stomach knotted with dread. At the top of the hill her worst fears were realized. As far as she could see the ground was covered with blackened trunks. The earth was bare of life, and the trees stood in stark nakedness, their limbs like twisted fingers reaching for the sky.

She stared, horrified at the destruction, yet too absorbed by it to pull her gaze away. In breathless shock she whispered, "It's like a blight, or a curse. What would cause such an appalling thing?" Before Bran could answer, something moved in the dimness below.

"Did you see that?" he asked.

Teya strained to see it again, but there was nothing. "I'm not sure. Maybe it was a shadow." A chill ran up her spine. This place made her skin crawl.

"How much further?" Bran asked.

"The pull of magic is strong here. We have to be close, but it leads straight through that."

"Maybe the Kaloriahns caused this to discourage outsiders. Whatever the reason, the only way we'll know is to keep going."

"You're right, but what if they're not there?" She couldn't say dead, even though it was what she meant.

"It's a possibility. Do you want to keep going?"

With a deep breath she nodded. "Of course. It's just hard. This blight feels wrong. Evil. I don't think my people would do this, but I don't know. I want to find them, but going through this could be dangerous."

"Then we'll just have to be careful." He scanned the landscape, "See that outcropping of rocks in the distance?" It was so far away she could barely make it out. "We'll head for that. Maybe we'll see something from there."

"All right," she agreed.

"I want you to have this." Bran pulled a short sword from his saddlebags. "Do you know how to use it?"

"Are you kidding? I wasn't allowed anywhere near something as lethal as that. My weapon is my voice, I don't need anything else."

"You're probably right, but since I don't have that luxury, I'm not going to take any chances." Bran strapped the sword to his back and then took out another belt that held a weapon Teya had never seen before.

"What's that?"

"This is a gun. It works like this." He held it in his hand with the barrel pointed outward and opened the chamber. "You put bullets in here and when you pull the trigger, the mechanism will fire the bullet out the barrel. Depending on how good your aim is, you can hit something at least fifty feet away maybe more."

"And how good are you?"

"I'm not bad," his lips quirked up in a smile. "But if anything should happen to me..."

"Nothing's going to happen," she said firmly. "Between the two of us, we'll be fine."

"Good, because you're right about this." He gestured around him. "It makes me uneasy." He loaded the gun, then settled the holster around his waist. Ready, he glanced at her with grim determination. "Let's go."

As they started through the dead trees, Teya kept her senses alert. Once or twice she thought there was a flicker of movement, but when she looked, nothing was there.

The sound of loose gravel came from behind, and she jerked around, but there was nothing she could see. "Keep going," Bran said. "Stay focused on the rocks. If we get separated, head for them."

Alarmed, Teya shook her head. "No. We should stay together."

"If I have to fight for your safety the least you can do is stay out of my way."

"All right," she said to ease the tension. The horses pulled on their reins, prancing with alarm. Something was out there, but it wasn't anything she could see. In an effort to calm the horses, she hummed a tune. The effect was immediate and the threat seemed to diminish.

She kept up the tune until they reached the shelter of rocks and she breathed a sigh of relief. Her throat was dry, and she needed a drink. "Do you think it's safe to rest here for a few minutes?" she asked Bran.

He nodded, but his face was grave. "Maybe we should stay here for the night."

"Why? Is it that late already?"

"No, but…take a look at that." He pointed back the way they had come. The gray twilight was enveloped in a dark mist that was slowly creeping toward them. Behind that, huge dark clouds followed. It looked like a terrible storm, getting bigger and bigger with each passing moment.

Teya was transfixed by the sheer enormity of it, and could hardly tear her eyes away. As it neared, a faint breeze carried the echoes of a low moan and the stench of decay. It came closer, and the dark mist coalesced into the form of a body that seemed to fall apart and come together in a horrible aberration. An inhuman cry shook her to the bone.

"No!" Teya cried, clutching Bran. Her heart pounded. "We have to make a run for it! We've got to get out of here!"

"What is it?"

"It's death! And it's coming for us!"

CHAPTER THREE

The Grove

Teya glanced back in horror. The dark form seemed to be gathering speed. It howled toward them as if hungry for living flesh. She kicked her horse in panic, needing every second of swiftness it could give. On her left, Bran shouted something, but she couldn't understand what he said.

She scanned the horizon for signs of the Kaloriahns, but there was nothing. Was anyplace safe? Bran shouted and veered further to the left. Teya strained to keep up and was almost knocked off her horse by a blackened tree limb. She kept her head down and thundered on. The light was fading fast and it was hard to see Bran in the gray shadows. She focused on his back and hoped he knew where he was going.

An eerie quiet was the only warning that the mist was at her heels. A cold tendril of shadow touched her back and slowly crept up her spine. Icy fingers caressed her cheek and she flinched, shaking it off. The mist withdrew and she took a quick breath before she felt it again. This time, the shadow penetrated into her back and she gasped in pain.

Her horse floundered in terror, and she lost sight of Bran. As the burning pain entered her chest she heard a high whistle. It sounded like reeds blowing in the wind. All at once, the pain lessened and she was able to breathe again. Concentrating with all her senses, she sang the exact same tones she heard. Immediately, the darkness recoiled and she was free.

Giddy with relief, she searched for Bran and found him a short distance away slumped over his horse. The mist receded as she approached with her song, releasing Bran from death's grip. His face was ashen, but he took a deep breath when she reached for him. She stopped singing to say something, but the mist started to come back and she began the tones again. Bran was slipping from his horse when she reached his side, but Teya grabbed him, using all her strength to hold him upright until he was steady. She motioned for him to follow her and focused on the tones she heard.

The mist thickened into a solid wall around them, and she tried not to panic. She closed her eyes and concentrated, knowing their only hope lay in finding the source of the music. At last, a faint breeze carried the tones to her and she jerked her horse toward the sound. Bran tensed when he heard them, finally understanding what she was doing.

As they got closer to the tones, the darkness thinned in front of them, and disappeared. What she had imagined as reeds were actually pipes, turned to catch the wind and placed on a wooden stand. About ten feet in both directions, more pipes were forming a barrier against the mist. With a cry of relief, she and Bran surged between them to safety. Gasping, Teya slid off her horse and almost fell to her knees.

A sudden moaning shriek came from behind. Her horse reared in fright, jerking from her grasp and galloped away. Teya turned to face the darkness and it roiled into a churning mass of turbid malevolence. She recoiled in horror and stepped back from the small tendrils of mist that crept forward, finding purchase between the pipes and straining to reach her. Instinctively, Teya lashed out with her song and the mist fell back as if stung. She strengthened her tones, and the darkness hung in the air for a few moments before disappearing into the dead countryside.

Taking huge breaths, Teya could hardly stand. Bran came to her side, his breath shallow and uneven. "That thing almost had us," he said. "Where did it come from?"

"I don't know." Her legs were trembling so hard she couldn't stand up. Bran caught her and they clung to each other as the shock of their narrow escape washed over them. Teya's trembling subsided with Bran's arms around her. When she was calm enough to notice her surroundings, she pulled back in astonishment.

"Look!" she exclaimed. "Grass! We're standing on it!" The green carpet began a few feet beyond the barrier of pipes and continued up a slope. With the darkness gone, the setting sun cast orange-gold rays across the land.

"There, in the distance," Bran said, pointing past the slope. "It looks like trees. Real trees." Golden light caught the tips of the trees in shimmering brilliance.

"That must be the grove," Teya agreed hopefully. "The pipes are the handiwork of my people. They have to be here."

They scrambled up the slope and the vista opened up to a scene of green grass covering the rolling countryside. At the center, stood a large stand of trees, glowing in the last rays of the sunset. It was beautiful, but seemed so small compared to what she remembered. Was this all that remained of the grove and her people?

Bran gathered the horses and followed Teya toward the trees. The setting sun left them in a gray twilight, taking the golden light with it, and they continued on in subdued silence. It didn't take long before they were close enough to see that the trees were spread out over a small valley. Nearby, a stream gurgled, but it was the glow of a campfire nestled in the trees that sent her heart racing.

She grabbed Bran's arm and pointed. "Can you see it? Someone's there!" She didn't wait for a reply and started to run. By the time she entered the trees, she was gasping for breath. The campfire was easy to find, but when she burst into the clearing, no one was there. "Hello?" she shouted, checking the length of the clearing. "Is anyone here?" No one answered and she hoped she hadn't scared them off. "I don't mean any harm. Please come out."

A rustling of hooves marked Bran's arrival and she turned to him. "Did you see anyone?"

He shook his head. "Not a soul."

"Where do you think they've gone?"

"Not far," Bran said quietly and nodded toward a tree.

Teya jerked in that direction and her breath caught. "Grandmother?" A small woman with long white hair and a surprisingly unlined face stepped into the light. She wore a simple gown of white muslin and her bearing was as regal as a queen. Her turquoise eyes grew bright with unshed tears.

"Teya?"

"Grandma!" Teya flew into her grandmother's welcoming arms. Tears ran unchecked down her face and soon she was sobbing uncontrollably. Grief for all she'd lost and suffered warred with the joy of seeing her grandmother again.

Her grandmother held her close, letting her emotions run their course. "There now, it's over," she said in a soothing voice, shedding tears of her own.

Teya drank in the familiar scent of lavender and sage that was her grandmother. It quieted her ravaged heart, and brought peace to her soul. The tears slowed and she took a deep breath, while her grandmother dabbed at her face with a handkerchief.

"You've grown into a beautiful woman, just like your mother. There," she said and handed the cloth to Teya. "That's enough crying to last a lifetime. Please…" She motioned toward Bran. "Introduce me to your friend. I think all these tears have made him uncomfortable."

Before Bran could protest, Teya made the introductions. "This is Bran. He rescued me, Grandmother. He is the reason I'm here."

Her grandmother took Bran's hands into her own. "Please, call me Leona. I owe you more than my thanks. If there is anything you wish that is in my power to grant, it is yours."

Bran graciously bowed his head, "Thank you, but rescuing Teya was easy compared to what we ran into out there. We're lucky we made it here alive."

"What's going on?" Teya asked. "What happened to the grove?"

"It is a long story, but one that you must know." She hummed a few notes and a small globe of light appeared in the palm of her hand. "Come with me." She led them deeper into the trees than Teya thought possible, but instead of coming out on the other side, the forest seemed to expand. The trail continued until at last, the woods opened to a natural clearing. At the center stood an immense tree. The trunk was several feet wide, and bending her neck all the way back, she couldn't see the top. From its roots, a small spring bubbled up, sending water into a pool. Soft, velvety grass surrounded the pool, and a wooden table and chairs sat off to one side.

"Teya, fetch some water from the spring with that pitcher so you and Bran can have a drink." The pitcher and glasses sat on the small table near the tree. Her grandmother hummed another tune and several hundred small spheres of light shone down from the tree limbs. Teya caught her breath. The tree filled the grove with its magnificence and beauty, and her blood stirred with recognition. This tree was the source of her magic.

With reverence, she filled the pitcher with flowing water. As she poured the clear liquid into crystal goblets and handed one to Bran, she realized how dry her mouth was. The cold water tasted sweet and pure, sending a wave of freshness that permeated every cell in her body. She drank deeply; emptying her cup, then poured and drank more. Bran did the same until they were both satisfied.

"This is a sacred place," Leona said. "It is the birthplace of our world. As a people, the Kaloriahns took an oath long ago to protect and guard this grove. In return, we were given special gifts of magic and promised immortality. We have been doing this since the dawn of time. But now, our people are gone and the grove is dying."

"Tell me what has happened. Are my parents…?" Teya paused to gather her courage. "Are they dead?"

"Oh, my child, I wish I could spare you more pain."

Teya swallowed, this was not the homecoming she had dreamed of. When tears threatened, she pushed her sorrow deep inside, and found her voice. "It's all right, just tell me what happened."

"Let me start from the beginning. The day you were kidnapped, my younger brother Korban had come to see me. A few years before, he used his power for evil and deceived and manipulated many of our people. He spread lies and rumors that got out of hand. In the end, he killed one of the elders.

"As a result, he was banished from the grove. All his rights and privileges were revoked and his magic taken from him. But in this he tricked us. During the ritual to strip him of his magic, he was able to hide a small portion of it in darkness. He used it to escape. After that, I never thought I would see him again. To return meant death.

"He came to me that day with a grand plan. These trees form a sacred grove and the spring water is special and life sustaining. It is all one needs to live forever. Korban wanted the water, and I am the only one who can lift the veil of magic to this tree." She motioned with her hand. "I don't think he realized that I also knew the secret that with the proper song, the water would restore his lost magic.

"I had the elders bind and hold him for execution. Even his dark magic wasn't strong enough to free him, but he was one step ahead of me. He had seen you Teya, and knew you were special to me, and our people. Your gift shines. He knew you were to be the next Songmistress."

Teya blinked in surprise. "He had me kidnapped?"

"Yes. After you were gone, he threatened your life if we did not let him go and do as he said. The elders would not compromise, and after a long debate, decided to execute him the next day. Unfortunately for us, he had accomplices and slipped from our grasp.

"Your mother was inconsolable. We searched for you, but you were not to be found. A few weeks later, Korban took his revenge. We found a box on the outskirts of our city. Your clothes were inside. They were soaked in blood and wrapped around a human heart. We thought you were dead."

"I always wondered if you had forgotten me."

"Never that my precious child. I've held you close in my heart everyday you've been gone. Your mother was never the same after that. She was a gentle soul and felt things very deeply. The strife and pain of this life were too much for her, and she died a year later."

Teya closed her eyes to hold back the tears. When she was under control, she asked. "What about my father and brother?"

"Your father lost both of you, but he did not give in to grief and pain like your mother. He turned his anger toward revenge and was pivotal in the decisions of the elders during the next few years. Hewson followed your father's example and talked of weaponry and war.

"I had underestimated Korban's craving for magic and his desire for immortality. During his first years of banishment he used his dark magic to create the *kundar*. Somehow, it acts as a shield to our magic so we can't use it."

Teya nodded. "I wore one until Bran removed it."

"You must tell me how he accomplished that," Leona said, "but first I must finish the story. After you were gone, our people began to disappear. Just a few at first, but enough to make us suspicious of everyone who entered our lands. Then Korban came later that year with an army of hardened men. Our magic was barely strong enough to stop them, and we were not fully prepared with sword and shield. We won the day, but many of our people were killed or taken prisoner.

"Weapons had long been forbidden, but with your father's influence it was decided that we should defend ourselves rather than perish or be captured. The forges took the first of the trees. Iron was plentiful, but the mining of it also changed the beauty of the grove. Learning how to fight brought changes within the people.

"After a few years, Korban returned, and even though we were better prepared, more of our people were slain. Your father was one of the first to die. With his dying breath, he made Hewson promise to help our people escape and forget about revenge. Living, he said, was more important.

"Korban tried bargaining with me again, telling me that he would leave us in peace if I would let him have access to the water. He even told me about you, that you were not dead, but alive and a slave to the king. He promised he would return you to me if I would cooperate." Leona's voice wavered with emotion. "I was so tired of the constant provocation. How could we fulfill our covenant to protect the grove if we were always fighting? The grove had withered with our people, and the bloodshed caused the land to dry up. Soon there would be nothing left."

Leona rubbed her temples, then took a long drink of precious water. "I met with Korban not far from here, ready to kill him. He was different from the last time I saw him, and it was almost too late before I realized what it was. His magic had returned! It wasn't the same, not nearly as powerful as it was before, but the combination of the dark magic with the light nearly overcame me. He lulled me with his beautiful voice, and then tried to capture me with a *kundar*. Luckily, I had shielded myself from a possible attack and he was unsuccessful. I screamed for guards to seize him, but he was already gone.

"I knew it was only a matter of time before he returned, and I was more troubled than ever. How had he regained the magic of our people without the grove water? It is something that I still don't understand. After his visit, we held a grand council. With our numbers dwindling, we knew this was a war we could not win.

"It was determined that our people would leave the grove and return later when it was safe. It was the only way to survive. A few of our best warriors went after Korban. We prayed for their success. The others began to leave that same night along with your brother. When Hewson heard the news that you were a captive of the king, he was determined to set you free and bring you back."

Teya straightened. "When was this?"

"Two years ago. Something must have happened. I had nearly given up hope until tonight when I heard your strong voice and I thought he had succeeded." Anxiety shone in her eyes and she sighed heavily. "Now I wonder if any of our people made it to safety."

Leona's shoulders sagged and she suddenly seemed very old. "With the loss of our people, the grove began to shrink. We were losing the battle and I needed to do something to protect what remained of the grove. I knew Korban would return and bring others with him, so I released the Destroyer."

Teya's mouth dropped open in astonishment. "The dark mist out there is your doing?"

"Yes," Leona sighed. "I knew it would keep all but true Kaloriahns out of the grove. What I didn't know was that it would slowly destroy it. I can't bind the Destroyer by myself. I've done what I can with the pipes, but everyday, the Destroyer grows in strength. It kills every living thing in its path and with each death, grows more powerful. Soon, even I will not be able to hold it back, and the grove will fail."

"Is there nothing we can do?"

Leona smiled sadly. "Yes, my child, there are two possibilities. If the people return to tend the grove, it will flourish once again and we can seal the Destroyer away. They must be found and brought back. This will be your burden. If this cannot be done, there is something else."

She reached up to the tree and it seemed one of the branches lowered to her. She tugged something away from the branch and held it out to Teya. "This is a seed." The seed was hardly bigger than an acorn. In oval shape, it glistened with shades of green and blue that swirled around a white pinpoint of light at its center. Teya couldn't look away from the dazzling brilliance.

Leona carefully placed it in a small leather pouch and gave it to Teya. "Safeguard this with your life. If this grove is destroyed, it will be the end of the Kaloriahns. The time of magic will be over, but this world can still go on if this seed is planted. The new tree will balance the destruction of evil. It will not fail because it will not need our magic to survive."

"I don't know if I can do this. What if I fail? Are you sure it's not something you should do?" Teya shrank from this heavy responsibility.

"I am not strong enough to leave the grove. I'm a lot older than you think. It is only the water that preserves me, and if I'm away from it too long I will die." She squeezed Teya's hands reassuringly. "I don't think it is a coincidence that you are here at this moment. Perhaps all you have been through was meant to happen, so that you could be here now, when you're needed most. You have a great gift, and properly trained, no one can stand against you."

"But I'm not trained," Teya said. "I don't know what I'm doing or how to do it."

"I can help you learn in a short time. Together we can strengthen the grove before you leave and that should help. I can teach you the basics and how to open yourself to your gift. After that, you will learn to recognize how to use it."

Teya sat quietly, absorbed in her grandmother's words. The grove was hushed and heavy, even the spring seemed frozen, waiting for her reply. In all the years she'd been held captive, all she'd really wanted was to come home. Now, the home she knew no longer existed. There was no choice in the matter. It was only fear that held her silent. Could she save her people and the grove? If she couldn't do it, no one would. "When do you want to start?"

⤳≈

All the next day Leona taught Teya everything she knew, leaving Bran mostly to himself. He hadn't minded too much, but time was slipping away and he was getting anxious. Checking on the pipes around the grove was Leona's idea, and even though he was grateful for something to do, he figured the real reason was to give Leona and Teya some time alone.

He was amazed at how resilient Teya was in the face of all her hardships. She had gone through so much as a child, being ripped from her family and all she knew, only to spend the next ten years in captivity. Enduring time in the 'box' and all kinds of cruelty. Something like that could twist a person, make them unpredictable, and unstable, yet here she was, taking on the responsibility of restoring the grove and her people.

At first, he thought she would refuse, but he sensed when she accepted the responsibility because a mantle of strength and determination fell over her. He was humbled by her courage in the face of such overwhelming odds. She had come through so much with an indomitable spirit, and his heart swelled with admiration. He knew that hardships often brought strength, but until now, he never understood how deep it went.

By horseback, it didn't take long to reach the periphery between the grove and the wasteland. There was no sign of the Destroyer in the stark countryside, but he couldn't help the shiver of unease that coursed through his veins. The pipes seemed to be working as long as there was a breeze. Spaced ten feet apart, at least a few of them caught the breeze most of the time. This helped settle his nerves, but he decided not to venture too close to the edge. Already, he could see that the grass around the pipes was turning yellow. How much longer could the pipes hold the Destroyer back?

One thing was certain; his plans had changed. Finding the Kaloriahns took precedence over everything else. He still needed to find *sym*, but he felt that the Kaloriahns were the key to that as well. If Korban had new magic as Leona said, Bran had a sneaking suspicion that *sym* was involved. Korban seemed to be the link to everything. Now he just had to figure out a way to find him.

The other thing that Bran marveled at was the water. With nothing else to eat or drink, Bran was surprised at how healthy and satisfied he felt. Not only that, but he knew he was stronger. Just this morning, after a quick bath he noticed that the scars from an old wound were gone. He cranked out push-ups and sit-ups without breaking a sweat, and his muscles were actually bulging! He was toned before, but nothing like this.

Bran could hardly fault Korban for wanting the water. If there was a way to save the grove, it had to be done. Bran wanted to take as much water as he could when he left. Just for him. He could imagine the benefits to everything he did, especially in his line of work. The possibilities were endless. A lot of people could be helped by just a small amount. It could be the cure for many illnesses. And it could make him rich.

Bran jerked away from that train of thought before it could take root. Thoughts like that never brought about any good, and deep down, he knew the water wasn't meant to be used that way. Best not to think about the water at all.

With that, he turned his thoughts to Jax and Clare, and hoped they had left the city in one piece. While Bran was gone, their job was to track *sym*, but Bran worried about the king's guard. With them out in force searching for Teya, he hoped Jax and Clare stayed out of sight. Especially Clare. The king would give a lot to have her back. She had risked so much to help Bran, and he didn't want anything to happen to her.

The fact that they were followed to the cabin bothered him as well, although if he thought about it, what Teya said made sense. If the *kundar* released some sort of magic when he took it off, it could have alerted a search party nearby if someone was using *sym* and felt it. He just didn't know. At least he didn't have to worry about being followed to the grove. The Destroyer would see to that.

A slight chill settled over him and the sunshine dimmed. With it came a sudden silence that shocked Bran into action. Before him, three of the pipe stands were down, and the dark mist was coalescing to strike. With enhanced speed from the grove water, Bran got the first one up, then the second, before the mist broke through. It surrounded him as he reached the third and his strength ebbed.

It was like wading through mud to lift the pipes from the ground, and with no breeze to blow through them, he put them to his lips and blew. The tones broke through the mist around him, giving him a moment's respite. He used that time to take a deep breath and blow harder. The mist recoiled from his immediate vicinity, but without the backup of the other pipes, it waited like a coiled snake to strike. He kept blowing, and within minutes began to feel light-headed. If a breeze didn't come soon, he was going to black out.

As his vision narrowed, a breeze ruffled his hair and a chorus of pipes broke through the silence. The mist recoiled and suddenly withdrew into the waste, leaving Bran out of breath, but alive. With the notes singing from the pipes, he caught his breath and shivered in the last rays of sunset. That was too close!

When his heart settled down, he drew his waterbag and took a long drink. Instantly refreshed, he turned his attention to the pipe stands and pushed them solidly into the ground so the wind couldn't blow them over again. He shuddered to think that the wind and pipes were the only things that held the Destroyer back. It seemed such a tenuous hold and he knew time was running out. With a quick look into the wasteland, he headed back to the grove.

Teya was waiting for him. She was dressed in a shimmering white gown that seemed to be covered with starlight. Her beauty astounded him and scattered his thoughts. Once more, he was speechless in her presence. She seemed more exotic than ever, almost like she didn't belong to this world.

"Come," Teya said. "Tonight my grandmother and I sing to strengthen the grove against the Destroyer. Tomorrow we will leave." Bran swallowed as she took his hand and led him into the meadow. She addressed him with a formality he wasn't used to. "Grandmother and I have prepared some things for you." She motioned toward some clothes lying on a chair. "Please do us the honor of wearing them tonight." Before he could say anything she continued. "I also have another request." She paused, a bit unsure of herself, and Bran wondered what he was getting into.

"We need you to help us with the song. It's not much, but if you could add your lower tones to ours, the outcome will be much stronger."

"What?" Nothing could have surprised him more. "I have no magic, and my voice is barely passable compared to you and your grandmother. I am sure there is nothing you could possibly gain from adding me. What makes you think I can sing anyway?"

"Oh, but there is. You underestimate yourself. Your speaking voice has a wonderful resonance, and I'm sure your singing voice does as well. There's not much you need to do, just hum the low tones that match ours. If it gets too hard, you can stop."

This was ridiculous. She made it sound so easy, but what if he sang the wrong notes? Wouldn't that ruin what they were doing? What if he made it worse? She didn't know what she was asking. He was on the point of refusal when Leona joined them.

"It is not so much your voice we need, as your participation," she added. "These groves are sustained by life and living beings. Three of us would be better than two, and the fact that you are a man is even more important. I would not ask if it would do any harm."

What could he say to that? "All right, I'll try."

"Thank you," Teya said, touching his arm gently. "It will be fine."

Looking deep into her aqua-blue eyes, he almost believed her. "I'll be back."

He grabbed the clothes and walked downstream to wash and change. Teya had a profound effect on him and he wasn't sure he liked it. Time with her grandmother had changed her; she didn't seem as young or innocent. She seemed more alluring and confident than ever, and it was hard for him to hold back his attraction to her.

He nimbly stripped off his clothes, and waded into the water. The cold had the desired effect, and after a quick scrub, he dried off, and pulled on the gray pants and shirt Teya left him. They were soft and fit him surprisingly well. Once his boots were on, all that was left was the coat. It was a strange design, with a high collar at the neck and longer than anything he had ever worn. It buttoned down the front to a place just below his waist, then tapered off in a flowing line below his knees. The sleeves were the perfect length for his long arms, and he was surprised again at the fit.

He supposed that these clothes were some of the remnants left behind when the Kaloriahns fled. Even though they weren't his, he was comfortable in them, and more self-assured. He stood a little taller and more confident about his participation. If he couldn't keep up with the singing, at least he looked good.

Twilight turned to darkness and Bran followed Leona's soft lights back to the meadow. Tonight the woods were hushed and seemed to hold an air of wistful expectancy. Teya and Leona were softly conversing when Bran approached. He smiled at Teya's quick intake of breath, and Leona's appreciative nod. Maybe this wouldn't be so bad after all.

"What do you want me to do?" he asked.

"It is a simple ceremony," Leona said. "If you can let the music be your guide, you will lose yourself in the song, and the notes will follow. Just open your heart. Are you ready?"

Bran nodded, realizing he was totally unprepared for this, but in an odd way, looking forward to the experience. The last time he heard Teya sing was still etched in his memory as one of the most extraordinary moments in his life, and his heart yearned to hear that sweet voice again.

Leona directed them to the other side of the tree where a white stone pedestal with a large bowl was balanced on top. The white bowl was filled with water so clear it was like looking in a mirror. They took positions around the bowl and satisfied, Leona spoke. "Join hands."

Teya smiled encouragingly when she took his hand, and he couldn't help smiling in return. Leona began a simple tune, with her voice light as the wind. Soon, Teya joined her, turning the simple melody into harmony so beautiful that chills ran down his spine. As their voices rose and fell the notes seemed to twine around him, lifting him to a dreamlike state.

Yet in this state he felt more real and alive than he ever had in his life. A fresh breeze caressed his skin, filling his nostrils with the scent of new cut grass and spring rain. He breathed deeply and his chest swelled, buoyed by the strength in the air. The grove began to thrum with a pulse of its own, and every leaf and blade of grass shimmered to the beat of newfound life.

Without thought, he began to sing, and his voice found a place in the song that anchored the melody, holding the ethereal notes firmly to the earth. All at once, the water began to rise from the bowl in a fine mist. It swirled in a never-ending funnel higher and higher above the meadow. Soon a cloudy haze overshadowed the entire grove. It hung suspended by a pure sweet note from Teya that held every living thing in thrall. As the tension mounted, Bran could not fathom how she could hold the note so long.

Then Leona's voice faded out and Bran was caught up in an intricate harmonic dance with Teya. His added strength changed the tempo and mingled with hers in a dance of creation. Soon they merged in an intimate caress. The rhythm intensified, leaving him bare and defenseless. In the magic of the moment he lost himself in the celebration of life.

Then all at once it was over. With the music's end, the mist hanging above them coalesced and fell to the earth as dewdrops from heaven. Each drop echoed the music like a tinkling chime and filled the grove with a resonance of light. It was as if the grove itself held the power of the sun.

A wholeness encompassed Bran as he radiated the light. His senses seemed on fire with broader depth and understanding, as though he had never used them before. It was as if he had transcended humanity and become something more. He glimpsed a place beyond the grove of shining light and towering cathedrals. The streets seemed paved in gold and the buildings sparkled like diamonds. This place of indescribable beauty and brightness was more than he could endure.

Reflexively pulling back, the light faded, and awareness of his surroundings pulled him into consciousness. Visions of grandeur became a star-studded night sky, and he realized he was lying on his back. He slowly sat up and found Teya next to him, staring wide-eyed into the heavens.

"Teya." She didn't respond. He clutched her hands and grew alarmed at how cold they were. "Teya!" He pulled her into his arms and with a hand on her cold cheek, searched her eyes, willing them to come into focus. Gradually, they lost that far-off look and she seemed to see him for the first time.

"Bran," she said, breathing his name like a prayer.

He smiled with relief, wanting more from this intimate moment. Unable to resist his desires, he leaned forward and brushed his lips against hers. Soft and welcoming, he kissed her thoroughly, finding a flame to match his own. Her arms twined around his neck and he couldn't seem to get enough of her. He deepened the kiss and his body responded with wild passion. His blood pulsed with a thundering rhythm that could not be denied.

Teya pulled away, leaving him breathless and unfulfilled. With guilt and bewilderment, she looked over her shoulder. Leona was leaning against the tree, watching them with unbridled interest.

"You don't have to stop on my account, but I wouldn't mind some water to quench my thirst. When you're through, of course." A faint blush spread over Teya's smooth skin and she smiled apologetically before slipping out from under him. Her leaving left a hollow ache in his groin, and Bran tried to get himself under control. After a few minutes, his harsh breathing settled down, and he was able to sit up.

"Come to the table," Leona said. "I have a few things I need to tell you."

Teya dutifully helped Leona to the table while Bran got to his feet, and with deliberate slowness, filled the pitcher with water. He was thirsty, but that was secondary to his real desire. He was so consumed with wanting Teya that he could hardly think straight. With trembling hands, he somehow managed to fill Leona's cup.

"Thank you Bran," Leona said, and took a long drink of water. Bran filled the other cups, then drank deeply from his own. The water satisfied the hunger that had been drained by the ritual and strengthened him, but did nothing to cool his passion. He closed his eyes in concentration and sat down, feeling a portion of sanity return. Once his heart settled into a normal rhythm, he was calm enough to open his eyes.

This was what Leona seemed to be waiting for. "Tomorrow, you will leave here," she said. "I have taught Teya the basics. That will have to be enough, as there is no time for more. Our singing has strengthened the grove for a little longer at least. You did surprisingly well for an outlander, Bran. Are you sure you don't have some Kaloriahn blood in you?"

Bran shrugged, but his voice was strained. "Not that I know of."

"You can see why we needed you. The song of life is only half filled without male participation because it is also a song of creation, hence the need for both man and woman. Your efforts made a dramatic difference to our success. The outcome will be felt for days and perhaps weeks to come. It has also affected both of you."

That was an understatement. If he had wanted Teya before, it was nothing compared to how he felt now. How could he acknowledge this attraction and not fulfill his desires? Something extraordinary had happened during the ceremony. Something he had no words to explain or ever felt before. As he searched within himself, he knew it was more than a connection with Teya. He felt changed somehow. What had Leona and Teya done to him?

"I have prepared a few things for you to take," Leona said. She pulled a small set of pipes from her pocket and handed them to Bran. "This will protect you from the Destroyer when you cross back. I meant to send them with you today when you checked on the perimeter, but I forgot. I trust all went well?"

"Yes." he could hardly remember his close call, and didn't see the need to tell her what had happened now.

"Good. All that remains is that you find our people and bring them back. I will keep the grove safe as long as I can, but I fear I am fading. Tonight proved it to me. I saw the White City and it was no longer a vision, it was real, and it called to me. It was difficult to return here. Next time, I might not be able to."

"What is the White City?" Bran asked, trying to focus. Is that what he had seen? He felt out of balance.

"It is our true home. When my work here is done, I will return there. You must understand; Kaloriahns are not quite human." Bran sighed with the effort of trying to comprehend what Leona was saying. Her voice seemed disembodied as she continued. "Tonight, you will sleep peacefully. Tomorrow, I will send you with as much water as I can. Drink it for extra strength and it will protect you. If you find Korban, it would be best if you killed him. Now, find your beds and rest peacefully."

Bran didn't remember lying down, only that the soft grass cushioned his head and a sweet melody filled his senses. He tried to think. Wasn't there a question? It was too hard to remember. He fought the haze that settled over him but his body was filled with a languor he couldn't resist, and after a brief struggle, he quit trying.

Chapter Four

The Search Begins

Bran woke to the sound of chirping birds and dappled sunlight. He sat up to clear his head and realized he was on a bed of grass in the grove. He still had on the clothes Leona had given him from the day before, but lying next to him were the contents of his pack and his regular clothes. They were freshly cleaned and ready to wear.

As he changed into them, he had a nagging sense of irritation. It wasn't that he was upset with his participation in the ritual; although this morning, it seemed more like a dream. He tried to remember exactly what happened, but it all seemed unreal, and he couldn't explain it with words. He felt suspiciously out of control. He also wasn't sure he liked the way Leona had used her magic on him in sending him to sleep. Maybe it wasn't the first time she had done it, and that bothered him even more.

He gathered everything together, leaving the clothes from Leona behind. Even if he was meant to keep them, he didn't have room in his bags. Teya was at the tree, filling the water pitcher. She was clothed in a simple shirt and long tunic with black pants tucked into her boots and a belt around her waist. The shirt was a deep jungle green that managed to make her turquoise eyes seem more green than blue. She smiled shyly at him and his heart skipped a beat. Magic or not, he couldn't deny his strong attraction to her and was glad that at least he remembered kissing her. With a quick greeting, she poured water into their goblets.

"Where's Leona?" Bran asked.

"She's resting, last night took a lot out of her. She won't be joining us this morning, but she did give me these waterskins to take with us. Once we've filled them, we can leave."

Bran was unhappy that Leona wasn't coming to see them off. He still had some questions he wanted to ask her. Was she really that frail? He quickly drained his goblet of water, and realized how much he missed eating. He looked forward to a satisfying meal along with a hefty pint of ale.

"Did Leona have any idea where your people might have gone? If we're to find them it would be nice to know."

Teya seemed to catch the note of annoyance in Bran's tone. "That's just it, she doesn't know. The people left in a hurry and they went in different directions in case Korban was waiting for them." She looked like she was about to say something else, then changed her mind.

Bran didn't press her, there were things he wanted to talk about as well, but decided to wait until they left the grove. He didn't know where Leona was, and didn't want her to hear what he had to say. "All right, let's fill up our waterbags and go. I suggest we head back to the city, only by a different route. We came from the west, so let's circle around and enter from the east this time. It's a more populated route, and maybe we can find some traces of your people along the way."

"That sounds like a good idea." Teya handed him two waterbags and began to fill the other two. Bran left to get the waterbags from his supplies, and after he filled them, took a small flask out of his coat pocket to fill as well. That was all the room he had and he still wished he could take more.

With the horses saddled, and their gear stowed away, they were ready to leave. "Are you going to say goodbye to your grandmother?"

"No," Teya answered. "I already did earlier." Her glance strayed to the hidden depths of the grove where her grandmother was resting, then with a sigh she turned to him and said. "Let's go."

A shadow seemed to fall over her and Bran knew it was hard to leave after waiting so long to come back. They mounted their horses and turned them east toward the rising sun. Once they were out of the grove, the velvet grass stretched green toward the lifeless boundary. Teya glanced over her shoulder and Bran was surprised at the frown on her face.

"We'll come back," Bran reassured her.

Teya smiled tightly. "I hope so, and she'd better be alive when we do. There's so much more she could teach me, and now I'm not sure I'll ever learn. I feel like a ship without a rudder, and no one to tell me where to go or how to get there."

"You certainly seemed to know what you were doing last night. Did Leona tell you what to do?"

Teya shook her head. "No, all I did was follow her lead. The rest just happened." She seemed uncomfortable.

"You'll do fine," Bran said. "Leona said after you knew the basics, the rest would come to you."

"Maybe, but I still worry. There's so much I don't know, and she won't be there to help me. What if I fail?"

Bran understood her concern. "That's a risk you have to take, but you'll fail for sure if you don't try."

Teya sighed. "That's true. I'll try not to worry so much. Besides, I have you to help me. You will, won't you?"

Bran nodded, maybe now was a good time to tell her his own worries. "There is one thing I would like to ask you." He paused at the discomfort in her eyes, like she knew what he was going to ask and dreaded it. "This may sound strange, but after last night, I have to clear this up. I know your grandmother used her magic on me. I was going to ask her some questions, and next thing I know, I can't keep my eyes open.

"Maybe she thought it was necessary," he continued. "But I didn't like it. At least she could have asked, but I was given no choice. I need to have a choice, Teya. I want you to promise that you won't use magic on me. I'm sorry I have to ask, but I need to be able to trust you."

"Of course," Teya bristled. "She wanted you to sleep well, that's the only reason she did it."

"That's good to know," Bran said. He hoped it was the truth. There was something else Leona said last night that bothered him, but through the haze of sleep, he couldn't remember what it was. He racked his brain trying to think what she said, but came up empty-handed. It seemed important, and he was frustrated that he couldn't remember. Was his lack of memory one of Leona's tricks as well?

Soon they were within sight of the pipes and the border. From this distance, the sound of the pipes seemed to cry out a warning and Bran shivered. Teya turned for one last look at the grove. It stood out fresh and green like an oasis in the desert. Bran was surprised to find that the green continued a good five feet beyond the pipes. The grove had grown as a result of last night's ritual. They paused within the boundary and stared at the vast emptiness before them. Was the Destroyer somewhere close, waiting for them?

"Do you have the pipes my grandmother gave you?" Teya asked.

"Yes." Bran pulled them from inside his shirt where he had tied them with a string around his neck. "If the Destroyer finds us before we get very far, we could end up wandering in that wilderness for days. I have a compass I can keep handy." He pulled it out of his pocket. "If we head due east, we should reach the borderlands. We can go south from there. Is there anything else I need to know?"

"Just stay close to me, all right? I don't want to lose you."

There was a double meaning in her eyes, and his heart quickened. "Don't worry," he responded. "I'm not letting you out of my sight." It was true, and not just because of the Destroyer. He was drawn to her in more ways than he cared to admit, and felt instinctively that something had happened during the ritual that bound them together. He just wished he knew what it was.

"Should we make a run for it?" Teya asked, a light shining in her eyes.

"Sure," Bran agreed. "As long as we don't push the horses too hard."

Teya took off before Bran finished, but he quickly caught up. The horses seemed eager for a run, and for the moment Bran forgot the threat. At the crest of a hill, the blackened trees and dusty earth were a startling contrast to the green grove they just left. It spread for miles in all directions, and put a damper on Bran's enthusiasm.

Slowing the horses, they kept on a straight course and barely spoke to each other, worried that speaking might draw the Destroyer to them. Soon the trees disappeared and the hard cracked earth turned to sand and rock. Oppression seemed to seep into his skin, and Bran settled into watchful silence. Soon, a brittle breeze brought a scent of decay that turned Bran's stomach. The source lay not too far from their path, and Bran swung down from his horse to investigate.

At first it looked like a heap of sun-bleached clothing and discarded blankets. As Bran got closer, the strange pile became the remains of a horse and rider, dead for several weeks. Oddly, there were no flies or carrion birds to eat the flesh. The shrunken skin made the grotesque features stand out, with the jaw and mouth opened in a silent scream of terror. Bran choked back his revulsion and motioned Teya to stay away.

He had seen death before, but not as bad as this. He forced himself to search the pockets for clues to the man's identity. He searched quickly, holding his breath as much as he could. The inner pocket of the jacket held several gold coins, an immense amount for anyone to carry. Bran felt around the lining and came upon a bulge, like a package of some sort. With his knife, he cut the lining and found two vials of a coppery red liquid. *Sym.* Frustratingly enough, there were no other clues to indicate who this man was. Bran pocketed the coins and *sym* before backing away.

He mounted up with an acute desire to put as much distance as he could between him and the corpse. Tension dropped over him like a net, and he scanned the vast waste for signs of darkness. Nothing. "Keep close," he whispered.

"Do you know who he was?" Teya asked.

"No, but I found gold in his pocket along with *sym*."

Teya shivered, and they urged their horses on, desperate to leave this place un-scathed. Several times in the next few hours, they came upon small mounds of bones held together by strips of cloth. Bran could only determine that this was a frequently traveled route. He wondered if the remains could have been some of the Kaloriahns, or possibly Korban's people trying to find a way to the grove.

It was late afternoon before they glimpsed the end of the waste. Ahead, was a pass between a rocky crag, and a barren hill. On the other side, a wide expanse of grassland spread for several miles. The waves of green and gold were a bright contrast to the colorless waste. The oppression they had endured during the entire day lifted. Teya glanced at Bran with delight and he smiled in return. They were almost there.

With the sun behind them, Bran didn't notice the looming shadow until it was upon them. Teya shouted a warning and voiced the notes of the grove. The darkness hovered above, waiting to strike. Bran checked his compass for the coordinates of the pass and shouted at Teya to ride hard.

The dark cloud seemed to grow in fury, only held back by Teya's voice. As it sur-rounded them, Bran fumbled for his pipes and began to blow. The darkness receded, leaving an angry buzz that hurt Bran's ears. He kept blowing his pipes in the race to the gap, and soon burst through and down the other side.

Breathing raggedly, he and Teya watched the dark cloud lift into the air and fall back in on itself. It hovered for a moment before disappearing. Teya mumbled something, but Bran couldn't understand what she said. His head pounded with a low buzz that wouldn't go away. In agony, Bran slid from his horse, clutching his head. Soon Teya's voice cut through the pain and Bran relaxed. She held his head and the buzzing faded until it too, was gone.

"Thank you," he said, breathing heavily. "I guess I have to eat my words about using your magic on me without asking."

She fell beside him, sweat dampening her face. "Well, I wouldn't mind lording it over you, but I think magic is what caused your pain. Sometimes the vibrations cause a buzzing in your ears that can be very painful. It's happened to me before so I know how it feels. Anyway, I'm glad we made it out. Are you all right now? I know I could use a drink of water. You rest and I'll get it."

It took him a minute to get up, but after a long drink, the water refreshed them both. Bran pulled a small map from his saddlebags and studied it. "According to this there should be a town not far from here." He checked the position of the sun. "We should reach it before nightfall if you want to keep going."

"I do. Before we left, my grandmother taught me a couple of songs that will help me find my people. I was thinking we could pass ourselves off as entertainers and sing in some of the towns along the way. If any of the Kaloriahns are around, they will know the songs."

Bran pursed his lips, his brows drawn together in concern. "What if you're rec-ognized? Don't you think you're taking a chance, especially if you use your magic?"

"No one in these towns will know me, and I can be careful with my magic. No one will know I'm using it except the Kaloriahns." When Bran didn't respond she continued. "Do you have a better plan?"

"Yes, let's go back to the city and find Jax and Clare. They have contacts and information we can trust. They may also have a lead on *sym*. I can go to the palace in my role as an ambassador and dig around. I'm sure something will turn up."

"But this is more important than finding *sym*! I thought you understood that."

"Of course I understand, but I have a feeling that if we find one, we'll find the other, and I've learned to trust my feelings. I think we should lay low until we reach the city. The king probably has people out looking for you everywhere. What you want to do isn't safe."

"How about a compromise," she said, her voice hard with determination. "We can decide if it's safe after we see what the towns are like. Some of my people could be close, and I can't let the chance to contact them pass by if they are."

Bran tried not to show his irritation. What she said did have some merit, but she didn't realize how dangerous it was. He decided to humor her. "All right. We'll check it out first, but please let me make the decision, I know what I'm doing and you need to trust me."

Teya shrugged. "Let's go then."

She stood to leave, and would have turned from him, but Bran stopped her. "Teya, you don't seem to realize one very important thing. The king will do anything to get you back, and Korban has to be part of his plans. Maybe Korban is the king, have you ever thought of that? If you are captured and collared, all that we're trying to do is for nothing. Without you, we will fail."

Teya didn't back down and kept her gaze steady on his. "All right, since you've had more experience, I'll trust your judgment, but in order for me to feel good about it, I have to know that you will consider my ideas as well."

Her eyes were hard and bright as sapphires, and Bran was surprised at her cold stare. "There's no reason why we can't work together."

She nodded, mollified for now, but Bran knew he had his work cut out for him. "The nearest town is Somara. From the map it looks like a major crossroad between several towns."

Teya's face lit up. "Then there might be some Kaloriahns there. I was thinking that if I had left the grove, I would go someplace where I could blend in with other people. That way Korban or his men would never find me. I bet that's what most of the Kaloriahns have done."

"You're probably right. I don't think they'd stray too far from the grove, unless they were in danger, but who knows, maybe Korban has people watching for newcomers." He paused, weighing his words. "There's something I have to ask you. Last night with the ritual, things are kind of blurry for me. Did something happen I should know about?"

Teya's eyes widened with alarm and she blushed. "You don't remember?"

"I don't have words for what happened. It was such a different experience that I find it hard to describe, so I wonder if it really happened. I remember the light and the water spiraling up over the grove. I remember singing with you and the intimacy that we shared. Then it seemed like the sky opened and I saw a city, but it was too bright for me to look at without hurting my eyes. Was any of that real?"

Teya pursed her lips. "Yes. All of it was real. The city you saw is the White City my grandmother was talking about. It's where my people hope to go after our work is finished here."

"You mean when you die?" She nodded, but didn't look at him, and Bran was immediately suspicious that she was hiding something. "I remember our kiss and wanting more." She ducked her head, refusing to look at him. "It seemed like it was important at the time. Why is that?"

"It was only a by-product of the ritual. The ceremony we performed to strengthen the grove is founded on the principle of creation. It's only natural that we felt the impulse to act it out that way." Her cheeks were stained with a rosy blush that deepened the color of her eyes and made her even more alluring.

"I see. And that's all that happened?" Bran wasn't going to let her off that easy. "Is there anything else I should know?"

"I don't think so."

Why wouldn't she tell him? Had he only imagined that something had happened? He wished he could remember everything Leona had said, but it was still fuzzy. Teya was uneasy, and that made Bran more certain that he was right. He decided to try another approach. "I could get used to it."

"What?"

"Kissing you, except that I think it would lead to something more." He smiled at her discomposure.

"You're teasing me, and I don't think it's funny."

"I know how we can settle the matter." He waited until he had her full attention. "We can try it again."

Teya opened her mouth to say something, then thought better of it when she caught the gleam in his eyes. Her expression changed to calculating mischief. "Perhaps you're right." The seductive curve of her lips took him off-guard. "I'll let you know when I'm ready." She coaxed her horse forward, leaving him to trail behind.

He couldn't help the leap of his pulse, but managed to maintain his cool demeanor, while inside he wondered what the hell he was doing.

✒︎❧

They reached the outskirts of Somara near sundown. It was larger than Teya expected, with a bustling community. Bran seemed obsessed about watching the people and keeping her safe. When a couple of riders passed them and one kept looking back at her, Bran bristled with annoyance.

Teya began to notice other people's stares, and wondered if something was strange about her appearance. Was she dressed wrong? Most people were friendly enough, and nodded or smiled politely. Teya had to conclude that she and Bran drew attention because they were strangers. Realizing this, she thought her plan had more merit than ever and would be a simple way to explain why they were there.

She was afraid that Bran wouldn't agree with her, because his scowl deepened the further into town they went. The worst of it was that he scowled at her just as much as anyone else. He was clearly upset with the attention they were getting and acted like it was her fault.

Ever since their discussion earlier, there was an underlying tension between them. Both of them tried to act as though nothing had happened, but it was draining. Teya hadn't been totally honest with Bran, but it was better if he didn't know everything. At least for now, although the guilt it caused was hard to bear. She kept wondering when Bran would recognize it and confront her. That thought alone was enough to dampen her spirits.

"This looks like a reputable place to spend the night," Bran said. He stopped in front of a three-story building with a beautifully carved sign that said 'Aris Inn' on it. Teya was intrigued, especially when they entered to find the large hall filled with people sitting at tables, eating and drinking. There was even a small stage for entertaining along the far end. As far as she was concerned, this was the perfect place for her plan.

Bran found them a seat at a side table, and Teya couldn't help the pulse of excitement that leapt within her. "I don't remember ever being in a place like this before."

Bran seemed surprised, then shook his head. "I keep forgetting where you've been all your life. Look, I know we didn't discuss this, but I want to share a room tonight. It will be safer that way. Is that all right with you?"

"Sure, that's fine."

He seemed surprised at how easily she agreed. "Good, I'll go make arrangements and get the horses stabled for the night. Stay put, and if anyone asks, I'm your husband."

He was gone before she could say a word and she was grateful he didn't see the blush that crept up her cheeks. How long could she go before he found out the truth? She hoped he didn't try kissing her again. He would know what she'd done and probably never forgive her. There had to be a way to tell him before that happened, but for the life of her, she couldn't figure out how. What had her grandmother been thinking?

Her thoughts were interrupted when a serving girl set a steaming platter of food on the table. "Your husband said to bring you some food." She expertly placed a pitcher of ale and two mugs beside the plates. "Hope you enjoy it."

The aroma of roast beef made her mouth water and she forgot everything else. She filled her plate, and with enthusiasm, took a bite. It was delicious. She was on her second bite when the music began and banished all thoughts of food. On the small stage, the singer sat on a stool with a guitar in his lap. He was singing an old lover's ballad and his rich voice flooded her senses with the emotion of love and longing.

The room had quieted, but most of the people kept talking as if nothing special was happening. Teya was amazed. She knew he was using magic, but maybe she was more sensitive to it than others. Her grandmother had told her that sometimes the magic had no effect when people's hearts were too hard to feel it. That was one reason the Kaloriahns had failed against Korban's army. But her magic was different. She could touch a king's cruel heart with truth and make him cringe with pain.

Bran was suddenly beside her. "That took longer than I thought. How's the food? It sure smells good." When she didn't respond right away he stopped what he was doing and gave her his full attention. "What's going on?"

Teya took a deep breath, hoping she didn't look as guilty as she felt. "Nothing, I've just been thinking." She waited until Bran began to eat before she spoke. "Did you notice the entertainer?" At Bran's nod she continued. "What do you think of his singing?" She had to know if Bran could tell he was using magic.

Bran listened while he ate, and after a couple of minutes he responded. "He's got talent. His voice is rich and beautiful, and you feel that his heart is in the song, like it really means something. I would imagine that if you listened closely, his song could move you to tears."

Teya was surprised. Was that how magic sounded to most people? The way Bran explained it, there was no magic involved. He called it talent. "Is that what you think when I sing? That I'm talented?"

Now it was Bran who was surprised. "Are you kidding? I mean, of course you are talented, I've never heard a more beautiful voice in my life, but that doesn't begin to explain how your music touches everyone who hears it. There's no doubt you have more to offer than a singer like him."

"So as far as you can tell, this singer has no magic?"

Bran paused in sudden understanding and once again concentrated on the singer. "If he's using magic, it's very subtle, but now that you mention it, I can feel a difference. The atmosphere in this room has changed. The people seem more subdued than when we first came in."

Teya smiled. Bran had recognized it; it just took him a little longer to understand what it was. Either the singer only had a limited use of magic, or else he was very good at using it. "That singer is using magic. He could very well be a Kaloriahn."

She knew this was not what Bran wanted to hear, but he only sighed. "I suppose you want to check this out."

"Yes, of course."

"Then we'll do it my way, like we discussed earlier. You've hardly touched your dinner. Why don't you finish up, and I'll make some inquiries about him, then maybe later, we can ask him to join us."

His way seemed like a waste of time. "Why don't you just let me talk to him? It would save you a lot of trouble."

"You can talk to him later. I want to know more about him first, and it's not any trouble." She could tell he knew she was holding something back from him and because of it, couldn't completely trust her. Her stomach clenched with a pang of regret. Her grandmother had been so sure, but now Teya wondered if they had done the right thing. They should have explained it all. Unfortunately, it was too late for second guesses.

"All right."

Bran nodded, the suspicion bright in his eyes, and left their table. She sighed and turned her attention to the singer. At least this was something she knew about. He was just finishing up a set of three love ballads and she quickly lost herself in the song, feeling the pain of the young man who had returned to find his love married to another. After the last note faded, a smattering of applause broke out and the singer announced he was taking a short break. His attention fixed on her, and with undeniable interest, he made his way to her table.

"I couldn't help noticing that you seemed to enjoy my music. May I join you?"

Teya couldn't believe her good fortune. Wouldn't Bran be surprised? "Of course, please sit down." She hadn't touched her mug of ale and eagerly passed it to him. "Would you like a drink? You're singing was wonderful."

"Thank you. My name's Jesse and I must admit that it's very gratifying to please such a beautiful woman."

"I'm Teya." She blushed, and then caught her breath when he took her hand and kissed the back of it. He was younger than she first thought and had a fair complexion with wavy golden hair and penetrating hazel eyes. His lips tickled her hand, sending shivers up her arm and she quickly pulled it away.

"You remind me of someone I knew a long time ago. Are you from around here?"

"No, I'm from the city." She hoped that was the right thing to say.

"Ah, well, I've never been to the city. They say it's a beautiful place, and maybe someday I'll go there, but for now, I'm enjoying the country. Singing is my first love and what makes it even better is that I get paid for it."

Teya smiled. "You have a beautiful voice."

"It's passable, but there are those much better."

"And those much worse!" Teya added.

Jesse laughed. "You have a point there. Well, it's about time I went back. Do you have a favorite song you'd like to hear?"

Teya's heart leapt, this was her chance. "Yes, do you know 'Fair Ones'?"

Jesse's gaze caught hers with a penetrating glance before he shook his head. "I don't think so, but I'd love to hear it. Would you like to join me on stage and give it a go?"

She didn't know what to say. Bran would have a fit if she went up there to sing.

"I promise no one will bite. Most of them are drunk and won't care if you mess up, as long as you've a pretty face. And yours is exceptional."

"All right," she gave in. "But you go sing some more first. I'll come up later."

That seemed to appease him. "Until later then." He bowed and left.

Teya's heart pounded with something akin to fear at what she had done. Jesse seemed to take it all in stride and began his next set with a rousing jig. Joining him on the stage was a drummer and a fiddle player. As they got going, people began to clap and sing along with great gusto. Soon, a space was cleared in front of the stage and couples began to dance. The drummer and fiddler were excellent musicians and sang the harmonies along with Jesse. The music was so engaging that before she knew it, she was tapping her foot and humming along.

Bran finally returned, sitting beside her and smiling at her enthusiasm. Guilt turned her cheeks red and she quit clapping. "Did you find out anything?"

"Yes. They're a group that travels around the towns in this area. Apparently, they've been playing together for the last few months. They make quite a bit of money, in fact, the innkeeper said they were in high demand."

"What does that mean?" she asked.

"It could mean a lot of things." Bran shrugged. "They're good, and they're doing well for themselves. Maybe they have some Kaloriahn blood in them."

The tension eased from Teya's shoulders. Maybe she hadn't been so stupid after all. If they were Kaloriahns, she'd know when she sang. And if they weren't? What was the worst thing that could happen? They'd go their separate ways and that would be the end of it.

"Let's talk to them after," Bran suggested.

Teya nodded. She was suddenly thirsty and took a drink of ale from her mug, then realized it was the same one Jesse had drunk from, and guilt made her put it down. She needed to tell Bran what had happened, but the music was so loud that she decided to wait until things calmed down. The ebullience of the crowd kept the flavor of the beat going for a long time and Teya despaired she would ever get the break she needed.

Amid exhausted applause, the drummer and fiddler put their instruments away while Jesse strummed a few soothing chords. "I have a treat for you tonight," he said, and Teya's heart sank. She had waited too long. "I've talked a bonnie lass into sharing a song with us before we go. She's from the city, so let's show her some country hospitality." The crowd clapped enthusiastically and Jesse motioned for Teya to join him. "There she is, at that table there. Come on lassie, don't be shy."

Teya swallowed under Bran's incredulous frown, but with the urging of the people around her, she had no choice but to join Jesse on the stage.

"Don't be frightened," Jesse whispered, taking her hand and helping her onto the stage. "They'll love you no matter what."

Teya couldn't help producing a small smile. He must think her reticence was due to a lack of singing ability. He was in for a surprise. She caught a warning glance from Bran and nodded to reassure him that she understood her precarious position. She wasn't going to blow it.

"May I?" she motioned to Jesse's guitar. With surprise, he handed it over. As a child she was taught how to play many instruments, but the guitar was her favorite, and the one instrument the king had allowed her to use.

She took Jesse's place on the stool and began to pick the strings in a haunting rhythm. An expectant hush fell over the crowd and pulled them to her mastery. When the tension reached its zenith, her clear voice filled the abyss and floated in airy wonder. In a spell woven of magic, she sang softly of a legendary place of beauty and mystery.

Restraining the images was hard, but she held back and sang only the simple melody. The clear message touched the hearts of the people with a longing for hearth and home. As the last notes left her mouth a collective sigh escaped the audience, followed by a reverent silence. Then as if coming from a trance, one by one they burst into appreciative applause.

Teya bowed respectfully and handed the guitar to Jesse who stared at her in fascination. The crowd called for more and Teya tried to leave the stage, but they protested so vehemently that she finally gave in to their demands. Their behavior was disconcerting and she wasn't sure how to handle it. She glanced at Bran for support, knowing she was in over her head, and was surprised to find him coming toward the stage. His expression was so cold and dour that she took a step back without realizing it.

In tightly controlled anger he whispered, "Don't sing again unless you can do so without using magic! It's too dangerous. For your protection, I'll stay on the stage. If anything threatening happens, run to me."

Teya swallowed. What had she done? Bran must have sensed danger or he wouldn't be so upset. She decided to sing something lively and engaging to put everyone in a good mood. At her urging, Jesse sang the familiar tune with her. The crowd relaxed and soon most everyone joined in with clapping and singing. The next song was like the first, only this time Teya sang harmony, leaving the main focus for Jesse. By the third song Teya was ready to leave the audience in Jesse's capable hands.

As she was moving away, Jesse urgently whispered that he needed to see her. "I'll come to your room when I'm done."

She nodded, eager to get off the stage. With Bran at her side, glaring at the crowd, no one dared approach her, and soon they were out of the hall.

"Our room's up here." He motioned up the stairs. At the top, he took a key from his pocket and, unlocking the door, ushered her in. A lamp glowing on the small table lit the empty room, but Bran held her back while he checked the dark corners. Satisfied, he turned to face her. "We have to leave. It's not safe here."

"Why? Did you see something?"

"Teya." He took her by the arms, as if to shake her. "Do you want a *kundar* put back on your neck? There were plenty of people in that crowd who aren't as stupid as you think. They're trained to spot magic like yours and make a profit from it."

"But what about Jesse? He was using magic."

"It's nothing like yours! He's hardly worth the time. You, on the other hand, are a goldmine. We never should have come here." Bran paced over to the window and gauged the distance to the ground.

Teya sank to the bed with a shiver of fear. Her hands strayed to her throat, remembering all the years spent wearing the *kundar*. She had to find her people, but this was not the way. Bran was right, she shouldn't have sung, and now they were both in danger. A thundering knock at the door made her jump. Before she could blink, Bran had the gun in his hand.

"Teya, it's me, Jesse. Please let me in!"

Bran was at the door in a heartbeat, his gun ready to fire. He opened the door a crack. "What do you want?"

"I came to warn you, but there's not a lot of time." Bran opened the door enough to scan the hallway. When he was satisfied that Jesse was alone he let him inside, keeping his gun ready.

Jesse eyed Bran's gun with apprehension. "There are some men down there who want Teya. I can get you to safety, but we have to leave now."

"Why are you helping us?" Teya asked.

"You're a Kaloriahn," he said simply. "Our kind need to stick together."

Chapter Five

The Hunter

"There's a back way out of here, grab your things and let's go," Jesse said.

Teya caught her breath, and excitement shone from her eyes. Bran could tell she believed Jesse's declaration and his heart sank. Maybe it was true, but it could just as easily be a lie. Bran wasn't about to believe him without more proof, although he was right about the men downstairs. Bran had singled them out while Teya was busy singing. If nothing else, Jesse could get them out of the inn, but Bran kept his guard up just the same.

He put his gun away and gathered the few things he'd brought upstairs. Most of their belongings were still with the horses, but he'd just have to come back and get them later. Jesse led them down the upstairs hallway to the other side of the building. At the end of the hall was a door that opened to an outside staircase and soon they were in an alleyway between the buildings.

Jesse motioned for them to follow, but Bran had other plans. "That's far enough, I can get us out of here now."

A shadow crossed Jesse's features, but cleared when he spoke. "All right, but go quickly."

"Wait," Teya said to Bran. "I don't want to go until I've had a chance to talk to him." She turned to Jesse and continued. "Can you take us somewhere safe?"

Jesse nodded eagerly. "Yes, come this way."

Bran swallowed his misgiving and followed behind, knowing Teya would not change her mind. What was it about Jesse that made him uncomfortable? Teya believed that Jesse was a Kaloriahn, but he wasn't so sure. *Sym* could also give him magical abilities.

Jesse led them through several streets toward the outskirts of town. At a corner house, he led them around the back and unlocked the door. "You'll be safe here," he said while lighting a candle, then motioned them toward a table and chairs. "Please sit down. It's not much, but it's home to me." His living quarters consisted of a bed on one side of the room, and a table with chairs on the other. Bran peered into the dark corners, but couldn't see anything amiss.

"How did you know I was a Kaloriahn?" Teya asked.

"That was easy." Jesse smiled. "Your magic is pure. There aren't many like that anymore. There are a few of us who have been here for a few months trying to scrape by, but it's difficult because of the hunters."

Teya glanced at Bran before answering. "Who are they?"

Jesse narrowed his eyes as his gaze went from one to the other, and he tensed, suddenly wary. "Where have you been? Every Kaloriahn knows about the hunters."

Bran wasn't about to let Jesse know who Teya really was. "We'll answer your questions, but first explain who these hunters are." Teya gave him an exasperated look, but didn't say anything.

"They're people who get paid to catch Kaloriahns. They use a *kundar,* and take them captive. I don't know where they are taken. I tried to follow a group once, and got as far as the Wynd River, before I lost them."

"We need to find them," Teya said. "And gather all the Kaloriahns that are still free and return to the grove. We don't have much time."

"What's wrong with the grove?"

"It's in bad shape. Leona's powers are dwindling and the grove is dying. Without the strength of the Kaloriahns it will be destroyed."

Jesse stared at her while comprehension flooded over him. "You've been to the grove. How did you get past that black thing?"

Bran tried to stop Teya, but she seemed oblivious to his cautioning glance. "With magic and luck. I know the notes that will hold it back."

"So that's it," Jesse breathed. "There is a way. What about the tree? Is it still standing?"

"Yes," Teya said. "But we need to find all the Kaloriahns we can and bring them back or it will die. Can you help us?"

"Yes, of course. There are a few other Kaloriahns here besides me, and I know they'll help. In fact, there's a man who has spent years looking for them because his sister was taken. He moves around a lot, but I know how to reach him. I could get a message off to him tonight, but I don't know how soon he'll get back to me."

Teya's eyes brightened with excitement. "Do you know the man's name?"

"No," Jesse said. "He's secretive, and doesn't trust anyone, but I think if he knows someone has been to the grove and the situation there, he'll come out of hiding. I've helped him out a few times, so he knows me. If nothing else, at least you could talk to him. It might make all the difference. If he's close by, he might even be in contact as soon as tomorrow."

Bran could see that Teya thought the man Jesse was talking about was her brother Hewson. He admitted that it could be him, but it seemed unlikely. If Hewson had gone after Teya two years ago, and knew she was at the palace, what would he be doing around here?

"I don't think we should stay here," Bran said. "It's too dangerous."

"But what about this man Jesse's talking about?" Teya asked. "We can't leave until we find him."

"What is your involvement in all this?" Jesse broke in. "I know you're not one of us."

"He's from Braemar," Teya answered. She opened her mouth to explain further, but Bran stopped her.

"I have my reasons," Bran glanced fiercely at Teya. "But my main focus is protecting her." Teya's eyes widened in surprise at the unspoken rebuke.

Jesse looked between the two of them before speaking. "You're right. It's not safe here. Too many people heard Teya sing tonight."

"But we can't leave until we get in contact with this man," Teya said. "Isn't there a way to get a message to him tonight?"

"Yes," Jesse answered. "But the way we set it up involves going back into town, and I don't want to get caught. Maybe we should wait a few days until things settle down."

Teya frowned. "We don't have a lot of time to wait. Couldn't Bran help you?" Her eyes lifted with hope. "No one knows him here, he could take the message."

"It would take both of us," Jesse said. "There's someone at a tavern I need to talk to, but I think we could do it. Are you game?"

Bran pursed his lips. It seemed like the best solution, and he was willing to take the risk. But leaving Teya didn't sit right. Of course, taking her would be worse. At least if he went with Jesse he could keep an eye on him. If things went bad, he could leave Jesse and get Teya safely away. "All right, but Teya stays here."

"But I could help…"

"No." Bran's voice was gruff, but she needed to know he was serious. "It's the only way I'll do it."

Teya shrugged. "All right. I'll wait here."

"He's right," Jesse said. "It won't take long with both of us. You sit tight, and we'll be back before you know it." He smiled at Teya, touching her arm reassuringly.

Bran wanted to punch him. "Let's go," he said instead. "You can fill me in on the way."

Jesse glanced at Bran with a flicker of anger before he masked it with an agreeable nod. He grabbed a floppy hat and pulled it low over his eyes, effectively hiding his hair and face. "Lock the door when we leave," he said to Teya.

She nodded, and followed them out. Before she could close the door Bran whispered urgently. "If I don't come back, get away from him. Understand?"

"What?"

"There's no time to explain. Just be careful." With a quick glance at her puzzled expression, he closed the door behind him and waited to hear the bolt catch before he caught up with Jesse. Hopefully, there would be no need for her to heed his warning, but this was almost too easy, and there was a hunger in Jesse's eyes that Bran didn't like.

"The tavern's on the other side of town," Jesse said. "But if we keep away from the main roads it will be easy to reach without much trouble. One of the serving girls is my contact. When we get there, you can go inside and I'll wait out back." He described the table where he normally sat and what the girl looked like. "Just tell her that I need to leave a message for our mutual friend, but couldn't come in. She'll know what to do."

"All right," Bran agreed.

As they made their way back to the center of town, Jesse shook his head and smiled with incredulity. "You're lucky you ran into me and not someone else. This is a dangerous place for someone like Teya. I'm surprised you let her sing in public."

Bran bristled at the criticism. "It seems to me that you're the one who lured her up on the stage. Not me."

Jesse frowned. "But I didn't know what she was then. All I knew was that she liked my music, and once I saw her, I couldn't take my eyes off her. I've never seen anyone with that color of eyes before."

Bran wanted to slap that silly smile off his face. Jesse may be a Kaloriahn, but he seemed too self-assured for someone on the run. It bothered him on a deep level, raising his hackles and putting him on guard. If things didn't feel right, he wanted to be ready.

After walking several blocks, they stopped in front of a tavern that looked like it had seen better days. Filth and grime covered the walks and walls. Through a window, Jesse pointed out the table and girl, then disappeared around the back.

Raucous laughter spilled from the doorway when Bran entered. He made his way to the back table with casual ease, all the while scanning the room for trouble. After sitting down, the serving girl approached with a glass of ale.

"What can I get for you, sir?"

Bran set a gold piece on the table where only she could see it. "I'm here for Jesse. He needs to get a message to your mutual friend."

"Jesse?" Her brows rose. "That blackguard? If this is one of his jokes…"

Bran surged to his feet with a growl of anger. He rushed out of the tavern and around to the back where he'd last seen Jesse. There was no sign of him, and Bran turned toward the street, anxious to get to Teya before Jesse.

As he ran down the alley, a black shape flew out of the darkness, shoving him into the wall. Caught off-guard, Bran fought to stay on his feet. More men joined the first and a blow to the jaw and stomach sent him to his knees.

"Enough." Jesse hissed. "Tie him up and get him out of here."

"What should we do with him?"

"Take him to the woods and kill him."

Bran's arms were jerked roughly behind him and tied together. A rope was thrown over his head and tightened around his neck.

"Wait." Jesse bent down and pulled Bran's gun from his waist. "I don't think you'll be needing this anymore."

They pulled Bran to his feet and he struggled against them, hot with anger until they tightened the rope around his neck and he nearly choked.

"Go!" Jesse hissed. "Before anyone sees you."

Bran stumbled onto one knee, and gasped for breath. He almost passed out before they loosened the rope, giving him enough slack to walk and breathe at the same time. They got him to his feet, and pushed him down the alley, skirting the tavern and other buildings where they might be seen. Struggling did him no good, and Bran fought to hold down the panic. How was he going to get out of this?

Jesse's men kept pushing him forward, and he fell to his knees several times before coming to the edge of town. The woods loomed dark before them and one of the men paused to light a torch before leading the way deep into the forest. Crackling twigs and the rustle of small animals scurrying through the brush accompanied their steps. The path took them past a creek before opening into a secluded clearing.

"This is far enough," one of them said. They pushed Bran down in the dirt, and he knew there was only one chance he could escape alive.

"Wait," he panted. "If I'm going to die, at least give me the dignity to stand up and fight."

"Go ahead," one of them said. "Stand up."

He struggled to his feet before the first blow knocked him down. Stunned, he got back to his feet, blood trickling from a gash on his forehead. "Come on," he cajoled. "Cut me loose, give me a chance."

Another blow to the stomach had him doubled over in pain. Before he fell one of the men jerked him back by the arms. "We don't mind having a little sport," the man said, and cut the ropes binding him. "Either way you will die. If you haven't noticed, you're outnumbered. No one's coming to help you." That brought a chorus of laughter.

The loose ropes fell and he pushed them off before straightening to confront them. He raised his fists and managed to land a few punches before the breath was knocked out of him. It wasn't a fight, it was a beating, but at least he wasn't completely defenseless. He had the satisfaction of hurting them a little before all three joined in together, and he couldn't keep up.

He tried to stay on his feet, but soon even that was too hard. Curled into a ball, he struggled to protect himself from the vicious kicks that rained down on him. His last conscious thought was that he must be dead, because nothing hurt anymore.

                         ≈≈

Teya didn't like waiting, but after ten years of captivity she'd grown used to spending time alone. Once Bran and Jesse left, she lit more candles because it seemed like the walls were closing in. The soft light gave off a warm glow that helped settle her nerves.

Bran had warned her to be careful, but she didn't understand why. Jesse was helping them. She couldn't think of anything in their conversation that seemed threatening. Still, she couldn't help being nervous. If Bran didn't come back that would mean she had made a terrible mistake. She pushed the thought away. He would come back.

Time passed slowly, adding fuel to her frayed nerves. What was taking them so long? Had King Thesald sent men looking for her this far away? She wondered how King Thesald was taking her escape and perversely hoped he was suffering. Then her thoughts went to Leona, and she hoped her grandmother was all right. Teya hated seeing her so frail. The night of the ritual had been wonderful, but it had taken a toll on her.

Teya blushed at what Leona had done, and almost wished Bran hadn't kissed her after the ceremony. He had inadvertently sealed the bond Leona had created, and if he ever kissed her again, he would know something was there. He would be furious, and she could hardly blame him. They should have given Bran a choice, but Leona wasn't about to let fate determine their future. His help was too important.

She froze at the sound of footsteps and jumped when the lock in the door rattled. The door opened, and Jesse came inside. He was alone. "Where's Bran? Did you get the message sent?" Sudden coldness settled in her stomach.

"Yes, we should hear back from him by tomorrow. Bran went back to the inn for your horses. He'll be here in a minute, but I couldn't wait. I wanted to make sure you were safe." Jesse came to her side and studied her face. "You don't know what a chance you took singing with me tonight. I'm glad you did, but it was dangerous. Your beauty is like a beacon. You're not someone that could ever go unnoticed."

His frank perusal was uncomfortable. "What do you mean?"

He smiled. "I know who you are. You're the Songbird. Everyone knows about you. You're legendary. People tell all kinds of stories about you. I wonder how many of them are true."

Teya's heart pounded. Had he known who she was all along? He reached out to touch her cheek, but when she flinched away his hand dropped. "Sorry, I didn't mean to offend you. You're just…you fascinate me." He took a step back with a placating smile. "While we're waiting for Bran why don't you tell me about the grove. It's not far from here is it?"

"Not too far." She tried to appear calm, even though her legs were trembling.

"I wish we could go there now. The grove has pulled at me for a long time. Don't you feel it in your blood?"

"Yes, but we need to find the others first."

Jesse nodded absently. "You're right, of course." He began to prowl around the small space.

Dread tightened her stomach and she asked, "Is something wrong?"

Her perception startled him and his gaze locked with hers. "As a matter of fact, we were followed by a hunter, but we managed to turn the tables and capture him. Bran's questioning him right now. He wouldn't rest until he'd talked to him. We're hoping the hunter knows where the captured Kaloriahns are."

"I thought you said Bran was getting the horses."

"He's doing that too…they're at the same inn."

Teya swallowed, feeling trapped. She needed to get out of there. "I'd better go see if I can help." She started toward the door, but Jesse caught her.

"No. It's not safe. You need to stay here." His fingers dug into her arms and when she tried to pull away, he jerked her against his body. She struggled to get free, and took a breath to use her magic. Before she could utter a sound, his mouth came down on hers, effectively cutting her off.

She fought against him, but it only served to tighten his hold. When he finally broke the kiss, he breathed a single tone that fell over her in a wave. Even though it wasn't powerful, the tone reverberated through her head, drowning her in a pool of darkness. Her arms fell limply to her sides and her vision blurred. Jesse caught her in his arms and carried her to his bed. He gently stroked her hair while she lay stunned and powerless.

"I'm sorry I had to hurt you, but I promise if you help me it won't happen again."

The pounding in her head lifted, and she fought against the darkness his tone had cast over her. It slowly gave way, but before she could summon her magic, Jesse pulled a handkerchief out of his pocket and gagged her. He left her side for a moment, bringing back a piece of rope and bound her hands together.

"I'm doing this so I won't have to hurt you again. I need you to be still and listen to what I have to say. The king was livid when you escaped, and he called on me to find you. I'm the best hunter there is, and he paid me well, but that's not the reason I wanted to get to you first."

He finished tying the rope and sat beside her, his brows drawn together. "I've seen you many times at the palace. Your song always touched me here." He gestured to his heart, and her eyes widened. He smiled at her surprise. "I kept out of sight. You never saw me, but I've always felt bad about how you were treated. I decided if there was a chance I could help you, I would. When word came that you escaped, I thought you might try to reach the grove, and since this city is near the border, I took a chance you'd come through here. It certainly paid off tonight." His eyes held hers and she shivered at the speculation gleaming in them.

"What you told me about the grove is fascinating. I've been trying to find a way in there for a long time. Several of my associates have died trying to get past that black thing. But now you've given me hope. I'll make you a deal. Share the tones with me, and I won't take you back to the king. I'll even tell you where the rest of the Kaloriahns are. We can go to the grove together."

Teya's stomach clenched. How could Jesse be a true Kaloriahn and betray his people, hunting them down like animals? He was crazy to think she would ever bargain with him. If he could do this to her, he would say anything to get what he wanted, and still take her back to the king. Then a new thought sent terror racing through her veins. Where was Bran? What had Jesse done to Bran?

Jesse stood at the approach of footsteps, and Teya tried to calm her racing heart. Three men came through the doorway looking disheveled and dirty. She recognized two of them from Jesse's band. The third was sporting a swollen eye, but they all seemed pleased with themselves.

"That her?" The third one said, and started toward her. Jesse blocked his way.

"She's Kaloriahn, but I don't want any of you near her. She's too valuable to be damaged—in any way."

The man shrugged, and Teya shivered when his cold stare crawled over her body. She knew he was only biding his time until he could get her alone. The others weren't quite as obvious, but dangerous just the same. At least Jesse hadn't told them who she was.

"We took care of him," the man said. "He's dead."

Bewildered panic rose in a scream that tore through her throat. Bran! Had they killed him? She twisted to her feet and was struck by Jesse's dark tone of magic. The pain knocked the breath from her, and she fell back against the bed. She doubled over with sudden nausea, and with the gag in her mouth, started to choke. Jesse leaned over her with startled concern and pulled the gag away.

"I told you to be still and I wouldn't have to hurt you again." Sighing, Jesse helped her lay back on the bed. "If you don't cooperate, I'll have to put a *kundar* around your neck. You don't want that do you?"

Helpless in a dark haze of pain she whispered, "A true Kaloriahn would never do anything like this. You can't be one of my people. You aren't worthy of the name. Bran took the *kundar* off to help me. He was a much better man than you'll ever be. You disgust me." His tones covered her in a blanket of darkness, while the anguished screams in her mind died, along with all hope that she would ever see Bran again.

～～

Soft moaning brought him awake and he realized it was coming from his own throat. Pain tore through his body like lightning, and he struggled for breath. Slowly, he managed to turn onto his back and gaze into the night sky. One of his eyes was swollen shut, but from the position of the stars, he knew he hadn't been out long, and he marveled that he was still alive.

Thirst and pain were dark friends in those first waking moments, and it was only thoughts of Teya that kept him from letting go of life. He dreamed of water and in his dream remembered the flask he had stored in his pocket. Grove water. With quiet determination, he willed his arm to move to his pocket. His searching fingers touched the silver flask and he nearly cried at this small victory. After a long rest, he brought the flask to his swollen lips, but couldn't get the lid open.

Using his teeth, he managed to loosen the lid until a few drops of water dripped into his mouth. It was difficult to swallow, but thirst and a will to live drove him past the pain. After an eternity of slow drips, he finally got the flask open and the life-sustaining water poured into him.

He drank carefully, needing each drop of the healing strength it carried. The flask was empty long before his thirst was quenched. The pain lessened and he breathed easier. As time passed, he tested his arms and legs with slight movements. Although his fingers and wrists were swollen, only a few bones seemed to be broken. He couldn't say that about his ribs. Every time he moved they grated against each other in excruciating pain.

He needed more grove water, but the waterbags were with the saddles and horses back at the inn. He didn't think he could possibly make it that far. Where was Teya now? Had Jesse taken her away? He hated to think of a *kundar* around her neck and blamed himself. He should have been more careful. He needed to find her before they took her back to the king, an impossible task in his condition.

As he mulled over his predicament, he remembered the *sym* he had taken from the body in the waste. It was in his pocket, and if he were lucky it would still be there. He gingerly rummaged inside and found one of the cylinders pushed into a corner. Relief coursed through him that it was unbroken and full of crimson liquid. He'd never taken *sym* before, and was reluctant to do so now, but if it would heal him for just a few hours, he could get the grove water he needed. More important, he could begin his search for Teya.

Not daring to wait any longer, he gently twisted the cap off and raised it carefully to his lips. The liquid tasted slightly coppery, but he quickly drained the cylinder and waited for a miracle. Would it work?

The seconds slowly passed, each with a new wave of anticipation. How long would it take before he knew it was working? So far, nothing seemed to change. The seconds turned to minutes and Bran blew out his breath in frustration. That was when he noticed his ribs didn't hurt. He took another breath, deepening it until his lungs were full. The pain was gone!

In wonder, he smiled and noticed that his lips weren't cracked and bleeding. His hands and wrists moved with ease and his vision cleared. With a racing heart, he stood and breathed in the cool night air with a sense of awe. A part of him had never believed that *sym* would work. How could it, unless it was magic. Real magic.

He knew it wouldn't last long, so he focused on the tasks at hand and found the trail that took him through the woods and back to the edge of town. It was still dark and although his first impulse was to get Teya, he knew getting the horses from the stable at the inn was his first priority.

The town stretched out endlessly before he found the way to the inn. It was further than he thought and precious time was slipping away. The stables were in the back, far from the main building, and he managed to slip in unnoticed. Relief coursed through him to find his horses and supplies still there. The only things missing were the clothes he had taken with them to Jesse's. He washed the blood from his face and hands in a bucket of water beside the stalls. Then he saddled both horses, pausing to take a long drink of grove water to sustain him. Ready to leave, he took the horses out of a side entrance.

With the inn behind him, he breathed easier. Now, all he had to do was find Teya. He hoped she was still at the house. If Jesse thought Bran was dead, there'd be no need to worry about him trying to rescue Teya. Bran reasoned that it would be easier for Jesse to leave her there.

He found a secluded place in the woods not far from Jesse's house, and tethered the horses. Needing a weapon, he rummaged through his saddlebags until he found a knife. He was sorry Jesse had taken his gun and perversely hoped he'd shoot himself trying to figure out how to use it.

As he headed back, he kept to the walls and shadows, being careful not to make any noise. For all his planning, he knew the possibility existed that Teya had already left town. If that was the case, he'd have to find her trail fast.

He entered the outskirts of town and followed a street that led toward the area he remembered. At the end of the block, he turned the corner, and there it was. A single candle glowed through a window, and he wondered how many men he would have to fight to free Teya. Thoughts of another fight made him nauseous, but this time, surprise would be on his side. He watched a few moments from a shadowed corner until he was satisfied that no one was coming, then stole across to the building.

He glanced through the window and was relieved to see Teya sleeping on a bed. Her hands were tied in front of her, and roped to the bedpost. A gag was tied around her mouth, and his heart lifted to see they hadn't put a *kundar* around her neck. One of his attackers was sprawled in a chair across the room, asleep. There was no sign of Jesse.

Knowing he had to hurry, he crept noiselessly to the back of the house. He found a large rock and edged to the door. To his surprise, it wasn't locked. He gingerly turned the handle and pushed it open. Stepping inside, he paused when the man stirred, but remained asleep, and Bran made his move. In three strides he reached the man and hit him over the head with the rock, knocking him out with one blow.

When he turned to Teya, she was staring at him in wide-eyed wonder. Her eyes filled with unshed tears. "Shh...I'm here now, it's going to be all right." His fingers shook as he loosened the gag and pulled it away from her mouth.

"Bran! I thought you were dead," Her voice was thick with emotion.

He pulled out his knife and cut through the ropes binding her hands. "I got lucky," he said. "Where's Jesse?"

"He's meeting someone. He'll be back any minute."

"There, you're free." Teya was unsteady when she stood, and Bran put his arm around her for support. She clung to him for a moment before he urged her toward the door. "I have the horses tethered nearby. Can you make a run for it?"

"Yes," she whispered.

Bran glanced out the door, and seeing no one, opened it wide. With Teya's hand in his they dashed to the other side of the street, pausing at the corner. With no one about, they continued on, waiting in shadows, watching and listening for signs of people. Finally, the way to the woods was clear, and as they entered, the trees seemed to wrap them in a cocoon of protection. Bran led her further, keeping up the pace, until he felt it was safe to stop and rest.

"Oh, Bran," Teya sobbed, breathless. "You were right. How could I be so stupid?"

He held her tightly against him. She was like a breath of fresh air after rain, and he realized he never wanted to let her go. "It's all right sweetheart." He lifted her face in his hands and gently wiped the tears away. The early light of dawn reflected in her luminous eyes and with sweeping tenderness, his lips moved to hers. In that moment, it felt as though their hearts beat in perfect harmony and a shock of recognition shuddered through Bran. It was as if they were tied together in some part of their souls.

Bran pulled away with a gasp at the powerful bond that linked them. Unsure of what it meant, but having no time to discuss it, he said, "We've got to go. Do you know what Jesse's plans are?"

Teya seemed almost as shaken as he was. Trembling, she answered, "He left to get a *kundar*. I can't believe how stupid I was. When you didn't come back with him, like an idiot, I panicked. He gagged me so I couldn't use my magic and tied me up. I didn't think I'd ever see you again."

Hot anger surged through Bran along with a wave of protectiveness. "I'm here now, and I won't leave you again." He hugged her, then took her hand and led her through the trees. "The horses aren't much further, we'll be there soon."

The horses nickered a greeting when they reached them, and Bran pulled a waterbag from his pack. "Here, have a drink." When she finished, he drank some as well. The grove water had a calming affect, and helped restore his jumbled wits. "We need to find a place to lay low for awhile, preferably far from here. It will be rough going through the trees, but I don't want to use the main roads. Let's go."

They traveled for several hours through the forest, continually alert for sounds of pursuit. Bran's thoughts kept turning back to the current of energy that pulled him to Teya. It was almost like she was a part of him. This powerful attachment must be linked to the *sym* he had used. At least that was the only explanation he could think of. Using the magic must have bonded them. Once the *sym* wore off, it would be gone. Instead of relief, this brought a tinge of regret that surprised him, but he pushed it to the back of his mind. He had other things he needed to concentrate on now.

It was late afternoon when Bran had to stop for a rest. Too soon, his body was beginning to tire and he needed to tell Teya what had happened before the *sym* stopped working.

"We're headed south toward the city," he said. "But I don't know exactly where we are. The map should help, but before we go any further I need to tell you what happened." He took a deep breath, and hoped Teya could handle what he had to say. "Jesse's men beat me up pretty bad. Luckily, I had a flask of grove water that helped a little, but I used something else. Remember the body we found in the waste?"

"Yes."

"I found two cylinders of *sym* in his pocket. I drank one earlier, and it healed me enough to come to you. The problem is, I don't know how much longer it's going to work, and when it wears off, I'm going to be a mess." Already his ribs were starting to ache.

"Oh, Bran, I'm so sorry. Is it wearing off now?"

"A little." He took short breaths, no longer able to disguise the pain. "We need to find a place to stop." He swallowed, and realized his lips were puffy and swollen. The *sym* was wearing off, only it was too fast.

"Over here," Teya urged him. "There's a small clearing."

He followed her, hoping he could stay on his horse long enough to reach it. He couldn't seem to hold the reins with his swollen fingers. Teya reached up for him and he managed to swing his leg off the horse. He stumbled when she led him to a space under a tree. At that moment his ribs gave way and his gasp of pain made it worse. Unable to stand, he sank to the ground in an agonized heap. Teya's sharp intake of breath and startled cry was the last thing he heard before darkness claimed him.

≈≈

Teya knelt beside Bran in shock at the sight of his discolored and swollen face. When he told her they beat him, she never expected it to be this bad. She swallowed her tears and tried to think. She carefully straightened his legs so he was laying flat on his back and wished she'd been able to get a blanket under him. He moaned softly and a knot formed in the pit her stomach. This was all her fault! Without the grove water and *sym*, he would be dead by now.

He seemed to have trouble breathing and she unbuttoned his shirt. His chest was black and blue with bruises, and several of his ribs shown through his skin as jagged pieces of bone. If the grove water had helped, she hated to think what he had looked like before. She closed his shirt and got the blankets out. As she placed one under his head, his eyes fluttered open.

"Are you crying again?" he slurred.

She dashed the tears from her cheeks and tried to sound confident. "Just rest Bran, I'm going to see if I can fix this."

His brows drew together, but the effort seemed to hurt. "You can do that?"

"I think so." Then as an afterthought she added, "Is that all right with you?"

"Hell yes," he croaked, then added through cracked lips. "I'm sorry I ever told you not to use your magic on me. Please feel free. Anytime soon would be good."

She smiled in spite of the gravity of the situation. She would have helped him whether he wanted her to or not. Closing her eyes, she concentrated on the basics her grandmother had taught her. In this case, she needed tones that brought completion and wholeness. A small doubt assailed her, but she pushed it away, she had to believe she could do this. It should be easier because of the bond they shared. With a deep breath, she began.

The music softly unfolded, gently covering Bran in a smooth blanket of protection. She wove the strings of magic to settle above and beneath him, until he was completely encased within it. Slowly, the threads began to sink into his skin, first, mending his bruises and then sinking lower to the deep wounds within, and finally knitting his bones back together.

Teya didn't know how long she sang, only that she had to keep going until he was whole again. When she finished, it was dark with only the moon and stars for light. Bran was resting peacefully, his face unmarred by cuts and bruises. He had always been handsome, but now something about him was different. He carried a part of her magic in him. Her grandmother had said the bond was necessary, but Teya still regretted what they had done without telling him. Their kiss had unlocked the awareness of it, and she knew he had felt it. He still might not comprehend the implications and she wasn't sure she should tell him.

The energy it took to heal him had sapped her strength. She drank some of the grove water before leaning back against the tree beside Bran. She hoped they were far enough from the road to be safe and wondered how long it would take before Jesse was on their trail. There was no doubt in her mind that he would come after her.

At least Bran was alive and they had escaped. Teya's world shattered when she realized Jesse had ordered his death. It was all her fault. She vowed that no one would ever take advantage of her again. Next time, she would be ready to use her magic.

There were a few things she knew she could do, the rest shouldn't be too hard to learn. An image of what she could do to Jesse flooded her thoughts. She could use the same dark notes he had used on her, only twist them to intensify the pain. She could make him suffer.

She could do the same thing to the king. She would relish singing to him again, and when he began to cringe, she wouldn't stop until he screamed in agony. Deep down, she knew it was wrong to feel this way, but it was hard to control the burning anger. She was tired of shutting these feelings away as if they didn't exist. Why should someone like him be allowed to hurt others anyway? If it was wrong, then someone had to stop him. It might as well be her.

Bone weary and tired, she gave in to her yearning to be close to Bran. She cuddled up next to him and his warmth brought some humanity back into her angry heart. Exhaustion settled over her, and rather than face what she was becoming, she let herself drift into sleep and oblivion.

∽≈

"Teya?"

She drowsily turned to her side and draped an arm across his chest. His chin brushed the top of her head and he pulled her closer. Early morning light filtered through the trees and her heart lifted to feel Bran's strong heartbeat beneath her hand. He was alive and they had escaped! She pulled away to take a good look at him. "Are you feeling better?"

"Yes, thanks to you." He took a deep breath to test his ribs and grinned. "It's nice to be able to breath again."

She smiled, grateful she had eased his pain. Especially since it was all her fault. "But can you stand? That's the real test."

"I don't know. I kind of like it right where I am." With a quick jerk, he pulled her down on top of him. She weakly protested with a laugh before relaxing against him. Her heart pounded furiously as their lips met in a soft kiss. She knew it would raise questions she didn't want to answer, but she was so grateful he was alive and well, that she couldn't help herself. Just like the night before, their heart and souls met in quiet greeting. Before it could go any further, Teya pulled away, breathless and scared.

He would know something was different, and she didn't know what to tell him. He gazed at her with sudden comprehension. "Will you tell me what this is all about? Why does it frighten you?"

Maybe he didn't know after all. When she didn't answer, he continued. "I've never felt this way before. When I kiss you, it's like we're joined together somehow." When her eyes widened, he grew cautious. "Don't you feel it?" At her nod, he continued. "Tell me what it means?"

"I'm not sure you'll be glad to hear it." She sat up and straightened her clothes, then started folding the blankets.

"Why? Because you don't want it?"

That question caught her off-guard. "It's not a question of wanting, it's just something that happened." His face fell, and Teya knew she'd hurt him without meaning to.

"So these feelings I have don't mean anything to you?" His voice was flat.

"Of course they do, but it's more complicated than that."

Bran sat up and took a deep breath. "Does this have something to do with the ceremony in the grove?"

"Yes," she confessed. "I promise I'll tell you everything, but right now, we'd probably better go." She knew Bran wanted an explanation, but she wasn't ready to tell him yet.

"Sometimes not telling is worse than telling. Especially if it's the truth." As he gingerly pushed to his feet, the tension ebbed between them. After he got his balance, he carefully stretched his arms and legs, testing his muscles for movement and strength. "Everything seems to be working," he admitted with a lighter tone. "In fact, I may be better than I was before. Thank you."

Teya spoke quickly. "You're welcome. At least my magic won't wear off like *sym*."

Bran's eyes widened. "Thank goodness for that."

"What should we do now?"

The first rays of sunlight cast long shadows through the trees. "It looks like we've slept the night away. Where are the horses?" At Teya's shrug Bran continued. "We'd better find them and get going."

In her worry for Bran, she had forgotten all about them. Thankfully, they hadn't wandered far. She handed Bran the blankets, and they finished off one of the bags of grove water.

"Did you find out anything about Jesse?" Bran asked. "Do you think he'll come after you?"

"Yes, he'll come. He's a hunter. The king sent him to find me, and he won't go back empty handed. What I don't understand is how he tricked me. His magic seemed so real, not at all how I expected *sym* to feel. He told me he was a Kaloriahn, but how could he turn on his own people?" The thought made her sick to her stomach.

"Who knows? I guess it's possible, if he has enough to gain like Korban."

A terrible idea formed in Teya's mind. "Jesse's too young to be Korban, isn't he?"

Bran considered it. "Yes, I think so. But whoever he is, he's dangerous. We'll have to change our plans. What I'd really like to do is get you to Braemar and safety, but for now I think we should concentrate on making it back to the city where we can meet up with Jax and Clare. We need to find out what's been going on in our absence."

"There's something else you should know," Teya said. "He wanted me to tell him how to get past the Destroyer. I think he knows about the grove water and what it can do. He also said he knew where the Kaloriahns were."

"That would make sense if he's a hunter," Bran said. "We're just lucky he didn't have a *kundar* handy. If he had taken you anywhere else, I would have been hard pressed to find you in time."

Bran froze and motioned for Teya to be still. Several moments passed in silence and Teya tensed, wondering if Jesse had already picked up their trail.

"I thought I heard something," Bran whispered, his hand automatically reaching for the gun that wasn't there. He swore softly before urging Teya to mount her horse. "Stay close."

Teya suppressed a shiver and followed Bran south where the trees soon thinned out, leaving them more exposed. When the road came into view, her spine tingled with foreboding that something was behind them. At that moment, the baying of a hound broke the stillness and was quickly joined by a chorus of barking dogs. Jesse was coming!

CHAPTER SIX

The Bond

"We'll make better time on the road," Bran shouted and spurred his mount forward. They gained the road, as the first dark shape broke through the trees, hot on their trail. Following the dogs came four men on horseback, and Teya groaned. Was there some way to stop them with her magic?

A loud crack pierced the air and a searing pain tore through Teya's arm, throwing her forward. With the shock, she fumbled the reins and lost her hold. Her left arm went numb and hung loosely at her side while blood ran down her fingers. Her horse slowed in the confusion, but she managed to move her arm to her lap and urged the horse forward. Pain replaced the numbness and she fought to stay in the saddle. Bran pulled up beside her, his face white with rage, and she realized she'd been shot with his gun.

"Keep going," she yelled. "I'll try and stop them with my magic." Her arm burned in agony, but she could still use it, and she needed time to figure out what to do.

Bran closed the distance, putting himself between her and their pursuers. "No!" she shouted. But Bran ignored her. The men were gaining on them, and another loud crack sent a wave of panic over her. She ducked, hearing the faint sound as the bullet whizzed past, and knew it was only a matter of time before one of them was hit again.

Teya did the only thing she could think of and sang, throwing wild tones to the sky. She twisted the elements against each other, calling them down, until they burst into a blast of heat. She barely caught the energy with her song in time to direct it into the earth behind her. The ground shook with a loud boom while earth and rock flew into the air.

Behind her, a horse screamed. When the dust settled one rider lay on the ground, and the others were galloping back the way they had come. Teya drew on the energy once more and flung it toward the retreating men. It fell short and they disappeared from sight. In reckless abandon, she started after them, her mind raging with anger. She wanted this nightmare to end, even if it meant killing them all.

Somewhere within this red haze she heard her name. The searing urgency of his voice stopped her headlong rush and she turned to find Bran dashing toward her. Fear radiated from him in waves through their bond, and she wondered what terrible thing had happened to cause it. In her concern for him, the rage pouring through her heart subsided, and the cause of Bran's distress became clear. He was afraid of her!

The fight and anger went out of her in an instant. Breathless and weak, Teya slid off her horse and held her bleeding arm. The power of her song echoed through her body and caused her to tremble and shake. The energy in the air vibrated in little bursts around her. In reaction, tears gathered in her eyes and rolled down her cheeks.

Without warning, quiet drops of rain mingled with her tears, accompanied by a low rumble above her. The once-blue sky now roiled with dark clouds that clashed with energy. Flashes of lightning and thunder boomed above her and she cringed. What had she done?

Nearby, the fallen rider stared sightlessly into the sky. Blood covered his head and his hair was smoking in the rain. The scent of burning flesh made her stomach queasy, and she twisted away to stifle a gag.

Bran picked up his gun and came to her side. "Come on, we need to get out of this rain." When the thunder rolled again, Bran gently steered her toward a stand of trees. Her legs trembled with each step and the storm seemed to mirror the tumult within her. She tried to gain some calm by taking deep breaths, but all it did was make her face go stiff and she realized she was losing what little control she had.

Bran sensed her turmoil. "It will be all right, Teya. I know this is hard, but don't shut down on me. We need to find shelter and tend to your arm."

With detached fascination, Teya watched the blood drip from her fingers and became aware of the pulsing pain in her arm. She focused on the pain, clearing her mind of everything else and found a measure of sanity return. Bran put his arm around her for support and his touch calmed her racing heart.

Once they reached the canopy of trees, Teya slid to the ground, leaning back against a tree. "I'll get the horses and my medicine kit and be right back," Bran said.

Teya laid her head against the tree and closed her eyes. Her loss of control frightened her, but it wasn't as bad as the look on Bran's face. She had done what was necessary, but that didn't make her a monster. Next time, she would have to make sure her feelings were locked away so she wouldn't lose control.

Bran returned and gently tore the fabric from her sleeve to check her wound. "This isn't too bad," he said reassuringly. "It looks like the bullet passed right through. This might hurt a little."

He cleaned it off and wrapped a bandage around her arm. "That should stop the bleeding." He held it tight for a moment while he studied her. "We can't stay. They might be coming back any minute. Can you ride?"

"Yes. Just give me a drink of grove water, that should help."

Bran held the bag while she drank, then put the supplies back in his saddlebags. He came to her side and helped her stand. The shock had pretty much worn off, and the grove water helped steady her. She mounted carefully, signaling with a nod to show she was ready.

As they moved out, Bran stayed close to her side and kept an eye on the road behind. They kept at a steady pace, and the road soon leveled out. With no sign of pursuit, he relaxed his guard. "I can't believe they used my gun!" he growled. "They must be complete idiots! They could have killed you!"

Teya was surprised at the direction of his thoughts. She thought he would focus on what she had done instead of his gun. "What I did was a lot worse," she managed. "I not only killed that man, but I let my emotions get away from me." There, she said it.

"You did what you had to. I don't think we could have escaped from them without your magic."

His acceptance encouraged her. "I had to do something, especially since they were shooting at us, but it got out of hand. I still feel a little off balance." Tears gathered in her eyes, but she held them back. "You brought me back, but the way you looked at me, like I was some kind of a monster..."

"You just scared me," Bran said. "Running after them like that. I wasn't expecting it, and you looked...angry."

"I don't know what I was thinking. I was kind of lost in the moment. I probably would have tried to kill them all. Why did you stop me?"

"I didn't want you to get hurt. Sometimes when someone gets out of control like that, they can do crazy, dangerous things."

"You mean like a crazed monster or wild animal? Is that why you were afraid of me?"

"I was trying to protect you. I was afraid for you, not of you. I know you would never hurt me. Anyone who has gone through what you have, could go a little crazy. I'm amazed at how stable you are after enduring all those years of captivity, but add that to your power and it makes a deadly combination."

At least he was being honest, and she couldn't argue with that. But she still didn't know what to say. Should she thank him for stopping her? She wasn't sure what was right anymore. If she couldn't trust herself, then she shouldn't use her powers. What if she did something wrong?

"Jesse's still back there," Bran said. "And I don't think he's going to give up. Next time, he'll be more careful. If we stay on this road, we should reach the city by nightfall. There's an inn outside the gates where I keep a room. We can contact Jax from there and find out what's been going on in our absence."

Teya nodded, unable to speak. Without Bran she would be completely lost. She didn't know what to do or where to go anymore, and she had just proven that her magic was deadly. It wasn't the most comfortable thought, and she knew it was urgent that she learn how to master it. Not the magic so much as herself. That was the key, but doing that was easier said than done.

The rain slowed to a drizzle, and the clouds receded, letting soft rays of sunshine filter through. With a fresh breeze and the sun, her clothes soon dried, but she was still a little lightheaded.

She glanced over her shoulder every now and then, but never saw any sign of pursuit. Still, she couldn't shake the feeling that Jesse was there, just out of sight, and it grated on her nerves. She wasn't ready to face him. Her tenuous hold over her emotions was too frightening.

They kept up a steady pace and made good time until they came to a small town. Bran insisted that they go around it and Teya agreed. By the time they got back to the main road, Bran worried that they'd lost their lead over Jesse.

From then on, Teya kept a steady watch behind them. As they traveled, the farms got closer together, and soon there were houses spread all over the countryside. With each one they skirted, they lost time and ran the risk of running into Jesse.

"We can't keep going this way," Bran said. "We'll have to follow another route. Jesse will probably get ahead of us, but it can't be helped. We'll cut toward the mountains and follow the foothills until we're closer to the city."

"All right," Teya agreed. Her arm was throbbing and she was hungry, but she didn't want to stop until he did. She didn't want him to think she couldn't keep up or take care of herself. He had almost died for her, and was doing all he could to keep her safe. Guilt over her grandmother's deception rose in burning intensity. He had trusted her, and she was using him. She had to tell him, but didn't know how she could stand to see the hurt her betrayal would cause.

The next few hours went by in a blur with the pain in her arm growing worse. When they finally stopped, she could hardly wait to get off her horse. In her hurry, she stumbled and had to grab onto the saddle with her good arm to keep her knees from buckling.

Bran noticed her clumsy dismount and came to her side. "Here, let me help you."

"No, I'm fine. Just a little tired." Bran ignored her and slipped an arm around her waist, then carefully led her to a shady spot under a tree.

"I'm sorry I pushed you so hard. Here, drink this," he ordered. She eagerly took the waterbag and forced herself to take slow drinks. Bran checked her bandage and swore under his breath.

"What's wrong?" she asked.

"This is worse than I thought." Teya turned to look, but Bran stopped her. "Just lie back for a minute and I'll clean it up." He took the grove water and was about to pour it over her wound when she pulled away from him.

"No! Don't use that! We're almost out!"

"It might help, unless you can heal yourself."

Teya didn't have the energy to even think about it. "I'm sure I can do something later, after I've rested for a few minutes."

"Fine. While you're resting, I'll wash this off. Try not to move." He gently poured the water over the wound and rubbed. It burned at first, but after a minute she relaxed while coolness spread from the wound up her arm. Finally released from the steady, throbbing pain, she took a deep breath and silently slipped into sleep.

≈≈

Bran cursed his stupidity. He should have checked her arm before now, but all he could think about was getting Teya away from Jesse. At least the grove water seemed to have an effect. It congealed when it came in contact with her broken skin. The redness and swelling began to lessen while he rubbed it into the wound and over her arm. The tension left Teya's body and soon her even breathing signaled that she was asleep.

He wiped away the blood and went to his saddlebags to find a clean bandage. After he wrapped her arm, he drank the last of the grove water and sat beside Teya. The sun was low on the horizon and they were a couple of hours away from their destination. An hour here wouldn't hurt, even if it meant Jesse got there before them. He would undoubtedly be watching the road, but it couldn't be helped.

There were more dimensions to Teya's power than he realized. The way she had brought down the lightning was frightening. It had come on so quickly that he thought it surprised her as much as him. His hair was standing on end when it flew over them before hitting the man behind.

Then Teya went charging after them. He was so surprised he almost didn't catch her in time. He reacted more to the way she looked than what she was doing. Her eyes had a wild intensity that frightened him. Like she had lost all ability to reason. Like she wasn't quite human.

That was the other thing that bothered him. Bran had called to her, but he didn't remember shouting her name. He thought he called her in his mind. And she heard.

What was that all about? What was it that she didn't dare tell him?

Ever since their kiss in the woods, he had an uncanny awareness of Teya. It was more than just his thoughts, almost like she occupied a place in the back of his mind. This awareness hadn't been there until he kissed her, but he had felt a change between them after the ritual in the grove.

He remembered that her grandmother had called the ceremony a song of life and creation. Had his participation brought out these feelings of connection between them? He had kissed her when it was over, unable to deny the desire that throbbed deep inside him. It felt right, like the completion of something more. Without her grandmother's presence, he would have made love to Teya and never doubted the reasons, but what if it was a compulsion brought on by the magic?

Teya had asked him to sing, but that was all he had agreed to. Now it looked like there was more to it, and it bothered him that she hadn't told him. Why? The only reason that made sense was because he probably wouldn't have agreed.

Teya moaned softly in her sleep, and Bran studied her. It was almost like she was reacting to his frustration. He thought she'd gone back to sleep until he realized her eyes were open and watching him. She frowned, and her eyes were silvery pools of concentration in the deepening twilight. He got the distinct impression she was trying to read his mind. With a suddenness he wasn't expecting, she rose to her feet and mumbled something about needing some privacy before scrambling up the rocky hillside behind them.

He opened his mouth to speak, then decided to try a different approach. Concentrating, he shifted his focus to Teya and got the distinct impression that she was afraid. He pushed deeper, and abruptly slammed against a mental barrier. He physically jerked and would have fallen over if he weren't already sitting on the ground. Astonishment and a sense of dread drove him to his feet, but he somehow mastered the impulse to charge after her.

In a steady climb over the rocks, she was soon at the top of the rise. Without breaking stride, she stepped around a large boulder and disappeared from sight. Bran took a deep breath to calm down. As hard as it was, he knew it was important to wait a few minutes before he followed. He made it to thirty seconds before starting up the hill, barely managing to take slow, deliberate steps.

She was sitting at the top of the craggy rocks facing the fading light. A gentle breeze tossed her hair, but other than that, she was still as a statue. The blankness on her face reminded him of when he first saw her at the palace, and he couldn't help the small shiver that coursed through him. This was who she was when she locked away her feelings and humanity.

With the gray hues of evening, her face was chalk-white against the darkness of her hair, giving her an ethereal glow. He could almost feel the power emanating from her. When she fixed her attention on him, his breath caught at how cold and predatory she seemed.

A barrier between them opened like a deep chasm, too wide to cross. He remembered her grandmother's words, and his heart beat furiously at the implication that Teya wasn't quite human. But if she wasn't human, what was she?

She held his gaze like a predator contemplating its prey before a flicker of emotion broke the spell and she sighed. The world tilted back to normal and Bran swallowed. She was warm and real, not a specter to be frightened of. Still, he couldn't help the nervous tension in his legs as he climbed the short distance to her.

He sat down and glanced out over the countryside. "The view from here is beautiful. The transition between night and day has always been a magical time for me. I like watching the moonrise, and see the first star in the darkening sky. Have you ever made a wish on a star?"

The tautness went out of Teya, and she took a deep breath, but didn't turn to look at him. "I don't think so." She let down her guard and Bran was relieved to feel some emotion through the bond, even if it was distant. As she relaxed, Bran was more sensitive to the turmoil within her. There was fear, but a thread of warmth flowed between them and overshadowed it.

"I can't remember what I wished for as a child," Bran said. "But right now, I think I'd wish to hear you sing." Her surprise wafted over him. "There's nothing more beautiful, anywhere...than you." A heartfelt smile lit up her face. "So what do you say?"

She took a quick breath and shook her head, but he wouldn't let her get off that easy. "Please?"

With a sigh, she gave in. Focusing on the night sky, she sang a simple melody that wove through the fabric of his imagination. She sang of a journey to the stars filled with wishes and dreams, a journey fraught with uncertainty, but undertaken for a noble purpose. A journey that ended with a return to a home filled with love and peace.

It reflected the journey they were on now. "Thank you." Bran took her hand. "Someday, I'd like to sing that song with you."

Teya pulled away, her face pale. "There's something I need to tell you." Several moments passed while she gathered her courage. "Something happened in the grove. But I'm afraid to tell you, because I don't want you to hate me."

Bran took a deep breath, stealing himself for what she had to say. "I don't think it's as bad as you make it out to be. I could never hate you. I could be angry, but hate? That's pretty strong."

"Just remember, it was Leona's idea."

Bran smiled despite the gravity of the situation. "I'll keep that in mind."

She steadied herself, then looked at him with such earnestness that his heart softened. "Leona wanted to do more than strengthen the grove, she wanted to protect me. I didn't understand the full measure of what she did until later, after it was done. You have to believe that."

She waited until Bran nodded before continuing. "It was during the ceremony. The powers of creation and life are also the same powers that are used to bond a man and woman. She helped create a link between us that has opened a connection to our feelings. She did this so that I could draw on your strength and your protection.

"It was selfish, and done without your consent, which is totally wrong. I hope you can forgive me, but she gave me little choice."

"How is this supposed to help?"

She hesitated and took a deep breath. "I'm not sure. I just know she didn't want you to leave me, and with this connection, you wouldn't be able to." Her eyes flashed with desperate entreaty. "Please understand, I don't intend to hold you to this when you never meant for it to happen. When this is all over, the bond can be broken and I will release you, I promise."

After the initial shock, Bran couldn't help the surge of anger that poured over him. "I'm not sure I understand why your grandmother thought she needed to do that. I would never have agreed to it." At her stricken expression he continued. "But only because I don't need this bond to help you. I wouldn't leave you unprotected and alone."

With his words, the tension seeped out of her. "My grandmother had good intentions, but she didn't know you, and after Korban, she doesn't trust easily. I can't sever the bond, only Grandmother can do that, but I can shield you from my feelings."

Something clicked into place and Bran paused. Maybe Leona created this bond between them for an entirely different reason. "There might be something else that we don't understand yet. I don't think you should block your feelings from me."

"It's best if I do," Teya explained. "When I was a captive of the king, I never seemed to feel things as much as I have lately. I used to shut my feelings into an imaginary box, so I could cope with things I couldn't control. I kept that box locked up tight so my emotions wouldn't touch me. I'm used to shutting my feelings away. I don't want to lose control. Not like I did today. You saw what happened."

"After being in captivity that long," Bran said. "It's amazing you kept your sanity at all. You remained true to yourself, even though it was at the cost of your feelings. That is an amazing feat for anyone, let alone a child. Most people would have done whatever their captors wanted for acceptance and love, and become like a puppet."

"I was ready to give up," Teya confessed. She glanced at him, her face glowing with wonder and gratitude. "Then you came and took me away from all that. You took me home to the grove, and even though it had changed, it was the first time I have ever felt at peace. To use my abilities to nurture and protect life filled me with more joy than anything I have ever known. That's where I belong. I realize that now, this world is foreign to me. My power was not meant to kill."

"Maybe not, but today you didn't have a choice."

"I know. It was something I had to do, but it goes against my nature. If I am to continue, I'm going to have to lock my feelings away again. Don't you see? Feelings make me lose control of my power and I can't risk making a mistake."

She stood, separating from him in both body and mind, and slammed hard shields over her feelings. Closed away, she took on the predatory blankness of a bird of prey and he shivered. Was that why Leona did it? Without this connection with him, would she lose control and become the monster everyone feared?

"No." In one swift motion Bran stood at her side with a boldness that surprised her. "You need me, Teya. Don't let your fear shut me out. You're not facing this alone." She needed his humanity, his reasoning, and his common sense.

Her sudden hope turned into a cynical smile. "Yes, Grandmother made sure of that, didn't she?"

"This bond has nothing to do with it."

"Are you sure of that?" Teya asked.

"Yes." He could tell she wanted to believe him, but didn't quite know how. "I stopped you from going after those men, didn't I? We can do this together. You just have to trust me."

"But the bond…"

"It can help us. We don't know exactly what is coming, but we'd be fools not to use what we have if it will help us."

"You're right." Teya gave in. "But I can't help feeling guilty that you got more than you bargained for."

Bran tried to keep a straight face. "Well, you are kind of hard to put up with, but I'll try to make the best of it." The look of outrage on her face was priceless and he laughed. "It was a joke," he said, then sobered at her pained expression. "It's hard for you to laugh isn't it?"

"I guess I'll have to work on that."

It was on the tip of his tongue to tell her he'd be happy to help her learn, but he didn't want to push too hard. In time, he knew she would be able to laugh at herself, but not just yet.

"How much longer before we get to the city?" she asked.

"A couple of hours. We'd better get going. Is your arm feeling better?"

"Yes, it doesn't hurt at all."

"Good." He followed her down the steep trail to the horses. It was full dark when they left the trees, and Bran deemed it safe to travel on the road. There was a chill in the wind, and both of them huddled in their cloaks for warmth. It didn't compare with the warmth that passed between them and Bran savored this moment of peace. He was lighthearted that they finally had everything out in the open. He enjoyed the easy banter they shared, and it was nice to have Teya open up to him for a change. Even talking, he loved the sound of her voice.

The hour it took to reach the outskirts of the city passed too quickly. Now it was time to get serious. "This close to the city we need to be careful. Besides the soldiers, it's a pretty sure thing that Jesse passed this way ahead of us. Is there anything you can do to keep us from being seen?"

"I don't know. Maybe I could try something that would make people not want to look at us, but we'd better be careful just in case."

"All right. Stay close. Once we get to the inn outside the city gates, we can go directly to my room."

Teya nodded. As they took to the road, she chanted in a soft whisper and soon darkness settled over him like a shadow. He led the way by an indirect path through back roads and alleys. At this time of night, the only people wandering around were usually drunk, but he knew others would be watching for them.

He breathed easier when the first person they encountered didn't seem to notice them. Teya's magic was working. When they reached the stables of the inn without incident, Bran relaxed his guard. After settling the horses, Bran took Teya up an outside staircase to a balcony around the second floor. At the door to his room, he paused to pull up a wooden plank where a key was hidden. With a flourish, he unlocked the door but held her back.

"Wait here," he whispered, then crept inside and felt for the lamp. In the flicker of light, everything looked as he had left it. The big bed took up most of the space, and a table and chairs sat in one corner with the armoire in the other.

He beckoned Teya inside. Even though they'd spent the last hour in relative peace, the strain of their journey was reflected in the dark smudges under her eyes.

"You'll be happy to know that my room has indoor plumbing. I have my own bathroom with a tub and everything." She perked up and eagerly opened the bathroom door. "Go ahead and get cleaned up. I'll get some food and leave a message for Jax. If there's any trouble, call me through this bond we've got." She looked at him like he was nuts. "Or doesn't it work that way?"

"I don't think so."

"Well," he shrugged, "you never know. I'll be back soon." After locking the balcony door, he crossed the room and opened another door to an inside hallway. Teya had already commandeered the bathroom and Bran could hear the water running. He shut the door and locked it, happy to feel her pleasure through the bond.

Downstairs, he found the innkeeper, who greeted him with a hearty slap on the back. "Master Will, it's good to see you. I take it you have already been to your room? I hope everything was satisfactory. Would you like some food? I'm sure we can find you something. There are a couple of messages for you. Why don't you go into the kitchen and I'll bring them to you."

"Thanks." Bran had taken an instant liking to the innkeeper when he took his room a month ago, paying in advance. The innkeeper never asked questions and was always discreet, a quality that was indispensable to Bran. The cook quickly filled his request for a tray of food and soon he was headed back to his room with two messages in hand, both from Jax.

Teya was humming from the bathroom when he entered, and a warm glow of contentment surrounded him. He set the tray on the table and ripped open the letters. The first message was short, but hastily written with a plea to contact Jax as soon as he got there. The second left no doubt that Bran was in trouble, and to lay low until Jax contacted him. Bran placed a candle in the window so Jax would know he was there and began to eat.

He had trouble concentrating on his food with Teya splashing in the other room. Soon, he heard the water draining from the tub and found it hard to swallow. He was so intent on what was going on inside the bathroom that the light rapping confused him. He realized it was coming from the balcony door and hurried over to unlock it.

Jax slipped inside and his jaw dropped at the sight of Teya coming out of the bathroom. From the look on his face Bran wondered if she was dressed. He turned and was almost disappointed to find her in clean clothes and buttoning up her shirt. His heart skipped a beat when she smiled at him.

"She's here?" Jax blurted. "Oh man, you're in one hell of a mess." Jax blew out the candle and pulled the window curtains together. He wore ragged old clothes and his hair was poking out in all directions. His disguise was complete with a few days growth of beard on his face. It would be hard for anyone who'd seen him to recognize him as Bran's assistant.

Dread tightened Bran's stomach. "What's going on?"

"It's Chancellor Turner. He knows you took Teya."

"How?" Bran asked.

"He wanted to question you when Teya disappeared, and when you couldn't be found, things escalated. He accused you of kidnapping Teya on behalf of our government, and holding her hostage in Braemar. You can imagine how upset Rasmussen is about this."

Bran groaned. Rasmussen was his superior and head of the diplomatic league. He may have condoned what Bran did in private, but would hang him out to dry if it was known. "Turner has no proof. Didn't anyone try to hold him off?"

"Of course. Rasmussen did everything he could to give you time to get back, but you've been gone too long, and Turner might know more than you think. He hasn't shown any proof that you took Teya, but he must have a reason to lay the blame on you."

"So what am I supposed to do?"

Jax shook his head. "If you go to Turner without Teya, he will probably kill you." At Bran's surprise, Jax continued. "You don't know the half of it. The king went crazy after her disappearance. Everyone at the palace was put to the question. Her guards were tortured, and two of them killed for letting her escape. The servants, the guests, and anyone connected to the palace during the celebration were found or detained. Everyone but you, me, and Clare."

"Is Clare all right?"

"Yes, she's in Braemar under Rasmussen's protection. I barely got her out in time, which is a whole different story." Jax paused and took a deep breath. "There's more. The king is making preparations to send his army across the wall."

"What? You mean he's declared war?"

"Not openly, but his meaning is clear. If Teya's not back by day after tomorrow, he's going to retaliate for our interference. He's out for blood, and he doesn't care whose blood it is. Rasmussen is denying the whole thing. He's keeping to the story that if you took her, you acted on your own without Braemar's sanction. You know what that means, don't you?"

Bran sighed. "I'm the fall guy."

"Where have you been? Did you find the Kaloriahns?"

Bran told Jax everything that had happened except for the ceremony in the grove. That was too personal. Jesse's involvement made things worse.

"I'll help you however I can," Jax said. "But you need to know that Rasmussen wants you to take Teya back."

"But doesn't he understand that Teya was being held against her will?"

"Of course, but that's not our problem. Rasmussen was furious when I told him you had taken her. He thought you'd lost your mind. He kept saying that we were not to interfere or meddle in this kingdom's affairs, especially with the king's Songbird. Our job was to track down *sym*, and nothing more."

"He knew my plans about taking her to her people," Bran interjected. "He wanted the Kaloriahns on our side if there was going to be trouble. Now he's denying the whole thing? Well, I'm not taking her back."

Silence stretched out between them before Jax abruptly nodded. "I never thought you would."

"That's a relief," Teya said, catching them both by surprise. Bran realized they'd been talking about her as if she wasn't there. Her face was pale and her hands trembled when she pulled her hair away from her face. With a deep breath, she pulled herself together and met his eyes with raw determination. "Day after tomorrow doesn't give us much time, but I think I might have an idea."

The hardness of her voice put Bran on his guard. "What are you thinking?"

"That there is someone who knows where the Kaloriahns are, and if we caught him, I'm sure he could be persuaded to tell us."

Bran narrowed his eyes. "And use you for bait, I suppose."

"Yes."

"No," he said forcefully. "We can't risk it."

"Who are you talking about?" Jax asked.

"Jesse, the hunter who's been following us," Bran answered.

"I've been thinking a lot about this," Teya said. "I think it could work. Jax could tell the right people that he had information about me, and for the right price, he'd be willing to share it with Jesse. We could have the place staked out and set up a trap for him. I could hold him with my magic and make him talk."

"But Jesse wouldn't come alone. What about his men?"

"Jax could insist that he talk to Jesse alone. They could meet in a tavern or something, and then go somewhere else to talk. We could be waiting for him there and his men wouldn't know."

"I think it might be worth a try," Jax said, much to Bran's consternation. "Let's see if we can come up with a plan that will work and then decide. The first thing we need to figure out is where to have this meeting. And I think I know just the place."

At the gleam in his eyes, Bran knew Jax could make Teya's plan work, and he inwardly groaned. Jax began by telling them of a tavern with a back room he could rent that would suit their purposes not far from the inn. It wouldn't come cheap, but Bran had gold stashed away for this kind of an emergency. Jax had several contacts in the city that he could use to relay a message to Jesse. The way things were coming together, Bran had to admit that this plan might work, but he couldn't help having some misgivings. "Jesse doesn't play fair," he said. "I'm not sure I like this."

"What other choice do we have?" Teya asked. "We're out of options. If we do nothing, there will be a war between our countries. If we go to Braemar, they'll throw you in jail and send me back to the king. If we stay here we risk being caught by Jesse or the king, while none of this gets us any closer to the Kaloriahns. At least going after Jesse will give us a chance to find them."

She was right. There was no other way, but Bran couldn't help thinking this was just the beginning. Once they found the Kaloriahns, they would have to free them, and somehow get them back to the grove, probably with Korban, the king, and Jesse on their tail. He wasn't sure how they were ever going to accomplish it.

"Jax and I will go to the tavern to make sure it suits our purposes," Bran said. "I'll come back here, while Jax makes the rounds to set up a meeting with Jesse." Teya didn't seem pleased with this arrangement, but she didn't complain. "I'll be back as soon as I can." He almost added that she was not to open the door to anyone else, but caught himself in time.

"Take your gun," she said. "And be careful."

Sudden warmth flooded over him, and he knew it came from Teya. "I will," he nodded, and hoped nothing would go wrong this time. He gathered what he needed and left the room with Jax, grateful to be doing something now that the decision was made. "Do you think this plan will work?"

"I don't know," Jax said. "It all depends on Jesse. He doesn't sound like someone who'd fall for a trap."

"No, but he's desperate enough to check it out. We'll just have to be one step ahead of him. I hate to put you in danger like this. I still don't have evidence that the Kaloriahns have anything to do with *sym*, except for my gut feelings. But I think finding them is the key."

"It is if you want Rasmussen's help," Jax said. "I can't think of any other way to get out of this mess besides giving Teya back. Even then, your head is on the line. No, this is the only way. And don't worry about me, I can take care of myself."

They crossed the crowded street and followed it for a few blocks until they came to the tavern. It was full of patrons, and the noise and smell of whiskey and smoke was nearly overpowering. They found the tavern keeper and rented the back room for that night and the next day. The room was perfectly situated in a secluded corner of the building. Inside, a curtain divided the room in half, leaving a place for concealment. When Bran parted the curtain, he found a door that opened to an outside alley. Perfect.

Jax decided to stay right where he was and took a seat at the bar. There were plenty of people here who could spread the word that Jax wanted to talk to Jesse. Bran hesitated, wondering if he really needed to involve Teya in this. Once Jesse was here in the back room, Bran could take care of him. Teya would be furious, but at least she wouldn't be in danger.

He never got the chance to find out. At that moment, Jesse and his men entered the tavern, and spotted Bran before he could leave. With a shout, Jesse lunged for Bran while his men blocked the door. Bran rushed toward the back room where he knew he could get out the secret door. The confused crowd got in his way, but he pushed around them, toppling chairs as he went. He wrenched the door open and was halfway across the room when Jesse's voice cut through the air like a hammer, sending a wave of shock into his head. He yelled in agony, but only managed a few more steps before he sank into black oblivion.

CHAPTER SEVEN

Braemar

After a relaxing bath, and the first real food Teya had in days, she fought against falling asleep. With Bran gone, she couldn't afford that luxury until she knew all was well. At least her arm wasn't bothering her. When she took off the bandage to bathe, all that remained of her injury was the puffy redness of new skin. It would scar, but that was the least of it.

The grove water was truly miraculous. No wonder Korban wanted it so badly. Korban. Every time she thought of him, deep anger stirred, shattering her calm. He was the reason for everything that was wrong. The far-reaching effects of his evil and greed were astounding. How could one person be the downfall of an entire race?

She closed her eyes and breathed deeply. It had been a harrowing day. The slight twinge in her arm attested to that. In escaping Jesse, she had called down lightning and killed one of Jesse's men. The power had raged through her with such intensity that she nearly lost control. Sharing this burden with Bran seemed a good idea at the time, but she wondered if it was the right decision.

It frightened her to think what could happen if her magic got away from her. It almost seemed like something separate from her, with a will of its own, but she knew that wasn't true. Magic was all about control. A wave of doubt assailed her. Was she strong enough to handle it? She knew Bran would help, but he didn't understand the anger that she locked away. Anger she'd hidden from herself for so long. Anger so deep, she didn't know how she could ever let it go.

She tried to focus her thoughts, but kept hearing Jax tell Bran what the king had done to her guards and countless others after her escape. Thoughts of the king torturing innocent people made her palms sweat. If there was a monster here, it was the king, not her.

To quell the growing anger, she focused on Bran. He had surprised her with his acceptance of the bond. His reaction melted a part of her heart and dared her to hope that what they shared between them was real, and not a by-product of the bond. Maybe she'd been looking at it all wrong, and the bond only magnified feelings they already had.

Teya sighed. It was hard to leave it alone, and she realized that she was the one who hadn't accepted it. But how could she when Bran had never agreed to it in the first place? It was difficult to understand why her grandmother thought it was necessary. Bran said himself that he wouldn't leave her, but if she ever lost control, what would happen to him? She couldn't bear it if she hurt him because of her weakness.

From what Jax told them, it looked like they were in more trouble than ever, with Bran caught in the middle of both countries. She knew the king wouldn't hesitate to kill him, and it sounded like his superior, Rasmussen, wasn't in a position to help him either. Their only way out of this mess was to find the Kaloriahns. Where could they be? And what about Korban? Who was he? Jesse knew him. It was one more thing she meant to find out once they caught Jesse.

The minutes passed into an hour with no sign of Bran, and Teya's stomach began to churn with unease. Where was he? Unless he was helping Jax spread the word, he should have been back by now, but with Jesse after them, she hoped he wouldn't risk it.

After fifteen more minutes she changed into her dark clothing and paced the room in restless energy while more time passed. This wasn't working. Something was wrong. She pulled her cloak over her shoulders. With the hood pulled up to hide her face, she was ready to go. Indecision held her there for a few more minutes. She didn't know exactly where this tavern was, but something must have gone wrong or Bran would be back by now. Could she do anything to help without making matters worse?

With startling clarity, she cursed herself for not thinking of it before and opened her feelings to the bond between them. She had no idea if she could find Bran this way, but anything was worth a try. Concentrating, she sent out her awareness and searched for the thread that tied them together. Nothing. If he was there, she could find no trace of him. Why hadn't she tried this before to see if it worked?

Maybe she was doing it wrong. Instead of concentrating on what she could do, she concentrated on Bran, and opened herself to him. There! She caught a faint glimpse of light in the darkness but it was shrouded in magic. It was barely bright enough to follow, but she knew where to go.

Without thinking it through, she pulled the broken *kundar* out of her jacket pocket and put it around her neck. It had no power over her now, but it might save her from having a real one put on if something went wrong.

A quick knock at the door startled her. "Teya, it's Jax. Open up!" With trembling fingers, she unlocked the door and he burst in. "Jesse's got Bran." Jax closed the door behind him and continued. "We had everything set up, and Bran was just leaving the tavern when Jesse walked in. Bran tried to outrun him but didn't make it. Jesse must have used magic on him. He's holding him in the same room we were going to use. They didn't know about me, so I slipped out when things calmed down."

"We'll have to get him out," she said, trying to stay calm.

"How?"

"I've got magic of my own. It's time I used it." She opened the door and waited for Jax to follow. "Show me where he is."

"But we need to have a plan," he argued. "You can't just go in there."

"I can find him without you." She started out the door, her heart pounding fiercely.

"Wait, I'll come. We can go around back to the alley. There's a door we can get in from there."

Teya nodded and waited for him to lead the way. With practice born from years of captivity, she locked away her fear and let calm determination wash over her. With a simple tone of magic, she cloaked herself and Jax from view, and followed Jax down the steps and into the street. He cut through a side street and down another alley to a corner, then hurried across the street and followed it until it came to the main street. The tavern was on the far side, facing the street in full view. From here, nothing looked out of the ordinary.

"We need to cross the street and head into that alleyway," Jax said. "The door is at the end." Teya increased her concentration and they slipped unnoticed across the street and into the alley. When they got to the door, she opened the bond with Bran and felt his frustration and fear. She knew when he sensed her because a rush of conflicting emotions came through the link. First, relief was followed by worry, then an urgency to act.

He wasn't in pain so she assumed he was tied up. Now how to get in? She tested the door. It wasn't locked. She kept the cloak of magic around her and slid inside. A black curtain strung across the wall, obstructed her view, but she knew Bran was on the other side. Someone else was there as well, quiet with anticipation.

Teya could feel the magic around him, just waiting for her to make a move. She needed a diversion and quickly ushered Jax inside. She motioned him to go around the other way. Without her cloak of magic he was easily noticed, but whoever was there allowed him to move to the edge of the curtain. Then everything happened at once.

Jax sprang from his hiding place and was thrown back by a burst of magic. Teya took that moment to slip around the other side of the curtain. Jesse didn't have time to change direction before Teya threw the low tone of darkness at him. He gasped and clutched at his head before sliding to the floor. Teya held him there for a moment longer, and anger rose with unbidden intensity. It was hard to let go, and when she finally did, the effort left her breathless.

Bran was tied up in a chair and Jax was loosening his bonds. Teya hurried over and removed the gag from his mouth. "We've got to get out of here," Bran gasped. "Jesse sent for the king's soldiers. They'll be here any minute."

"We can't leave until we know where the Kaloriahns are." She turned back and knelt by Jesse's side, touching his face. The magic she had felt around him was gone. For a moment she thought he was dead, then he took in a shallow breath and she sighed with relief.

"I know where the Kaloriahns are," Bran said, kneeling beside her. "He told me."

"He did?" Teya's mind went blank. "Why?"

"I don't think he thought I'd ever get away. Come on, we need to leave."

Teya nodded, but didn't stand. Jesse had survived her magic, but she almost wished he hadn't. She wanted to kill him, and that's what bothered her the most. Even if he deserved it, killing Jesse would make her no better than him.

"Teya!"

At Bran's urging, she swallowed her anger and followed him out of the room. They slipped into the alley and ran to the end, stopping when they heard sounds of a large group of riders coming from the street. Jax took the lead and led them into a side street where they waited while the soldiers passed.

Teya held her breath until the soldiers were gone, then silently followed Jax and Bran in a roundabout way back to their room. Once inside, Bran turned the lock in the door and leaned against it with relief. "I can't believe we made it," he said. "You came at the perfect time. Jesse was going to use me as bait, but you came before he was ready. It was lucky he didn't know about Jax."

Teya shuddered to think what could have happened. "That was almost too easy," she said. "But I won't complain. Are you all right?" Bran's lip was bleeding and the side of his face was discolored. She gently touched the bruise with her cool fingers.

"I'm fine." He took her hand in his and spoke gently, "Your people are in Braemar. I overheard Jesse gloating about how they were right under our noses all this time. From what he said, I think they're in a building someplace close to the wall. It must be some kind of church, because he talked about all the praying that went on there. If we can look at a map, I bet we could figure it out. I can get us back into the city from here, but I don't know how we are going to get through the city and past the wall between the Old Country and Braemar."

"I know a way," Jax said. "And if Jesse doesn't wake up for awhile, we'll have a head start. What do you think?"

"I think I hurt him pretty bad, but if he sent for the soldiers and told them he had Bran, they'll start looking for us. I can use my magic as a shield, but someone using *sym* might be able to see through it."

"Then we'd better get going, there's just one more thing you should know." Bran took hold of Teya's hands. "The easiest way into the city from here is the way we came out, through the vault in the cemetery. Can you handle that?"

Teya's heart sank at the prospect of going back down into that hole, but she swallowed her revulsion and nodded. Bran squeezed her arm reassuringly, and turned to gather his things.

"We'll have to leave the horses there," he said. "And go through the city on foot so bring only what you need. If all goes well, by morning we'll be in Braemar."

The confidence Bran radiated gave Teya a quick burst of energy and she hurriedly looked through her things, reaching for the pouch that held the seed from her grandmother. It was all she really needed to take with her, but she was afraid to lose it. With sudden inspiration, she borrowed Bran's knife and loosened the lining of her jacket. When the opening was big enough, she slipped the pouch inside where it was well hidden. Pleased, she put the jacket back on and handed the knife back to Bran.

"I think you should keep it," he said. "Here's the sheath. It should fit in your pocket." She accepted it with a nod, but didn't think she'd ever need it, not with her magic, but if Bran wanted her to keep it, she would. "I noticed you put the *kundar* on," he said, giving her an admiring glance. "That was a good idea." Warmth flooded through the bond, and she smiled unexpectedly.

He smiled back, then reached above the armoire. He brought down a small case, and opening it, revealed a pair of guns and ammunition. He strapped them on and gave his other gun to Jax before turning to Teya. "Let's go."

With only two horses, Teya rode behind Bran, but she didn't mind. It gave her an excuse to touch him. She sang the notes to cloak them from sight, and they started out. She had to adjust the tones several times before she muffled the sound of the horses' hooves. Soon after, several riders came barreling toward them.

Beneath her arms she felt Bran hold his breath when they passed, then let it out in relief. After that, he turned off the main street and followed a different path. Soldiers were everywhere searching for them. Teya strained to keep the shield around them, while Bran worked to keep them off the main streets and out of sight.

They were near the end of a main road when Teya felt a pulse of magic come from behind. A lone rider came into view, and paused to search with his magic. Teya strengthened the shield, and sat stiffly until the rider continued on. When she relaxed, Bran let out his breath and she realized how tight she had held him. She was about to explain, but found she didn't need to. Bran had felt it through the bond and she realized she hadn't shielded her feelings from him since their agreement. Maybe this bond was useful after all.

They left the soldiers behind at the outskirts of town and rode quickly to the eastern side of the city wall. The hill was exactly how she remembered it, and when Bran removed the covering only the first two rungs of the ladder could be seen in the inky blackness below. Teya shuddered involuntarily and was relieved when Jax said he'd go first and find the torch Bran left behind.

After Jax lit the torch, the faint glow coming from the tunnel didn't make it any better, because now she could see exactly how small and narrow the passage was. How was she ever going to do this? Already, her palms were moist with sweat and her stomach churned.

"Come on," Bran said, and she felt his strength pour over her. This was easy, nothing to be afraid of. She focused on the feelings he shared and stepped into the hole, following the ladder until she felt the ground under her feet. Bran appeared beside her, leading her along the passage and into the vault.

The torch went out, sending her into a brief panic in the inky blackness. Thankfully, Jax opened the door, and she was breathing in the cool night air. They crept through the grounds to the gate, and Teya realized she hadn't let go of Bran, nor did she want to. When he ushered her through the gate, she kept hold of his hand. It was like a lifeline, and despite everything, he was right, she needed him.

"At this time of night the gates at the great wall are locked and barred," Jax said. "But there's another way out. It's near the palace, so stay low."

Teya was not happy to go anywhere near the palace, but followed Jax anyway. It was several hours after midnight, and the city was quiet, but she tensed, attuning her senses for anything unusual. Jax hadn't asked her to use magic to cloak them, but she did anyway.

A few blocks from the wall between their countries, Jax veered toward the palace and Teya's anxiety grew. She didn't like being this close to the king and his soldiers. From where they hid, the entrance to the palace was at the end of the street and illuminated by several street lamps. Two guards were conversing in low tones as they paced back and forth in front of the gate. A guardhouse was just inside the gate, and even though a light shown through the window, Teya couldn't tell if anyone else was in there.

"Below that guardhouse is a tunnel that leads to the outer side of the wall and Braemar. The tunnel is big enough for a small army of men to pass through quickly. It comes out about a hundred yards down the wall.

"This late, there's usually just the two men standing guard in front of the palace. If Teya can get them to take a little nap, we could slip into the guardhouse, then through the tunnel, and be in Braemar in no time."

"How did you know this?" Bran asked.

Jax smiled, showing his teeth. "I have my sources. Can you do it Teya?"

"I have to get a little closer, but yes, I can do it. You two stay here, I don't think the guards will be suspicious if I approach alone." Teya walked off before either of them could protest. She could feel Bran's disapproval through the link and was afraid he would follow until Jax stopped him.

Both guards noticed her at the same time, but only stared in appreciation. She smiled to put them at ease and then wove a song of sleep into their minds. She hated the thought of these men getting in trouble or dying because of her, so she made sure they would only think she was a part of their dreams. With their eyes a vacant stare, she motioned Bran and Jax forward. They passed the guards quietly, slipped through the gate, and entered the silent guardhouse.

Inside, there was no sign of a door that would lead anywhere.

"Where is it?" Bran asked, slightly panicked.

"It's here, we just need to look harder," Jax said, then pointed. "Try behind there." Along the back wall hung a large tapestry. Bran parted the hanging from the wall, revealing doors behind it. Unfortunately, they were bound with a padlock.

"Where's the key?" Bran asked.

Jax shrugged. "I didn't know it was locked. It's got to be around here somewhere."

"While you're looking, I'll try and get this open." Bran took a sharp metal object out of his pocket and inserted it in the lock. He maneuvered it around but wasn't having any luck. Jax returned empty-handed.

"The guards must have it. I'll go get it." Jax started toward the door when a shout came from the palace, and several soldiers rushed toward the guardhouse.

Teya ducked behind the hanging beside Bran. She heard an officer tell the guards that the watch at the gates was to be doubled and absolutely no one was allowed to leave the city. There was some shuffling as several soldiers continued toward the wall, but the officer remained, and Teya was sure he was going to come into the guardhouse.

In desperation, she spun a thread of magic into the lock to make it break and pulled on it. The metal snapped off in her hand and she stumbled. Bran caught her and pulled open the door, propelling them both inside. As footsteps echoed outside the entrance, Jax dove through the opening, and Bran swung the door shut behind him.

Teya hardly dared breathe, waiting for the officer to yell, but nothing happened. Bran carefully let go of the door handle and it held. It was pitch black except for the light that came from under the door, and that was scarce. After adjusting to the darkness, the outline of a landing dropped off at the beginning of a huge staircase that led down into a black maw. The panic this normally caused Teya was lessened by the larger space. Still, it helped that Bran took her arm before starting down the stairs.

Jax was several feet in front of them when he came to the bottom and continued into the tunnel. On the verge of panic, Teya's breath was coming faster. From somewhere up ahead came a scraping sound and Teya jerked to a halt. "Jax?" Bran whispered. A sudden flame burst in front of them and there was Jax, holding a lighted torch. "Come on!" he said urgently and started to jog down the tunnel.

That was enough encouragement for Teya. The bare stone walls and floor passed quickly under her feet. She ran longer than she thought possible, keeping up with Bran until she got a stitch in her side. They slowed, but kept up a steady pace until they finally came to another staircase leading upward.

At the top was a single door of heavy wood covered in cobwebs that didn't look like it had ever been opened. It was bolted on the inside but had no lock. Bran threw the bolt and pulled, but the door didn't budge. Jax joined him and the door moved a few inches. As the door opened further, Teya felt a jolt of magic leap around the doorframe and pulse past her. In a whirl the magic was gone, and her mouth went dry.

"Hurry," she said, turning back toward the struggling men. "When you opened the door, it released magic of some kind. It won't be long before somebody comes."

Teya joined them, pulling with a growl of impatience that sent the door flying open. When they stepped through, she sang a few notes and tugged on the ring. It swung shut with a clang and the deadbolt slammed home.

Both men looked at her with exasperation. "What?" she asked. Then they looked at each other and something unspoken passed between them. "I didn't know it would be so easy or I would have helped sooner. Where do we go from here?"

Turning, she realized that the door was actually part of the great wall, and she was on the other side. In Braemar. The land next to the wall was bare of trees and vegetation for several yards, then it opened up into a beautiful rolling countryside. In the dark it was hard to see what lay beyond, but Bran and Jax knew where to go and they surged ahead.

"There's an outpost not far from here," Bran explained. "And a garrison to house soldiers. I imagine it will be full because of the king's threat, but they'll have maps, and it shouldn't take long to figure out where the Kaloriahns are."

"Will they try to stop us?" Teya asked.

"I don't know who will be in charge, but if it's a friend, we might get some help."

"And if it's not," Jax interjected. "They'll try to arrest Bran."

"I won't let them," Teya said heatedly. "Just see if they try, I'll show them something they won't easily forget."

"Thanks," Bran said dryly. "But let's see what happens first. We don't want to bring the whole army down on us."

Teya knew he was right, but it wasn't what she wanted. She wanted to break something. So much had happened that was beyond her control, and she was tired of running. She glanced back at the city. Above the wall, the top spires of the palace were visible, and she imagined how easy it would be to call down lightning and blast it to bits. She could do a lot of damage in a short amount of time.

Anger swelled to a boiling point, dangerously close to exploding. Cold fury settled over her like a shroud and she wondered what it would be like to let it go.

"Teya."

Bran. Lost in this red haze, she'd almost forgotten him. She swallowed against her unbidden thoughts, and tried to act like nothing was wrong. The anger still burned, but she tried to push it aside. He wasn't fooled; something of it passed to him through the bond.

"You're so angry it's almost frightening," he said evenly. "Anger like that is always destructive. It will destroy you."

"I know," she gasped. "But it's so hard. Being this close to the palace brought it all back, and I can't seem to let it go. How can I, after what they did to me? Show me how to let it go and I will. I don't want to be a monster."

"If you really want to let it go, you can. All you have to do is open the box and let it out. Take it from your heart and free it. Think of it as something dark that you're going to replace with something light."

"But Korban, and the king. What they did..."

"It was wrong, and they hurt you. But the anger is hurting you more. Free yourself and you win against them."

"But if I let it go, that means I would have to forgive them, and I don't know if I can. Not yet."

"Letting go of your anger is a beginning. That's where it starts. Forgiveness can come later, once you've let yourself heal."

Calm returned, along with the balance she'd lost. The anger was gone for now, but she didn't know if she could keep it that way. "All right. I'll make you a deal. I'll give up my anger, as long as it means that Korban will still pay for what he's done."

Bran smiled. "Oh, he'll pay. In fact, I'm looking forward to meting out the justice he deserves." This time his smile was dangerous. "But first, we have to find him."

Together, they started down the narrow track and Teya's heart lifted. For the first time, she felt a control she'd never imagined. It was going to be all right. Without anger, her magic would come to her pure and free, a tool for justice. To think of it this way was exhilarating and a sudden love for Bran swelled in her heart. A love that had been building for days, but now deepened into something sustaining and substantial. He shook her world and made it better. She squeezed his hand, letting her appreciation flow through the bond. Maybe when this was over, she could let him know how she felt. Maybe by then, he would feel the same way.

The outpost was larger than she first thought. The main building had an air of efficiency about it that bolstered her confidence. Bran stood a little straighter when golden light spilled through the open door, and the officer on duty greeted them.

"Who's the commanding officer here?" Bran asked the soldier.

"It's Colonel Porter."

"I know who Colonel Porter is, can you get him for me? This is an urgent matter."

"He's asleep." The soldier's eyes narrowed with suspicion.

"Then wake him, he'll want to see me." Bran's voice resonated with authority, but the soldier hesitated.

"Not until you give me your name, and state your business."

Bran huffed his displeasure, then shrugged. "I'm Ambassador Havil, this is my assistant Jax Weyland, and this..." he paused dramatically, "is the king's Songbird."

The soldier's eyes widened. "You...?" His jaw moved up and down before any words came out. "Come inside and I'll get him. And...don't go anywhere." He held the door open for them, and hurried up a staircase to the second floor.

Bran turned to Teya. "I hope you're not upset that I told him who you were, but I thought if I did, we would get faster results."

Teya had time to nod before the soldier returned, breathless from his errand. "The Colonel will be right down. He asked me to have you wait in his office. It's through here." He led them down a hallway and opened a door. "Make yourselves comfortable."

"Thanks," Bran said. The soldier nodded politely and closed the door behind him. The colonel's office was surprisingly well furnished with a beautiful dark wooden desk and plush chair. Several cushioned chairs were situated around the desk and a bookcase covered one wall. At the other end of the room between two large windows, the wall was covered with maps. A long rectangular table with several chairs took up the space beneath the maps.

A door closed above them and they heard footsteps hurrying down the hall toward them. The colonel burst through the door, still buttoning up his shirt. He swept a glance over them before addressing Bran. "Ambassador Havil? Didn't think you'd dare show your face here." He shook Bran's hand in a friendly manner, then turned to Jax and offered his hand as well. "This must be Jax. Rasmussen is frantic about your return, by the way."

The man had hawk-like features and wavy silver hair. A protruding brow hooded his piercing blue eyes and Teya was instantly wary of him without knowing why. He looked them over, his eyes lingering on Teya, before settling on Bran. "You do know the trouble you're in?"

Bran nodded before making a formal introduction. "Teya, this is Colonel Porter, acting commander of the army along the border, and also a ranking officer in our government. Colonel, may I introduce Teya, the king's Songbird."

The Colonel took her hand, his eyes flicking to her neck before he smiled at her. "Although it is a pleasure to meet you, I had not expected that Ambassador Havil would bring you here." His touch was firm, but he held her hand longer than necessary.

"We've run out of options, Colonel," Bran said. "Or we wouldn't be here. The only way to avoid a war is to help Teya. Her people are being held against their will in our country. That makes it our problem. We need to find them."

"How is that going to stop a war?"

"The Kaloriahns are my people," Teya said. "They have the magic you need to stop the king." When he didn't respond, she continued. "Believe me, the king's soldiers are coming, whether you help us or not."

Porter rubbed his chin thoughtfully, then turned to Jax. "I was serious when I said that Rasmussen was looking for you. He urged me to send you to him as soon as possible if you showed up here."

Jax glanced at Bran who nodded and said, "You'd better report to him. Besides, we could use his help."

"Are you sure?" Jax asked.

"Yes." Bran answered, and Teya knew something only they understood passed between them. "I'm sure Colonel Porter can spare you a motorbike."

"Of course," Porter said. "Tell Rasmussen to advise me if this changes our plans. He'll know what I mean. Let him know I'll contact him if we find out anything new." Porter called to the guard outside the door and told him to see that Jax got whatever he needed. With a piercing glance at Bran, Jax left the room.

Teya wondered what was going on between them, but decided not to say anything in front of Porter. "Where were we?" Porter asked her. "Oh yes, where do you think your people are?"

"Somewhere close to the wall," Bran answered, and wandered over to the wall that was covered with charts and maps. Porter followed and soon they were scouring the maps of the countryside nearest the city. "Look," Bran pointed, "this is an old monastery not three miles from here. It would be the perfect place to keep a bunch of people you didn't want anyone to know about."

Teya looked at the map. There wasn't another place like it for miles, and from Jesse's description, it had to be where the Kaloriahns were kept. "I think you're right."

"Ambassador," Colonel Porter said. "The Songbird is supposed to go back to the king. You must realize that I won't disobey orders."

"We can't take her back, she's too valuable, and if we find her people, we will have an advantage over the king. This war can be averted. I've been charged with finding the source of *sym*, and I think the Kaloriahns are involved. We must find them before any other decisions are made. I'm sure Rasmussen will agree, once he finds out about it. Jax will see to that."

Porter glanced between Bran and Teya, his brow creased in contemplation. "All right," he grimaced. "You've made your point, and although it goes against my orders, I happen to agree with you. Since I'm already up, I suppose we can go check it out. Reinforcements are due to arrive this morning. If you're right, this discovery will probably change things." He hesitated. "I'm taking a chance for you Ambassador. My orders are clear that Teya be returned to King Thesald. You see what a bind this puts me in. If this doesn't work out, I will have to abide by the terms of the agreement and send her back to avoid a war."

Teya knew Bran would never agree if it meant sending her back to the king, but she didn't think the Colonel needed to know that. She opened the bond to Bran and urged him to accept. He glanced at her sharply before he replied. "They'll be there Colonel, but thanks for the warning."

It wasn't exactly the answer the Colonel was looking for, but he nodded curtly and led them down the hall toward the entrance. He beckoned to the guard who had just returned from helping Jax. "Lieutenant, get thirty men assembled immediately. I want them armed and ready for action." As the soldier left, Porter glanced at Bran. "To be honest, when I heard they suspected you of taking the king's Songbird, I didn't believe it. Now you're both here seeking my help. Why didn't you come back sooner? Rasmussen may have been able to smooth things over and we could have avoided this mess."

"Not without taking Teya back, and I won't do that. There's more to this than you realize," Bran explained. "I think the Kaloriahns might have something to do with *sym*, so I freed Teya to help me find them. We went back to their homeland, but Teya's grandmother was the only one left. It's important that the Kaloriahns return to their home, and we've been searching for them. After we left the grove we ran into a man named Jesse. Apparently he tracks down Kaloriahns and brings them across the border."

"He's the one who told us that the Kaloriahns were here in Braemar," Teya added.

"If *sym* is part of this, then I understand your involvement," Porter said to Bran. "But why do the Kaloriahns need to return to their home?"

"It's because of the grove," Teya answered. "When my people left, the grove began to shrivel and die. Unless they return, it will be lost and magic will be taken from the land. We'll lose everything without the grove. I can't let that happen."

Porter nodded in understanding before he asked, "Is that a *kundar* you're wearing? I thought it kept you from using your magic."

This change of subject took Teya by surprise. Her fingers absently brushed against the metal before she spoke. "It's..."

"We took the first one off," Bran broke in, "but before we got away, Jesse put that one on her. I haven't had a chance to take it off yet. I thought we'd take it off at the same time as the other Kaloriahns."

What was he saying? Teya tried to hide her confusion with a nod, then blurted, "The sooner, the better, if you ask me."

Porter raised his eyebrows. "You're going to take all of them off?"

"The Kaloriahns are not monsters," Teya replied. "They're people just like you and me, and deserve their freedom. The magic they have can help us against the king if it comes to that, but I hope we can resolve things peacefully."

"Yes, of course, that would be best." He seemed to accept the explanation. "We should be able to leave in a few minutes. I imagine you're tired and hungry. I'll have my steward bring you something to eat and drink while I get my things together."

Once he was gone, Teya lowered her voice. "Why did you tell him this was real?" she asked, tugging on the *kundar.*

Bran shrugged. "I don't know. He's a trusted aide in our government, so I'm probably overreacting, but I don't know much about him and I'd rather not tell him everything. At least he's willing to take us to the monastery, and his men will be able to help us if we need them."

"That's true," Teya agreed. "Since we have no idea what to expect."

"I wish I had time to check it out and see what we're getting into. I hate going in cold. Chances are, Korban will be there. I want you to be extra careful when we arrive. Be ready for anything."

Facing Korban so soon made Teya's heart race, but she wouldn't be alone and that bolstered her courage. "The main thing is to find the Kaloriahns and release them. If Korban's there, I won't hesitate to use my powers on him. He'll be sorry to see me." She was nervous, but ready just the same. It was time for Korban to be held accountable for his actions. He was a monster, and he needed to be stopped.

A sleepy-eyed man carried a tray to them. "These biscuits are from last night, but it's the best I could do on short notice. The wine is good."

"Thank you," Bran said. The man nodded and placed the tray on the small table, then left. Bran picked up a roll and poured glasses of watered wine. "I'm glad Jax was able to leave."

"Is he really going to Rasmussen?"

"Yes. We need Rasmussen on our side, and if anyone can persuade him to help, it would be Jax."

That was reassuring. Teya ate quickly and had just finished drinking her wine when the lieutenant came in and told them everything was ready. The food gave her some needed energy, especially since she hadn't had enough sleep for the past few nights.

Colonel Porter joined them at the entrance and ushered them out to the cool night air. Teya stopped short at the sight that greeted her. Bran quickly explained. "It's a motorcar. We use them to travel in, and believe me, they're much more comfortable than the back of a horse. Here, I'll show you." He opened the door to the inside which held a cushioned seat, much like those in an open carriage, only both seats faced forward. The lieutenant climbed behind a protruding wheel in the front seat and the colonel entered from the other side. "Get in, you'll love it."

It was clear that Bran had no qualms about the strange machine, so Teya climbed in. The cushions were soft, and once she was settled with Bran beside her, the thing started to move. "There's an engine that makes it run," he said enthusiastically. "On a good road it can get up to forty miles an hour, much faster than a horse."

Teya felt her initial wariness turn into astonishment as they picked up speed. Larger motorcars both in front and behind them carried the other soldiers. She was pleasantly surprised at how quickly and efficiently they were all moving.

Braemar was full of wonders and she eagerly surveyed the passing countryside. In the early gray light of dawn, the rolling hills didn't seem much different, but at the speed they were going it was hard to tell. At this rate they would be to the monastery in no time.

Coming over a rise, she glimpsed a group of buildings in the distance. "That's it." Bran pointed toward them. Trees and gardens with neat rows of well-tended vegetables surrounded the large compound of several buildings. The main building was two stories high with a bell tower above it, and had to be their place of worship, while the other buildings were living quarters. She could picture the Kaloriahns inside the compound, held within its boundaries. Her heart stirred with anticipation that they were so close.

Her motorcar pulled up at the front of the main building, and she waited tensely for guards to come rushing toward them. When a few moments passed, it was apparent that no one was coming. She and Bran got out of the car and cautiously approached the building, while Porter gave orders to his men. Halfway there, a man in brown robes approached. He asked, "How may I be of service to you?"

He looked and acted like a real monk and Teya wondered if they had made a mistake. Her heart sank with sudden realization. Had Jesse lied to Bran? If the Kaloriahns weren't here, then where were they?

"We are seeking sanctuary and a place to rest for a few hours," Bran answered. The monk merely nodded and motioned for them to follow. "Once we're inside, we can begin our search," Bran whispered. At least Bran thought there was a chance they were here, and her step lightened.

Colonel Porter and three soldiers followed behind, leaving the others to stand guard outside. They entered the dimly lit interior and the monk hastened to light more candles and torches. As she moved further into the building, the pungent odor of incense overwhelmed her and she held back a cough. The monk motioned them down a long hallway, and as they moved, she became aware of a low chanting coming from deep in the bowels of the stone. She caught her breath and coughed on fumes of billowing incense.

With her head swimming and unable to focus, she leaned toward Bran and found the same confusion in his eyes. Something was wrong! She concentrated on drawing her magic, but a sudden lethargy left her numb. Her mind screamed in terror and she fought against it, but it was too late to do any good. With bleak despair, she sank into darkness.

CHAPTER EIGHT

Korban

Voices penetrated the drugged veil of sleep. Teya focused on the sounds and listened through the fog of darkness until she could understand what they were saying.

"...But we have to tell the king something."

"That's easy. Just tell him I have her, and will bring her to him when it's safe. That should appease him, and the Braemarians will think I single-handedly stopped a war. I'll have the governor of Braemar eating out of the palm of my hand, and in a few days we'll take Teya back under a large guard of Braemarian soldiers. When the king opens the palace to let us in, we'll make our move and be rid of him once and for all. The Old Country will be mine. I'll convince the governor that the king attacked us, and we had to defend ourselves. After that I'm sure the governor will beg me to stay and take charge."

"What about Teya and the Kaloriahns?

"Once the kingdom is in my control, we'll take them back to the grove. Don't worry, Jesse, I've been planning this for a long time. Everything will work out."

"But Teya said the grove was dying. Leona's the only one left to keep back the Destroyer."

Teya's numb mind tried to make sense of what she was hearing. One of them was Jesse, but the other? It sounded like Colonel Porter, but how could he be involved?

"We'll deal with that when we get there."

"All right, I'm ready," Jesse said. "Are you sure you want to do this now? Remember how some of the others reacted."

"I'm only taking enough for you and me, she'll be fine. Besides, once the Kaloriahns know she's here, I think they'll stop dying. Especially when we tell them that we're taking them back to the grove."

A sharp pain in the tender part of her arm caused her to moan, but the influence of the drug kept her from moving. What were they doing to her? She tried to open her eyes, but couldn't. Soon, she became aware of a different sensation, like all her energy was draining out of her.

"That's enough," Jesse said.

"A couple more vials won't hurt her. She's strong. The *sym* from this blood will be enough to last until we reach the grove. By then, I'll have my full power again, along with everything else I deserve." A small tug released the pain from her arm, but not the greater one gathering in her heart. "There, all done. Here, hold that down." Someone applied pressure to her arm, then bent it at the elbow. "You're drawn to her, aren't you? I can tell by the way you look at her."

"She's exotically beautiful."

"Yes. She looks a lot like her mother with her black hair. When Teya was a child it was lighter, almost blond, like yours, but that was many years ago. Why don't you finish up? I'll get this ready."

Teya struggled to open her eyes. The man leaving could only be one person. The person who had destroyed her life, and she was lying there helpless.

"I know you're awake Teya. Don't worry. I made sure he didn't take too much of your blood. You'll recover quickly, but it would be best if you slept. Go ahead, you're safe now, and you have me to keep watch over you." He hummed a few notes that wove through her consciousness and then pulled her back into oblivion.

Gradual awareness brought Teya awake. This time the lethargy of the drug was gone and she opened her eyes with ease. The ceiling was far above her head in a room much larger than she was used to. Thick maroon curtains kept the sunlight at bay, leaving the room bathed in a dim, gray light. Portraits and paintings decorated the walls, and a fireplace took up the opposite side of the room. She was lying fully clothed in a large four-poster bed, covered with a maroon comforter.

She tried to sit up but fell back, faint and weak. Her arm was bandaged where they had taken her blood. Blood they meant to make into *sym*. That's how they did it, by taking blood from the Kaloriahns. Were any of them left? From what she could recall, it seemed like Jesse said they were dying. She had to get out of here.

Bran! What had happened to him? She tried not to panic and took a deep breath. The incense must have drugged them when they entered the monastery. It was Colonel Porter's doing, only that wasn't who he really was. Her stomach clenched with the realization that he was actually Korban.

Teya's throat was dry and she swallowed. The familiar feel of the *kundar* sent a small wave of panic through her, and she feverishly ran her fingers over the gold. There! The rough edge of the broken seam caught her skin. It was hers! Through some miracle, they didn't know!

Tears of relief and hope filled her eyes, but she hastily dashed them away. She had a chance now, but only if she stayed in control. Her first impulse to jump out of bed and kill them all was quickly checked by controlled determination. She was not going to blow it this time. She needed to find out what was going on, and the only way to do that was to play along with Korban. Let him think she was helpless until the time was right, then she could blast him to pieces.

Her hands were clenched and shaking, so she took a calming breath and tried to relax. It wasn't easy, especially when she wondered what had happened to Bran. There was a way to find him. All she had to do was open the bond. She gathered her courage and let down her guard, opening herself to him. At first, all she felt was a flicker of emotion, but it was enough to guide her to the light of his essence. He was alive and nearby. But nothing else came through. Maybe he was still drugged.

A sudden burst of warmth thundered into her, spreading through her body with welcome comfort. She gasped with relief and her heart overflowed. With impulsive abandon, she sent her love through the bond to him in a wave of tenderness. His warmth was more than a feeling of love, it carried with it a resonance of strength, and her heart constricted. He believed in her, and because of that, she knew she could do whatever it took to win her way free.

A soft knock was the only warning she got before Jesse came into the room. Teya tried to compose her features into something bland, but couldn't mask the defiance before Jesse saw it.

"Good, you're awake," he said cheerfully, choosing to ignore the venom she directed his way. He motioned to someone in the hall. "Bring it in." A young woman entered with a tray of food and set it on the table. The woman kept her head lowered while she worked, but Teya caught a glimpse of a gold circlet around her neck. She was Kaloriahn! The girl glanced at Teya with curiosity before she hurried out.

"Wait," Teya cried, but the girl didn't come back. She directed her anger at Jesse. "What's going on? What do you want with me? Where's Bran?"

Frowning, Jesse pulled a chair from the table, his earlier cheer gone. Asking about Bran clearly upset him and she hoped it wasn't a mistake that Bran would pay for later. "Come to the table and have something to eat. You must be starving."

He was right. She was hungry. She sat up and swung her legs over the bed to stand, but the movement brought a wave of dizziness and she lost her balance, toppling forward. Jesse caught her, and settled her back against the pillows. She glared at him. "What did you do to me?"

His face clouded with contrition. "It was just some blood. Not that much, really. If you'll eat something, you'll feel better. Here, I'll bring the tray over to the bed."

She was too angry to eat, and wanted nothing to do with him. But the aroma of bacon and eggs, and the sight of warm biscuits and jam, sparked a burning hunger she couldn't deny. She didn't want to eat just to spite him, but swallowed her pride and took a bite of eggs. Each mouthful strengthened her, and gradually, she felt better.

Jesse wandered about the room while she ate and stopped to open the curtains. With the slant of the sun, Teya guessed it had to be late morning. The bright rays fell on Jesse, and his golden hair shone with luminous brilliance while softening his chiseled features with a warm glow. In this light she couldn't help realizing how handsome he was, and for some reason, it fueled her anger.

"How long have I been asleep?"

He didn't turn to her, but kept his gaze focused on the world outside the window. "Since yesterday. It took a while for the drug to wear off. Then after...you needed to recover."

Was that guilt she detected? "That's how you make *sym*, isn't it? With the blood of my people." When he didn't respond, she continued. "How many have you killed for this counterfeit magic of yours?"

His blue eyes blazed. "It doesn't kill them anymore because I've intervened. I'm trying to save them. Korban doesn't realize what he's doing."

She didn't believe him. "What do you mean?"

"Korban is my father."

Teya could hardly contain her astonishment. "Your father?" Her heart raced as the pieces began to fit together. "But, what about *sym*? Korban said he was taking my blood for both of you to use. Why do you need my blood?"

His eyes narrowed. "I didn't realize you overheard our conversation." His voice hardened. "That means you must have heard everything else."

"Your plans to kill the king?" She tried to sound nonchalant. "As if I care about that. You forget how much I hate him." Hate she still held in her heart. He could not mistake the truth in her tone, and the intensity of it surprised her. She really did wish the king dead. Jesse studied her shrewdly; she had surprised him as well. "The king is cruel and heartless," she continued, "a lot like your father."

He smiled at the jibe. "You surprise me princess. I didn't know you possessed such venom."

"You never answered my question. If you have your own magic, why use *sym?*"

"It augments what I have. And my father doesn't mind. After all, *sym* has always been plentiful for me."

Teya shook her head, confused. "Then why intervene? Why try to help the Kaloriahns against your father's wishes?"

Jesse filled a glass with wine and took a drink, then sat on the edge of the bed next to her. "I'm tired of it all. I can't stand back and watch him destroy us. Up until now, all I've been able to do is stop him from taking too much blood and killing any more Kaloriahns, but with you here we can go back to the grove where we belong.

"I want to find my true heritage. My true nature. I wasn't born there, but something inside of me is pulling me toward the grove, almost against my will. It's like I'm yearning for something that isn't here, and the only place I'll find it is in the grove."

Teya was stunned. It was exactly how she felt. She caught herself nodding in agreement.

His brows lifted. "You feel it too."

"But what about the Kaloriahns?" she asked. "What about the *kundar?* How could you allow this captivity, this exploitation of your own people?"

"Allow it?" He stood and began to pace in agitation. "How could I stop it? It began long before I could do anything about it." With an air of exasperation, he came to her side. "I know you find this hard to believe, but it's true. I want to restore the Kaloriahns to the grove. I want to return with you. Even if it means defying my father."

"You're good," she whispered. "For a minute, you almost had me fooled."

"I'm telling the truth."

"No, you're only telling me what you want me to believe." But was he? How could she believe him? Besides being Korban's son, he was a hunter. He'd hunted down her people and captured them like dogs.

"I understand it's too early for you to believe me now, but in time, you'll see that I mean every word." He took the tray from her lap and set it on the table. "I'll send someone in to draw your bath, and bring fresh clothes. When you're ready, Korban wants to see you." He paused, and with an undercurrent of warning said, "Be careful with him. It's better to appease him when you can. At least appear to go along with him for now. I promise it won't always be this way." He didn't wait for a reply and was soon shutting the door behind him.

Teya took a deep breath. His advice was what she'd planned to do all along, and it rattled her that he suggested it. Still, she wasn't going to let Korban bully her. She was going to insist that she see Bran and her people. He could hardly deny her that.

Now that she knew Korban's plans to displace the king, she didn't know what to do. Should she wait until Korban was in control, and they were on their way to the grove or do something now? She needed to talk to Bran. He could help her decide what was best.

It was a dangerous game she was playing. Both Korban and Jesse must think the other put the *kundar* on her, and if they ever talked about it they would know.

A real *kundar* would be the end. She couldn't let that happen.

A quick knock came from the door and a young woman entered. She dipped her head shyly, and laid out the clothes she brought at the end of the bed. "I'm Cherie, and I'm to help you with your bath."

"You're Kaloriahn," Teya said.

"I'm not supposed to talk to you, but yes, I'm Kaloriahn. And it looks like you are too. I see they took some of your blood." She shook her head. "Don't worry, you should feel better in a day or two, depending on how much they took. Lucky for me, they quit taking mine when I nearly died. I'd better get your bath started." She opened a door and disappeared inside a large bathroom. The sound of splashing water filled the echoing chamber and after a moment, Cherie returned. "Do you need help getting in there?"

"No, I can manage."

"Then, I'd better go."

"Wait, I have a million questions..."

"Not for me," Cherie protested. "Please...I don't want to get in trouble. We can talk...later."

"All right," Teya said. "And thank you." Cherie nodded and left in a hurry, clearly uneasy about being there. Teya sighed and got out of bed. She stood carefully, still slightly dizzy.

Her lightheadedness passed, but left her shaken. It took some time to get to the bathroom and once she settled inside, the water was barely warm. On impulse, she breathed a simple tone to heat it up. That small burst of power sent her reeling, and she clutched at the tub until the dizziness subsided. Taking her blood had more of an effect on her than she realized, and it would mean precious time before she was back to her full strength. She shivered, knowing that until then, she was quite helpless.

Something else bothered her, perhaps even frightened her. Would the *sym* from her blood make Korban or Jesse more powerful than her? She couldn't believe it was possible, but there were a lot of things that were hard to believe. One of them was Jesse. Why had he confided in her? What did he really want?

Dressed and ready to go, she sat on the bed to gather her composure. Korban was waiting for her, and she was too weak to summon her magic. It was not the meeting she envisioned, especially with Bran locked up somewhere. If they were ever to escape, it all depended on her. She reached for Bran. It took a moment to find him, but when she did, his warmth flooded over her.

It washed through her like a soothing balm, and strengthened her at the same time. Bran. Where would she be without her link to him? Thoughts of him bound in chains brought fresh anxiety. She needed him, and hoped he wasn't suffering. His warmth energized her more than anything else could. Soothed and strengthened, she locked away her fear, and opened the door.

Two soldiers quickly came to attention and beckoned her to follow them. Their presence took her by surprise, even though she should have known she would be guarded. No wonder Cherie had been so nervous with these two so close.

Confronted with guards, it was easy to slip into the haughty disdain she had always worn in the palace. It helped settle her down, even though her heart pounded with trepidation. She followed the guards down the hall, where they paused before a set of double doors. After a quick knock, they ushered her inside.

It was a large room, made elegant with dark wood siding. The man she had known as Colonel Porter was sitting behind a thick mahogany desk. Korban. He wasn't alone. A tall man with black hair stood facing him. When he turned, a shock of recognition swept over Teya and her knees nearly buckled. Her brother was the last person she had expected to see.

"Hewson?" Her voice faltered.

"Teya!" In two strides he was beside her and holding her in a crushing embrace. Teya could hardly breathe before he pulled back. He wasn't well. There were dark smudges under his eyes and his skin held an unhealthy pallor. His eyes took on a feverish brilliance, with the same turquoise color as hers. "When I found out the king was holding you, I tried to get you out of the palace. But I failed. They caught me and I've been here ever since. Are you all right?" He searched her face. "You look so pale." With this realization he took hold of her arm and pushed up her sleeve, uncovering the bandage. He uttered a silent curse before confronting Korban.

"You've already taken her blood? This has to stop! Our people are dying because of your greed. What will you do then?"

"Calm down, Hewson." Korban's deep voice ordered obedience. "With Teya, I can put my plan into action. Once I take care of my business here, I'm taking all of you back to the grove. I won't need your blood then." Hewson stiffened with distrust and Korban continued. "Teya can tell you why, since she just came from there, but before she does, I would like a moment alone with her. You may wait outside the door."

Hewson's lips parted to protest, but with visible effort, he held it back. "I'll be waiting." He took her hand and gave it a squeeze.

When the door closed behind Hewson, Teya's heart raced. She was alone with her enemy. Studying Korban, she realized that he was not as old as she had imagined. Closer to the age of her father than her grandmother. He emanated an aura of power, and she nearly took a step back, but determinedly held her ground. After all, it was probably just the effects of *sym*. With startling clarity, she knew he was using *sym* at this very moment, possibly hers, and her stomach clenched. The thought that she enabled him to have such power was nauseating.

"From the loathing on your face, I can see your grandmother filled you with her lies." Straining with effort, Teya closed off her feelings before anger inflamed her. Protected in this shell of indifference, she listened without pain to his speech.

"I'll admit that some of it is probably true, but I'm not the demon she has made me out to be. If she wouldn't have been so obstinate, none of this would have happened." He met her blank stare with one of his own, and unnerved, she dropped her gaze.

"But that is beside the point," he continued. "Tomorrow, I'm taking my army to the palace. You will be coming with me. The rest of the Kaloriahns will remain here. Only when the palace is secure, will we continue our journey to the grove. How many of the Kaloriahns go with us, will depend on you."

"Why is that?"

"I need to know I have your cooperation. You know how to get past the destroyer. You need the Kaloriahns to restore the grove, and I need the water to restore my power. It's a mutually beneficial arrangement." He paused to gauge her reaction and when none came, he grew annoyed. "Your companion, Bran, is also here. I haven't decided what to do with him yet."

She couldn't help the faint flush that spread over her face, and nearly blanched at the sudden gleam in his eyes. He would use her feelings for Bran if he could, and she fought to quell her anxiety.

"The king is eagerly awaiting your arrival, and bringing Bran along might help sweeten the deal, and lessen any suspicions he may have about me and Braemar. After all, Bran is from the country I represent. It would be a small matter to wait until after his execution to take over the palace."

"No! Leave him here. I'll do what you want."

That was the reaction he'd been waiting for, and a sardonic smile lifted his lips. "I need your full cooperation, not only for him, but your brother and the rest of them."

"Doesn't the king already know who you are? After all, it was you who gave me to him in the first place."

"I was never involved in that. Is that what Leona told you?"

Her eyes narrowed. "It's what happened."

"Why would I have given you to the king when I could have used you for myself?"

She had no answer for that question because he was right. It didn't make any sense. But there had to be a logical explanation, so she chose to ignore it. "Once we get to the grove, and your powers are restored, what then?"

"I'm sure we can learn to exist side by side. There will be no need for further bloodshed among the Kaloriahns with your cooperation as the Songmistress. That is your rightful place, and I intend to honor it as you honor my right to rule." He came around the desk with a conciliatory smile. "I'm sure your grandmother didn't tell you that I am the rightful heir to the Grove of Kalore. Leona wanted it passed on to her son, and deceitfully planted evidence that had me banished. That is what she didn't tell you. The fate of the Kaloriahns is her fault, but I intend to rectify that and restore the grove to its former glory. It will be beautiful once again."

She didn't believe him for a minute. Leona wouldn't do anything like that. He began to speak of the grove, regaling her with visions of glory and power, and the tones of his voice eased the confusion in her heart. A tendril of quiet peacefulness laced a way into her thoughts and she fought against an overwhelming desire to believe him. She shook her head. What was happening? Was he using magic on her? He took her hands in his and with passion said, "The grove calls to us. It is where we belong. Help me make it what it once was."

The feeling grew, and with it came a vision of the grove, more beautiful than she had ever seen it. A deep longing to return surged over her. It pulled at her soul, and with anguished yearning, she answered the call. "Yes. I will help you."

"Good." Korban led her toward the door "Tomorrow is the beginning of our journey home."

He ushered her out the door and she was startled to find Hewson waiting for her. With sudden clarity, the spell was broken, and in a flash of anger she turned back toward Korban. As she raised her fists to strike, the door clicked shut. Hewson pulled her away, and she choked on an angry cry.

"Don't," he said, carting her down the hall.

"I hate him!" she hissed. "He's a monster."

"Yes, you're right. But throwing a fit isn't going to help."

She quit struggling, already out of breath in her weakened state, and tried to regain her composure. "I'm all right now," she said. "Didn't he know using magic wouldn't work on me?"

"But it did. He let you see it. That's what he wanted you to know."

With that declaration, Teya would have stumbled without Hewson's hold on her. It was true. Korban had shown her what he was capable of, and the realization terrified her. Teya leaned on Hewson for support, hardly aware of where they were.

"We'll find a way out, Teya. I promise you." His beautiful eyes were filled with remorse. "I'm sorry I failed you."

"Please don't say that. When Grandmother told me you left the grove to rescue me, I thought you must have been killed. I never thought I'd find you alive."

"I'm not sure this is living. But at least now I finally have you. It's been so long," he smiled wistfully. "Just look at you, you're all grown up." She smiled back at him, and a flood of memories filled her mind. She'd lost so much.

"Come on. I want you to meet the others, and then tell me what Korban is planning." He led her down the hallway past her room, and through the double doors to the outside of the building. One of the guards followed them, but Hewson didn't seem to care. They crossed a beautiful courtyard before entering a second structure similar to the first, but on a smaller scale.

Inside the building, Hewson led Teya to a dining hall with tables and chairs filling the room. He motioned Teya to a chair, and she gratefully sat down while he spread the word for the Kaloriahns to gather. The guard following them waited at the entrance within hearing distance, but did nothing to interfere.

The room filled with people from all stages of life. Besides the gold band around their necks, they also shared the trait of looking pale and sick. Some of them did not have the energy to walk on their own, and leaned on others. Even the few children in the group were not spared the bloodletting. As they were, she doubted that many of them could make it to the grove, and silent rage filled her heart. She welcomed the rage. It was easier to cope with than fear.

Hewson joined her and whispered, "They don't have hope anymore, so I'm asking you to give it to them. Even if it's not true, they need something to live for."

"Is this all of them?" Her heart sank. There were only about fifty people.

"There are a few who are too sick to leave their beds, but other than that, they're all here. Just remember, Korban has more than one guard listening."

Only Cherie's face was familiar, but she still felt a kinship with the others. Something in their eyes spoke to her heart, and she concentrated on that instead of her anger. After Hewson introduced her as Leona's heir and the future Songmistress, she rose shakily to her feet.

"I came from the grove a few days ago. Leona is the only one left, and she charged me with the responsibility of bringing you all back." She paused, trying to find a way to soften what she had to say next, but couldn't. "The grove is dying, and without you it will be destroyed. I won't let that happen. I promised my grandmother, and I promise you, that we will return. All of us."

None of them said anything, but a wary hope sprang in their eyes. "I want you to be ready to leave at a moment's notice. It won't be tomorrow, but it will be soon." She wanted to heal them too, but didn't think she was strong enough. "I will try to visit with each of you personally. In the meantime, get your things together."

One by one, they stood and quietly bowed to her before leaving the hall. As sorrow lanced through her heart, tears pricked the back of her eyes. Her once proud people had been reduced to slaves, all for the greed of one man.

"You've given them hope, but you don't seem to have any," Hewson said, wiping a tear from her cheek. "Was it all a lie?"

"No, Hewson. It's true. You heard Korban say he is planning to take everyone back to the grove, but I have plans of my own and they don't include him. I don't want to tell you more, because it would put you in danger. Can you trust me?"

"Of course, but I don't want to see you get hurt. You must let me help if I can," he pleaded.

"I will." She couldn't tell him her true feelings—that she would rather die than become a slave again.

"All right. Now tell me how you got away from the king."

In soft whispered tones she told Hewson how Bran rescued her, and their return to the grove. Hewson didn't know about the Destroyer and was astonished that Leona had released it. "It has kept Korban away from the grove and now he wants me to take him back. We cannot let him return and restore his power."

"No," Hewson agreed. "There must be a way to stop him."

It was on the tip of her tongue to tell him that her *kundar* wasn't real, but after all her ruined plans, she didn't want to put him in danger.

"How did he catch you?"

She told him how they met Jesse and his final trap that led them straight to Korban. "I haven't seen Bran since, do you know where he is?"

"Yes. He's locked up in the cells below the building. I don't know if the guards will let us down there, but we can try."

"Thank you. And Hewson...we will be free. I promise." She needed to see Bran almost as much as she needed to breathe. Outside, the soldiers' presence was immediately felt and every eye seemed to follow her progress. Hewson led Teya down a dirty staircase at the back of the building. Inside were several rows of tiny cells that were locked and barred. The small space was dark and Teya fought against the suffocating feeling that closed around her. When a man's hands appeared on the bars, her heart leapt. Bran. She started toward him but a sturdy guard blocked her way.

"I'm here to see the prisoner," she said. The guard was huge and she had to crane her neck to see his face, but she wasn't going to let him stop her. Not when she was this close.

"Only you," he answered, then put a hand to Hewson's chest. "You will wait."

She hastily agreed and darted past him to Bran's cell a few feet away. She reached through the bars, clasping his hands and searching his face for signs of abuse. He pulled her to him with a gentle kiss, releasing her when the bars got in the way. His eyes shone with all that was in his heart and she caught her breath in the warmth of his love. Hiding nothing, she returned it without thought of consequence or reason. The intensity shook her, and she fought to hold back tears.

"Are you all right?" Bran asked. "Did he hurt you?"

"He took some of my blood. That's how he makes *sym*. He made my blood into *sym* for himself. The Kaloriahns are sick and dying because he's taken so much of it from them." She couldn't hide the anger in her tone, especially when she sensed Bran was in terrible pain. A bruise along his jaw was the least of it, but she focused on that anyway, not wanting Bran to know how angry she was. "What happened?"

"I tried to get past that big lug out there."

She shook her head, her heart pounding with anger. "How did this happen? I thought we were safe with Porter, and he led us straight into this trap."

"It's my fault. I trusted him. I never would have guessed he was really Korban. How did he get where he is? Here, in my own country?"

"Magic. He has magic, and he's used it to betray us all."

Bran glanced at the *kundar*. "Please tell me that's yours." When she nodded he let out a breath of relief. "Good. Do you know what his plans are?"

"Yes. Tomorrow, he's taking me back to the king, but it's all a sham. Now that he commands a large group of soldiers from Braemar, he's determined to kill the king and take over the Old Country using me to get into the palace. He's leaving the Kaloriahns here to insure my cooperation. Then he plans to take all of us back to the grove and regain his magic. He had the audacity to say that he was the rightful heir to the grove, and that Leona plotted his banishment." She couldn't control her anger and knew Bran felt it through the bond.

"Of course he would say something like that. But you can't let anger cloud your judgment."

"I could have killed him by now." She pulled away, suddenly cold. "But when he took my blood it weakened me, and I can't use my magic until I get stronger. I can't free you or the Kaloriahns. I can't get us out of here." Teya felt Bran's dismay along with the pain he tried not to show. "What am I going to do?"

"How long? When will your strength return?"

"I don't know, maybe tomorrow." She knew that was pushing it.

"Then you need to rest. You can't do anything until you have your full strength. Just don't let him take any more of your blood."

Teya shook her head. "I overheard him say that he took enough to last until he makes it to the grove, so I don't think we have to worry about it."

"Good," Bran sighed. "I guess you'll have to go to the palace without me. Just don't let him goad you into using your magic until you're ready. You can't take the chance of being collared again."

Teya took hold of his hands. "He threatened to take you with us and offer you to the king for execution unless I cooperate."

"If that happens…"

"No. I won't let it!"

Bran rubbed her hands through the bars. "I hate being so helpless. If there was a way out of here I could help you."

Teya sent a small tone toward the lock, but it died on her lips in a wave of dizziness. "I can't open it," she gasped.

"Don't try. It's all right," Bran said in a soothing voice. "Maybe you can come back later, when you're stronger, and try again."

"Yes. I'll come back as soon as I'm strong enough to open the lock."

"Time's up," the guard growled toward them.

"Be careful," Bran cautioned.

"Let's go." The guard clamped a meaty hand on her bandaged arm.

"Let go of me you big lug!" With surprise, he released her arm and waited to follow behind. She swallowed her anger and glanced at Bran, trying to show some control. "I'll be back later." The guard prodded her out before she could say anything else.

She reached the top of the stairs in a foul mood. Hewson was gone and a soldier stood in his place. "Where's my brother?"

"He had other things to do, and you are to return to your room."

"But I need to talk to him."

"Korban wants you back in your room."

She masked her anger with a blank stare and sullenly allowed him to lead her to her room. By the time she got there, she was too tired to do more than flop on her bed and close her eyes. As she puzzled out her next move, sleep drifted over her and she reluctantly gave in, hoping the next time she woke, her magic would be strong again. At this point, it was all she had to cling to.

≈≈

Bran slumped on the bench in his cell and held his side. It had taken all his control to hide his pain from Teya, but she had enough to worry about without him adding to it. At least his ribs were only bruised and not broken.

He'd never seen Teya so pale, and his blood boiled at what Korban had done. Not only to her, but Braemar as well. He was sure that no one in Braemar knew who 'Colonel Porter' really was. The fact that Bran had been charged to find out where *sym* came from, when it was right here in his own country, was humiliating. Now it looked like Korban had the use of the Braemarian soldiers at his disposal. He needed to be stopped, and Bran was powerless to do anything. He was grateful Jax left when he did. He was Bran's only hope of outside help.

Knowing that Teya wore her own *kundar* was the only thing that kept him sane. That, and the bond they shared. He had no words to describe his relief when he felt her through the bond. He didn't know what they had done with her, or where she was, until she opened the bond. He'd been so relieved that he didn't try to hide his feelings, and sent his relief and love spiraling toward her. The depth of his feelings surprised him, and he hoped he hadn't gone too far. When those same feelings came back, mirroring his own, it left him hopeful. He knew it wasn't a dream when she came to him and he finally saw it in her eyes.

The look she sent him when she left held more than anger, and he shifted with sudden unease when he recognized her fear. She was afraid for him, and he knew Korban would use him to insure her cooperation. Anger and frustration surged through him. Teya was strong, but he worried that a confrontation might push her over the edge. That the anger she'd been trying to control would get away from her. Would she become the monster everyone feared? How many people would she kill before it was over?

CHAPTER NINE

The Return

Teya shifted position so she could see out of her window without the bright morning light blinding her. Below, the preparations were now complete and two motorcars were leaving the yard. The last one waited in rumbling anticipation for the occupant who had not yet arrived. When Korban finally appeared, she stepped forward to witness his departure. As if sensing her interest, he turned and caught her gaze, holding it until she pulled away, breathless and shaken.

Not until the sound of his motorcar abated in the distance, could she look again into the empty yard. Korban was gone, but even now another motorcar moved to take the place his had vacated. This one was meant for her. It seemed she was poised on the edge of a cliff and the only way down was to jump.

She smoothed the silken folds of her shimmering dress. Korban made sure she was returned to the king dressed in the finery he would expect. The blue-black color was the king's favorite and suited her feeling of doom.

To his credit, Korban dazzled her with his efforts. Tiny black feathers were incorporated subtly into the material of the clothing, giving the effect of an exotic bird. More feathers adorned the neckline and wrists of the dress, and an intricate pattern of feathers and jeweled silver, twined through her hair. If she looked a little pale, it only reinforced her trepidation of being caught and brought back to face the rage of her owner. She stared at her reflection with cool appraisal and caught a glimpse of what others might call 'not quite human.'

Dressed like this, she could certainly play the part, even though deep inside she was trembling with fear. She had not recovered her full strength. Even though she was stronger than yesterday, she didn't think it was enough to win a confrontation with Korban. Besides him, she still had to face the king. She might have enough power for one of them, but not both.

The Kaloriahns would remain here as a lever for her cooperation, not that Korban needed it, but what about Bran? Korban hadn't allowed her to see him again, and she was sure he had something planned. The king wanted Bran almost as much as he wanted Teya. Would Korban take Bran with them to appease the king?

The soft knock at her door signaled the end of her time alone. Jesse entered, then halted in mid-stride with an expression of awe and appreciation. He swallowed to regain his composure, and she was grateful for all her finery if it threw him off-balance.

"You look...breathtaking," Jesse said. "Are you ready to leave?"

She couldn't contain her smile of irony. "I don't have much choice, do I?"

Annoyance crossed his features. "No, but I won't let anyone hurt you. That includes my father. No more blood, I promise."

"And are you using *sym* from my blood?" With a shake of his head, he opened his mouth to speak, but she cut him off. "Please don't lie to me. I may not be able to use much of my own magic, but we share the same Kaloriahn blood. I'll know."

He approached her with an earnestness that was surprising, his tall, lithe frame full of grace and poise. His blue eyes shone with regret and sobriety. "I have *sym* from your blood with me, but I haven't wanted to use it. I don't know how things are going to happen at the palace today, and it might come in handy, but I don't want to betray your trust."

"How can you, when you don't have it in the first place?"

He huffed in vexation. "True, but I'm trying to remedy that. I'm hoping that after today, you'll see we're on the same side. Come." He took her hand and led her out of the room in regal fashion. They swept down the stairs and through the outer rooms to the courtyard. Two guards were waiting at the motorcar, but it was their prisoner that brought Teya up short. They held Bran between them, disheveled and dirty, bound in chains.

"Where do you want him?" a guard asked.

"Put him in the next motorcar with you, and follow behind us," Jesse answered.

They started to pull Bran toward the car. "Wait!" Teya cried. "Jesse, you can't take him with us. The king will kill him."

"I have to. It's part of the deal my father made with the king."

"No! Please don't do this!"

Jesse pulled Teya back into the building, out of hearing distance from the others. "He has to come with us, or our plans won't work. You want to see King Thesald defeated don't you? Nothing will happen to Bran. The king will lock him up, and after that, we'll take over. Bran will be safe in a cell until then."

"You can't guarantee that," she spat. "If the king wants him executed, your father would go along with him, and you would be powerless to stop them." Teya couldn't seem to breathe. Jesse didn't care if Bran died. In fact, he probably wanted him out of the way. She tried a different tactic. "You said you wanted me to trust you. Leave Bran here. Tell the king that Bran's government wouldn't approve, or make something up. But leave him here. If you do this for me, I know I'll be able to trust you."

"You don't understand…my father…" Jesse broke off and paced a few steps away, his shoulders hunched and his face clouded with indecision. An anguished moment passed and Teya hardly dared to move. Jesse turned back to her, his eyes held bitter disdain. "You don't know what you ask of me. What this will cost me." He paused, looking deep into her eyes. "A true Kaloriahn would never do this, you told me that," he explained. "You said Bran was a better man than I'll ever be and that you despised me. You don't know how your words affected me, and now, I can't stand to see you look at me the same way you did then, with such distrust and abhorrence." He sighed heavily and lowered his gaze. "All right, I'll do it."

Before Teya could thank him, he was out the door, ordering the guards to take Bran back to the cells. She followed him out and caught a questioning glance from Bran before he was hauled away. A trickle of confusion and alarm came from him through the link. She sought to reassure him, but her own feelings were too far from that to be convincing. Instead, she sent what was in her heart and hoped he didn't pick up on her fear. She knew she failed when he responded with a wave of anxious helplessness. Not knowing what else to do, she closed the link on a whisper of love. He would hate it, but it was the only way she could face what she had to do.

Jesse helped settle her inside the motorcar, then climbed in beside her. As the car pulled away, she closed her eyes and took a deep breath. "Thank you," she whispered.

He shook his head before answering with a sarcastic twist of his lips. "For all the good it will do me, I may need that *sym* after all, especially since we can't take any guns into the city."

"Then you should use it," she answered. She could sense his turmoil over what he had done and wished there was a way placate him. "What will happen now?"

"We're meeting Korban in front of the wall to the city. He's planned a grand entrance with you in an open carriage, flanked by a couple hundred Braemarian soldiers on horseback. Hopefully, he won't notice Bran's absence until we're in the city. By then it will be too late to go back and get him."

"You'll stay by me?" she asked, suddenly nervous, realizing the king would be furious with her.

"As much as I can. Just try to keep your distance from the king."

"Right, as if that will happen. Once I'm in his hands, he won't let me out of his sight. I'll probably have to find a way to kill him myself."

He ignored her outburst. "At the palace, I'm not Korban's son, I'm the king's hunter. I won't be sitting with him at the high table, but I will be there. I'll look after you as much as I can, and I promise if there's a way, I'll not leave you alone with the bastard."

Her brows rose. The fact that he didn't like the king shouldn't have been a surprise, but she didn't expect it, and it helped quiet her nerves.

As much as she feared the king, she feared Korban more, and she didn't know how far she could depend on Jesse. If her full strength were back, it wouldn't matter.

"Are you riding in the carriage with me?"

"No, you'll be alone, but don't worry, whatever happens, I won't be far away."

The motorcar passed the outpost where she first met 'Colonel Porter' and climbed to the top of the ridge. Here, they pulled off the road behind other motorcars in the wide 'no-man's land' that separated the two kingdoms. Jesse helped her out and ushered her into a beautiful open carriage. Before leaving, he took her hand and kissed her palm. "For luck," he said. His blue eyes held her gaze for a moment, then he shut the door and told the driver to move out. She clenched her hand into a fist, not sure she liked what his kiss did to her.

The soldiers closed in and Jesse disappeared in the crowd. She swallowed her fear and straightened her spine. With an ease that came from years of practice, she closed off her feelings, locking them away in the small box where nothing could touch her.

The huge gateway in the wall to the city stood open, and as her company moved forward, she caught sight of Korban in all his military finery, standing beside Chancellor Turner in a beautiful carriage of their own. It was disconcerting to see Korban in a Braemarian uniform when she knew he was Kaloriahn, and she wondered how many people knew who he really was. When the chancellor caught sight of Teya, he visibly relaxed before nodding to Korban in satisfaction. When her carriage drew up behind theirs, they began the parade into the city.

Soldiers from the Old Country lined the road, while hundreds of people gathered behind to catch a glimpse of the returning Songbird. Some clapped and cheered as she passed, but most pointed with curious stares and whispered conjectures. She bore their discourteousness with feigned indifference and fleetingly wondered what they would do if she smiled and waved.

She glanced toward the palace and realized somewhere along the way her carriage had slowed, creating a distance between them. As she wondered about this, a rock flew past her shoulder, startling her out of her reverie. Another went wild and hit the side of the carriage. Before she knew what was happening, the horse pulling the carriage reared from being struck. In the ensuing chaos, King Thesald's soldiers drew their swords and bellowed at the surging crowd, chasing the miscreants away, and leaving Teya without protection. In the chaos, a few burly men broke through the ranks and advanced toward the disabled carriage.

Teya stared in morbid fascination as they proceeded toward her. Before she could gather her wits, Braemarian soldiers on horseback rushed to her aid. They rapidly surrounded her carriage and beat the attackers back with disciplined efficiency. It happened so fast that Teya was slightly bewildered when it was over.

It took a moment to grasp what had happened, but when Jesse appeared at her side and winked, she realized it had been staged to get the Braemarian soldiers into the palace as her escort. It was all part of Korban's grand scheme and she wondered what else he planned. She sat back with apprehension for the rest of the journey, and tensed when they passed through the palace gates. Before she was ready, they stopped in the plaza outside the palace. It was filled with dignitaries and nobles whose ranks spilled up the stairs. Beyond them, marble pillars held up the rounded towers of the palace.

She followed the line of people toward the top of the stairs and her heart lurched at the sight of King Thesald. He towered above them, a formidable figure in his regal robes. At her arrival, he began the long descent toward her with a look of zealous anticipation. She glanced around for Jesse and found him in arduous conversation with Korban. A quick movement brought an end to their words, and Korban hastily came around the carriage to open the door.

He reached in for Teya with pursed lips of dissatisfaction and anger rippling about him in waves. This close, she could feel the *sym* hovering around him like a second glove. She wondered how much he had taken to gather such power, and reflexively shrank back from his touch. His cold eyes locked with hers and she swallowed her revulsion before taking his proffered hand.

He led her out of the carriage and his countenance changed into cordial civility as he mounted the stairs toward the king. With a sweeping gesture of magnanimity, Korban bowed deeply before King Thesald and presented Teya to him. "Your Majesty, your prize is returned, unharmed and collared."

"I thank you Colonel Porter, and all of Braemar, for returning her to me." He searched the entourage and asked. "Where is the man who took her?"

"He was delayed by our governor for a brief questioning before turning him over to you. I assure you he will be here later."

Teya knew from the set of his jaw that the king was furious, and when his gaze turned on her she flinched. With narrowed eyes he took a step toward her and she backed into Korban's chest. The backhanded blow that hit her face might have snapped her neck if not for the cushion of *sym* that diffused much of the power. As it was, she tasted blood in her mouth, along with a slight ringing in her ears. Korban must have deflected the blow with his magic.

The king seemed satisfied with her dazed eyes and bloody lip. "Welcome back, my beauty. You will be thoroughly punished later, but in honor of our guests, we will call a truce." He offered her his hand, and trembling, she placed hers over it. As they began the ascent into the palace, he methodically scrutinized her face. "You seem different somehow. Pale, and not so haughty. It pleases me."

She said nothing, only concentrated on putting one foot in front of the other until the stairs were behind them and they were inside the main hall. Korban and Chancellor Turner followed them, along with two or three other dignitaries. A few select Braemarian guards kept pace beside them, and Teya wondered if the king realized how easily they had replaced the palace guards. Jesse was in the entourage behind Korban. In his courtly dress, he could not be mistaken for a Braemarian. This led Teya to wonder how many of the other people surrounding the king were actually loyal to him, or on Korban's side.

Inside the palace, King Thesald led her to the main hall where a small banquet had been set up. Instead of seating her at the high table, he walked her up a tiny set of stairs to a small rounded alcove in the palace wall, perched above the crowd. The statue that normally rested in this spot was gone.

"A living, breathing work of art is much better than cold marble. You will serve me well here." Triumph gleamed in his eyes. "Besides, I want you where no one can easily reach you. Any freedom you had before is lost. From now on, you will be isolated from everyone."

"As you wish." She inclined her head, and his eyes widened in surprise, then narrowed in suspicion before he turned away, his triumph gone.

Those three simple words settled Teya and helped restore the sense of balance she desperately needed. She never realized before, the power of such words. Bran's words to let go of her hate helped her stay focused. When Jesse told her how her words of being a true Kaloriahn had affected him, she was astonished. Because of them, Bran wasn't here. Words held as much power as her music, but in a different way. If she sang the truth to these people with her magic, would it change things?

The full use of her magic would return soon, if not today, then tomorrow. All she had to do was endure the present. It wouldn't be easy, but she could do it. In a way, she was grateful for this perch. From here, she could see what was going on. She settled lightly on the small stool that was the only comfort she was allowed, and scanned the room.

Chancellor Turner, Korban, and three members of the king's council joined King Thesald's table. The occupants of the other tables varied between Braemarian officers and Old Country dignitaries. Jesse was seated between two of the king's advisors and others she didn't know. It was a small gathering by the king's standards, with only five tables in all.

King Thesald stood. "For the safe return of my Songbird, I thank Colonel Porter and Braemar. Hopefully, we can put our differences aside and forge a new alliance for the future. To that end, this banquet was prepared. However," he paused and motioned toward the back of the hall, "I hope you don't mind the presence of a few more guards. I do not want to lose my Songbird a second time."

A troop of the king's soldiers entered the hall and took up positions along the walls. Was it possible King Thesald suspected something? Teya didn't know what Korban had planned, but this would complicate things. Korban graciously inclined his head, seemingly nonplussed by this show of dominance.

Teya sat through dinner, relieved that she was momentarily forgotten and wondered if Jesse had actually drunk the *sym* he had in his pocket. He glanced at Teya a few times, but never for long. After dinner was cleared away, the king stood again, only this time he turned to Teya. She tensed under his dark gaze.

"I wish to hear you sing."

An undercurrent of tension filled the chamber and echoed through her blood. The king was up to something and her singing would put his plan in motion. She stood, her heart pounding as if poised on the edge of a massacre. Korban was a fool to think he could dislodge the king. Without Bran to make an example of, King Thesald was going to do something else. Korban seemed to realize it as well, but instead of fear, an odd light shone in his eyes.

The first few notes were hardly out of her mouth before the palace guards attacked. Several guards took position around the king for his protection, while others fell on the Braemarian officers. To her astonishment, a large group of Braemarian soldiers flooded the hall and the fight began in earnest.

Korban disarmed two of the king's councilors and Teya received another shock when Chancellor Turner joined him, easily disarming the others. The rest of the dignitaries gave up without a fight, persuaded by Turner's betrayal. Jesse tried to get to the king, but was waylaid by palace guards, who outnumbered the Braemarian soldiers.

At this turn of events, the king's face was red and livid with rage. Even though the Braemarians were outnumbered, they seemed to possess incredible fighting skills and the tide was turning in their favor. Teya knew it came from *sym*. When Korban turned his attention to the king, it was easy to see that his bodyguards wouldn't last long.

With everyone occupied, Teya jumped at the chance to escape. She quickly climbed down from her perch and dodged behind a guard. She nearly made it to the door behind the table, but was brought up short by King Thesald's strong grasp. "You're not leaving without me," he hissed. He held her as a shield and backed toward the door.

Teya went with him easily, knowing that once they were in the hall, she had enough strength to stop him with a dark tone of magic. As they backed through the door, Teya's heart raced to see Jesse running toward them and she cursed the promise he'd made to stay by her side. As he surged through the door after them, a shot rang out and Teya jumped. The king had fired a gun! Jesse clutched his chest and fell to his knees. Blood ran between his fingers.

"No!" Teya cried.

Jesse slid to the ground, his eyes full of pain and desperation. "Teya."

Suddenly, all the pent-up emotions of anger and rage broke through her carefully constructed barriers. In one breath, she directed them toward the king in a single harsh tone. He screamed in pain and clutched his head, dropping the gun. She intensified the tone and the king writhed in agony. His screams turned to a gurgling sound and he collapsed at her feet, his face a mottled purple, and his breathing shallow.

"Teya," Jesse whispered. He was trying to stand, but fell back in pain. "I think I'm dying."

Dazed, she ran to Jesse's side. "Lie still," she panted. Blood soaked his shirt, and she pulled it away to reveal a gaping wound in his chest, just below his heart. "I can help you, but you must promise not to tell anyone."

"Please," he gasped. "Whatever you want is yours."

Teya took a deep breath and placed her hands over the wound. With strength born of need, she poured a healing melody over him, binding the torn flesh while drawing the bullet out. Concentrating with heart and soul, the bullet was soon in her hand and the skin beneath it, whole.

She opened her eyes to find the world tilting at a crazy angle. Darkness buzzed at the outer edges of sight, and her face felt waxen and cold. She slid helplessly to Jesse's side and he gently cradled her in his arms.

The door burst open, and Korban frantically rushed in, then stopped abruptly. Jesse relaxed to see his father, and Teya fought to keep the darkness at bay. "Is she all right?" Korban asked.

"She's hurt, but she should be fine with some rest."

Korban rushed to the king. "What happened?"

"He was leaving with Teya. I came after them and we fought. Is he dead?"

"Not yet, but look at him. What did you do?"

Teya tried to open her eyes, but it was too much effort. Jesse was saying something about *sym* while other voices soon joined Korban's and Teya lost track of the words. She felt the sensation of weightlessness before coming to rest on something soft and warm. Comforted, she let go of her tenuous hold on awareness. As soft lips brushed her forehead, she fell into a deep sleep.

❧❧

Teya woke in a rush, pulled out of her sleep by awareness that she was not alone. The elegant room belonged to someone of wealth, and with sudden clarity it all came flooding back to her. She was in the palace and had nearly killed the king. What about Jesse? She had healed him and now he had to know that her *kundar* was a fake. She searched the room, feeling again that she was not alone, and there in the corner, sat Jesse, asleep in a large cushioned chair. His rumpled, bloodstained clothes left no doubt that he had stayed with her for as long as she'd been there.

On the bedside table was a pitcher of water and Teya was plagued by a sudden thirst. She shifted delicately into a sitting position and when the room stopped spinning, swung her legs over the side of the bed.

At the sound of her movements, Jesse came awake. He studied her for a moment before moving stiffly from the chair to her side. "Here, let me pour that for you." He took the glass out of her hand and poured the water. "You look better than you did a few hours ago."

She drank the water greedily before responding. "What about you?" He had changed his bloodstained shirt for another, but his trousers still carried splotches of red.

He pulled something from his pocket and opened his palm. There, in the center lay the gray stub of a bullet. "I've been waiting to hear how you did this, especially with that *kundar* on."

"You didn't say anything...?"

"No, of course not. But I'd like to know how you did it."

"What about the king, is he still alive?"

"Probably, but the way he is, it won't be long. His brain is fried. My father de-cided to let him die on his own. That way the transition won't seem so difficult for the advisors and people. This gives them a chance to get used to the idea. Not that many of them needed persuading. Most had already grown tired of Thesald's rule. Chancel-lor Turner's cooperation converted the rest of the councilors. He and my father have enjoyed a long and fruitful friendship. Turner practically ruled this country under Thesald, and will have more power than he did before, once we return to the grove.

"But right now I'd like to know what you did to the king? I had to lie through my teeth to convince Korban it was me who did it. He thinks I used *sym* and hit the king so hard it affected his brain. I'm not sure he believes me, but there was no one else who could have done it besides you, and with the *kundar*, that was impossible."

"I asked if I could trust you…"

He waved her words away. "You can. You saved my life with your magic. I didn't know it was even possible. The wound was mortal. I would have died."

Teya sighed, knowing she had to tell him the truth. "When the king grabbed me, it all happened so fast. I didn't even realize he had a gun until it went off. Then I had to stop him. It was a natural reaction. I don't regret what I did, as long as he can't tell anyone it was me."

Jesse shook his head. "If you saw him you'd know there's no chance of that."

"Good," she said with conviction, to ease the whisper of guilt for the king's plight. Jesse looked at her expectantly, and she knew she had to explain how she did it. "This *kundar* is mine. When Bran got it off, the dark magic inside was destroyed. I kept it, and after my first meeting with you, I put it back on for protection."

"Ah."

He didn't say anything more, and Teya had to ask, "What will you do now?"

He sighed deeply. "I won't tell anyone, just promise me you won't do anything rash with your power. I can't cover for you if Korban finds out."

"What about Korban," she finally dared to ask. "What are you going to do about him?"

"I don't know." He began to pace the room. The turmoil in his eyes matched his restless energy.

Teya was afraid this turn of conversation would make him leave. "What's going on in the palace now?"

"I'm not sure. I was so worried about you that I haven't been paying attention. If you're feeling better, I think I'll find out. You'd better stay here, out of sight."

"Does Korban know where I am?"

"He knows I'm with you and…he trusts me. I'd better go, I'll come back when I know anything more."

"Wait!" She looked deep into Jesse's eyes. She had to know he would keep her secret.

"I won't say anything."

She nodded numbly, realizing how precarious her position was. Jesse knew the truth. She hoped placing her trust in him wasn't a mistake. How long did she have before someone else figured it out? Did Korban suspect anything? That was the last thing she needed, and it was easy to see that this window of opportunity wouldn't last. She had to do something before it was too late.

Jesse surprised her by taking her hand. "You could have let me die today. With things the way they are maybe you should have." He stopped her protest with a finger to her lips. "It's all right. I'm glad you didn't. Just forgive me if I'm not sure about things, and know that I won't betray you."

He moved toward her for a kiss, but she lowered her face and his lips brushed her forehead. He sighed deeply, waiting for a response, and when she didn't look up, he left the room.

With his departure, she was able to breathe again. He wanted more from her than she was able to give, and her stomach clenched with turmoil. No matter what Jesse was now, she loved Bran. Jesse had probably saved Bran's life, but she had saved Jesse. They were even. Except now he knew about the *kundar*. Did he have a price for his trust? She hoped not, because she would never stop loving Bran. Thinking of Bran, she opened the link, not knowing if the distance was too great, but needing him all the same.

Only a hint of awareness came to her, but nothing solid. She tried again, with the same result, and wondered if the distance was to blame. It didn't help that she was tired, but the faint link with Bran unsettled her, and she worried that something was wrong.

Using her magic against the king and healing Jesse had laid her flat. She was surprised she could even get out of bed. The force of her anger had given her more power than she thought possible, but it seemed different from the power of the grove. The grove was filled with the miracle of life, but she had used her power to destroy and kill. She shivered. There was a world of difference between them, and she suddenly understood how her powers could be considered monstrous, especially used in anger.

If Korban regained his full powers, she had little doubt that he would use them to kill and subjugate. He was no different from the king, and perhaps even worse. Now, the king was dying. Unbidden, the moment she unleashed her magic on King Thesald flashed into her mind. She remembered with startling clarity the agonized contortions of his face. At the time, the red haze of rage and anger didn't make it seem so terrible. Thinking about it now disturbed her, and she quickly banished that train of thought with another. The king had killed and hurt many people. He deserved what he got, and those he hurt deserved justice.

She took a few unsteady steps to the window. The sun was setting and darkness stole across the sky in ever lengthening shadows. Shadows that fell across her heart and threatened to pull her into them with chains of hate and anger. It was clear that killing with her power was wrong, but what choice did she have?

Using her power in the grove was so different from using her power here. Going back would cleanse her soul from what she had done, but it wasn't over. She still had to face Korban.

Needing Bran, she tried to reach him again. This time, she felt his presence like he was beside her, but before she knew what to make of it, a sudden shock of pain washed over her. Like a broken dam, pain and despair flooded the link, withering to a steady throb of helplessness. Bran was in serious trouble.

In response, a protective surge of power rippled through her. Bran had to be somewhere close, maybe even in the palace. Korban must have brought him here after all. She swallowed her nausea and closed her eyes to concentrate on Bran. The murky darkness of semi-consciousness slithered through the link. Desperate to find him, she followed the bond to the door before hesitating.

If Korban had Bran here, why was he hurting him now? The king was dying; there was no reason for it. What if Jesse had decided to get rid of Bran? This was the perfect time to do it, before she knew he was here. Before she could stop him.

She opened the door, half expecting to see a guard, but the dimly lit hall was empty. In careful silence, she crept into the hallway toward the stairs. Trepidation set her heart beating furiously. Nothing looked familiar, and she had no idea where she was. Concentrating on the link, she felt Bran's presence above her. The staircase led upward to a landing that opened up into another hallway. This area seemed more familiar and as she ascended the stairs, she was certain that this floor contained the king's rooms.

Bran was close, but was Korban or Jesse with him? Approaching footsteps sent her to the first door she came to and she slid inside. The room was dark except for a single light on the bedside table. The man lying on the bed could have been asleep, but his eyes were open and staring. With awful lucidity, she realized it was the king, and he was dead.

A chill ran down her spine, and she stifled a small scream. The footsteps stopped outside the door, and she froze in place until they continued on. Relief surged through her, and she slumped against the door, wanting more than anything to be out of there. She focused on Bran and peered into the hallway. He was close. She had to find him. Korban couldn't find out about the bond they shared, or that she knew Bran was here. Now was her chance to rescue Bran and put an end to Korban.

With that thought bolstering her resolve, she stepped into the hallway and followed it until she felt Bran behind the closed door. Gathering her power to her, she quickly entered. Bran was lashed to a chair with his head lolling to the side. His face was bruised, and blood dripped from a cut over his eye.

Korban sat beside him with a gun to his head. "I thought you might come looking for me, so I brought some insurance."

Teya froze. "Don't."

"I won't as long as you do something for me."

Dread tightened her stomach. "What?"

"See that *kundar* on the desk? I want you to put it on."

"But…"

"I know the one around your neck isn't real." He pushed the gun against Bran's flesh. "Put it on or he's dead."

Bran moaned and opened his eyes. When he recognized her, his eyes widened. "No…don't…"

"Please, let me heal him first," she pleaded.

"I won't ask you again." Korban's voice sounded deadly. "Do it now." He cocked the gun and she flinched. There was no way out. She couldn't stop him with her magic before he pulled the trigger. As she crossed to the desk, sudden tears blinded her. When she touched the *kundar*, revulsion closed her throat. Swallowing the bile, she picked it up and put it around her neck.

"Push it closed."

She sucked in her breath and looked at Bran. His eyes held deep pain and remorse. He struggled to speak, but could barely stay conscious. Bran was the only reason she could lock away all that she was. The latch clicked on her choked sob, and

Korban finally withdrew the gun.

She almost gave in to her grief, but managed to hold it back, unwilling to give Korban that satisfaction. Still, her legs buckled and she sat down hard on the floor. Korban opened a drawer and set the gun inside before turning his attention to her.

"Thanks to you, the king is dead. I wasn't about to make that same mistake."

"How?" she asked. Was it Jesse? Did he betray her?

"When you showed up at the outpost, I knew it wasn't real. The *kundar* is a work of dark power that only I possess. I let you think I was fooled because it served my purposes. I thought that if things went wrong, you would take care of the king. It worked, but once you did that, I couldn't take any chances. I knew you'd come after me next, and even with your *sym* in my blood, I am no match against your power."

An overwhelming wave of hopelessness wrapped around Teya. It was over. He had won. She stared at him, her eyes devoid of hope, feeling as if she was already dead, and he flinched. "I would rather die than take you to the grove," she said calmly. The truth of her words rang free, even if she wasn't.

"I'm sure you would, but what about him? What about your brother and the rest of the Kaloriahns?" At this moment of defeat, she couldn't manage to care. His eyes narrowed with concern and a little worry when her expression didn't change. He called for one of his men, and when he opened the door, said, "Get this prisoner untied and follow me."

She didn't protest when Korban helped her stand, keeping hold of her arm. When the guard jerked Bran to his feet, he groaned in pain, then suddenly struck the guard with his tied hands. Korban lashed out with a dark tone and Bran slumped over, holding his head. "That will hold him for now. Let's go," Korban said.

With a firm grip, he led her up the stairs to her old room in the north tower. To her surprise Korban let the guard lay Bran down on her bed. Without a backward glance, he left, barring the door behind him. As the lock clicked into place, Teya let go of her control, and with anguished bitterness, finally wept.

Chapter Ten

Collared

His soft touch on her head quieted Teya's sobs—sobs that had pulled Bran from unconsciousness with rending intensity. Her silken hair fell through his fingers like soft feathers. His heart constricted when she looked up at him, her eyes burning with sorrow and pain. She rubbed away the tears and concentrated on untying his hands.

When the ropes fell away, he slid over on the bed and she came into his arms. He held her close, stroking her back, and made soothing noises until she quieted and relaxed. After a moment, she rose up on her elbow and lightly touched his swollen face, then with tenderness, leaned over and kissed him.

His lips were sore and bruised, but she was careful of his hurts and pulled away with sadness shining in her eyes. A bowl of water and a towel lay on the table, and she gently began to wash the blood from the cut over his eye. He saw the *kundar* then, the one Korban coerced her into wearing. His heart was heavy, knowing she had done it to save him. She continued to clean him, and he closed his eyes under her soothing ministrations.

"I recognize this room," he said when she was done. His voice rasped and his head still hurt. "Did anyone fix the bars on the window, or are they still apart?"

"It looks like someone tried to pull them back together, but they weren't quite successful. There's still a space between them, but I don't think it's big enough to fit through."

"That's all right. Listen," he took hold of her hands, "we'll find a way out of here. We can still make this work. You may not be able to use your magic on him, but he's still flesh and blood. He's not impervious to a gun or a knife. There are other ways to stop him. Don't forget, we got the *kundar* off of you once, we can do it again."

She bent over, covering her face with her hands, fighting to hold back tears. "You don't think it's over? That he's won?"

"No, of course not. Has he got his powers back? Is he in the grove? There's still time to stop him. You can't give up now."

"If I were dead, he wouldn't be able to enter the grove. You would all be safe."

"No! That's not true. He'd figure something out. Besides, this world will wither up and die if the Destroyer remains unbound. Don't give up. We need you...I need you. More than you know."

"All I've done is cause you grief and pain. You'd be a lot better off without ever knowing me."

"No, that's not true. I wouldn't give up any of the pain to have known you. My life is better because of you." When she started to protest, he stopped her. "We have something beautiful together, and it's just beginning. I don't want to lose it. I don't want to lose you. It's worth fighting for."

"It's so hard to have hope. Everything we've been through—now only to end up in the same place we started. I should have killed Korban the first chance I got. Now, look what he's done!"

Anger lit up her eyes, and Bran took heart. He realized it was better than the emptiness it replaced. "That's right. We can't let him get away with this. We need to fight back."

"But how?"

Bran eased back on the pillows. His whole body ached, and his head was pounding hard enough that even his hair hurt. "First, tell me what happened and how Korban knew the *kundar* wasn't real. I sort of missed that part."

Teya explained what Korban had done, and how he knew all along that it wasn't real. She played right into his schemes by killing the king herself. She also told Bran about Jesse and how he had agreed to leave Bran at the monastery in return for her trust, then later, how she had healed him after he'd been shot by the king.

"I wondered why he didn't bring me with you to the palace, especially when it was part of the deal Korban made with the king," Bran said. "But do you really think you can trust him?" Bran didn't like the thought of Jesse helping Teya. It bothered him that Jesse could change so quickly, especially after ordering Bran's death. He also didn't believe that Jesse's desire to find the grove was the only reason he helped Teya.

"At first I thought it was Jesse who told Korban about the *kundar*, but now I know it wasn't. Maybe Jesse will help us."

Bran fell silent. Jesse was not someone Bran wanted either of them indebted to. He'd rather figure a way out of this without Jesse. Bran swallowed against the pain in his head and tried to think. Seeing his discomfort, Teya placed the wet cloth on his forehead and he sighed. "Thanks. I'm not in the best shape right now, and my head is pounding like it's on fire."

"I wish there was something I could do to help. I hate to see you like this." Teya gently pushed his hair away from his eyes. "I can still use some of my magic, maybe if I try sending it through the bond it will make a difference."

"Sure, I'm willing to try anything." As she opened the bond, he felt her swirling emotions—despair, tenderness, and underneath them all, a solid wall of rage. He wondered if she was aware of this darkness locked deep inside. Soon, all of these emotions faded as a tendril of warmth flooded into him. He took a deep breath and was immediately consumed in a blanket of well-being. The heat spread into him and he relaxed under the ministrations of her magic. Then coming from a distance, he heard the sweet, healing tones of peace.

"It's all right," she whispered. "Sleep. We'll talk when you wake up." He fought against abandoning her again, but finally gave in. He only needed a few minutes rest, then he'd be in better shape to help her, and if he was lucky, he might even know how.

❧

The sun was shining when he woke, and he was dismayed that he had slept the rest of the night. He sat up, amazed that he felt no pain, in fact, his headache was gone, along with all the injuries he had suffered at Korban's hands. Somehow, Teya had healed him with her magic through the bond. Had it taken her all night?

His wonder turned to panic when he found no trace of her in the room. Where was she? He tried to reach for her through the bond, but felt only a vague impression of irritation. It irked him that she would block him out like that, and it was something he wanted to discuss, but had never had the chance. This bond was useful, but so far, it didn't seem like they had mastered how it worked.

Another idea popped into his head, and the ramifications were mind-boggling. If she had healed him with her power through the bond, could he use her magic in the same way? If she sent her power through the bond and he controlled it? It would take both of them working together, but what if it worked? He wished she were there so they could find out. Maybe it wouldn't be strong enough to do him much good, but it was worth a try.

A key jangled in the lock, and he was relieved that Teya had returned, until the door opened and two palace guards stood in the frame. Bran's heart sank. "You're to come with us," one said. They clapped manacles on his wrists and shoved him into the hall.

"Where?" he asked.

"Korban wants you locked up where he can keep an eye on you."

"But I was already locked up in there," he protested. When the guards ignored him, he knew that was all the explanation he was going to get. With a heavy heart he followed them through the palace. They took the servants' staircase and although Bran watched carefully, he never caught a glimpse of Teya. She probably didn't know. Far below the main floor of the palace, they came abreast a stone staircase with torches lighting the walls. The dank smell of wet stone and rotting wood filled his nostrils. At the bottom, prison cells lined the corridor. Reaching the nearest one, they unlocked the wooden door and pushed him inside.

It was dark, with the only light coming from under the door. It took some time before his eyes adjusted. When they did, he recoiled slightly, realizing he was not alone. Someone was sitting in the corner. The person stood, and with uneven steps, walked toward him. Bran stepped back and there was just enough light to see who it was.

"Jax!" Bran caught his breath.

"Bran?"

"What happened to you?"

Jax shook his head, his voice full of irony. "I got caught. Can you believe it? I watched you leave the outpost in the motorcars and followed at a safe distance. When you didn't come out of the monastery, I decided to find Rasmussen and tell him everything. I didn't get very far before they caught up with me. They brought me here, and I've been here ever since. Why would Colonel Porter do this?"

Bran heaved a huge sigh and sat down on the wooden bench. "You're not going to like it."

Bran explained everything to his friend, that Porter was really Korban, and using the Kaloriahns to make *sym.* "He's using the Braemarians as well, and now that the king is dead, he'll finally have what he wants."

"What's that?"

"Power. If he gets back to the grove, his magical powers will be restored, then what's to stop him from turning on Braemar?"

"Nothing," Jax said. "Nothing at all."

Teya fidgeted with the *kundar*, watching with disinterest as yet another dignitary pledged his loyalty to Chancellor Turner. Sitting on the dais with Turner, she had a clear view of the proceedings. The captain of the Palace Guard along with the military commanders seemed the most pleased. Turner easily won their allegiance.

She glanced at Korban, who sat beside Turner. Korban deferring rule to Turner came as a surprise, but since he was known as Colonel Porter of Braemar it made sense. He must need Braemar for something or he would have declared himself. It was easy to see that Korban and Turner had reached an understanding of some sort, but she could only guess at the details.

Korban's demand this morning that she attend and witness these formal events still irritated her, and she wondered if Bran had woken up yet. She hated leaving him there, but after helping him with her magic through the bond, she was hopeful that he was healed. She smiled to herself, pleased that she had defied Korban and the *kundar*. Hope blossomed to know there was a chance Bran could use her magic through the bond. This possibility was something she needed to talk to him about and sitting here was trying her patience.

She hadn't seen Jesse since he'd left her room the day before. She thought about asking where he was, but didn't want to make anyone suspicious. It was clear he was gone, and she wondered if Korban had sent him away. Did he suspect Jesse of anything?

She knew Bran disliked the thought of asking Jesse for help, but she didn't care. If he could help them, she would ask. How far was Jesse willing to go against Korban? Worse, she didn't know if Jesse had the strength to go against Korban. When it came right down to it, what would Jesse choose? His desire for the grove was real; she knew that, but what about anything else? What about proving he was a true Kaloriahn? What about his feelings for her? Would he go against Korban to win her trust, hoping to earn her love as well?

Finally, the proceedings were over and Turner stood, making a grand speech of peace and prosperity. He spoke of a new alliance with Braemar and 'Colonel Porter' then made a startling announcement that he wished for the wall between their countries to come down. The people seemed stunned at first, but then most began to nod as the idea took root. Change was coming.

Korban addressed the group and talked of bringing trade and commerce between the countries. This was readily accepted, and she could see the speculation of riches in the eyes of several prominent men. The changes this would bring to the Old Country were apparent, but no one seemed to mind.

At the end of his speech, Korban surprised her by making a request that Teya sing. Then Turner followed with his own request, asking with such civility, that she would have appeared mean-spirited to refuse.

She gathered her scattered thoughts together and wondered what to sing that would hurt Korban the most. His direct stare and the tightening around his eyes changed her mind. He had control of Bran's fate, and she must not forget that. She sang instead of loneliness and captivity. When she finished, the hall was hushed and Korban seemed flustered. Apparently that was not what he wanted. Turner graciously thanked her and dismissed the assembly.

"What do you think you're doing?" Korban's fingers dug into her arm. "What we need are feelings of goodwill, not guilt."

"Then don't ask me to sing without telling me what you want first."

"I want a change of attitude. Or do you want Bran dead?"

"Of course not."

"Then next time I ask, sing something that will have them more willing to do my bidding." He waited until she nodded before continuing. "You may go to your room."

It was easy to obey that command and she fled the hall before he changed his mind. She wanted to see Bran more than anything, and when she finally reached the north tower she was breathless. The guard standing at the door ushered her inside and then threw the bolts into place.

The sound echoed through her mind as she registered Bran's absence, and a wave of panic slammed into her chest. She turned and started pounding on the door until the guard opened it, concern spreading over his face. "Where's Bran?" she shouted at him. "Why isn't he here?"

Relief crossed his features. "He's in the dungeon." He pushed the door shut against her protests, and when the bolt dropped into place it was like an arrow through her heart. She sagged onto the bed and fought against the anger that billowed into a consuming cloud of rage. Rational thought fled, and a scream of hot temper tore from her throat. The magic she released rebounded from the *kundar* and back into her with a blinding shock of pain.

Her eyes watered and she gasped for breath, clutching the edge of the bed for balance as nausea tightened her stomach. Once her heart stopped racing, she concentrated on putting her scrambled thoughts into order. Why had Korban done this? Why did he let her have Bran only to take him away again?

Calm, but shaken, she opened the bond to Bran. He answered, strong and solid, and relief found a way into her heart. He strengthened her and she responded with a tone of magic through the bond. Gratitude rippled back to her and she knew whatever she'd done had helped him. It wasn't enough. She wanted him out of there, and vowed that she would not leave her room until Korban let her see him.

Later, when the guard opened her door to join Korban for dinner, she refused. Flustered, he threatened to carry her if she didn't come of her own free will.

"Don't you threaten me," she answered. "I'll use my magic on you if you come anywhere near me."

He laughed, but when he opened his mouth to speak, all that came out was a hoarse croak and Teya smiled knowingly at his discomfort. Sobered, he backed off, slamming the door behind him. It didn't take long before Korban was there. "What is this? What game are you playing?"

"I just want to see Bran, and make sure he's all right."

Korban shook his head in derision. "All you had to do was ask. You can see him in the morning."

"I'm not going anywhere until I see him first."

Korban considered her. "I guess you'll just have to stay here and miss your dinner then." He enjoyed her anger, and she knew it, but couldn't stop the feeling from surging inside. With intense hatred coursing through her veins, she said nothing as he walked out the door.

Her anger was so strong, she wanted to direct it at something, but it wasn't worth breaking her own things. Instead, she occupied herself trying to break the *kundar.* Her anger made her reckless and pushed her to try something she never would have before. She reasoned that if the *kundar* was made using dark power, maybe dark power would get it off. If Korban had the use of dark power, it had to be something she could tap into. Darkness was centered on anger, rage, or revenge, and she had plenty of that to last a lifetime. If she felt these things strong enough, maybe it would break.

It didn't work. No matter how full of anger and rage she became, the magic always bounced back at her through the *kundar.* She gave up trying after her head felt like it was going to explode, and she couldn't stop shaking. The power probably wasn't about dark or light, but more about what the person used it for that made it that way. If it was used for killing and destroying it became dark. She realized she walked a fine line when she let her anger control her. It was something she needed to think about.

She went to sleep that night exhausted and unhappy. Experimenting with her emotions led her to believe what she had thought all along. It was better to lock away her feelings. If she didn't care, she didn't hurt. But she found she couldn't do that anymore, because she realized that either way, she lost. Life wasn't worth living if she didn't have feelings, and without feelings, she wasn't human.

☙ ❧

She spent the next day and night in her room. The only time the door opened was when someone brought her food. It was Korban's way of letting her know he wasn't intimidated by her threats. She had communicated with Bran through the bond as best she could, so she knew he was all right, but it couldn't compare with seeing him.

When the door opened on the second morning, she was ready to do whatever Korban asked for just one glimpse of Bran. The slight figure that entered with a tray of food confused her for a moment. Then she realized it was Cherie, the Kaloriahn woman who had waited on her at the monastery.

"What's going on? Are all the Kaloriahns here?"

Cherie set the tray on the table before answering. "Yes Mistress, all of us are here. Jesse brought us. Most are in the army barracks, out of sight. Korban doesn't want people nervous with so many of us around. He brought me to the palace to serve you."

"How are they?"

"He's held off bleeding them, if that's what you mean. I think he must have enough *sym* to last for a while. He wants everyone to regain their strength for the journey to the grove."

"When does he plan to leave?"

Cherie sighed. "I don't know. I brought the clothes you left at the monastery. I can bring them to you if you like. My room's next door."

"That would be wonderful!" Teya had been worried about the seed, because she hadn't been able to bring her clothes with her. The morning Teya left, Cherie said she'd look after her things. Teya was grateful she kept her word. "Thank you. Please, sit down and eat with me. I've been stuck up here alone for two days. Do you know anything that's going on in the palace?"

"Not exactly. But something big is happening today. They're setting up the banquet tables and making all kinds of food."

"What about Hewson? Is he here too?"

"I think Korban may have brought him, but I'm not sure."

Teya was so grateful to talk to someone that she hardly registered the sound of the door unlocking. It swung open and she jerked with surprise, spilling her drink. Korban strode in with a scowl, and Cherie was so flustered that she jumped up to leave. Korban held up his hand. "You may stay. What I have to say involves you both."

After she sat in nervous silence, Korban began to pace the room. "Today, Rasmussen and the undersecretary of Braemar are coming to negotiate the terms of an alliance between our countries. Rasmussen has asked repeatedly to see you Teya, and I have promised him you will sing for us. I want your word that you will perform something pleasing and beautiful for our entertainment."

"Of course, as long as I can see Bran first."

He shot her a piercing glance and shook his head with annoyance. "I will arrange it, but I don't want Rasmussen to know he's here."

"Why?"

"Rasmussen wants him back, but that cannot happen. Bran knows too much."

"So what will you tell him?"

"That he's dead," he said bluntly. "And he will be too, if you say anything."

"I won't." Her heart skipped a beat. "Just let me see him."

"I'll have the guard escort you down when I leave. After that, I want you dressed in your finest and ready to attend me." He turned his attention to Cherie. "You will follow my earlier instructions."

"Yes sir," Cherie said, bowing slightly. Korban gave Teya a hard stare meant to intimidate her and left the room.

The tension drained away when Korban left, but Teya turned to Cherie with mild disappointment. "What instructions?"

"I was going to tell you before Korban came bursting in. It's nothing really. He has another dress he wants you to wear. I just didn't know he wanted you to wear it today. It's in my room. I'd better take this tray down before I get in trouble. When I get back, I'll bring your things in here."

"All right," Teya said numbly. She couldn't seem to think anymore. Nothing was going right and she didn't know what to do. She swallowed her fears and followed Cherie out the door to the waiting guard. At least she was going to see Bran.

The journey to the dungeons seemed to take forever. She was dismayed at the depths of the palace. She thought her 'box' in the cellar under the kitchens was bad, but now she found there were hidden staircases that she never knew existed. They kept going down until the light faded and they had to light torches to see the way. The final staircase loomed darkly before them, but Teya couldn't seem to move. The dank, clammy air made her skin crawl.

"Come on, then." The guard prodded. "We're almost there, or do you want to go back?"

She cursed her stupid weakness, and swallowing her revulsion, took a step forward. In desperation, she reached out to Bran, needing his strength to move down the last few steps. Assurance poured over her, blocking the fear, and in a moment she was in front of his locked cell.

As the door creaked open, Teya gasped to see two men shielding their eyes from the brightness of the torchlight. The guard nudged her inside and left a torch to burn in a bracket on the wall before closing her in. When Bran lowered his arm, she sagged in relief, just barely keeping the panic at bay.

"Teya! I didn't think they'd ever let you come," Bran said, gathering her in his arms. She couldn't stop trembling and was grateful for his strength.

"What have they done to you?" She pulled away from his awkward embrace and focused on the manacles around his wrists. "How long have these been on?" His wrists were rubbed raw and he was clearly in pain. She focused on the other prisoner and gasped. "Jax?"

"He was here when they brought me down," said Bran.

"That's right," Jax said. "They caught me the night you went to the monastery. I was on my way to tell Rasmussen the whole story, but never made it."

"He's coming here," Teya said.

"Who?"

"Rasmussen. Korban just told me he's coming to sign an alliance between our countries. They don't know who Korban is yet. They still think he's Colonel Porter. Korban let Turner take the king's place as ruler, probably because he's easier to control, and the Kaloriahns just arrived today. Jesse brought them." Teya spoke in a rush, knowing her time was short. "Rasmussen's been asking for you, so Korban's going to tell him you're dead. That the king had you killed for taking me." Bran swore under his breath.

"I had to bargain with Korban to see you," Teya said. "He wants me to sing for Rasmussen tonight, but I can't let him know you're here, or he'll kill you. He'll never let you go, Bran. You know too much. Once Rasmussen thinks you're dead, there's no reason for Korban to keep you alive. With the fate of the Kaloriahns resting on my head, he knows I'll do whatever he wants whether you're here or not."

Urgency flickered across Bran's face. "I've been thinking about this. I want you to send your magic through the bond and see if I can use it to unlock these manacles."

"I did this before from my room. Didn't you feel it?"

"Yes, but I think you were too far away for it to work. Try it now."

She took hold of his hands. "All right." Closing her eyes, she focused on the bond and sent a sweet tone to him. The *kundar* tingled with heat, but she kept the tone light and didn't feel any pain. To her amazement, the manacles popped open and fell to the ground. "It worked!"

"Let's try it on your *kundar*," Bran said.

Hope poured over Teya. If it worked, Korban would know the instant it came off, but she didn't care. With her full power, she could destroy him and anything else that stood in her way. "Go ahead." Again, she sent the magic to Bran. Heat pulsed into the *kundar* and for a moment, Teya thought it would shatter. Then a blinding pain shot through her head and she crumpled to the floor.

Bran sucked in a deep breath. "Damn, I thought we had it. Are you all right?"

The pain receded enough for Teya to open her eyes, but tears blinded her. Bran whispered that he was sorry before she finally got under control.

"It's all right," Teya said, breathlessly, an idea forming in her mind. As Bran helped her stand, she said, "We need to get you out of here. I'm going to ask for Jesse's help." Bran started to protest, but she continued. "He'll do it for me, and if you leave tonight during the reception and get to Rasmussen, you can join him when he crosses the wall and Korban won't know. You'll be away from here and safe. Then you can tell Rasmussen everything."

The jangling of keys in the lock warned them that their time was up. Teya took a startled breath. "Be careful. I'll keep the bond open and send what magic I can in case you can use it."

"I wish there was another way," Bran said.

"It's the only chance we have."

The door swung open, and the burly guard stepped inside. "Time's up. Let's go."

Teya hugged Bran quickly, then moved aside when the guard reached around her to take the torch. On impulse, Teya stopped him with a hand to his chest. "Leave it." Her tone carried the lilt of power not stopped by the *kundar*. It brought the guard up short, and with apprehension, he shrugged and left it, ushering her out and locking the door behind.

Once she started up the stairs, her strength faded and she leaned against the stones for support. Her head resonated with pain and her legs trembled. The guard grumbled at her slowness and took her arm, helping her up the rest of the way. By the time she reached the main hall, the pain had subsided to a dull ache, and she could think again.

Servants were everywhere, readying the palace for the evening's festivities and Teya searched among them hoping to catch sight of Jesse, but the guard would not let her linger. His orders to return her to her rooms left no time for delay.

Cherie was waiting in her rooms when Teya walked through the door. "You look pale, are you all right?"

Teya waited for the guard to leave, then eased into a chair. "Just trying to get this blasted *kundar* off. It backfired and left me with a terrible headache."

"Nothing will take it off."

"Gunpowder will, but it is beyond my reach." Teya sat up, contemplating her next move. "I need to get a message to Jesse. Can you do it? I need to speak to him, but without Korban knowing."

Cherie's eyes clouded with doubt. "Jesse?" Teya could understand her hesitation. Trusting Jesse came hard, but it was a risk she had to take.

"Yes." Teya didn't elaborate. She didn't want Cherie to know more than was absolutely necessary for her own sake.

"I suppose I can get clean towels for you, and accidentally run into him. What should I tell him?"

"Just tell him I need to speak with him privately, before tonight."

Cherie hesitated, her mouth twisting in a frown. "All right."

"Don't worry, I know what I'm going, and I can get ready while you're gone." Cherie straightened her shoulders before turning toward the door. At her knock, the guard opened the door. When she explained what she needed, he let her out, and Teya sighed with relief.

Now all she had to do was convince Jesse to release Bran and Jax. She had saved his life, but was it enough to get him to help her? These questions and more plagued her while she quickly bathed. With the *kundar* around her neck she was helpless against Korban, and Jesse could lose everything if he helped her. Why would he risk it?

The dress Cherie had laid out on the bed was like nothing Teya had ever seen before. The sheer white fabric was iridescent and shimmered with underlying tones of turquoise blue. The bodice molded to her body while the sleeves and skirt feathered out in scarf-like folds. When she looked in the mirror, she was startled by the effect the color had on her eyes. In her oval face, and framed by black hair, her eyes held hidden depths that seemed to capture the light and made them sparkle like jewels. She caught her breath, uncomfortable with the strange image she conjured. There was something about her that didn't look quite normal.

She let out her breath with a huff. Her 'other-worldly' look was just the effect Korban would want, especially in front of Rasmussen and the undersecretary of Braemar. Angry, she contemplated changing into something else when Jesse came through the door, his eyes a haunting mixture of hope and wariness.

Words caught in his throat when he saw her, leaving him momentarily speechless. She took advantage of his silence, realizing her power over him. His desire for her left him vulnerable, and she could use it to suit her needs. She could manipulate him however she wanted and he would do her bidding.

Guilt battled with necessity. It wasn't right, but neither was what they had done to her and her people. How guiltless was Jesse? Whose side was he really on? Could she promise him things she never intended to give?

She lifted her chin and pointed to the *kundar*. "Did you know what Korban did to me? This is real. He coerced me into putting it on with my own hands." Her voice shook with emotion. "A part of me died that night. I am bound. For the sake of my people, I must take Korban to the grove."

Jesse came to her. "I didn't betray you Teya. I didn't tell him it wasn't real. He must have figured it out on his own. Believe me, I'm sorry it happened."

"There is a way to take the *kundar* off." She decided against telling him how, in case he refused. "Bran did it, and I know you can do it too. With my full strength, I am stronger than Korban. He told me this himself. I can defeat him. Let's work together. Take it off me. Tonight. Now."

Jesse went still, his brows drawn low, then shook his head. "Not tonight. There's too much to risk. Korban's always surrounded by soldiers, and with Turner's cooperation, the odds against us are too great. I can do it once we leave here, on the way to the grove. Our chances for success will be better then."

Did he really mean it, or was he just putting her off? Sensing her doubt, he suddenly reached for her hands. "I will do it Teya." He gently cupped her face. "You mean more to me than any ties I have with Korban. I see a future for us in the grove. We're both Kaloriahns, we belong together. It's what I want, but I don't know where you stand, or how you feel."

She flinched at the raw need in him. He wanted her. Would she have to give up Bran in order to save him? Would Jesse help her if she didn't? He studied her, knowing she struggled. "It's Bran, isn't it?" He started to pull away.

"Yes." She drew him back. "He's in the dungeon with Jax. Help them escape. Tonight," she pleaded. "I owe him that much. It will save his life. After he's gone, we can work everything else out together. Just you and me, the way you want."

Conflicting emotions of hope and doubt flooded Jesse's face. As he gazed in her eyes, the hope slowly died, and was replaced with cold calculation. He didn't believe her. Something in her eyes must have given her away. His face was like chiseled stone when he finally spoke. "There might be a way I can free them, so Korban won't know it's me. I'll have to use *sym*." He tightly gripped Teya's arms. "He'll kill me if he finds out. You know that don't you?"

"Yes." She held her breath.

"All right then, I'll do it—for you." He released his crushing hold, but barely held his emotions in check. "And then later, when I remove your *kundar*, you'll have everything you want. But what will I have, Teya? What will you give me?" When she couldn't answer, he turned on his heel, and left.

CHAPTER ELEVEN

A Doubtful Alliance

Teya drew a ragged breath to quell the thundering storm of emotion. Before, it had always been easy to fix an unwavering blankness on her face. Now she could hardly keep her focus centered on one thing. Jesse had upset her with his questions. He was right. Teya was asking a lot of him, and what could she give him in return? She would never give up Bran. Did that make it wrong to ask for his help? At least he hadn't given her an ultimatum.

Cherie entered the room, and after taking one look at Teya, quickly ushered her to a chair and gave her a drink of water. She deftly began to comb Teya's hair while she hummed a soothing melody. Teya closed her eyes and let the melody enfold her, easing out the knots in her shoulders and neck. While Cherie expertly entwined a jeweled circlet into her hair, Teya opened the link to Bran.

Relief and strength flooded into her, quieting the storm. Flowing within this quiet river came another feeling that held everything else together. Love. He loved her. She suddenly wished she had spoken the words while she was with him, but the moment was lost. Instead she sent the feeling to him in a wave. She could almost see his smile of pleasure. It was enough to bring tears to her eyes. His life was all that mattered to her now. Even if she could never share it with him.

Squaring her shoulders and her resolve, she was ready. "Thank you Cherie, you've helped me a great deal."

"Good luck tonight, Mistress," she said. "I'll let them know you're ready."

It seemed like hours before the door opened again and three palace guards escorted her down to the main staircase above the great hall. Korban was waiting on the landing, and took her arm in a courtly manner. "I offered Jesse the honor of escorting you into the hall, but he refused. Did you have an argument?"

"Of course not," Teya protested, but color stained her cheeks.

"Hmm." Korban scrutinized her. "Jesse covered for you when you killed the king. I've been watching him ever since. He was covered in blood that night, but I never understood that it was his. You saved his life didn't you?" Her silence was all the confirmation he needed. "Maybe for that I won't kill Bran. It will depend on how convincing you are tonight. I want Rasmussen to think you are acting of your own free will."

"Kindness would go a lot further than your threats Colonel Porter, but have no fear, I won't let you down."

He smiled at her comeback, as if he was pleased, and she didn't know if it was sincere, or only for the benefit of the large crowd watching them. It was a huge gathering. The vast hall was filled with all the high-ranking officials in the kingdom. At the high table, everyone stood as she was introduced. Rasmussen was an imposing figure who took in everything with analytical consideration. He would be a hard man to lie to. It was on the tip of her tongue to tell him that Bran and Jax were in the dungeon below them.

"After spending the last few hours working out the fine print of the alliance, it's a welcome break to finally meet you," Rasmussen said. "Now seeing you, I can understand why Bran was so willing to help you escape. With King Thesald dead, I suppose that's no longer a problem. I was half expecting to see him here with you. He doesn't have to run anymore. In view of these latest developments, all charges have been dropped."

There was an awkward silence before Korban spoke. "Tell him Songbird."

Only Korban would be so cruel, and she was sorely tempted to tell Rasmussen the truth. Teya cleared her throat. "It's difficult for me to say," she stammered, to cover her hesitation. Korban frowned with warning and she haltingly continued. "You see...the king...had Bran...killed when we first got here."

Rasmussen paled at the news. "I had no idea. What happened?"

"King Thesald was furious," Turner said when Teya was silent. "He had Bran executed before the large crowd we had here, and in front of Colonel Porter and his soldiers. Bran may have been out of favor with your government, but you can imagine the outrage this act sparked among your soldiers. It was in the commotion that followed between our soldiers and yours, that the king received the fatal blow that killed him. Luckily, more of us wanted an alliance than a war, and cooler heads prevailed. Colonel Porter and his men did an excellent job of maintaining peace. I credit him for this alliance now."

"Thank you for telling me what happened, Chancellor Turner," Rasmussen regained his composure. "Colonel Porter was too modest to tell me his part in all this. Bran was a good man. I am saddened to hear he is gone."

Turner motioned to Teya. "Perhaps our Songbird can ease some of your sorrow with her beautiful voice."

Rasmussen keenly scrutinized her. "Are you sure you're up to it? I would be happy to wait if now is not a good time."

"No. I would be honored to sing for you in his memory." Teya dutifully went to her place on the dais, hating this charade she was forced to play. She could imagine Rasmussen's reaction if he found out both Bran and Jax were being held against their will. And how disturbed he would be to know she had killed the king. She hoped she didn't regret not telling him the truth, but there was too much to lose if it went wrong.

After being part of such blatant lies about the events of that day, it was difficult to center herself, and find the proper voice to sing. She had to be careful. Bran's life depended on this moment and how she handled it.

That gave her an idea. As her tones of a lilting melody filled the hall, she opened the bond to Bran. By funneling the magic to him, she was able to increase the tolerance of her power over the *kundar*. With the bond siphoning off the magic that would normally bounce back at her, she was much stronger than before. She funneled as much magic to Bran as she could, hoping he could use it, despite the distance between them.

Once her song took hold of the people listening, she magnified their feelings of contentment and well-being, then sent them back in an ever-widening circle. The effect was a beautiful kaleidoscope of color that laced through the air and flickered over the room like a prism. The reaction was awe-inspiring, and she integrated that emotion as well, heightening the experience into ripples of pleasure. Even Korban seemed spellbound.

When her gaze fell on Jesse, his attention was focused, not on the effects of the song, but on her mastery of it. He was studying how she wove the tones together and used emotion to bring the crowd under her control. His concentration centered within the music, like he was trying to understand what she was doing and how it worked.

In a way it unnerved her that he could see the patterns behind the magic. It also confirmed that he was a true Kaloriahn. Ready to finish, she brought the music to a climax and began the slow descent back to reality. It was then that she heard the barely audible undertones that flowed beside her own. It was Jesse. As her tones melted into the air, his did as well, leaving the hall adrift in an aching silence.

The power dissipated, and the crowd leapt as one in overflowing appreciation. They clapped and cheered with approval, begging for more. Korban seemed pleased, although a bit taken back by the phenomenon, and she realized he had never been present when she'd sung. It was the first time he had experienced her power the way it was meant to be. She detected an unguarded vulnerability about him before the fissure closed into something hard and cold.

Turner led her to an empty chair beside his and she gratefully sat at the high table, drained from the exertion. She had a vague sense of Bran, but nothing more. Jesse moved his chair to her side and deftly fielded the questions that arose. Several key officials surrounded her, remarking on her beauty and offering their services. Others petitioned Turner for the chance to have her attend their various functions as an honored guest.

With her song, the attitude of the people changed. She lost the enmity of the crowd. Suddenly, she was not a monster, but someone to admire and adore. They were no longer afraid. Already, people were jostling for her favor. They were in awe of her, and treated her with a fevered reverence that made the hairs stand on the back of her neck. It was almost like they wanted a piece of her. Already, more than one person had tried to take her hand and kiss it. Someone touched her arm, then another patted her back.

A strange buzzing settled around her, growing like a swarm of bees. She felt like bait for a wild predator, and if she wasn't careful, she would be eaten alive.

She stood abruptly and the whole room tensed in watchfulness. Her mouth went dry, but she managed to say, "Please, may I be excused?" Turner quickly acquiesced and Korban announced that he would escort her to her rooms, taking the opportunity away from Jesse, who frowned at being thwarted. As Korban took her arm, the speculation in his eyes distressed her, and she tensed in response.

"That was an interesting display," Korban said under his breath. "Your power seemed stronger. Are you sure that *kundar* is working?"

She flashed him a quelling look. "Of course it's working. You'd be dead if it wasn't."

Korban's suspicion turned to relief, and he smiled, appreciating her audacity. "Don't you see what happened back there? You had complete control of the crowd. With your full magic, you could convince everyone within the sound of your voice to do whatever you wanted. I can use magic on one or two people at once, but my influence usually doesn't last long. But you could control and manipulate anyone, and half of them would thank you for it. They adore you. In time, they could begin to worship you."

"They only want me for what it would get them. Like you."

"You're wrong. You didn't feel the change come over them, but if you think about it, you'll see what I mean. They know you are more than human. In time, with or without fear, they would do anything you asked."

"True or not, it's not right. People should have choices."

"Not if it's for their own good."

"And who determines that? You?" Teya could see where he was going with this and it sickened her.

"You've just given me the hope I need to fulfill my dreams. Once I get to the grove and have my powers restored, I can do much more than conquer Braemar."

His meaning wasn't lost on her. "That's not our way. Kaloriahns are the keepers of creation. Our magic will only survive as long as the grove is protected and we uphold the sanctity of life."

"That's true. Our magic is tied to the grove, and we must return, but we are a far superior race than the race of man. We have been given magic and immortality because we were chosen to be rulers. Leona never told you that we are also the chosen guardians of men. It is through us that men survive. Now is the time for Kaloriahns to take back their rightful place in the world. The revered place of the Immortals."

Teya was unnerved by his vehement declaration. He had taken the commitment of the Kaloriahns and the grove, and twisted it into something dark and self-serving, all the while making it appear good and right. Using these god-given powers to obtain the loyalty of men, and then dominating and controlling them with it.

"You don't understand who we are and what we are capable of becoming," he said reasonably. "Until you do, you will always limit yourself. Open your mind to the possibilities. Immortality and magic point to one thing. When you figure it out, we will talk again."

They were standing in front of her door. Korban opened it and ushered her in before Teya could respond. As the lock clicked into place she sank down onto the bed with a troubled frown. Korban was mad. And dangerous. She had no doubt what he meant, and it made her blood turn to ice. He spoke of being a god.

⁂

Bran sensed the moment Teya used her magic. Echoes of her song drifted through the cracks of the palace and came to rest over everything like a fine mist. When she opened the bond, it flowed into him with a warmth that took his breath away. Somehow, she was circumventing the *kundar* and sending the magic to him.

He shifted his concentration to the wooden door of his cell and breathed out tones that he prayed would open the lock. Metal strained against his tones and he pushed harder until there came a definite snap. He grinned at Jax who stared with open-mouthed amazement. "It's Teya," he reassured him. "She's sending the magic to me through the bond." Bran had tried to explain to Jax what the bond was all about, but wasn't sure Jax understood. Not that it mattered; it was something Bran hardly understood himself.

Bran scanned the lower reaches of the dark hall, and seeing no one, hurried out. With Jax behind him, they moved stealthily toward the staircase and the flickering torches. Two guards were stationed in the upper hallway, but neither was at their post. Bran caught sight of them at the foot of the next staircase listening to Teya sing.

He wasn't sure where this hallway went, but motioned Jax to follow him in the opposite direction of the guards. Luckily, most of the inhabitants of the palace had congregated near the banquet hall to listen to Teya and the hallways were deserted. They took several turns before coming to an outside wall and window where Bran could get his bearings. The window was about six feet above the ground and close to the outer gardens. Hope flared, he knew this area from before, and all they needed to do was get outside.

The window was stuck shut, but Bran directed the still-pulsing magic to it, and when it swung open, hurried out. Jax followed and they quickly covered the ground toward the stables and waiting Braemarian carriages. The crunch of boots on gravel spurred them to dive into the bushes for cover, and Bran was grateful for his dirt-streaked face when two palace guards walked past.

While waiting to make sure they weren't coming back, Bran felt the magic thin as Teya's song ended, leaving him on his own. A sense of loss was tempered by the necessity to get out of there as fast as possible. From the corner of the palace garden, the carriages stood waiting on the gravel path. The only problem lay in getting past the guards standing between them.

Jax nudged Bran. "We'll have to go around. See over there?" He pointed to the dense foliage on the other side of the carriage path. "The guards aren't watching that side. We might be able to climb aboard before we're seen."

Bran nodded and they began the long trek around the gardens and outbuildings. With the stables and carriage house in the way, it took precious time to get to the other side, especially when they had to keep to the shadows and slip between the large numbers of stable hands wandering around. It was a relief to finally get to the trees on the other side. Several yards from his goal, Bran's heart nearly stopped when Rasmussen and the others came out of the palace. Within moments they were boarding the carriages.

Bran was just about to make a run for it when Jax stumbled and fell. Lurching to help him up, the unmistakable whoosh of an arrow sailed past his head. He ducked to get out of the way, and pulled Jax down after him. They scrambled on hands and knees toward the carriages, but didn't get far before he and Jax were immediately surrounded.

With arrows pointing directly at their hearts, Bran and Jax raised their hands in surrender.

"Good decision," the officer said, then spoke to the others. "Tie them up and take them to the guard house."

Including the officer, there were five of them. They were King Thesald's soldiers, now loyal to Chancellor Turner. Bitter disappointment churned through Bran. They were so close! The soldiers bound his hands tightly behind his back, then tied his legs so he could barely shuffle. If not for that, Bran would have run for it. He cringed at the sound of the carriages passing beyond the palace grounds. His chance for escape was gone.

They were marched to the guardhouse, then taken inside to a tiny cell and locked up. One man stayed beside the cell, but the others left and Bran wondered why they had been brought here instead of the palace dungeon. This guardhouse was at the far end of the palace grounds, and bordered a street into the city. It was different from the one with the tunnel to Braemar under it, and Bran doubted that this guardhouse held any kind of escape route.

"Let's see if we can get these off," Bran said. Jax agreed and they turned back-to-back and fumbled with the knots in the rope. It was slow going, but they were soon rewarded when the ropes loosened. Impatiently, Bran tugged at the rope until he got his right hand free, and the rest fell away.

Jax slumped down to the ground and rubbed his twisted ankle. Bran got the ropes untied from his legs and set to searching the walls and window for any kind of weakness. His search was fruitless and he threw himself next to Jax in defeat, realizing it was over. They were stuck here.

The night progressed into the early hours of morning before the crunch of gravel roused him. He came to his feet, but staggered back when a bright light shone through the bars in the door.

"I wondered if you would try to escape, and I still don't know how you did it." The voice belonged to Chancellor Turner, and he sounded quite pleased. The guard opened the door and preceded Turner, training a gun on them. "I hope you don't mind the extra precautions, but I can't be too careful." Turner strolled to a bench along the far wall and sat, leaning forward as he spoke.

"I have to admit, you two are pretty resourceful, that's why I have a proposition for you."

"For us?" Bran could hardly believe what he was hearing.

"That's right," Turner continued noting his surprise, "I want to work together. I know who Colonel Porter really is. I had to support him to get rid of the king, but now I find myself in a precarious position. Korban has big plans, but he's dangerous.

"I've known Korban for a long time. He brought the Songbird to me as a gift for the king. He made an alliance with the king by supplying him with *sym* in exchange for anything Korban wanted. First, the Kaloriahns were hunted down and turned over to Korban at his request. He controlled the amount of *sym* that came into our country, and now yours. He has grown rich and powerful, but it wasn't enough.

"What I didn't know until now was that he is a Kaloriahn." Turner paused, and Bran could sense his revulsion. "He even brought the Kaloriahns here, but luckily they are all collared. Apparently, Korban lost his power, but now he says he knows how to get it back. I can't let that happen.

"He commands a small army of his own, but I am the commander of the king's soldiers. Their allegiance is to me. If it comes to a fight, they will fight against him."

"What do you want with us?" Bran asked.

"Korban is planning to return to this lost grove of his. It has something to do with restoring his powers, but that's all he will say. He told me that you know where the grove is. I was thinking that you could lead us there ahead of him. He has to be stopped before he gets to the grove, and it can only be done with your help."

Bran's mind raced with the turn of events. He never thought Turner would betray Korban, but given his dislike of the Kaloriahns, he could understand why. "Not all Kaloriahns would misuse their power, but you are right about Korban. I agree that he needs to be stopped. I have only one request."

"Teya," Turner said.

"Yes. She's mine."

"Agreed. It's settled then, you'll help us?"

"Yes, we'll help."

The guard had lowered his gun a long time ago and now put it away. "I need to keep your presence a secret, but I'll have clothing and food brought. You'll be dressed as the king's soldiers and will probably leave tomorrow. If I don't get back before you go, Robert here will deliver our messages. Is there anything else?"

"Yes," Bran said. "Who will be commanding your army?"

"Me. Don't worry, I have it all worked out." Turner stood to leave. "I'll have Robert show you to your new quarters. Now get some sleep if you can."

Sleep? Bran doubted that would happen for a long time. Robert ushered them into a different room, a bunkhouse with mattresses and blankets. "I'm keeping watch for the night, so let me know if you need anything," he added, before closing the door behind him. Bran tested the door. It wasn't locked.

"What do you think?" Bran asked Jax. "Can we trust Turner?"

"It's hard to say," Jax answered. "He's sincere about stopping Korban."

"True. I wish I knew more about his plans. His dislike of the Kaloriahns bothers me, but this turn of events is a complete surprise."

"I know. Did you ever think we'd be helping Turner get rid of Korban?" Jax shook his head with disbelief.

"No. That's what makes me uneasy. But he has his reasons, and they make sense. That doesn't mean we can't make plans of our own." Bran refused to let anyone dictate his own actions, especially with something as uncertain as this. He was convinced Turner hadn't told him everything, but it was the chance he was looking for to stop Korban. It would work as long as Teya and the Kaloriahns made it to the grove. That was something Turner didn't need to know about, along with the fact that Bran meant to take off their collars.

❧

Teya was eating breakfast when Korban burst in. "You," he pointed at Cherie, "out! Go to your room and stay there!" After casting a worried glance at Teya, Cherie calmly left the room. Teya swallowed back her fear and settled the mask of indifferent boredom over her features. It had served her well with the king; it would do the same with Korban.

"I don't know how you did it, but Bran and Jax are gone."

She hid her surprise, careful not to let him know how his news affected her. She had hardly slept last night, worrying if Jesse would follow through with her request. Then later, worrying that Bran would get caught and killed. She'd tried to reach him several times through the bond, but the only thing that came was a lingering awareness that he was there. She understood it now.

Korban stopped pacing and jerked her up by the arms. "It doesn't matter where they've gone. I will find them, but don't think you can get away with it. If that *kundar* won't hold back enough of your power, I know something else that will." He began to pull her toward the door, and she knew he meant to take her blood.

"Wait! I can't help you get past the Destroyer if I'm too weak." She didn't want to lay suspicion for Bran's disappearance on Jesse, but neither did she want to endure another bloodletting.

Her outburst seemed to restore a sense of calm to Korban and he slowed his angry steps. "By the time we get to the grove, you will be well enough. It didn't kill you last time. It is the present that concerns me. I don't have time to waste on you." His black eyes were hot with anger, and she flinched away from his malevolent gaze. As they continued out the door, he jerked hard on her arm and she stumbled.

He pulled her down the stairs so fast it was all she could do to keep up without falling. They rounded the corner to what used to be the king's rooms, and continued down the hall, passing several rooms until coming to another flight of stairs. At the bottom of this staircase, they came to a halt in front of the room she had been in that first day after saving Jesse.

The door was open and Jesse was sitting at a desk with a quill in his hand. His startled glance indicated he knew nothing about Korban's plans. He stood, and in a calm, soothing voice asked, "What's going on?"

"I need your help to draw her blood." He shoved Teya down on the bed. "She is responsible for Bran's escape, and I intend to stop her from doing any more damage."

Jesse plastered an agreeable expression on his face, and Teya felt sure he had dealt with his father like this many times before. "Certainly. Let me get my things. I've finished with the letter you asked me to write. If it needs to be off soon, I'd better find a messenger now, or do you want me to wait?"

Korban stilled while his anger subsided and focused on Jesse. "It needs to go now."

"Why don't you let me take care of this unpleasantness with Teya? You've got more important things to do. I can manage her."

Korban's eyes narrowed shrewdly at Jesse, not missing the meaning behind his words. "I suppose you're right. Here, give me that letter and I'll send it off." He took the envelope from Jesse and looked at Teya. "You probably won't take as much blood as I would. Maybe that's a good thing. In the state I'm in, I'd probably kill her, and that would put a damper on my plans." He turned back to Jesse. "Go ahead. Just be sure to take her back to her room after you're done." There was a veiled threat in that statement. Did Korban suspect she and Jesse had talked, or worse, made plans of their own? Korban stalked from the room and Jesse followed, closing the door as he left.

A troubled frown creased his brow when he came to Teya's side. "We can't let him know we're working together," he said under his breath. "If he suspects anything at all, he'll keep us apart."

"Why do you think I kept my mouth shut about Bran's escape? He thinks I did it with my power, and that this *kundar* isn't strong enough," she said, pausing. "Korban knows I healed you. He knows you covered for me that day, but it didn't stop him from bringing me to you now. He obviously has no idea you're the one who got Bran out." Thoughts of losing her blood curdled her stomach. "Are you sure you have to do this? It's only been a few days since the last time. It will weaken me too much. What if it makes me sick?"

"You'll be fine. I'll make sure of it. But I have to do this or Korban will know." Jesse pulled a black bag from a dresser drawer and set it on the bed beside her. He took out several instruments and arranged them in order, working with an air of efficiency that sent a chill through her. How many times had he done this to his own people?

"Your frown isn't making this any easier," Jesse said. "But I have to take some blood, even if it's not very much." When she didn't look at him he continued. "I promise it won't hurt you. By tonight you'll be back to normal."

His earnest expression eased her distrust, even though it wasn't enough to quell the ugliness of what he was going to do. She didn't know which punishment was worse, the box, or this.

"It will be easier if you lie back on the pillows."

This was ridiculous! In a burst of anger, she shot off the bed and ran to the door.

Jesse got there first. "Don't fight me Teya, please." He grabbed hold of her arms, his fingers digging into her soft flesh. "This is hard for me too." She struggled until she was breathless, then sagged against him. He loosened his hold and held her tenderly until her breathing settled down.

She pulled away. "Are you sure you have to do this? It's so wrong!"

"I know," he said. "But for now, we have to do what he says. Once we're away from here, it will be different. I'm making plans, but I can't implement them until we're on our way to the grove. It's too dangerous here. Too many people are watching."

"All right." She knew people were watching, but would it be any different when they left? Jesse thought it would, so for now, she'd have to believe him. "The only reason I can do this is because you helped Bran. I know I probably seem ungrateful, but this is a bitter thing for me to do." She took her place on the bed, and when he didn't say anything, realized he was still upset with her. "I'll be good, I promise." A faint smile creased his face while he pushed the sleeve of her shirt above her elbow.

The silence stretched between them while he got everything ready and she realized there was a lot she didn't know about him. "Where did you learn to do all this?"

"In Braemar," he answered. "I grew up there from the time I was about seven."

"With Korban?"

"Yes. When Korban left the grove, my mother went with him. I was born shortly after that, but we didn't see much of my father. He spent most of his time trying to find a way back into the grove. When I was seven, my mother got sick and sent for him. I think she died partly because of her yearning for the grove. It was home to her, and something she never got over. After we buried her, Korban stopped trying to go back to the grove, and we left for Braemar shortly after that."

Teya was surprised that Jesse's mother left the grove. Korban was banished, but it was hard to believe they'd banish his wife as well. Maybe Korban forced her to leave because of the child. His son. She shivered, realizing how important Jesse was to Korban. They'd made a life together, and Teya wondered if Jesse would have the will to defy his father when the time came.

Before she knew it, Jesse was filling up a small bottle with her blood. Her stomach went queasy at the sight, and she closed her eyes, hoping Jesse would stop. With each small bottle she willed it to be enough, but he kept going until she wasn't sure he would ever stop. Finally, he pulled the needle from her arm and had her hold a piece of cloth over the wound.

"I know that looks like a lot of blood," Jesse said, motioning to the five small bottles he had filled. "But you would have to lose a lot more than that to really feel the effects. It's probably not enough to satisfy Korban, but it will have to do. At least you won't be so weak this time."

Teya watched while Jesse carefully poured the blood into smaller vials. Next, he added several drops of a milky-white substance that caused the blood to bubble and change to a rusty pink color. Then, he corked the vials to seal them. *Sym*. And Jesse made it.

"What is that white liquid you put in it?"

"It's a plant extract. It preserves the blood, and enhances the ability to ingest it into your own body. At first, Korban tried drinking pure blood, but it always made him sick. The plant extract alters it enough to make it digestible."

Teya was sickened by a momentary vision of Korban drinking blood. She wondered if he would ever resort to actually doing that if he ran out of *sym*, and small tremors of revulsion shivered over her.

"Are you cold?" Jesse asked.

"I'm fine." She lied, not wanting Jesse to know her thoughts.

His eyebrows drew together quizzically, but he didn't say anything, and she was relieved he let it go. She was uncomfortable with his casualness toward *sym*, and his ease in making it, like it was nothing out of the ordinary. Especially when it had cost some of her people their own lives.

She closed her eyes against the repulsiveness of it all and took a deep breath. At least Bran had escaped, and she focused on that. She must have dozed off for a minute, because the next thing she knew, Jesse was gently shaking her shoulder.

"I need to take you back to your room," Jesse said.

"I guess I fell asleep." Teya sat up and waited for the room to stop spinning before she stood. Jesse put an arm around her waist to steady her before they began the trek up the stairs. Teya needed his strength and didn't pull away, even though it was his fault she was weak. Not him, she amended—Korban. This was Korban's doing, but even as she thought it, a part of her couldn't help blame Jesse as well. The only thing that made it easier was the fact that Jesse had helped Bran escape. If not, Bran would probably be dead by now. She owed Jesse a lot for that.

They reached her room, and her stomach growled when the aroma of food from the table reached her nose. She was suddenly famished.

"It will do you good to eat," Jesse said. His tone of compassion caught her off-guard, and when she studied him, she could feel his struggle with guilt for what he had done. "I'm sorry for taking your blood," he continued. "I didn't want to, and I wish I had a choice, but it was the only thing I could do."

"It's all right. I understand you had to do it." His relief seemed forced, and she wondered if there was something else he wasn't happy about.

"I'd better go." He turned to leave.

"Wait. We didn't get a chance to talk about your plans. Can you stay for a few more minutes?"

He shook his head. "I can't. I've got to get back. Korban wants to leave for the grove in a few days, and there's a lot I have to do before then. Just try and stay out of his way, all right?"

His comment triggered a question she'd been wondering about. "Do you know where Bran went? Did he get out with Rasmussen?"

Jesse shrugged. "I don't know for sure, but I suspect that's what happened. It wasn't until after Rasmussen was gone that Bran and Jax were discovered missing. There's been no trace of them since."

"At least Korban doesn't suspect you. That's good."

"Yes. I have you to thank for that. Get some rest. I'll try and come back later and let you know what's going on."

"Wait." She hated to sound so needy, but he was all she had. "I know the other Kaloriahns are here. Do you think Korban would let me stay with them? He doesn't need me here anymore, does he? I would like to see my brother."

Jesse huffed and crossed to the door. His voice was harsh when he spoke. "I don't know, and I don't think now is a good time to ask. Maybe tomorrow he'll be in a better mood. I really need to go."

After he shut the door, the lock clicked into place, leaving her alone and confused. She tried to make sense of everything that had happened, but she was too tired. She didn't feel much different from the first time they'd taken her blood. But it was easy to tell she couldn't have used her magic, even without the *kundar*. Korban had made sure of that.

She wondered if Jesse had a special place put aside for her *sym*, and if he kept any for himself. Why wouldn't he? He was certainly used to using it. Where did he keep all the vials of *sym* anyway? A sudden vision of breaking them all gave her a sense of satisfaction, but it didn't last long. Korban would probably take it out on her or someone she loved. At least it wouldn't be Bran.

Bran was gone. Hopefully, he had made it out with Rasmussen. She hated to think about him being caught, and tried to open the link between them, but nothing happened. What if taking so much of her blood had broken the link? A melancholy sadness came over her and she realized how much she depended on Bran. His strength was what kept her going. She was relieved that he was gone, but it felt like a bright light had been taken from her, and she panicked. Did this mean that he was dead? No, of course not. She was only tired.

He was probably far away in Braemar. Hopefully, he was making plans with Rasmussen to come after them. When she was stronger tomorrow, she would try the link again, and this time, he would be there.

She only had to hold out for a few more days. If they left for the grove then, she would have enough strength built up so that once Jesse took off her *kundar*, she could defeat Korban. It would work out. She had to believe that. Otherwise, she might as well be dead.

CHAPTER TWELVE

Road to the Grove

Bran rolled his shoulders against the tightness of his new uniform and was grateful to still have full movement in his arms. It would take him a while to get used to wearing the king's colors, but he had to admit, it was nice to have a sword, knife and gun again. He was still shocked that Turner allowed him the weapons, even though a king's soldier wouldn't look right without them. It meant Turner was holding up his side of the bargain and trusted their arrangement. Turner probably understood how Bran felt about Teya, which was a far more compelling reason to cooperate than any other.

He smoothed his hair away from his face one last time before slipping on his gloves. With several days' growth of beard, and his hair slicked back, he definitely looked like a king's soldier. Most people never looked a soldier in the face, but that didn't mean he shouldn't stay in the background as much as possible. As long as Korban's men didn't notice him, he should be all right.

With the Kaloriahns staying in the barracks along with Korban's army, they had displaced the king's soldiers. Turner had to move them to the garrison outside the city gates. This served Turner well, since he didn't want Korban suspicious of his preparations for a confrontation.

Jax entered the room and Bran hardly recognized him. He had trimmed his shaggy hair and beard, and with the uniform, looked like a different person. That was the thing about Jax, his nondescript features always made it easy for him to blend in.

"They're waiting," Jax announced.

Bran nodded and followed him out the door. Ten soldiers on horseback had arrived, and adding Bran and Jax, made an even dozen. They mounted up and took position within the group before riding out. Bran took a quick glance at the palace and the north tower, wondering how Teya was and what she was doing. Did she know he had escaped because of her magic?

Soon, they were passing through the palace gate into the city. With the passing of the king, the mood of the city had changed. Furtive glances were replaced by easy greetings and friendly banter. The king's soldiers drew hardly a glance, and before long they neared the northern garrison just outside the city wall.

Bran breathed easier after leaving the city behind, certain no one would recognize him here. Turner wanted to leave today, but Bran didn't know how he would explain that to Korban. He found out once they entered the garrison. It was half-empty.

"Most of the men have gone on ahead," Robert, Turner's aide, said. "The Chancellor didn't want anyone to be aware that a large group of King Thesald's soldiers was gathering here. We will combine forces with them at the next garrison. In the meantime, we're to wait here for the Chancellor, he'll be riding with us."

Bran dismounted and joined the other soldiers as if he belonged. There was plenty to do, and soon he was busy making preparations and gathering supplies. He wanted to make sure he had enough ammunition, and sent Jax to find the wire they needed to take the *kundar* off each of the Kaloriahns. The day passed quickly, but as evening approached with no sign of Turner, Bran grew uneasy. All of them did. Had Turner run into a problem? What about Teya? Had Korban found out she had helped him escape? He was consoled by the distant, but steady awareness of her through the bond, and relaxed his vigil.

They slept that night with their clothes on, ready to leave at a moment's notice. It was all in vain. The morning came with no word from Turner, and Bran quelled his uneasiness by reaching for Teya through the bond. The contrast between yesterday and today hit him with such force, that his stomach clenched with fear. The steady awareness had changed into sudden heat. It was like hitting a wall of fire and he knew that something was desperately wrong. Teya was in trouble.

✲✲

Teya woke with a pounding headache. She had thrown off the covers sometime in the night and now lay shivering, covered in a sheen of sweat. Hot and cold at the same time, all she wanted was a drink of water. The room swam when she sat up and she fought back sudden nausea. After a few deep breaths, things settled down and she reached for the glass of water on the bed stand.

Her fingers shook, but the water cooled her parched throat. Having never been sick a day in her life, it took a moment for her to realize what was wrong. Her head was hot and feverish, her throat sore and dry, and her hands trembled with weakness. She groaned inwardly, realizing that taking her blood had caused this to happen. Korban was an idiot, and so was Jesse.

The lock rattled in the door and Cherie entered with a tray of food. She took one look at Teya and gasped before muttering under her breath, "Those stupid fools. You'd think they'd learn." After touching Teya's forehead she announced, "You're burning up. Lie back down and rest. You need a healer, and only Hewson can help you now. I'll have to tell Korban to send for him."

Hewson? Just the thought of being able to see her brother made the fever bearable. She didn't realize Hewson knew how to heal, but it made sense. His power was stronger than most, but with the *kundar* stifling him, it couldn't be much. She hoped it was enough to help her.

Cherie returned with a pot of tea, Korban right behind her. He came to Teya's bedside and stood over her with a scowl. Teya weakly sat up in alarm, but Korban left without saying a word.

"Don't worry," Cherie said. "He had to see for himself. Now he'll send for Hewson. Sit up and let's get some tea down you."

Grateful for Cherie's intervention, she eagerly took the proffered cup, but it wasn't until after the second refill that she started to feel better. "It has ground willow bark in it," Cherie explained. "It helps lower the fever."

"Sounds like you've done this before," Teya said.

"Yes. We Kaloriahns never get sick unless we take too much blood, and that varies from person to person. We never know how much is too much, so it's happened quite a bit. Korban is so greedy, he never seems to know when to stop."

Cherie's disgust floated over Teya in a wave that quickly dissipated when Hewson came through the door. He hurried to her side and gently held her hand. "It's good to see you," Teya said. "It's worth being sick for." That brought a smile to his face and eased the concern. With his black hair and turquoise eyes she was struck again at how much they resembled each other. And how much she had missed over the years.

"I'm glad to see you too. When I heard you had the fever, I was upset. Furious is more like it. I can't believe he took more of your blood! What did you do to deserve this?"

"Bran and Jax escaped and Korban blamed me," she explained. "He was livid! But with Bran gone, I'm hoping he will bring some men from Braemar to help free us."

"Bran would do that?"

"Yes, of course."

"Then we'd better get to work. With Cherie's help we'll have you better in no time."

He glanced at Cherie and something radiant passed between them, then he focused his attention back on Teya. "I want you to close your eyes and relax." Teya did as he asked and felt the soothing tones of his beautiful voice immediately. Cherie's harmonic tones joined his, and the fire raging through her body was soon cooled by a penetrating resonance that swept over her in a wave. The tones became deeper, soaking into her bones with soothing clarity before coming to a sudden halt.

The healing in her blood had barely begun before Hewson stopped in pain, and the tones were ripped away. Hewson breathed heavily, his mouth open and beads of perspiration dotting his forehead. Healing her had cost him dearly, and he slumped in frustration. "The *kundar*," he panted. "I couldn't finish."

"I feel better," she said earnestly. "I'm sure it helped."

"Good." He nodded. "But until your blood rebuilds, the fever will probably come back. We might need to do this again."

Teya understood they were too exhausted to be of any more help right now. Grateful for what he had done, she hugged him tightly. "Thanks." His arms wrapped around her. "Take me back with you. I want to be with you and the others."

He started to speak, but the opening door cut him off. Korban and Jesse strode in and Hewson slowly pulled away. "Is she any better?" Korban asked.

"For now," Hewson answered. "But I couldn't heal her completely. She'll probably have a relapse." He stood and faced Korban with a fierceness Teya hadn't expected. "Don't bleed her again. She might die the next time."

Korban stiffened before he spoke. "Don't make me regret sending for you." Neither spoke for a long time.

"How are you feeling now?" Jesse asked Teya, breaking the tension.

"Better," she said, grateful for the diversion.

"Good, because we wanted to talk about how soon we can leave for the grove," Jesse said.

"I want to leave today," Korban said harshly. "If you're not well enough, you can ride in a supply wagon, but I don't want to delay any longer."

"That's fine with me," she agreed. "If I start to feel sick, I can find the wagon."

"You don't know what you're saying," Hewson argued. "You may feel fine now, but the fever will come back."

"Then you can help me." Teya knew it didn't matter to Korban if she was well enough, and Hewson would only make things worse. "We can ride together. Korban is right. We need to get to the grove as soon as we can. Grandmother needs us." She hated being on Korban's side, but if it would stop the arguing it was worth it. Besides, there was no point in staying here, especially if Jesse was going to help her get the *kundar* off. Of course, having the *kundar* off wouldn't help her much if she was too weak to use her magic, but it would help her heal faster.

"We'll leave within the hour." Korban turned to Hewson. "Make sure your people are ready."

Hewson said nothing and Korban left the room, followed by Jesse, who glanced at her meaningfully.

"I think Korban's afraid of you," Hewson said. "Afraid of your power even with the *kundar* on."

"That's why he took my blood—to weaken me. For some reason, he thought I helped Bran and Jax escape. He scares me, yet when I sang the other day, I sensed a vulnerability in him."

"Don't let him fool you," Hewson said. "He is a master manipulator, and will stop at nothing to get what he wants. Nothing. Remember that. And don't forget, Jesse's not much better. Look who he's learned from."

Hewson had a point, but he didn't know what Jesse had done for her, and she decided now was not the time to tell him. "I'd better go," he said. "But I'll see you again soon." With a departing glance at Cherie, he left the room.

"We'll have to make sure we take plenty of that tea," Teya said to Cherie. "I have a feeling I'm going to need it."

"That and more time to heal. Why didn't you tell Korban you were too sick to leave? I think he might have delayed our departure."

"No, you're wrong. It wouldn't have changed a thing, and I wanted to make sure Hewson didn't get caught in the middle. Besides, I feel a lot better, and I'm stronger than you think." Teya wondered about Cherie's relationship with Hewson. Something electric had passed between them, she was sure of it, but didn't know if it was her place to ask. It was on the tip of her tongue, but Cherie surprised her by speaking first.

"You're looking at me strange. Is it because of Hewson?"

Teya shrugged. "You sang beautifully together," she said. "He's my brother, but I don't know him that well. Sometimes it's hard to imagine what having a brother means. I've been gone for so long that I don't remember much about him. I wish things were different. I hate what's happened to me, but I can't change it. What's Hewson like?"

"He's taken the responsibility of our people on his shoulders, and it's been difficult to say the least. Captivity for all of us has been a nightmare. I wish you could talk to him. You told him you had a plan, but he needs to know more, especially now that Korban is taking us back to the grove."

"I know," Teya said. "That's why it's been so hard to be separated from all of you. If my being sick makes it so we can travel together, it will be worth it." She didn't want to tell Cherie that all her plans failed when Korban put the *kundar* around her neck. Jesse better come through and take it off soon. Whatever the cost, Korban could never be allowed to regain his power.

Bran was coming out of the stables when sounds of a large traveling party reached him. He hurried across the grounds toward the street to see what was going on. He ducked into the shadows when he caught sight of a group of soldiers, followed by Korban astride his black horse. For a moment he panicked, thinking they had come for him, but as they continued on, his fear turned to dismay. They were leaving. Ahead of him.

The procession stretched out, and among the soldiers, he found pockets of people who could only be Kaloriahns. Where was Teya? Ever since this morning, his worry for her had grown, even though the heat coming through the bond had diminished. She wasn't well, but it didn't look like it had stopped Korban.

He caught sight of Jesse and his blood rose when his gaze found Teya, riding beside him. Her pale face was pinched with fatigue, and she swayed in the saddle. Faced with her exhaustion, he started walking toward her without realizing what he was doing. It was Jax's constraining grip that held him back.

Without thinking, he reached out to her through the bond with a purpose he'd never had before. The link flew open without hint of a barrier and he poured his strength and determination to her. She straightened with a gasp and immediately started searching the street for him. He stepped into view and his heart stopped when she caught sight of him. He started to raise his hand when Jax jerked him around. "You fool!" he said. "Jesse will see you! He's looking this way."

For a heartbeat everything stopped, then Bran moved, quickly ducking into the shadows. He waited breathlessly for the command from Jesse to seize him. When no alarm sounded, he relaxed his tight shoulders and leaned back against the wall next to Jax. "Sorry. I wasn't prepared to see her."

"They've passed," Jax sighed heavily. "I don't think Jesse saw you, unless he's really helping Teya like she said."

"Helping her? I doubt it. He'd like her to think that, but who knows what he'll do on his own. That was stupid of me. If Jesse knows we're here, it could ruin everything."

Jax shook his head. "If he didn't see you, we have nothing to worry about."

"Unless Teya tells him." Bran closed his eyes in consternation. "But maybe I can do something about that." Again, he opened the link to her and sent what he hoped she would understand as a warning. He felt a slight acknowledgment that could mean almost anything before the link closed. What was she thinking? He took another look at the departing horses and supply wagons. "Did you notice who else was riding with them?"

"Yes. A man with black hair was on the other side of her."

Bran sighed. "I thought I recognized him. Good, that was her brother, Hewson. I know he'll protect her as much as he can. She was sick this morning. Weak. I wonder what happened."

"They probably took more of her blood."

Bran stood up straight. "I'll bet you're right, even though Korban told her he wouldn't, I can't think of anything else that would affect her like that. So why was Korban in such a hurry to leave? I don't think Turner was expecting him to go so soon."

"I don't know, but I don't think it will be too hard to get ahead of them. They've got women and children to slow them down. We can travel faster and farther than they can."

Bran nodded his agreement. "I hope Turner gets here soon, this waiting is killing me. Maybe we should follow them." It was hard not to jump on his horse this minute and ride out after her.

"No," Jax countered. "She's too heavily guarded. We need to stick to the plan. The right time will come. You just need to be patient."

It was a long wait. The sun had set before Turner came through the gates. He barreled through the garrison door, and called for everyone left there to gather. He was grim-faced, but a light of excitement shone in his eyes. "I had a difficult time leaving. Korban had me watched, and it took awhile to find out who was behind it and persuade him to tell me what he knew. But it was worth it." He opened the bag he brought with him and pulled out several vials of *sym*. "This was the king's supply. Korban was looking for it, but I found it first. I don't like using it, but you saw how Korban and his soldiers fought. We will have a better chance against him if we are prepared. I want everyone here to take a couple of vials and use them when you think it's necessary in the upcoming fight.

"I don't know why Korban was in such a hurry to leave. I don't think he knows my plans, but we'll have to be careful. I know the general route they are taking, so tonight, we'll bypass them and meet up with the rest of our men. After a few hours rest, we'll continue on with Bran as our guide. Any questions?" When no one responded he continued. "Let's head out."

As Bran and Jax turned to leave, Turner stopped them. "Don't forget these." He handed both of them several vials of *sym*. "I know you don't like it any better than me, but you'll use it if you need it."

Bran studied the vial, wondering if it was from Teya's blood. Turner was right, he didn't like using it, but he would if he had to. A small seed of satisfaction rose when he realized that with *sym*, he could even have a shot at Korban.

⁊⁊

Teya woke in the gray light of dawn, tired and hot. Her fever was back, but she was too tired to care. As the sounds of breaking camp reached her, she burrowed under the covers wishing to be left alone. Yesterday, her pride had not allowed her to ride in the baggage wagons, but that wouldn't happen today.

Cherie came through the flap of the small tent they shared with a mug of steaming tea. "Here, drink this," she told Teya.

"Thank you." Teya fought dizziness as she sat up.

"I've sent for Hewson," Cherie said. "You were moaning in your sleep all night. You may be able to cover it when you're awake, but I know better."

"Just let me ride with the baggage. Being away from Korban should improve my health immensely."

Cherie chuckled. "That's not a bad idea."

Hewson entered, stoic as ever, and once again, sang with Cherie in beautiful healing tones. When Hewson pulled away this time, the pain etched on his face didn't seem quite so bad. After recovering for a minute, Teya whispered, "We need to talk."

"I'll keep watch outside." Cherie ducked out of the tent and began to pack their bedding.

"I saw Bran yesterday at the garrison just outside the city gates," Teya whispered eagerly. "He was with the king's soldiers and was wearing their uniform. I don't know what's happened. I thought he left with Rasmussen. Anyway, I'm sure he's planning to help us. I just don't know how."

"That doesn't make sense. The king's soldiers are loyal to Korban now."

"No, you're wrong. It's Chancellor Turner they swore fealty to. He ran the country, even when the king was alive."

"So maybe Turner has plans of his own." Hewson frowned. "What about the *kundar?* Cherie said you know a way to get it off."

Teya considered telling Hewson about Jesse. She didn't have the nerve to tell him before now, but putting it off didn't make it any easier. She took a deep breath. "Jesse wants to help. He's the one who helped Bran and Jax escape. He told me he'd help get the *kundar* off before we reach the grove. He has plans to go against Korban, but I don't know what they are. He hasn't told me yet."

Hewson's mouth dropped open, then snapped shut with anger. "You don't know Jesse. You can't trust him. This is ridiculous. He's Korban's son—he'd never go against his father." Hewson's eyes smoldered. "He took our blood. He took your blood! He's been doing it for years. Not only that, he's hunted us down like animals. He's a lying, manipulative…" Hewson trailed off. His voice had risen in volume and his chest heaved. He took a deep breath in an effort to gain control. "No. There's no way he'll help you. He couldn't mean it. I don't know what he's up to, but it's not anything good."

Teya swallowed. Hewson was so upset that a part of her couldn't help believing him. Then she thought about Jesse's confession. Couldn't someone change? Maybe all he needed was a chance. What choice had Korban given Jesse in all this? Couldn't Jesse be a victim like the rest of them?

"You want to trust him," Hewson said accusingly.

"I want this *kundar* off," she whispered. "I can't do it alone. Even Korban told me I could defeat him without it. Once Korban's powers are restored, it will be too late."

"I'll kill Korban," Hewson said. "It's not something you should have to do anyway, and it's not something you need magic for either. Between here and the grove, I'll find a way to do it." His cold and unfeeling voice made Teya shiver. "I'm sorry you ever thought it was your responsibility." She opened her mouth to speak, but Hewson stopped her. "Don't. You're not the only person here with plans. Korban watches us, but not closely enough. He thinks we have no spirit, and so grateful to be going home that we will follow him blindly. That's just what I want him to think."

He paused when Cherie poked her head through the flap to warn them that Korban and two guards were approaching.

"Don't do anything foolish," Hewson told her urgently. "I don't need to worry about you getting in my way."

"Hewson I…"

"Shh…I'm glad you've decided to ride in the wagon today," he said for Korban's benefit, then left the tent. She heard him exchange a few words with Korban and with worried exhaustion laid back down on her pillow.

Korban didn't even bother talking to her, instead sending Cherie to gather her things and situate her in the wagon. It wasn't until they were on the road again that Teya finally concentrated on what Hewson had said. If he planned on killing Korban, it would have to be with a knife or gun. Maybe he thought he could filch one from a guard. What if he already had, and was just waiting for an opportunity?

Her stomach clenched with fear at the risk he was taking. Since beginning their journey, Korban kept a tight guard on the Kaloriahns. He had to know they would escape if they could. Guards were everywhere. Korban never came to them alone and unarmed. Someone was always with him, even if it was only Jesse.

Teya needed to talk to Jesse and find out what he was planning. When he took her blood, he told her that she had to wait until they were on the road before he could help her. They were on the road now. Were all his words lies?

After stewing for an hour, Teya was ready to get back on a horse. The enclosed wagon was too stifling for her, and she needed to see what was going on outside. She pulled on her boots and opened the flap in the back. When two startled guards looked up at her, she quickly let the flap fall. That left only one other option and she took it, stepping over some supplies toward the front. She climbed over the back of the seat and sat down next to the wagon driver, who was disconcerted at having her sit beside him. "You should be resting, miss."

"I'm not tired anymore," she said, realizing it was true. She felt stronger today. "If you don't want me here, then get someone to find my horse and I'll gladly leave."

He shrugged. "Stay then. I'm not going to stop the whole procession just for one girl. Korban wouldn't like it, and I don't want to be on his bad side."

"That makes two of us," she said, and caught the barest hint of a smile on his face. They rode in amiable silence while she studied the terrain. It wouldn't be long before they reached the plateau and the stunted trees. Beyond that, came the boundary of the Destroyer and her blood ran cold knowing she would be unable to stop it with the *kundar* still around her neck.

Korban expected her to give him the tones that would keep it at bay. He would probably use *sym* made from her blood to do it. With a huff of despair, she looked for Jesse, but was too far back in the line to see much of anything. She needed to know if he was going to help her or not, and she needed to know now.

A short time later, they stopped for the noonday meal, and she scrambled down from the wagon. Finding her strength improved, she strode toward the front of the procession. The startled cry of the driver alerted the guards and they surged after her. She panicked, and turned to run, but didn't get far before someone grabbed her.

Instinctively struggling against the firm hold, she didn't realize it was Jesse until he spoke. "Hold on," he said. She quieted while he turned to the guards and told them to return to their places. "Where were you going in such a hurry?"

"To find you," she gasped. "We need to talk."

He nodded. "Let's go back to the wagon. That's where I was headed in the first place." His tone held a hint of exasperation. "I told Korban I would check on you, and it would help if you'd stay put. And if you're going to plead illness, at least you could act like it."

She held back a retort, realizing that he was probably right. What had possessed her to take off like that? Fear. Time was running short. By tomorrow they would be in the Destroyer's path.

She waited until they were back at the wagon before speaking. "We're getting close to the boundary," she said. "If you're going to do anything, it needs to be now."

He handed her some bread before he replied. "Tonight," he whispered. "I'll take the *kundar* off. Until then, try not to do anything conspicuous. I'll come to you."

He seemed so earnest it was hard not to believe him. Hewson had to be wrong about Jesse. "Do you really mean that?"

There was a light in his eyes she'd never seen before. "Yes. Can't you feel it? The grove. I know where it is from here."

Sadness overcame Teya. "No. With the *kundar* on, it is lost to me."

Jesse's face crumpled in sympathy and he touched her cheek with tenderness. "Not for long. Tonight we'll take it off. What do I need? How did Bran do it before?"

She swallowed before answering, hoping she wasn't making a mistake. "He used a string of some kind that was coated with gun powder. It melted through the metal and let the darkness escape. Korban will feel it when the *kundar* is broken."

Jesse nodded solemnly. "I know, but I plan to be far away from here when that happens."

"What do you mean?" Teya tensed in alarm.

Jesse knew he had said too much and tried to cover it. "I mean we need to leave camp to be safe from Korban. Otherwise, we'll never get the chance to take it off."

"I don't think that's what you meant at all," Teya said. Silence slipped between them like an open chasm, too wide to cross. "What are you planning?" He didn't answer immediately, and something inside Teya snapped shut. "You want to go ahead, don't you? Get to the grove before your father?"

"Yes, I want to go to the grove, and if there's some way to stop my father without killing him, I want to do that too." When Teya didn't respond, he continued. "Korban kept me with him and took care of me. He's not all bad."

"No, but what he intends is." Teya bit back her frustration. Jesse wasn't listening. Korban would never give up until he had what he wanted, at the cost of everything else.

"I've got to get back," he said, his jaw clenched. "I'm going to get what I need to take it off. Think about it. I'll come to you tonight."

He walked away, leaving her in turmoil. Was taking the *kundar* off, better than staying here with it on? Whatever happened, there was one thing she could take care of right now. "I'm ready to ride. I want my horse," she told the guard. He motioned to another guard to get it and once she was in the saddle, she rode eagerly up the ranks toward her brother.

Hewson was closer to Korban than Teya wished and she knew he was trying to carry out his plan. When she drew up next to him, he jerked back, startled, then slowed until they were in the midst of the Kaloriahns.

"I thought you were resting," he growled. "You should not be here."

"There's something you need to know. We'll be reaching the boundary of the Destroyer soon. I want to give you and our people the tones that will hold it back. If we band together, our combined voices might be enough to save us from the Destroyer." She looked around carefully to make sure no one would hear what she had to say next. "I won't give Korban the same tones."

Understanding lit Hewson's eyes. If they could save themselves, the Destroyer would take care of Korban and his soldiers. Hewson nodded with approval, but Teya stopped him. "I don't know if we're strong enough. Do you want to chance it?"

"If there's nothing better, yes."

She knew he still meant to put his plan into action, and there was nothing she could do to stop him. With great reluctance, she nodded and sent the tones floating to him in a gentle whisper. "For the Destroyer." These words of explanation traveled through the Kaloriahns like a wild fire, followed by the tones until everyone knew and heard. The Kaloriahns had become expert at sending messages in this subtle way, without the guards' knowledge. They covered it by making idle conversation, and drawing away the guards' attention with their limited magic.

Teya fought her trepidation that she had just doomed all of her people. The Destroyer was strong while they were shackled by the *kundar*. Taking her *kundar* off before they faced the Destroyer might make the only difference between life and death for them all.

The rest of the day Teya's stomach was tied up in knots. She decided that Hewson had a knife hidden somewhere, because he watched Korban like a bird of prey and a couple of times appeared to be moving in for the kill. Each time her breath caught in her throat. After the second time he was thwarted, she was afraid he would recklessly rush in and be cut down before her eyes. Luckily, he was levelheaded enough to know when he couldn't succeed.

Evening came, and with it, the landscape changed. The leaves on the trees were no longer green, but withered to a dull brown. The yellowed grass and moldy bracken leant an air of foul smelling decay. Over the rise, the trees took on the shape of twisted monsters, and not far beyond lay complete desolation.

Under Korban's direction, they retraced their route to the last small stream of fresh water to wait out the night. He placed a heavy guard around the Kaloriahns, splitting them into two groups, the men in one, and the women in the other, with the heaviest guard on the men. Only one tent was set up for privacy, and that was his.

Teya sat beside Cherie and tried to get comfortable. She shivered in the gathering darkness and huddled with the other women and children around the fire Korban had allowed them. This heightened security was different from the night before and Teya wondered if Korban was doing it because of their closer proximity to the grove, or if he suspected they were planning something against him.

It certainly thwarted Jesse's plan to take Teya and leave. Had Korban found out about that? She was just beginning to drowse off when muffled footfalls warned her of someone's approach, and she sat up to find Jesse standing over her. He motioned her to be quiet and helped her up. Once they were out of hearing, he spoke. "Korban wants to see you."

Teya was prepared to tell Jesse that she wouldn't leave her people, so was surprised with his request. "Why?" she asked. "What does he want?"

"He didn't say, only that he wants to talk to you."

Even though that was reassuring, she could hardly stop her growing anxiety. She wanted to ask Jesse if he was still planning to leave, but there were too many people who might hear.

Golden light spilled out of the tent when Jesse ushered her inside, temporarily blinding her. Korban sat at a table, finishing off his glass of wine. "Have a seat." Jesse remained by the entrance, while Teya sat across from Korban. He said nothing, and she straightened her spine and endured his rudeness, deciding not to speak first.

"You're probably wondering what you're doing here," he finally said. "We're almost there. In fact all that stands between us and the grove is the Destroyer. I need the tones that will keep all of us safe."

Of course that was what this was about. She let out a breath before answering. "It takes magic to keep the Destroyer back. Magic you don't have."

"I have plenty of *sym* for me and my men. We can protect the rest of you, but only with the proper tones."

Now was her only chance to bargain for her release from the *kundar*. "If I promise to help you against the Destroyer, will you take this off me?"

He smiled indulgently. "So you can turn on me? No, my dear, I don't think so. Once we get to the grove and I have secured my powers, all the Kaloriahns will be freed, but not before then."

"How do I know you'll free us then?"

"There will be no reason to keep you bound. You won't be a threat to me, and the grove will need your powers to survive."

His words hung in the silence and she knew further discussion would get her nowhere. "All right, listen carefully." She picked three tones that were similar to the real ones and let them resonate in the air. They held a hint of the power needed to stop the Destroyer, but would never be enough.

Korban's expression blanked, then drew into a frown of displeasure. "What was that?"

Teya sucked in a nervous breath. She hadn't fooled him. "What do you mean?"

"Those were not the same tones you gave the Kaloriahns today."

Her stomach dropped. How did Korban know? Had someone betrayed her? She glanced surreptitiously at Jesse only to find him frowning with confusion. He obviously knew nothing. She drew in a deep breath. Was Korban bluffing? One look into his eyes told her more than any spoken words. She felt the magic in him then, the magic of *sym* that was vaguely familiar. She shuddered with recognition. It was hers.

Korban smiled at her horrified understanding. "I have enough of your *sym* to last me quite awhile and have decided to keep using it until I reach my goals. Naturally, I picked up on the magic that you passed to the Kaloriahns. I wanted to know what you had planned." He took a sip of wine before speaking again. "I also had to know if Jesse was in on your plans. I see that he wasn't."

Jesse's expression hardened with comprehension, and Teya fought against sinking despair. "Since Jesse doesn't know the tones," Korban said. "Why don't you sing them for him?"

She wondered if this was another test of some kind. Was Korban mocking her? "Why don't you?" The defiance came without thought of the consequences. The danger brought an exhilarating freedom, and her heart pounded.

"I admire your spunk," Korban said. "It's lucky for you this wine has dulled my wits. Otherwise, I might be tempted to punish you severely for that. As it is, I will only insist that you do as I ask. Sing the tones for Jesse."

She was backed into a corner. Korban wasn't bluffing now. Only her pride kept her from singing. Knowing defeat, she let the tones curl into the air, taking her hopes for defeating Korban with them.

"Good," he said, satisfied. "Take her back, Jesse."

As they left the tent a cold chill settled over Teya. Jesse led her partway back, before skirting into the trees for privacy. Surprisingly, his voice carried no hint of anger. "Was he telling the truth?"

There was no point in lying now. "Yes. I didn't want to leave the Kaloriahns without protecting them from the Destroyer. Not telling Korban the right tones seemed like a good idea."

Jesse wrestled with her confession for a moment. "I'm not sure he already knew them."

"What? You think he was bluffing?"

"I don't know. Do you think he could have picked up on the magic you passed to the Kaloriahns today?"

"Using *sym*—probably."

"Now I know he's suspicious of me. I will have to be careful." His faraway gaze came to rest on her. "I have what I need to take the *kundar* off. Stay close to me tomorrow. When we encounter the Destroyer, Korban will be too busy to notice, and I'll take it off."

"Why not take it off now?"

"Too risky. The Destroyer is the perfect diversion. It will keep Korban busy and by the time he realizes your *kundar* is off, it will be too late to do anything about it."

"How do I know you mean it? Especially after Korban told you what I'd done."

"What we do now will determine the balance of things in the future. I don't want the future Korban has planned. The only future I want is one with you in it, free and unharmed. I have chosen my path. I choose you."

Teya didn't know how to respond. His declaration left her speechless. "I'd better get back." He took her hand and led her back to the low-burning fire. With a quick squeeze of her fingers, he left.

She looked after him for a moment before finding her discarded blankets and lying down next to Cherie. The stars were bright in the night sky, but offered her no comfort. It was a long time before she fell asleep.

CHAPTER THIRTEEN
The Destroyer

I choose you.

Those words had haunted her through the long night. It was hard to believe Jesse had made his choice. He was going to free her from the *kundar*. Today.

The day dawned with the threat of rain, but Teya hardly noticed. Her thoughts were centered on the battle she knew was coming. Her stomach roiled in nervous anticipation, there was so much that could go wrong. Today would decide the fate of her people, and it was up to her to stop Korban.

After washing up at the stream and eating a quick breakfast, she watched for Jesse, hoping he would speak to her before they left. He never came. Preparations to leave passed in tense anxiety. Teya watched for her chance to warn Hewson, but it wasn't until they were readying the horses that she snuck between them to his side. He frowned at the risk she was taking, clearly displeased with what he perceived as her interference. "Korban is using *sym* from my blood," she whispered breathlessly. "All the time. Anything you try against him will fail. You must leave him to me."

His brows drew down and his nostrils flared. "No! It's not for you."

"Yes, it is. I can do it. Look to our people. They need you now."

"How? What do you have planned?"

"I can't explain it right now. But it will work. When we reach the path of the Destroyer, hold our people together. Sing the tones with as much power as you can." She prayed it would be enough. She didn't want Hewson to know that Korban also knew the tones and her plan had failed. What about Jesse? Hewson wouldn't believe that he was helping her, so there was no point in telling him.

A guard noticed them talking. "Hey," he yelled and started in their direction. His coming precluded further explanation, which was probably just as well. After a nod to Hewson, Teya ducked under the horse and skirted a few others, before finding her way back to Cherie and the rest of the women.

"Did he listen to you?" Cherie asked anxiously.

"Yes," Teya said. "But keep an eye on him just the same. Keep everyone together as we travel, I'm going to see if I can get closer to Jesse." She told Cherie as little as possible, barely hinting at Jesse's involvement, then pressed her to take charge of the women. Cherie wasn't pleased, but agreed anyway.

Before they left, Korban passed a command to his soldiers that puzzled her until she saw the vials. They all drank *sym* and she knew it was in preparation for their meeting with the Destroyer. Anger bristled that her people were left shackled by the *kundar*, while Korban's men were protected because of them.

They were soon mounted and began the journey toward the fractured trees. Korban remained in the forefront with Jesse, flanked by his men. Jesse dropped back every now and then to check the company's progress, but Teya knew his real reason was to check on her.

The Kaloriahns were heavily guarded, but Teya moved toward the outside edge of her people as close to the guards as she dared. From this side, she had better access to Jesse. Hewson kept an eye on her as well, but with his close proximity to Korban, he didn't look like he was giving up on his own plans. She silently cursed his stubbornness, but there was nothing she could do about it now.

They entered the fractured trees, with knotted trunks twisted like broken fingers. The birds were gone and in the eerie quiet, the overcast sky brought a gray bleakness. The jingle of harness and bridle echoed, and all conversation ceased. The tension increased, encompassing them with strains of unease and discomfort. This was the last boundary between them and the Destroyer.

For a brief moment, Teya felt a startling pulse of awareness through her link to Bran. She twisted to look behind her when a shocked cry came from the guard at her side. An arrow sliced into his back, and he fell from his horse. Other arrows rained down upon them, and the guards yelled, warning of an attack.

At that moment a large group of the king's soldiers came at them from behind. The roar of their cries filled her with terror. Teya kicked her horse forward, running into Korban's men who turned to meet the soldiers. She fought to keep her horse from turning, but on the outside fringe of the Kaloriahns, was caught in their advance. Her horse reared and she barely managed to hold on before it turned with the advancing guards. As she fought for control, someone was calling her name, and she twisted to find Jesse closing in. He cut around her horse and managed to turn it away from the fighting.

Gunfire erupted behind them and Teya winced, ducking instinctively. Jesse urged her to flee while fighting broke out on every side. One of Korban's soldiers grabbed for Teya. She lost her balance and fell from the saddle. The soldier reached down for her again, but was stopped by a bullet from Jesse's gun. Jesse made it to her side, and grabbing her arms, swung her onto the back of his horse. He galloped through the trees, keeping the advancing soldiers from pursuit with gunfire.

The sounds of fighting grew muted when Jesse pulled the horse to an abrupt stop between the trees in a rocky outcropping. Before them spread the desolate land of the Destroyer. From behind came the sounds of pursuit, but far enough away that she couldn't see who it was. Could it be Bran? She knew Bran was with the king's soldiers, probably searching for her.

"Now's our chance to take the *kundar* off." Jesse helped Teya down, then dismounted.

He rifled through his pockets, pulling out a small packet, and unwrapped the cloth. Inside was a wire coated with gunpowder. "How do we do this without burning your neck?" he asked.

Teya was concentrating on the approaching hooves. The sounds seemed to be coming closer, but from a different direction. "There's no time, just wrap it around the *kundar* and light it. Hurry!" Teya could feel magic pulsing in the air, along with something dark. She tried to focus on the link to Bran, but could barely concentrate.

Jesse fumbled with the string, his fingers stiff in his hurry. "I can't light this without protecting you." He tore off his leather tunic. At the same time, a dark shadow hurtled from the rocks above.

Teya screamed. Jesse drew his gun, but was knocked sideways by a vicious blow. He staggered to his feet, but the magic held him in a vise-like grip. Korban lowered his tone and Jesse was flung backward onto the ground. Korban towered over him, breathing heavily. Jesse gasped for air, clutching at his throat.

"I knew you would try to take her for yourself. I hoped against it, but I could see the way you looked at her." He released his magic and Jesse drew in a strangled breath. "The strange thing is, it's something I probably would have done."

Jesse lunged to his feet, and held back Korban's strangling tones with magic of his own. "You're learning," Korban ground out. "But you're not as strong as me." Korban pushed with a harsh cry that broke through Jesse's defenses and he flew back against the stones.

"Stop it!" Teya ran to Jesse's side. His eyes were glazed and blood ran from the back of his head. "You're going to kill him!"

"Isn't that what he wanted you to do to me?"

"No. He never wanted you killed."

Korban stood over her. "Then I'll let him live, but you're coming with me."

"You can't leave Jesse here, they'll kill him." The fighting was closing in on them. Only the rocky outcropping kept them from being seen.

"I can't worry about him now," Korban said. "I sent the Kaloriahns across the way. We need to catch up with them before the Destroyer does."

Jesse held his head, but lurched to his feet with a groan. "I'm coming with you."

Korban shrugged. "Then hurry, I won't be waiting if you fall behind."

Teya grabbed the reins of Jesse's horse and quickly helped him up. He swayed in the saddle, but kept his seat. He helped pull her up behind him and they burst out of their rocky concealment, following closely behind Korban.

Below them, the Kaloriahns traveled rapidly, putting distance between them and their attackers. Korban's army was still holding the king's soldiers back, but they were vastly outnumbered and wouldn't hold for long. As they raced toward the Kaloriahns, the king's soldiers spotted Korban and several riders took off after them.

Teya glanced behind and thought she recognized Bran as one of them. She tried to focus on the link with him, but was suddenly distracted by a dark, looming cloud. The shadow lengthened, and the gathering darkness coalesced into a monstrous shape. The black seething bulk formed enormous wings and a hulking head dotted with two flaming eyes. Teya cringed with horror. The Destroyer had changed. Dark power writhed within the smoky outline of a bird of prey.

Korban cursed and quickly changed course. Instead of joining the Kaloriahns, he raced to put them between him and the Destroyer. "Our only hope is to race directly to the grove," he shouted.

"No!" Teya screamed. "They'll all be killed. We have to help them."

"Against that? Nothing will stop it. The Kaloriahns are beyond our help. You'll only end up dying too. Jesse! Come on!" Korban kicked his horse and raced forward. Jesse started after him.

"Jesse! No!" Teya grabbed Jesse's arms to stop him. "We can't leave them!"

"But we'll die!"

"I don't care!" The horse slowed and Teya slipped off. As her feet touched the ground, she fell, rolling to a stop. She jumped to her feet and began to run.

"Teya! Wait!" Jesse reined the horse beside her. "I'll take you. Give me your hand!" When Teya hesitated, he continued. "You'll never make it in time." She reached up to him and he swung her back on, then spurred his horse toward the Kaloriahns.

Teya's stomach clenched and a cry of terror caught in her throat. The Destroyer had completely formed, and with a shriek of decaying breath, rose into the air. It attacked the border first, where men still fought. It landed heavily, then writhed into the form of a black wave, eating up everyone in its path. Some escaped into the trees, others weren't so lucky and screamed as the life was sucked out of them.

"Jesse, listen! I need you to use your magic and break my *kundar*. I know you can do it. Use the tones to draw out the darkness!"

"I don't know how!"

"Just try!"

They were almost to the Kaloriahns, but she needed her full magic to succeed. She felt the metal grow hot before Jesse let out his breath. "Did it work?" he asked.

She knew it hadn't. "Keep trying," she told him, but knew it wouldn't matter. Time was running out. They reached the Kaloriahns and she shouted at them to sing the tones with her. "No matter what happens, keep to the grove!"

A rider garbed in the king's uniform had dodged the path of the Destroyer and raced into their midst. Jesse raised his gun to fire, but Teya pushed it down and slid off the horse. She rushed into Bran's outstretched arms, weary with relief and deep sadness that he would die with her. A deafening screech brought them around. The Destroyer landed not far away, and began advancing slowly toward them.

Bran opened a packet. "I've got wire and matches." He quickly wrapped the wire around her *kundar* and with his gloved hand as a shield, lit the wire. The *kundar* sizzled apart, releasing the dark power and Teya gasped with hope. "Help the others."

She began to sing the tones with the Kaloriahns. Their voices rose as one, and the magic coruscated around her. Suddenly, something inside her rose up, responding to the magic with a deep sense of urgency. Magic sang through her blood, rising in power, seeking release. She walked toward the Destroyer and it screeched in bellowing hatred, then with a wail of rage, unfolded its wings and lifted skyward.

It circled the Kaloriahns, then came to ground on the other side away from Teya, and began advancing toward them. Here, the tones were weak, leaving them vulnerable to a vicious death.

Something snapped in Teya and her voice rose in a challenging echo. The deep stirring inside her began to pulse with new power. She abandoned her will and let the power consume her. It surged through her body with a life of its own, changing her into a creature of its own making.

Light shot out of her fingers and cascaded over her transcending form. The power filled her lungs while her heart slowed and her vision narrowed. Tiny pin-pricks sent a tingling rush through her body, hitting her skin like hard drops of ice. Before panic set in, her heart beat to a new rhythm and her vision cleared. Taking a deep breath she raised her arms and was surprised at how light they felt. Her body shook, emerging from the whirling power into the feathered wings and sweeping tail of a human-sized bird.

Flexing her wings, Teya's breath caught with wonder and excitement. She reveled in her newfound glory, instinctively knowing what to do. With a sweep of her wings, she jumped into the sky. Soaring over her people, she left a streak of light in her wake, and dove toward the Destroyer. It reared back as she passed, blocking her attack with a sweep of its wings. The song she trilled cut through the mass of darkness and it shrank in on itself before exploding upward into the air with a cry of rage.

Caught in the updraft, Teya spun out of control. Fighting for balance, she pulled in her wings to stop the spinning, and fell diving toward the ground. As the rocks rose up before her, she opened her wings and pulled up, narrowly missing the hard earth. Fear sent rippling waves through her feathers, and she leveled out, testing the strength of her wings. That was close, but new confidence in her abilities settled her nerves. With power bolstering her courage, she swept across the ground and vaulted into the sky. Determined to win, no matter the cost, she sailed back toward the Kaloriahns and the hovering Destroyer.

This time her opponent charged her, attacking with a malevolent energy that was surprising. Her small form was no match for the larger Destroyer, but it gave her the advantage of speed and stealth. She dodged the gaping maw and outstretched claws, leaving burning marks of her own across its back.

It snapped at her and she darted between its outstretched feathers, skimming under its belly. She dodged the raking claws by an inch and dove to the other side. When she came about the Destroyer was on top of her with open beak and deafening roar. Her sharp trill repelled the attack, but it came back in a gliding sweep straight at her.

Teya sang with a burst of magic that pushed the attack aside, but not in time to dodge the outstretched wing. It clipped her wing and sent her spinning toward the ground. She managed to slow her descent, but could not stop her fall.

She hit the ground and rolled to a stop, where she lay in a dazed heap on the rocky soil. The stink of decay and death warned her of the Destroyer's approach. She hobbled to her feet, her broken wing hanging crookedly at her side. The power still coursed through her, but she didn't know what to do. The Destroyer was death, and it seemed too big for her to conquer alone.

As she faced this ancient foe, the power shimmered through her body with a rush, changing her back to her true form. She instinctively cradled her arm, and her hand brushed against the tiny bulge in her jacket. The seed. Her heart pounded with new hope, and she tore the lining, catching the small seed in her palm.

The Destroyer approached in the lopsided form of a man. The ragged edges of darkness lost shape, then reformed in patchy decay. The fight had weakened it, and she knew if she sang the tones, it would flee. But she needed to bind it, send it back to the darkness, and seal it away forever.

In the distance came the sound of approaching hoof beats. The Destroyer backed away, and she knew the time had come. She couldn't let this chance to banish it be lost. With a deep breath she walked toward the Destroyer in deathly silence. She closed her mind to the darkness that awaited her, concentrating instead on the seed.

The Destroyer smelled the life pulsing in her and rose in height until it overshadowed her. With an unearthly cry of victory, it enclosed her in a suffocating grip and she couldn't breathe. There was no way out. She couldn't sing without air. The darkness was thick, and permeated through her skin into her soul. Then it began to solidify. The pain shocked her. She hadn't expected it to hurt. Not this much.

Doubt rocked her. What was she thinking? No one could survive this. She was lost to the darkness now, never to return. Pain and panic crashed into her soul in waves, leaving little room for thought. She had to do something. But what? There was nothing she could do. It was over.

Suddenly a thread of awareness shattered the panic. A small flame of strength flowed into her and lessened the pain. She latched onto this light with the little strength she had left and the pain lifted, before leaving her entirely. Someone else was bearing it for her. Bran.

With her thoughts clear again, she remembered what it was she had to do. She opened her hand and poured magic into the seed. At first, the melody was hardly a whisper, but soon her breath came more easily and the tone brightened. The solid mass around her lost shape. Her melody stirred the seed to life, imbuing it with a pulsing light. The light sparked, then surged into a thousand tiny rays. As she sang, the rays grew, pulsing through her hand and cutting into the Destroyer. Suddenly, the darkness shattered into a million pieces. The pieces turned into mist, then shadow, before disappearing completely. The Destroyer was gone!

Teya gulped in a breath of fresh air, then collapsed. Spots clouded her vision, and she couldn't seem to breathe right. The hand she'd held the seed in burned, and her broken arm thudded with pain. Someone carefully lifted her head and cradled her in his arms. Bran. He really was here. She hadn't imagined him after all. She opened her mouth to speak, but all that came out was a croak.

"Don't try to talk," Bran said. "Someone's bringing water."

She couldn't see him very well, then realized tears blurred her vision. "Oh, Bran," she whispered. "You saved me."

He pulled her close and gently kissed her, then held her tight. His face was pale and strained when he looked deep into her eyes. "I thought I'd lost you. When you walked into the Destroyer like that, I couldn't imagine what you were thinking."

If she would have known how hard it was, she wasn't sure she could have done it. The pain was unbearable, and Bran had taken it for her. She searched his face for signs of his sacrifice. Sweat beaded his brow, and white lines of stress were etched into his forehead and around his mouth.

Someone handed them a waterskin, which she greedily accepted. The water eased the dryness in her throat and helped buoy her spirits. She gave it to Bran. "Here, you have some too." When he raised it to his lips she noticed his hands were trembling. "Are you going to be all right?"

"I'm just shaken up. I'll be fine."

"A fine pair we are," she said, trying to lighten the moment. Bran smiled, but it turned into a grimace. Her throat constricted and she fought back tears. She didn't want to cry now. It wasn't over yet, and she needed to be strong. She took a deep breath and steadied her composure.

Several people had gathered around them, but it was Hewson that knelt beside her. "Teya?" His tender concern brought the tears back. "*Songbird,* that's what you really are. It's not just a title is it?"

His declaration, along with the look of adulation in his eyes cleared her head. "I don't know what happened. It was the magic."

"How did you do it?" he asked. "The Destroyer—it's gone. Bran got here before the rest of us, but I saw you walk into it—almost like you were embracing death. I never thought I'd see you again. Then Bran doubled over in pain, and I thought it was because you were gone, but it was deeper than that, like he shared your burden. Then the darkness gathered in on you, like a solid mass of death, before it suddenly exploded, and there you were—alive!"

It was a miracle, she realized, although she didn't quite understand it herself. "It was the seed. When Bran and I came to the grove, Grandmother gave me a seed from the tree. I didn't realize until the end that the only way to banish the Destroyer was with the seed because it contains the miracle of life."

Hewson nodded in understanding. "I want to hear all of it when you're feeling better. For now, let's take a look at that arm."

Teya was grateful for the diversion. She was starting to get all teary-eyed again, besides the fact that her arm was throbbing. They brought blankets and Bran eased her off his lap. Cherie helped Hewson set the broken bones into place and she nearly passed out from the pain. The soothing tones of their healing voices brought gradual relief, and she eventually dozed off into a relaxed state of oblivion.

She woke to hushed voices and was surprised at how long she had slept. She was lying inside a hastily constructed lean-to, and the late afternoon sun on the shelter cast long, stretching shadows.

She sat up, careful of her arm. Someone had wrapped it in bandages and although it was healed, it was still tender. The voices rose in volume and Teya tried to catch what the arguing was about. She recognized the tone of anger in one of them. It was Jesse.

She slowly rose to her feet, grateful there was no dizziness. The conversation abruptly stopped with her appearance.

"Teya," Hewson said. "We didn't mean to wake you. How are you feeling?"

"Much better, thank you." She looked around. The Kaloriahns were all there, some with bandages, most waiting patiently. When they saw her, many of them gave the old Kaloriahn greeting of hand to heart and lips in an outward gesture of obeisance. It caught her off-guard and spots of color rose to her cheeks. "You should have woken me sooner."

"You needed the rest."

Her heart constricted. The one person she most wanted to see wasn't there. "Where's Bran?"

Hewson didn't seem happy to tell her. "He rode back. There was a friend, Jax, he was concerned about. We're not far from the border. In fact, you can make out the trees from here but I thought they'd be back by now."

Teya could see the tiny trees on the horizon. "Is it safe? What about Korban's men?"

"Bran came with Turner. It was Turner's idea to come after Korban. From what we could see, there aren't many of Korban's men left, and Bran wanted to make sure they would leave the rest of us alone."

"Did anyone go with him?" She fought the whisper of fear that curdled her stomach.

"Cherie. I should have gone, but I didn't want to leave you. She went because of her healing powers. Without the *kundar* there is a lot of good she can do."

With a shock, Teya realized that all of the Kaloriahns were free from the collars they had worn for so long. Because of Bran. Now he was gone again. She contemplated reaching out to him through the bond, but stopped when Jesse turned to her. The abject misery etched on his golden features caught at her heart.

"What's wrong?" She remembered he was arguing with Hewson.

He dropped his gaze, as if it hurt to look at her. "I'm concerned about my father. He went on to the grove." Jesse raised guilt-stricken eyes to her. "I want to go after him, but Hewson has a problem with that."

Teya understood that look. Jesse thought he failed her. "Can you excuse us Hewson? I'd like to talk to Jesse alone for a minute." She gathered her thoughts while Hewson withdrew. How could she convince Jesse that he hadn't failed? He wouldn't accept sympathy; he had too much pride for that.

"I'm worried too. Korban is probably at the grove by now." She measured her words carefully. "But I don't want you to go after him alone." He stiffened, and she realized she'd said the wrong thing.

"You don't think I can handle him." Anger tightened Jesse's mouth. "I saw you change shape, and witnessed your battle with the Destroyer. I don't know what that makes you, but we have the same Kaloriahn blood in our veins. Korban is my responsibility."

"No, not just yours."

"You think you're the only one who can stop him, but that's not true. Why won't you let me do something to prove my worth? Or do you want all the glory?"

Glory? She wasn't doing this for glory. His words stung, but she knew he was hurting. If he wanted to leave, did she have the right to stop him? Bran hadn't asked her permission to go back for Jax, despite the danger. Jesse didn't need it either. What he needed was her respect, but at the cost of his life?

"I have no doubt that Korban will want to kill you. You left him Jesse. You chose to follow me. He won't forgive that." She paused to let her words sink in. "I can't stop you from going after him. I can only ask that you wait for the rest of us. If he has somehow regained his powers...then maybe I am the only one who can stop him. You could die."

"What does that matter to me? I chose to follow you and now I've lost you... to someone else."

"You never had me Jesse. I was never yours, you know that."

He took a deep breath. "Yes, I guess you're right. It was just wishful thinking on my part. And I failed, where Bran stepped in. He got the *kundar* off of you when I couldn't. I've always been on the wrong side. I don't belong with the Kaloriahns either. They don't trust me. How could they when I'm the one who hunted them down like animals and captured them? I took their blood to make *sym*. They hate me Teya. Maybe, just maybe, if I stop my father, they won't see me as such a monster."

"You brought me to them when Korban went on to the grove," Teya said. "I'm sure they know that. It may take some time, but they'll see you've changed."

"You always want to give people the benefit of the doubt, but for once you're wrong. The whole time you were asleep, they were uncomfortable with me here. You didn't see how they glanced at me, with dark suspicion in their eyes, especially your brother. I thought I could be a true Kaloriahn, but unless I prove it to them by stopping my father, it won't happen."

"They will accept you if I do. Then it will only be a matter of time before they accept you on your own merit. You don't have to risk your life to prove anything."

His face hardened with resolve. "You don't understand. If I don't stop him, I'm not sure I've got it in me to face their hatred everyday. It's the only way I can make up for my past. I've done too much."

"You once told me that the grove called to you. Does it still?"

He thought about it for a moment, and she knew he would answer truthfully. "I thought at first it was only the lure of immortality and all of Korban's talk. But there were times when my mother spoke of the grove. Her face changed, and got all dreamy and soft, then she'd sing things that I've never heard since. Beautiful things. It must be a sacred place. She quit singing when all it did was make her cry, and died soon after that."

Teya felt the familiar pang of losing her own mother and understood his yearning for something lost to him. "My memories of the grove were a child's until I went back." It seemed ages ago now. "Being there changed me. I felt like I'd finally come home. It will be the same for you. I don't want you to throw your life away. The grove is worth living for."

"If I don't survive, at least I will die for a worthy cause. I'd rather have your respect in death, than your sympathy in life." At her stricken expression, he smiled. "Don't be so glum. I don't plan on losing. I know Korban better than you think, and I'm not without my own resources." He glanced past her toward the border and his face darkened. "It looks like Bran is returning."

Teya whirled around in anticipation, and spotted not two, but three riders. It took a moment to recognize the third rider. "It's Jax!" She turned to Jesse, but he was gone. Her heart sank, knowing he was bound for the grove and nothing would change his mind. She started after him anyway, and caught sight of him mounting his horse. Their eyes met across the distance, then he turned and galloped away.

"Jesse!" He slowed and almost looked over his shoulder, then spurred his horse forward without a backward glance. The horse carried him away until all that remained was the dust of his passing. She sighed, stricken that his perceived duty might also mean his death. His leaving left a hollow place in her heart.

She felt Bran's presence behind her, and turned to see his jaw harden as he watched Jesse ride away. His face relaxed when he caught her watching him, and he hurried over with Hewson and Jax trailing behind. "You look better," he said in greeting. "I had to see if Jax was all right. He wanted to come back with me." He seemed ill at ease. There was something he wasn't saying.

"What is it?" she asked.

"When we escaped from Korban, we were captured by Turner's men. The Chancellor wanted to stop Korban, and asked for our help. That's why we joined him and attacked this morning. Chancellor Turner and everyone else who survived saw you fight the Destroyer. As the Songbird. That's what they're calling you.

"They don't know what to make of it," he said. "But Turner is afraid of your power. He's afraid of what Korban might become. I convinced him that you and your people were going back to the grove where you belong, and that you would take care of Korban. He's satisfied for now, but you won't be welcome back. None of you will."

"What do you mean?"

"He's always been leery of your people. The power of your unrestricted magic could mean death and dominion for the rest of the human race. After Korban, he doesn't trust any Kaloriahn. I know he planned to stop Korban, but now I think there was more to it. I think he was planning to stop all of you. Permanently."

"You mean kill us?" She couldn't be more surprised.

"I think so. Especially now that you're all unleashed. He's seen what you can do with your power."

"But it was a good thing, stopping the Destroyer. How can he think otherwise?"

"Think about what Korban is planning."

"I see what you mean," she said with resignation. "Turner believes the worst of us, that we have the potential to be monsters and Korban is his proof. I suppose in a way he's right. My own grandmother released the Destroyer, and look at how it ravaged the land." She didn't want to talk about her own change. She didn't understand what that made her, but it wasn't evil. Urgency washed over her, and all she wanted to do was find the grove. "Is he going to come after us?"

"Not now, but he's leaving some men behind to guard the way back and report what happens."

A swell of protectiveness washed over Teya and she fought the urge to confront Turner. The magic grew inside her, threatening to overwhelm her. If she let it, the power would easily transform her again. What then? Turner was no Destroyer—only a man who was afraid. Feeding his fear was the last thing she wanted.

Korban and the grove awaited her; that was the direction she needed to take. She would deal with Turner later. "We'd better go." To Hewson she asked, "How soon can we leave?"

Hewson seemed relieved. "Right away. What happened with Jesse?"

"He went on ahead."

Hewson's mouth curled in disgust. "You shouldn't have let him go. Now he will help Korban."

Teya winced. Jesse was right. Everyone viewed him with suspicion. "He's gone to stop Korban, not help him. He wants to redeem himself, and show the rest of you that he's changed." No one would look her in the eye.

"Good," Bran said, and she was grateful for his support.

A pressing need to get to the grove as soon as possible came over her. Hewson took charge, and soon the rest of her people were getting their things together. It seemed everyone was anxious to leave, and why not? They were going home.

She greeted Jax with a warm smile, and although he smiled back when he spoke, he seemed in awe of her. What did she expect? The power had altered her into the form of a bird. Could it change her into something else? She knew if she wanted, she could sprout wings right now and fly to the grove. It made her different, and only in the direst need was she willing to widen the gap between them. She sensed the same awe from Bran and knew they needed to talk.

Jax volunteered to get her horse ready, and Teya realized she'd left it behind. Bran spoke up. "You can ride with me," he offered.

Teya smiled. That was exactly what she wanted. His answering smile quickened her breath, and with his help, she eagerly swung up behind him.

Hewson took the lead, and they were finally on their way. It was comforting to be close to Bran again. His presence was solid and reassuring. "I've missed you," she said, holding him tight. "The pain...how did you bear it for me?"

He shook his head. "Easily—since it meant saving you. You don't know how terrified I was. And before, when you changed." He paused. "I thought...I don't know what I thought, except that you had become something extraordinary. Like an avenging angel. I knew it was you, but something more. My heart stopped a thousand times when you flew at the Destroyer. I kept wondering how it was possible, but I couldn't deny what I was seeing. The light streaming from you was blinding, but I couldn't take my eyes off you."

He looked over his shoulder as if reassuring himself that she was still there. "I don't know what to think anymore. You're you, but you're more."

"No, I'm still the same." But was she? Could she honestly say she was the same person she was before? Bran wasn't speaking. He obviously disagreed. "What do you think I am? How do you think this has changed me?"

He took a deep breath and his brows furrowed, as if disturbed by his thoughts. "Some of Turner's men thought you were an angel sent by the gods to conquer a demon. Your own people look at you differently. They bow to you with respectful submission. Your grandmother told me something before we left the grove that I didn't understand. She told me that the Kaloriahns weren't quite human."

Teya swallowed. She remembered her grandmother saying that, but she thought she was referring to her magical abilities.

"I still don't know what that means," Bran said. "But when I think of the grove being the birthplace of life, I wonder if you are closer to the angels than you are to the world of men."

His words brought a sharp denial. "No, we're nothing of the kind. We're a different race. We have magic, but we're still human. The gods gave us this magic to protect the grove. The ability to use it in special ways, like changing me, is a gift from them, but we can still die." Her parents had both died, but her grandmother didn't call it dying. She called it returning to the White City, a place of infinite beauty and peace. Then she remembered Korban's words. With his magic restored, combined with the immortality of the grove, he believed he could become a god.

Where was he now? Had he found her grandmother? Unless Leona led Korban to the tree and the water, he would not be able to find it himself. She couldn't imagine her grandmother doing that. There was still time to stop him.

She rested her head against Bran's broad shoulder. She would have died without him, but he wasn't Kaloriahn. The grove was her home and where she belonged, but what about Bran? She loved him, and couldn't bear the thought of living without him. Did he love her enough to stay in the grove? Did she love him enough to leave?

CHAPTER FOURTEEN

Restoration

The sun was dipping toward the horizon when they came over the rise. Leona's pipes echoed with melodic tones when the wind blew, casting a strange accompaniment to the eerie scene beyond.

Teya's heart pounded and a lump rose in her throat. This was not what she expected. The oasis of green grass was yellowed and brown. The nearest trees were twisted and black. Further in, she strained to find green leaves above the blackened limbs. In the golden light of sunset, the trees had a gray cast to them as if the light had been sucked out, and her heart faltered. After all they'd been through, they couldn't lose the grove now!

All of them seemed rooted to the spot, and several gasped in despair. Then someone started to sing. Softly at first, and soon, all of them joined in. Magic pulsed in the air with the tones, and drew them forward to the grove.

At the outer edges, the yellow grass took on a hint of green. The Kaloriahns pressed on, passing the whistling pipes and coming to a stop at the edge of the grove. They sang of life and new birth, filling the air with promise.

Around them, the blackened trees seemed to wake to a memory of life. They stirred and creaked, as if taking a deep breath, slowly filling with light where a void of darkness had been.

It was a small start, and would take days and days of healing magic to bring the grove back to what it once was. Was it possible? Could this terrible destruction be reversed?

The Kaloriahns had made a start, but some of the older ones had tears streaming down their faces. To see their once beautiful and sacred grove reduced to this was heartbreaking. What about the Tree? Was it as still and silent as the trees here? And the water? Did it still flow?

As Songmistress, Teya knew instinctively where the Tree was, but hesitated to lead her people there. If Korban found the water, he would drink it, and restore his lost powers. She had to find Korban first and ensure that it never happened.

"Teya! Over here!" Hewson called.

Just inside the blackened trees Hewson knelt beside a fallen figure. Teya raced to his side, then faltered to see Jesse lying in silent repose. He was still as death, and Teya caught her breath as she knelt beside him. His ashen face was cool to the touch, but his heart still beat beneath her trembling fingers.

"He's alive," she breathed. "But just barely! Can you see a wound?" There was no evidence of blood or other injuries. Then Hewson turned him onto his side and

Teya found it. Someone had stabbed him in the back and the ground was coated in sticky, red blood. Korban. "Quick, get me something to bind this with!"

"He won't survive," Hewson said. "Without the combination of the healing waters and our magic. He's too far gone."

Teya could feel the life ebbing from him and knew Hewson was right. Cherie came with bandages, and together they wrapped him up, singing the healing tones that would stop the bleeding.

"The Tree's not far. Is there a way we can carry him?"

"Yes," Bran said. "I can fashion a stretcher for him."

"Thank you," Teya said, gratefully. "Hewson, see if you can find any trace of Korban. I don't want him following us. Have the people stay here and keep vigil until we return."

"If you must go, I'm coming with you," Hewson said. "Bran and I can carry the stretcher. Cherie can help us keep him alive. Why don't you look for Korban? See if you can sense him with your power. If he's anywhere near, you might feel his presence. I don't want to start for the Tree until I know it's safe."

"All right," Teya said. She left Jesse to their capable hands and stepped further into the grove. With her eyes closed and the power humming in her blood, she reached out with her senses. She felt the wrongness immediately, but it was all around her. It wasn't something that came from Korban. It was in the grove.

Pushing beyond the immediate vicinity, she felt the pulse of magic from the Kaloriahns' singing. It was a powerful force, changing the wrong back to right. Within that force came another tiny tendril of power that she recognized as her grandmother. Her small beacon of light pulsed from the direction of the Tree deep within the grove. But it was weak and erratic, like the fluttering heart of a dying bird, and surrounded with darkness. Teya caught her breath. Grandmother needed her. Now.

She couldn't wait. When Korban showed his face, she would be ready. Until then, there was work to do. Jesse was lying unconscious on a makeshift stretcher when she returned. "Let's go."

"What about Korban?" Hewson asked.

"I can't sense him anywhere and we can't wait. Grandmother needs us. She's keeping the Tree alive, but it's using up her life force. We must go to her aid now."

Hewson sighed, but nodded with agreement. The five of them began the trek to the Tree, keeping close watch for signs of Korban. Teya took the lead, gathering her power in readiness, leaving Hewson and Cherie to keep Jesse alive. Their footsteps rustled through the dead leaves, and echoed in the gathering twilight. It would be dark soon, and a gloomy shadow already seemed to overtake them.

The path lengthened unnaturally, seeming to grow beneath their feet and carry them beyond the normal boundaries of the valley. Teya stepped with unhurried determination, watching for movement in the shadows. Except for the low healing tones, all was silent and still. There were no birdcalls, or the rustling of small animals. Nothing moved but the breeze that rolled over them like a cold wraith.

As the grove darkened, she picked up a smooth, round stone and whispered a soft melody of light over it. At the core, a small flame flashed, then spread to fill the stone with a white glow. The light banished the shadows for several feet in all directions, and with lightened steps they hurried forward.

Teya heard the spring before she saw it. The water fell from the tree as before, and trailed away into the small pool. The large tree overwhelmed them with its size and living presence. But the leaves were brown with decay and carried the smell of mold.

Teya almost missed her grandmother. Lying against the trunk with ashen skin and clothes, she appeared as part of the roots. A vine had grown around her still form and blackened leaves wreathed her dress and crown. If not for the slight movement of her chest, Teya would have thought her turned to a wooden statue.

Something was vastly wrong. Through Teya's magical perception, she could feel Leona's life force draining into the tree, almost like it was being held captive. No, that couldn't be right. Leona was keeping the tree alive through her own free will.

The others came abreast of Teya and lowered the stretcher to the ground, then stood in baffled silence. Teya set the light stone on the small table near the tree. Empty glasses and the water pitcher were positioned appropriately there, as if awaiting guests. On an impulse, she picked up a glass and dipped it into the water, then carried it to Leona.

"Grandmother? Can you hear me? It's Teya." She sang a healing tone over Leona's inert body. Leona stirred, and Teya's heart quickened with hope. Something else shifted as well, something dark. Teya swallowed, then realized Leona's eyes were open, but unfocused. Her lips moved, but Teya couldn't make out the words. "Grandmother, I have some water for you to drink."

To Teya's chagrin, Leona moved her head away and wouldn't drink it. Teya sat back in confusion, then noticed that Hewson had filled the pitcher with water and was pouring it into the glasses. "Hewson," she whispered urgently. "Wait. Grandmother won't drink the water. Something's not right. We need to find out what it is before we give any to Jesse or take any for ourselves." His face drained of color. "Come," she added. "And help me strengthen her."

Hewson left Cherie and Bran to watch over Jesse. With both Teya and Hewson singing, Leona's breath quickened, and her eyes focused with clarity. She reached out with gnarled fingers and touched their faces. "You're both here," she whispered softly. "I hope there's enough time. The Destroyer invaded everything. Even the Tree." She stopped for breath before continuing. "The water is tainted. You must not drink it until it is purified by your magic." Again, she paused and Teya leaned forward to catch her words. "The Tree holds my life force, but the darkness is also there, battling for dominance. The Tree must be strengthened for the grove to survive."

Teya finally understood. Even though she had defeated the Destroyer, it came too late to stop the darkness from infecting the grove. "The Kaloriahns are here, and strengthening the grove as we speak. Should I bring them to the Tree?"

"No. It is enough that you are here." Leona searched Teya's face. "I feel your power, it has changed you, and marked you as a true Daughter of Kalore." Leona's eyes were full of wonder. "The gods have not deserted us after all. Quickly now, you must save the Tree."

A sudden splash broke the stillness and Teya jerked around to find Korban on the other side of the pool. He dipped his hand into the water and lifted it to his lips. "Don't drink it!" Teya cried. "It's poisoned!"

Korban hesitated, then smiled maliciously. "Of course you would say that." Before she could stop him, he quickly took several gulps of the water. "It tastes wonderful, better than I remember."

He drank more, and then splashed the water over his face before rising. He seemed to swell when he reached his full height, and a smile of satisfaction crossed his dark features. Suddenly, he gasped in surprise, and clutched at his stomach, then fell to his knees. He fought for breath while his whole body shook. Spasmodic waves shot through him in short blasts. When it was over, a dark essence glowed with unnatural light around his body. He straightened, and his eyes blazed red. "I see clearly now. I thought I understood what the grove was, but now I see I was wrong. The gate between light and dark is here. All the powers of creation and death are held in this place. I see my destiny now, and the only thing standing in my way is you. Back away or die, the Tree is mine."

Teya stepped in front of her grandmother and braced for Korban's attack. "Not while I live." The notes flew from her mouth before Korban moved, pinning him to the spot. She strengthened her voice and felt the magic coursing through her like liquid fire. In a blinding flare of light, magic flew from her outstretched fingers toward Korban.

He held it back with a shield of blood-red fire, then pushed the power back toward Teya. His strength unbalanced her, and she fought for control. He pushed harder and with easy steps started around the pool toward the tree. She knew she had to keep him away, and doubled her efforts. It slowed him, but he still came on.

The loud crack of gunfire startled her, and Korban faltered. Bran stood at the edge of the pool, and fired his gun again. Korban jerked from the impact, but with a sweep of his hand sent his power crashing into Bran. The blow sent Bran flying in the air where he landed with a loud smack against a tree. He lay unmoving and still. Teya's heart constricted with a spasm of pain. "Bran!" His efforts may have stopped Korban, but at what cost?

Korban straightened as a low wind whistled through the trees. Dark shadows coalesced around him like wraiths, and flowed to him in undulating waves. A small smile curved his lips, and when he opened his mouth, they disappeared down his throat. His body swelled again, and with a gasp, the bullets fell out of his chest. He grinned in defiance, more powerful than before.

"I am sorry to have to destroy you," he said. "But I can't let you stop me. You stand between me, and all I ever wanted. Everything I deserve after years of banishment and pain. In this sacred place, I can become a god. A god of death and life, darkness and light, joy and pain. This earth and everything in it belong to me."

"It will take more than a few wraiths to do that!" Teya shouted.

"But you forget the Tree. It is the conduit to all power. With the Tree, I can do anything."

The Tree was also Teya's only hope, but half-filled with darkness, how could she harness the light? She gently placed her fingertips, then her palm, on the smooth bark of the Tree, and felt an immediate response. Something stirred within it, like the shifting of a great door, and the balance of power changed. The darkness gave way to light.

Teya concentrated on drawing the light to fill the Tree, placing both hands on the trunk. Her clear voice rang out with startling purity, forcing the darkness to recede. Without warning, a driving shock shattered her focus and waves of pain lanced up her back. She screamed from the pain, but didn't release her hold on the Tree. It was crucial that she change the balance of power to her advantage before Korban got any closer. She managed to fling up a small shield of protection, and the pain receded.

Korban advanced with fierce determination, his contorted features a mask of death. Korban's power pounded into her, and in desperation, she wrenched one hand from the Tree and flung her own power at Korban. He shrank back and she doubled her efforts, reaching deep inside for strength she didn't know was there. Sparked by her power, a corridor opened in the Tree and sealed the darkness away. A blast of pure light coursed through her, and she glanced up to find the Tree smothered in a beam of light coming from above, like a conduit from another place!

Korban cried out in anger, and darkness pounded her, beating at her with un-broken fury. She dropped her hand from the tree, but the power stayed connected to her through the channel she'd formed. With light streaming into her, she sent a crushing wave into Korban. He flew back, landing in a tangled mass.

With pain still floating over her in a hazy cloud, she leaned over, breathing deeply to catch her breath. In this moment of inattention, Korban stood, his body ablaze with darkness, and rushed toward the Tree with amazing speed. His quick recovery shocked Teya into action. Dropping all her defenses, she opened herself to the light and sang. What came from her was not of her choosing, but dictated by the power itself. It was not a harsh tone, nor loud, but one never heard before, as if coming from another level of existence. It was powerful, yet small. Soft enough to pierce the depths of the soul, yet loud enough to spread before her like wildfire.

With Teya at the center, the music rippled outward in waves that caused the ground to tremble and shake. It crashed over Korban and he jerked spasmodically to a halt. He clutched at his chest and his mouth opened in a soundless scream. His whole body trembled, and the muscles stood out in cords around his neck and arms. He jerked stiffly upright, and like a statue made of stone, toppled to the ground.

The wave cascaded outward like a giant disk that penetrated through all living things. Immersed in the music of her voice, brown and decaying leaves suddenly turned green with new life. Yellow parched grass brightened with new growth. Black spiked trees trembled into soft flowing lines and graceful leafy branches.

The Tree became solid and strong once again, the pure water flowing true. Teya carried the tones as long as she could, buoyed by the power. Caught within this pure light, time seemed to stand still. The magic pulsed through her in strengthening waves. The outer appearance of decay was gone, but now she must work on the inner core. Even the smallest trace of darkness could not be allowed to exist for the grove to be purified. With the Tree as a conduit to sustain her, she drifted in a state of oblivion until the work was finally done. The power shrank to a small stream, then a thread, before vanishing all together.

Teya sank to the ground, overcome with more than exhaustion. Her heart burned like it was on fire, and her body tingled as if unbound and weightless. Her skin seemed to give off little sparks of light and there was a funny taste in her mouth.

Insistent thirst drove her to the foot of the Tree where she swallowed several gulps of water. The refreshing liquid soothed her trembling and relieved the burn-ing sensation in her chest to a small hum. Fortified, she realized the grove was filled with unnatural light. Wasn't it supposed to be night? Had purifying the grove taken that long? Although the gray sky was filled with sparkling stars, the light of dawn was not far off. Still, the grove carried a light of its own. With a jolt she realized her skin did the same thing, sending tiny sparks of light when she moved. The power that had channeled through the Tree and into her was gone, but the light was like a memory of all that had occured.

With wonder, she glanced to the spot where Korban fell. Was he still alive? She sensed no threat, but no life either. What about Bran and the others? Had Bran been seriously hurt when Korban turned on him? Leona and Hewson lay in peaceful repose against the trunk of the Tree, breathing deep and even. Cherie slept next to Jesse's stretcher, and color stained Jesse's cheeks with a healthy glow. She sensed his injuries were gone, healed through the cleansing power of the grove.

Teya rose carefully to her feet, hoping she could stand after her exhausting ordeal. The grove water must have helped because she felt no weakness. Relieved, she lightly stepped over the small stream of water flowing from the Tree. Bran had careened into a smaller tree on the far side of the grove, and collapsed in a heap. Now he lay stretched out on a soft bed of grass. She dared to breathe again when his chest rose in deep, even breaths. Like the others, he slept, healthy and alive.

Did this mean Korban was alive too? She didn't want to leave Bran's side, but this was something best taken care of now. If Korban wasn't dead, she meant to bind him. If he had survived the cleansing light, he deserved a second chance.

A tiny thread of apprehension curled through her when she approached Korban. From a distance, his features looked normal enough, but when she reached him, she recoiled. His body and clothing were the color of gray stone, and seemed to lay in several fractured pieces. He was dead, but she sensed his presence centered in the stone. As if he were hiding.

With a deep breath, she summoned her courage, knowing what she had to do, but dreading it all the same. She held her hands above the body and hummed a haunting tone to call him forth. The response was immediate. A small seed of light burst from his chest and hovered for a moment before vanishing into another dimension, but fear and anguish lingered long after he was gone. He wanted to become a god, now he must face the gods with what he'd done.

The broken stone of his body collapsed into dust, and a sudden breeze carried it away. Released from this dark burden, the grass below him changed from blackened gray to a cushion of green. Except for her, no one would know where Korban had met his end.

Was it over then? She took in a deep breath, savoring the fresh smell of dew and dark earth. The trees stood tall and strong once again. Ferns and wildflowers dotted the ground, the columbines and lupine swaying in the breeze. Somewhere high above, a bird began to sing, it's trilling notes a tribute to the beauty of life. In the dawn of a new day, the grove was reborn.

≈≈

In the place between wakefulness and sleep, Bran dreamed. He was lying comfortably on a soft bed of grass, aware of his surroundings through heightened senses. The fresh air seemed perfumed with a delightful bouquet of earth, grass, tree and flower. The gurgle of a spring bubbling from the ground came next, followed by the beautiful serenading of a bird. The breeze ruffled his hair and he took a deep breath, finally opening his eyes.

Coming toward him was the most beautiful being he had ever seen. Light rippled from her skin in tiny sparks and her eyes glittered like turquoise crystals. As the breeze caught her raven-black hair, it shimmered in the early light of dawn and feathered around her oval face. The light framed her head in a dazzling halo. He knew her, and yet he didn't. "Are you real?"

The warmth of her hand against his unshaven face jolted him into complete wakefulness. This wasn't a dream. "Teya." She leaned over him and their lips met. Her breath was sweet, the touch of her lips, feathery-soft and intoxicating.

"Are you all right?" she asked.

His heart pounded with sudden desire and he pulled her back against him with a groan. For this moment she was his, and his alone. Their lips met again and he deepened the kiss, wanting more and yet holding back. Even with his eyes closed, her brilliance dazzled him. She wasn't the same. There was a beauty and profoundness to her that seared through him with burning intensity.

It plunged deep to the depths of his soul, and he was suddenly aware of his human frailties and vulnerability. As pain seared through his chest, he ended the kiss abruptly, and took a steadying breath. She studied him with concern, but even looking into her eyes seemed to hurt.

She sat back on her heels, stunned. "I don't understand. I've given you pain." She was astonished and dismayed.

"I'll be all right. You're just...different somehow." He managed to catch his breath, and quickly sat up, but the burning still lodged in his heart. "What happened to Korban?"

"He's dead. There's nothing left of him."

"The grove," Bran said reverently, and studied his surroundings without sleep-clouded eyes. "You did it. It's beautiful beyond words!" He looked at her again. "Just like you. You shine."

She glanced at him with uncertainty before a small smile lit her face. "It is beautiful isn't it? My heart is so full, I feel like it could burst! I never imagined so much beauty before. There are no words to describe it."

She was right. Bran was nearly overcome by the radiant light that rested over everything. More than an outer glow, it seemed to flow from the very essence of the grove.

"I'd better check on the others," Teya said.

"I'll help you," he offered. She helped him to his feet and he was amazed at how good he felt. He remembered Korban slamming him into the tree and the terrible pain before he blacked out. "Did you heal me?" he asked.

"It happened when the grove was re-born I think. The power touched everything in its path and restored all life but Korban's. It killed him."

"Then shooting him didn't help?" Bran asked with mock severity.

"Oh, it helped me a great deal." She smiled up at him. "But in the end, that wasn't what killed him."

Teya knelt beside Jesse and Cherie who stirred at her touch. As Jesse glanced at his surroundings, his eyes widened in shock. "Did I die? Is this heaven?"

Teya laughed before replying. "No, but it's close."

With a burst of joyful energy, Jesse rose to his feet and caught her in a wild embrace. "You did it!" He set her down and rushed on. "With no help from me. I'm sorry I let you down. Korban and I argued for a long time. We saw you coming, and when my back was turned, he stabbed me. I never expected it. I should have, but I didn't."

Cherie woke Hewson and Leona, who joined them. "None of us understood Korban completely," Teya said. "But he's gone now." She turned toward Hewson and Leona, then rushed into Leona's outstretched arms. "Grandmother!"

Tears streamed down both their faces. "My child!" Leona cried. They embraced for several minutes. After shedding more tears, Teya reached out to Hewson, who hugged her tightly.

"Jesse," Leona said with outstretched hands. "Welcome home." With an awe-struck expression, Jesse took her hands, then quickly embraced her.

Bran took a deep breath, suddenly feeling like an intruder. Taking a few steps back, he leaned against a tree to stay out of the way. It was then that he noticed the glow from their bodies, and a chill tightened his heart. All of them gave off light. None of them shone as brightly as Teya, but he couldn't deny the similarity. He held out his own hands and examined them carefully. Nothing. No sparks, no glow, no light.

"Bran," Leona called.

He jerked his hands down. She came to him and took his hands in hers. "None of this could have happened without you." Her clear gray eyes shone with light and understanding. He swallowed, hardly knowing what to say or think. She squeezed his fingers before releasing him. "Come join us. Teya is going to tell us what happened." She steered him toward the others where he took a seat beside Teya.

"I'll start with the Destroyer," Teya said. "And save what happened when Bran and I left the grove for another time."

"I would greatly like to hear the whole of your tale, but you're right, later will be fine for now," said Leona.

Teya began and even though Bran had been there, it was still hard to believe all that had happened. When Teya told them Bran's part, he waved it away, but not before he noticed the approval in Leona's eyes. She must have known the link between him and Teya was all that would save her when she faced the Destroyer. The battle with Korban in the grove came next. He wished he could have seen the light come from the heavens and into the Tree, before it spread through the grove. Where had the power come from? That Korban turned to stone, and then to dust seemed a fitting end for someone who would stab his own son in the back.

Bran studied Teya while she spoke. The glow of light around her was vapor-like and ethereal. Her skin sparkled, almost like her bright spirit was bigger than her body and overlapped the edges. The light from the others wasn't quite as noticeable, but still there. What did it mean? His heart quickened with anxiety. Why didn't he glow? He had the sinking feeling that this change was permanent. If that were the case, would Teya still want him? He thought again about the kiss they had shared. He'd pulled away because it hurt him. He hadn't been able to endure the burning. If she remained like this, how could they be together?

Leona was anxious to meet with the rest of the Kaloriahns, but insisted everyone take a drink of water first. Before the cup reached Jesse's lips, he exchanged glances with Teya. She smiled at him encouragingly, and he drank with a reverence Bran didn't know he possessed. Afterward, his eyes shone with unbridled joy and Bran realized Jesse had finally found a place he could call home. Jesse belonged here because he was a Kaloriahn. Bran knew Jesse cared for Teya, maybe even loved her, and it hit him like a punch to the stomach.

Teya led the way to the others and motioned Bran to her side, but before he could reach her, Leona disrupted their plans. " Bran," she called. "Walk a little way with me." Teya frowned at her grandmother. "I'll send him back as soon as I've talked with him."

Leona waited until everyone was out of earshot, then took hold of Bran's arm. With arms linked they started down the trail. "I know how much you care for Teya, or you wouldn't have risked your life for her. That's why saying this is going to be hard." She paused and Bran braced for what was coming.

"I didn't expect things to work out in quite this way. Like the bond between you. It never would have taken if there weren't already a natural connection. The ceremony we performed only took what was there and strengthened it. Now, things are different. Teya has been changed by the power. She is no longer human."

Bran stopped and searched her face. "What do you mean?"

"Dear boy." She patted his hand. "She has been touched by the gods, and through her, all of our race. You see how we shine?"

"Yes," Bran could see the evidence in her glowing hand as she patted him. "But not me. Even though I was here, I wasn't changed."

"No. The Kaloriahns have a different task to fulfill that does not belong to you. And now that the task is done, we must leave this place."

"What? How can you? After all we went through to restore the grove you mean to leave?"

"You misunderstand. Not us. The grove. The grove must leave your world." She paused to let it sink in. "Teya restored the grove with power that came from the White City. Now we are prepared to take our place there. The grove can no longer exist in your world. The time for magic is over."

"How is that possible?" Bran's heart sank. He couldn't give up Teya so easily. There had to be a way for them to be together.

"Magic can no longer exist in this world. There is too much potential for abuse. We all witnessed what Korban did and how he nearly destroyed the grove."

"But it was one of your own who started it. Not us."

"Yes, and we paid a heavy price. But we have been redeemed. It is time for us to leave. I'm sorry you cannot come. Not that you don't deserve it, but your body could not survive the transcendence. I'm afraid it would kill you."

"What about Teya. Could she stay here?"

"Teya can only stay on the condition that she give up her magic. That will not be easy for her. You've seen how brightly she shines; it is what she was meant to be. If you press her, I'm afraid she will give it up. I'm asking you not to let that happen. She could never be happy after this, not when her heart burns with power. To give that up would destroy her."

"How can you be so certain? I think she could be happy here. Besides, I love her." He swallowed, knowing he sounded desperate and selfish.

"But do you love her enough to let her go? To do what's best for her?"

They had stopped walking a long time ago. Bran clenched his fists in anguish. "You're asking me to leave, aren't you? Without telling her or talking to her about it. You're asking me to walk away because it's what you think is best for her." He could hardly contain his frustration and pain.

Leona sighed and seemed to shrink in on herself. "This is not a contest between you and me. We both love her. It's not what I think. It's what is. You don't understand what she would give up to be with you."

"And if I don't ask, will she think I don't want her?"

"I would never tell her that."

Bran wasn't sure he could believe her. "What would you tell her?"

"That you loved her enough not to ask."

They were back where they started. Leona was adamant that Bran do this her way. "What if she wants to leave anyway? Will you let her go?"

Leona smiled slightly. "Do you think I could make her stay? If that is what she wants, she will have my blessing."

Bran came to a decision, even though it was not the one he wanted. "I'll leave tonight, but I'll wait on the ridge overlooking the valley for three days. If she hasn't come to me by then, I'll know she's staying with you. My only request is that you make sure she knows I'm waiting and that I haven't abandoned her if she wants to stay."

Leona nodded. "It is a fair thing you ask, but before I agree, do something for me. Watch her. See for yourself if you think she is happy here. Think of what she would give up to be with you, then we will speak again."

It took all the fortitude he had to agree, and his heart sank. Deep down he knew Leona was right. Teya had told him before that the grove was the only place she felt at home. It was where she belonged. How could he ask her to give that up? Someone who didn't love her enough could. Did he?

When Bran nodded his agreement, there were tears in Leona's eyes and she took his proffered arm with deep sorrow. She knew how much she was asking of him.

They soon emerged from the trail where the Kaloriahns surrounded them. Leona was caught up in the embrace of people she hadn't seen for years. Bran found Teya deep in conversation with Hewson and Jesse, and was loath to interrupt. How could he talk to her as if nothing were wrong? All around him, the Kaloriahns glowed, some brighter than others, but Teya, the brightest light of all.

He distanced himself from the others to watch her, but his heart broke with every glance. Still, he had to look at her. He needed to memorize everything about her. The quirk of her lips when she smiled, the way her eyebrows moved when she was concentrating. How she used her hands when she spoke. The melodic resonance of her voice. He was drawn to her like a moth to a flame. A flame that shone too brightly for him.

"What's going on?" Jax came to his side. "I've been looking everywhere for you."

Jax was a welcome relief and Bran clapped him on the back. "I think it's time we left." Jax was startled into silence and Bran continued. "Can you see the light around them or is it just me?"

"Oh, I see it all right. And I feel a lot better knowing you see it too. I wondered if something was wrong with my eyes. What happened back there?"

Bran told him everything, including Leona's request. "She's right, you know. Teya belongs here. I can't stay and I can't ask her to leave with me."

"That's a shame. Seems to me she should have a choice."

Bran stood with sudden energy. "I can't take this anymore. Let's find some horses and get out of here."

"Are you sure? Because I think she'll be pretty upset if you leave without explaining. Without saying something, even if it's goodbye."

"Leona will explain."

"What if she doesn't? Can you trust Leona to tell her how you feel?"

"I can't tell her myself!" He snarled. "Don't you see? I'd probably end up begging her to come with me. I've never run away from anything before, but I can't tell her to stay, even when it's what I should do. So the only thing left for me is to leave. If that makes me a coward or a fool, then so be it." He embraced the anger because it blocked the pain, making it bearable.

Anger carried him through the motions of finding a horse and getting it saddled and ready. It wasn't until he was mounted and riding away that his anger slipped. With a lump in his throat, he turned for one last look. Teya's back was to him, but Leona looked up. She raised her hand in farewell, before quickly turning away.

For a fleeting instant, Bran expected Teya to realize he was leaving and run to stop him. He held his breath, but the moment passed, and nothing happened. He set his jaw in bitter disappointment and turned away, cursing himself for a fool, and wondering if he had just made the biggest mistake of his life.

CHAPTER FIFTEEN

A New Day

At the top of the grassy ridge Jax stopped, but when Bran came abreast of him, he only paused before continuing on. He couldn't stay and watch for her, and he couldn't look back. Not now. He was too close. It wouldn't take much, just a thought of the kisses they'd shared, the turn of her lips when she smiled, and he would be riding back to her side. Bran and Jax spent the rest of the day on a course that would take them to the edge of the forest, where they'd left Turner and his men. Bran knew a few of Turner's soldiers would still be there, awaiting word of Korban and the outcome of the battle. Telling them Korban was no longer a problem was one thing Bran could take care of. After that, he wasn't sure what he would do.

Focused on getting away, he just now realized that the land they were traveling through was no longer dry and barren. All signs of the Destroyer were gone. Small green shoots of grass were already rising from the dust. The breeze carried a hint of moisture, and small streams bubbled from the earth, running in rivulets to the West. Life sprung anew all around them, flooding in an ever widening circle from the grove. The birthplace of life.

Toward evening, they spotted the tree line in the distance. The black spiked trees were now straight and dotted with new green leaves. Teya's power and her wielding of it in the grove had started a wave that was spreading for miles. Was it still going? Would it reach all the way to Braemar? The effects of what had transpired in the grove would linger for years. The sheer intensity of it caught him with a realization that running from Teya would never keep him from her. She was in every blade of grass that grew, every drop of rain that fell, and every breath of air he breathed.

For the first time, he slowed and looked behind him. Green verdant valleys with soft rolling hills set off the fiery sunset in a grand display of beauty. Far in the distance, a grove of trees in various shades of green seemed to shine with reflected light. He caught his breath at the sight. It filled him with a longing that caught at his heart. With deep regret, he pulled his gaze away and continued toward the trees, no longer sure of what he was doing.

They found the soldier's camp at the edge of the trees. Their exuberant faces held the excitement of yesterday's events, and they were eager to hear what had happened. The sergeant in charge told Bran of the bright burning light that rolled over them in the night, changing everything in its path. Those with new injuries were miraculously healed, even old injuries and scars were gone.

Bran explained what he could, and told them Korban was dead. He explained that the Kaloriahns were the guardians of the grove, and they were the ones who defeated the Destroyer and restored the grove's lost magic. When someone asked if he could travel to the grove, Bran held him back with an unequivocal no. He explained that the grove wouldn't be there much longer because the Kaloriahns were leaving. The whole grove would soon be taken away. How, he could not say, only that soon, the grove would be gone.

For his own piece of mind, Bran knew he could go no further. This was the place he would stand watch and be a witness to this event. He needed to see how it ended, especially when he had played such a vital role. It was hard to believe that in a few days, it could all be over. But not, he prayed, before Teya came to him. It was a small hope, with little chance of being fulfilled, but he held it close to his heart anyway.

When Bran announced he was staying for a few days, there were several others that wanted to stay with him. The sergeant sent a few soldiers on ahead to tell Turner the news, then chose to stay as well. Bran realized those who stayed did so out of more than curiosity. As witnesses to these strange events, they weren't ready to leave. There was no fear, and as the night grew dark, it was easy to understand their feelings. Far off in the distance an unnatural light shone as brightly as noonday. Rather than being frightened, most of them were fascinated by this uncanny anomaly.

Bran settled himself in a blanket for the night, and leaned against a tree where he could watch the light from the grove. He hardly dared close his eyes for fear he'd miss something. Jax kept him company. "What do you think will happen?" he asked.

"I don't know. When Leona said they were leaving, she meant the entire grove. How that will take place, I can't say, but with the strange happenings in the grove, it could be anything."

"How long do you plan on staying here?"

"Until Teya comes, or the grove disappears." It pained him to admit it out loud. "I'm not holding out much hope that she'll come, but I can't leave until I know." Bran glanced at his friend. "You don't have to stay."

"You kidding? I'm staying. I've seen some strange things in my day, but nothing like this. I don't intend to miss it." Jax spread his blankets on the ground not far from Bran. "But I think I'll sleep for awhile. Wake me if anything happens."

Bran nodded, knowing for him, sleep was out of the question. As the hours passed, the light in the distance never changed. He dozed off every now and then, but always jerked awake to find the light still there. Every once in a while, he studied the land for an approaching horse and rider, knowing it was futile, but unable to do otherwise.

In the dark of night when all was quiet, Bran nourished a small hope that Teya would choose him. With a deep breath, he took a chance and did something he'd wanted to do all day. He tried to reach Teya through the bond. He focused his energy on her and felt the bond shift and stretch, reaching into a vast sea of light. Bright radiance flooded the link, filling him with warmth that suddenly became so intense it burned. Grunting with pain, he severed the contact and doubled over, clutching at his chest. He concentrated on breathing until the burning receded and he was in control.

His hands shook and sweat beaded his brow. In a panic, he grabbed his waterbag and drank until the dryness in his throat was gone. Breathing hard, he leaned his head back and closed his eyes, fighting against the anguish filling his soul. She was lost to him; he could never endure her the way she was now. When the sky lightened in the east, it washed away his foolish dreams with stark reality. She would never give up who she was for him, and he shouldn't expect her to. It was in the early hours of dawn, that he gave up his vigil along with his small hope, and finally slept.

He woke a few hours later. The pinpoint of light in the distance hadn't changed. The Kaloriahns were still here. He didn't know why he was relieved, especially when he held no hope, but seeing it kept something in him alive.

The day passed in expectant watchfulness. Bran tried to convince himself to leave, but each time he made that decision, something stopped him. He couldn't go. Not until he knew. He filled the day with mundane chores, most of which entailed preparing for the journey home. Idle conversation and an occasional game of cards filled the hours. Bran had little patience for much of anything and quietly took up his vigil.

It was after the sun went down that he noticed a change. The light from the grove burned brighter and he jumped to his feet. Jax hastened to his side, but Bran didn't dare spare him a glance for fear he'd miss something. The light gathered in intensity, making him flinch, and his heart started to pound. This was it.

A breeze started to pick up, blowing gently into them before picking up speed. Carried on the wind came the symphonious tones of voices raised in song. The harmonic inflections were soft yet electrifying. The harmonies rose in spellbinding intensity, piercing his soul with unearthly fervor. The ground vibrated with power that resonated in the air, spreading into the earth like molten fire. As the silvery tones poured over him, a chill swept down Bran's back, and his whole body tingled. Although his feet touched the ground, it felt as if his soul was rising, lifting him into the air.

At that moment, the sky exploded above the grove in a burst of pulsating current. It erupted in a torrential line toward the trees as a channel of power held suspended in the air. The power held and widened into a circular conduit. With a racing heart, Bran followed the light upward into the dark sky, but couldn't see an end. It went on forever.

The bright light that was the grove suddenly lifted into the sky, and the channel closed beneath it. Carried on a tidal wave of power, it coursed upward, higher and higher, until disappearing as a shining circle of light in the darkness. Bran followed it as far as he could, where it seemed to hang suspended in the heavens like a burning star.

His eyes watered, but he was afraid to blink and lose this last sight of her.

All at once, the ground calmed and the wind died down, bringing with it a trailing echo of rapturous music that softly spun into profound silence. High in the heavens a new star burned brightly, shimmering with rainbows of light.

Bran took a deep breath of air and his legs shook. There were no words for what he had just witnessed. Indescribable in beauty and strength, it carried a sanctity he had felt only one other time. The time he sang with Teya in the grove and was carried to a far off place, a shining white city, too bright for him to endure.

It was over. Teya was gone. His eyes burned with unshed tears, and he swallowed back the deep sorrow that threatened to consume him. She was gone. Lost to him forever. She had made her choice, and it wasn't him. He couldn't blame her. What he had witnessed was bigger than him, bigger than her. He knew she was safe and happy. What he didn't know was how he was supposed to go on without her.

Nothing, and no one could ever compare to her. She left a hole in his heart that could never be filled. He tried not to think what his life would be like, but failed, knowing heart-wrenching pain and loneliness. A dark haired beauty with turquoise eyes had changed him. Taken him places he had never dreamed of. Above him, the star hung suspended in the sky, a constant reminder of her. He didn't know whether it was a curse or a blessing to see where she was, but never be able to reach her.

Deep weariness settled over him. As the men made plans to leave, he kept to himself. Luckily, Jax circumvented most of the questions directed his way, giving Bran the space he needed. Bone-tired, he laid down to sleep, knowing morning would come soon enough, bringing with it, the long journey home. To what, he wasn't sure. He only knew that life would never be the same.

⁂

Teya rubbed the sleep out of her eyes and took her time waking up. She stretched to get the kinks out and winced. How long had she been asleep? From the slant of the sun, it was well past noon and she moaned, disgruntled that she had slept so long.

The argument with her grandmother had done her in, not to mention the tremendous amount of concentration it took to open the channel. Now here she was, flat on her back lying in a soft bed of grass. Turning her head, she steeled herself to look at the empty place where the grove had been.

Tall trees surrounded a large meadow where new tufts of grass and a sprinkling of trees were already beginning to grow. She swallowed against the sudden tightness in her throat. The loss of all that power would take some time to get used to, but she'd really never had it that long. What she had now felt comfortable, more like her old self. Magic was still there, about what she had with the *kundar* on. Just enough, but not gone completely. To lose all her magic would have been unbearable.

She sat up, taking a deep breath of earth-scented air, and then checked her pouch. The seed caught the light and glowed back at her. Reassured, she tucked the pouch in its place against her heart and stood. Beside her lay several bags of water from the tree. Water she would need for her journey. She glanced once more at the empty meadow, remembering her last glimpse of Leona, Hewson and Jesse.

Each of them had begged her to let someone else stay and carry the seed, but there was no one else. She was the only one with a reason to stay other than the seed, and that reason was Bran. Still, it was hard to say goodbye, especially when Jesse told her he loved her.

Jesse understood that she loved Bran, but it didn't matter. He could live with it, hoping time and distance would change things. He needed her. She had shown him the way. They were both Kaloriahns, and could learn this new way of life and what it meant to be in this new place together. He couldn't bear to see her leave, not when their journey was just beginning.

His heartfelt declaration shook her. She cared for Jesse. He appealed to her with his boyish grin and quiet charm. He needed her guidance and companionship to complete himself. She could probably build a life with him, but never with the intensity she felt for Bran. Bran was like air to a drowning soul, water for a dying thirst. If there was a chance to be with Bran, she had to take it, no matter the cost.

Jesse didn't understand how she could give up so much to be with Bran. Giving up the kind of power she held was not something he would do, but when he could see she meant to go through with it, he gracefully bid her goodbye.

Leona knew. It wasn't what she wanted either, but ever since the day of their bonding, Leona knew it was Bran who won her heart. The bond testified of it. When

Leona confessed that the bond worked because Teya and Bran already had a connection, Teya's relief was palpable. She finally knew for certain that Bran's feelings were his own and not brought about because of the bond. It strengthened her resolve to stay.

She was still upset that Bran had left without talking to her, but she blamed Leona for that. Bran wouldn't have left without Leona's interference. Of course, the way Teya was then helped convince him that they could never be together, not when her kiss burned him. If only she could have explained that the painful burning was temporary.

At least he shouldn't be too far away. Bran told Leona he'd wait three days, so that gave her plenty of time. A good thing since the day was half over. Her heart beat a little faster in anticipation of seeing him again. She couldn't imagine her life without him. Together, they would plant the seed and the new Tree would be a link to her people. The Tree wouldn't be the same as the one in the grove, because it wouldn't need magic to survive, but it would keep the little magic left to this world alive, and serve as a buffer between darkness and light, keeping the powers in balance.

Her horse was grazing on the far side of the trees. She sang three notes and it perked up its ears in her direction before cantering over. It took awhile to get everything situated without help. The saddle had to be tightened twice, and blankets, supplies and waterbags secured. Not used to doing this work, her patience was frazzled by the time she mounted up. Finally on her way, she got her bearings and headed for the ridge.

It wasn't far, and as she got closer, she expected to see him standing on the top, watching for her. She could hardly contain her excitement, but her hopes were soon dashed when she came to the top, and the ridge was empty. Where was he? He must have continued on, but when? How far ahead had he gone?

Mild panic that he had left her set in, but she tamped it down. She could find him through the unbroken bond. Opening to him, she was dismayed to encounter a thick barrier. She concentrated on cutting through it, then reluctantly stopped, realizing it was too deep to penetrate. With cold comprehension, she recognized what it was. A wall of grief cut him off from her. She staggered under the weight. He carried it like a cloak of protection, a dark and solid presence, cutting him off from the rest of humanity. She understood how it hurt him. It went deep, too deep to break.

She hated to find him hurting so much, and there was nothing she could do. In sudden comprehension, she spurred her horse to a gallop. Without hope, Bran would never wait for her, and with the barrier, she didn't know how to find him.

She reasoned that he couldn't be too far ahead, and tried to think where he would go. He would probably head straight for Turner to explain what happened. Turner was the last person she wanted to see, but she could catch up to Bran long before that.

The line of trees came into view late that night. With the moon and stars to light the path, she continued on, hoping to find Bran there with the rest of Turner's men. Her hope turned to ashes when she came upon the deserted remnants of a camp. He had been here. She felt traces of him everywhere. It brought a certain amount of comfort, and she decided to rest here for a while. She unsaddled her horse and readied her blankets. The water gave her nourishment, and she determined only to sleep a few hours before starting on the trail again.

Before closing her eyes, she found the new star in the sky. With the Kaloriahns gone, and Bran so far ahead, she experienced a sudden stab of loneliness. It was a poor consolation for all she had gone through, but she was determined not to wallow in self-pity. She had a job to do that was more important than what happened to her.

She reached out to Bran again and managed to find a small crack in the barrier. It was probably there only because he was sleeping, but it gave her a chance to touch him, even if he was asleep. She poured her love through the crack and felt an immediate response. The barrier came partway down and she reached out to his essence in quiet greeting. Longing drenched her with sweet abandon, and she sent a pulse of steady reassurance that she was there, that he didn't need to grieve for her.

Like a dream she felt his arms around her, his warm breath stirring the hair on the top of her head. She breathed in the scent of him, luxuriating in his embrace. The steady beat of his heart was like a symphony to her ears, and she relaxed into the curve of his neck.

Sometime later, she awoke, disoriented to find herself alone. In quiet realization, it disturbed her to be so close to Bran and yet so far away. With frustrated energy, she gathered her things and set out in the early hours of dawn, determined to catch up with him. She couldn't bear to be apart, not when it was unnecessary, and not when Bran was filled with grief. As the day passed, she imagined each step bringing her closer. She kept watching ahead, hoping to see something of his camp, but each turn of the road was empty.

It seemed he was running away from her as quickly as she was trying to reach him. The bond was no help, with his barriers set in place it was almost stronger than before. As evening fell, the outskirts of the city were a welcome sight, and she picked a path toward the inn where they had met up with Jax, ages ago.

With a chance he was there, her heart swelled with anticipation. Passing through the city was difficult because it brought back the terror of their escape from the king's soldiers. At least things were different now. The king was dead and the supply of *sym* probably thin, if not completely gone. She couldn't sense anyone using it, and was grateful *sym* was gone forever.

Everyone seemed pleasant enough, but she kept a discreet vigil for anyone with more than a casual interest in her. It wouldn't do to have someone recognize her now. She had no desire for her presence to be known. The Songbird was gone, but she doubted Turner would see it that way.

Relief swept over her at the welcome sight of the inn. When she turned the corner to the back, the window to Bran's room was dark and her heart sank. Unless already asleep, he was long gone. The stairs creaked underfoot, and she held her breath when she knocked. No response. Remembering where Bran had left the key, she pried up the floorboard and sighed with relief to find it there. With a surge of hope, she inserted the key and opened the door.

The room was empty, but full of his presence. He had been here, maybe spent the night. That meant he was a full day ahead of her. She sighed with bitter resignation. How many days before he stopped long enough for her to catch up?

She stabled her horse with money from the stash hidden in his room, keeping the water with her. She couldn't take a chance on losing it, not when she needed it to plant the seed. At least she was sleeping in a real bed tonight, and that took away some of the sting. The pillow carried Bran's scent, and sometime in the night, she dreamed that he was beside her.

❧❧

When morning came, Teya blushed, remembering the turn her dream had taken. His kisses had felt so real, and her response full of passion. She flushed to realize that in his sleep, Bran had no barriers, and the bond between them opened freely. It was heartening, yet frustrating at the same time.

With the barriers down between them, he had to know she was close. Maybe now, she could finally reach him. She sat up, opened the bond, and was met by a solid, unyielding wall. This time, he seemed even more determined to block her out, and her shoulders sagged with discouragement. What was he thinking? Couldn't he realize she was here?

She shook her head, trying to see it from his point of view. If he really thought she was gone, these 'dreams' would be torture for him. It made sense that he would block her out if it caused him pain.

Disheartened, yet resigned, she released her hold on the bond, determined not to push him further away than she already had. She only hoped it didn't take much longer to find him.

If Bran went to Turner, he had probably gone yesterday. She debated that course as well. Chancellor Turner would know how to find Bran, but she couldn't trust him. What if he decided to detain her? More than that, she didn't want anyone to know she was here. The Kaloriahns were gone, and that was the way she wanted to keep it.

What would Bran do now? Where would she go if she were him? She'd go home. The more she thought about it, the more right it seemed. He could have crossed into Braemar yesterday, but there was a slight chance he would be going today. If she went straight to Braemar, she might catch up with him. She hoped that was the case, because once he made it to Braemar, she had no idea where to look for him.

❧❧

Bran woke, slightly disappointed that he hadn't dreamed of Teya. That made two nights in a row that she hadn't troubled his dreams. He didn't know which was worse. In his dreams, she was real, but waking to find her gone was like losing her all over again.

He swallowed. He didn't know how to let her go. The only thing that would banish thoughts of her was hard work. That's why he had volunteered for the Southern Boundary. It was about as far away from the Old Country as he could get, and the climate was hot and dry. Not a place most people wanted to go. But at least in that place, there were no reminders of her.

Rasmussen thought Bran was joking when he first requested it, but agreed willingly enough. Bran's command of the language made him invaluable. There was always room for another translator willing to help the people in distributing medicine and food, and building schools and homes, along with countless other projects. The work never seemed to end, which was just what he needed right now.

His train left at noon, but Bran was packed and ready to go. He spent the morning prowling through the house, and regretted the fact that he was leaving it empty again. It was a nice place, but he was never home much, and wondered if he should sell it. The rooms were comfortable, although sparsely furnished, but airy and light with large windows that let in lots of sunshine. When he first bought it, he imagined raising a family here, but now the only family he could see himself with included

Teya, and that would never be.

He ambled through the back courtyard and out into the trees. A soft breeze ruffled his hair, accompanied by the trilling of birds. The woods behind the house were another reason why he bought the property. It amazed him to realize that he owned half the forest spread out across the area. It was a beautiful place, and deep in his heart, he didn't want to give it up.

The gurgle of a small stream welcomed him and he stopped, letting the water run through his fingers. The solitude of the glade always brought him comfort before, but now it seemed to weigh him down with memories of another grove. This time, instead of pushing the memories away, he embraced them, feeling again the wonder of Teya's song. The song they had sung together in the grove. He remembered the haunting melody that whispered over him in a warm embrace and filled his soul, heightening the awareness of his senses.

With deep concentration, he closed his eyes and sang the notes he could recall, but only got so far before losing the tune. How did it go? He tried again. The first few notes came easily, but he faltered over the next and lost the tune again. Suddenly, the most important thing at this moment was remembering how it went, and with determination, he tried it again with a stronger voice.

He got even further this time and was on the verge of remembering the entire thing when he lost the direction and floundered. Out of the blue, another voice caught the unfinished melody; a sweet, pure voice that belonged to the one person he never thought he would see again.

Bran jerked shakily to his feet and spun around. There, not more than ten feet away, stood the most beautiful vision he had ever seen. His throat constricted in surprise, and he could scarcely believe what he was seeing. "Teya?" Trembling, he closed the distance between them and, as he reached for her, she fell into his arms. "It's really you! I didn't…how?…when?…I thought…"

She smothered him with kisses, and he finally quit talking and kissed her back. Deep inside, the black cord of grief cracked open and a shock of awareness flooded his senses. She became a part of him, tied through the bond with a connection that could never be broken. Her love resonated with his, augmenting his own until all he felt was liquid fire.

"Teya." he pulled away, breathless and nearly out of his mind.

"I'm here to stay," she answered his unspoken question. "I didn't go…I've been trying to catch up with you ever since the grove was taken. I didn't know where you were."

"Oh." He had no idea. Had she been trying to reach him all this time? "The dreams…that was really you?" When she nodded, he felt a chagrinned croak tumble from his lips. "Teya…don't ever leave me again." He held her as tight as he dared without hurting her.

"I didn't," she mumbled against his chest.

"Oh…right." He smiled sheepishly and looked deep into her eyes, still not daring to believe she was here. His voice lowered to a husky whisper. "If I start kissing you again, I'll never be able to stop."

"Bran," she breathed his name like a prayer. "It's all right. I don't want you to stop. Ever. I didn't tell you before, but the bond…it makes us…lifemates. What you call married." At his shocked expression she continued. "The ceremony in the grove…it's a joining of heart and soul. I belong to you, and you belong to me. We always will, because of our love."

He didn't know what she expected, but she held her breath as if waiting for him to be angry. Instead, he began to laugh. A small chuckle at first, then with more abandon until she joined him and laughter rang through the trees. He picked her off her feet and twirled her around in wild abandon, until they fell in a tangle of arms and legs.

With tender devotion he kissed her again, marveling that such a beautiful creature belonged to him. He had many unanswered questions, but put them aside. All that mattered now was that she was here and they were together. With nothing held back, their souls met in a torrent of cascading light. The bond sharpened and augmented the feelings of love between them, lifting them to a place beyond understanding.

Bran felt the familiar burning of her power, but this time it enfolded him in a warm embrace, welcoming him in a cataclysmic deluge of light and love. He entrusted her with everything that he was in a mutual sharing of heart and soul. Together, they soared on wings of light, exalting in this holy union of love.

She had chosen him, and in her sweet embrace, he was finally home.

≫≪

Later that day, they planted the seed in a simple ceremony. Teya chose to plant it in the glade where she found Bran that morning. Already nourished by their union, the glade held a special magic that would cultivate and nurture the seed.

She poured the water she had carried so many miles into the carefully turned well of earth, then placed the seed deep inside this womb of life. For a moment, she caught a glimpse of light that stretched upward to the heavens. Connecting mortal with immortal.

With Bran's help, she covered the seed, and began to sing the song of Creation. Bran joined her with his beautiful baritone voice, anchoring her lilting tones solidly to the dark earth beneath their fingers. The song resounded through the glade, piercing every living thing to the core.

When the tones faded to a reverent finish, a small beam of light angled through the forest from the heavens, and illuminated the earth over the seed like a benediction. In this soft glow came the warmth of love, and a small green shoot extended above the ground. The light expanded in an ever-widening circle. Where the light touched, the nature of the glade changed, taking on vibrant tones of color in glowing hues.

The light encircled Teya and Bran, suffusing them in a symbolic link to the heavens. When the light dissipated, Teya caught her breath, her heart full of wonder. This new grove sparkled with a light of its own, surrounding and nurturing the young shoot of a Silver Tree.

The song of Creation echoed all around. The earth shook, sending small tremors through the souls of her feet that filtered upward to flow throughout her entire body with an echoing thrum. Next to her, Bran trembled, and they held fast to each other, witnesses as well as participants in this extraordinary event.

It was a new beginning in a new age. This tree was a union of both heaven and earth, much like her and Bran. It didn't need magic to survive, just air and water. The cycle of life would go on, and with the birth of the Tree, the song of Creation would never end.

Epilogue

The young woman pushed through the undergrowth, searching for the path she had known as a child. It had been much easier to find then, but maybe that was because she was smaller. Today was her twenty-third birthday, and the day she was for-sworn to return.

Humming to herself, she let her thoughts drift, and suddenly there it was, stretched out before her like a red carpet. Smiling, she stepped to the path, fused with a rush of anticipation. For years, she had been awaiting this day.

Green ferns and mountain geraniums hung over the edge of the path, straddled by wild roses and dainty columbine. The trees branched overhead in leafy shadows and the breeze carried the scent of dark earth and pine. It had been raining earlier, but the sun broke through the clouds every now and then, lighting the shadowed way.

The path turned and, as she came around the bend, opened up into a beautiful shining glade. Even though it was a cloudy day, the glade seemed brighter than the rest of the forest. In the clearing at its center, stood the most beautiful tree she had ever seen. Larger than she remembered, it reached upward, towering above her in unequaled majesty.

The thick trunk was smooth and silvery white. Green leaves shimmered with glistening silver sparkles, giving off light that had nothing to do with the sunshine. When the wind shifted, the leaves rustled in faint musical tones, and she caught her breath. She knew that melody. From the edge of her memory she remembered her grandmother singing it to her many times when she was small.

The tree spoke to her in a way she couldn't express, as if she were linked to it somehow. She reached out and laid her palm against the smooth bark. It was surprisingly warm, and the perfumed scent caught at her senses with a profound feeling of peace. Like she was home.

She remembered the story of how her great-grandparents had planted the seed a long time ago. Teya and Bran. They brought it from another place that was gone, taken from the earth by magic. The seed had sprouted because of their love, and grown in this beautiful garden to keep watch over them and their posterity. It stood like a sentinel, guarding their love forever. That was the story. When she was young, she used to believe in magic, but that was a childhood fancy. Magic was only something told in tales. It wasn't real.

Yet, standing here in this grove, she could almost believe in it again. This place was different. The rest of the world may be turning sour with darkness and strife, but here, it was as if life had begun anew. This place held hope.

She sighed, and the tree seemed to shift in response, sending a faint intimation of melody. The musical tones grew and reverberated through her mind, then went deeper into her skin. With a smile and rash sense of buoyancy, she let the notes trickle off her tongue into the air. The leaves caught the tones of her clear voice and played with them in a counter melody that sent shivers up her spine.

In a burst of exaltation, she opened her mouth and sang the tones with unbound pleasure. She'd always held back before, keeping her voice in check because of the amazing feelings she could conjure. Here, she let it all out, and the grove filled with the sounds, echoing through the glade like a vast domed cathedral, spiraling upward to shower down in waves of resonant beauty.

Within this conduit of sound, a vision opened to her mind of a white city filled with shimmering buildings that reflected the light like prisms. These shining crystal towers stood amid silvery green trees and deep azure blue sky. Countless people inhabited this fathomless beauty, and in the midst of them, stood two whom she knew instinctively as her great-grandparents.

Their happiness was palpable, and spread through her like a brand of fire. Her great-grandmother's smile bridged the gap between time and space, sending a feeling of deep love that filled her heart with a sweet burning of truth. A connection ran between them and she knew in the core of her being, that this was part of her heritage, part of who she was. She realized that the magic of this legacy was imbedded deep inside of her, ready for her use. If the need ever arose it would be there for her and her posterity.

The vision cleared and she stood again in the shadow of the Silver Tree. Her heart pounded with new understanding and strength. Grateful for this gift of understanding, she vowed to carry on the birthright of her ancestors. Whatever the future held, this tree was part of her heritage and also part of her destiny.

A destiny her family would carry to the end of days.

About the Author

Colleen Helme lives in Salt Lake City, Utah with her husband and children. Her love of fantasy began as a child when she read *A Wrinkle in Time*, by Madeleine L'Engle and continues today not only as a writer, but a voracious reader. Her creative nature is also manifest as a watercolor artist and musician. Her hero is her son, Clayton, who as a teenager, faced cancer with faith and courage. He is now cancer-free and living proof that miracles do happen.